P9-AOO-275

"Given the current political climate [*Small Great Things*] is quite prescient and worthwhile. . . . This is a writer who understands her characters inside and out."
—ROXANE GAY, *The New York Times Book Review*

"**Picoult has outdone herself.**" —*St. Louis Post-Dispatch*

"**A courageous and important work.**" —Minneapolis *Star Tribune*

"**I couldn't put it down. Her best yet!**" —ALICE HOFFMAN

"[Picoult] offers a thought-provoking examination of racism in America today, both overt and subtle. Her many readers will find much to discuss in the pages of this topical, moving book." —*Booklist* (starred review)

"**[A] gem.**" —*Vox Magazine*

"*Small Great Things* embraces . . . empathy, hope and humility."
—*Newsday*

Praise for *Small Great Things*

"*Small Great Things* is the most important novel Jodi Picoult has ever written. . . . It will challenge her readers . . . [and] expand our cultural conversation about race and prejudice." —*The Washington Post*

"A gripping courtroom drama . . . Given the current political climate it is quite prescient and worthwhile. . . . This is a writer who understands her characters inside and out."

—Roxane Gay, *The New York Times Book Review*

"A novel that puts its finger on the very pulse of the nation that we live in today . . . A fantastic read from beginning to end, as can always be expected from Picoult, this novel maintains a steady, page-turning pace that makes it hard for readers to put down. It also allows for conversations to be had and for people to sit back and look at their lives, actions (past and present) and wonder how they will move forward. This is a fantastic book not only because it addresses something that happens in America and around the world every day, but it also shows us that change is possible too." —*San Francisco Book Review*

"Given that Picoult is wrestling with the subject of white privilege, writing Ruth's story in the first person might seem like an exercise of that very prerogative. Can Ruth be the hero of her own story? Or must she be saved by Kennedy? Turns out, this is Picoult's driving concern, too. That *Small Great Things* embraces this question with empathy, hope and humility is no small feat." —*Newsday*

"The gem of this novel lies in the characterization of Picoult's three narrators: Ruth; Ruth's white public defender, Kennedy McQuarrie, who prefers to keep race out of the courtroom; and Turk Bauer, the baby's father. As the narrators alternate throughout the novel, their perspectives on the case are strikingly distinct." —*Vox Magazine*

"It's Jodi Picoult, the prime provider of literary soul food. This riveting drama is sure to be supremely satisfying and a bravely thought-provoking tale on the dangers of prejudice." —*Redbook*

By Jodi Picoult

A Spark of Light

Small Great Things

Leaving Time

The Storyteller

Lone Wolf

Sing You Home

House Rules

Handle with Care

Change of Heart

Nineteen Minutes

The Tenth Circle

Vanishing Acts

My Sister's Keeper

Second Glance

Perfect Match

Salem Falls

Plain Truth

Keeping Faith

The Pact

Mercy

Picture Perfect

Harvesting the Heart

Songs of the Humpback Whale

For Young Adults

Off the Page

Between the Lines

And for the Stage

Over the Moon: An Original Musical for Teens

small
great
things

VINTAGE CANADA

small great things

A NOVEL

Jodi Picoult

Library and Archives Canada Cataloguing in Publication

Picoult, Jodi, 1966– , author
Small great things / Jodi Picoult

ISBN 978-0-345-81339-8
eBook ISBN 978-0-345-81340-4

I. Title.

PS3566.I372S63 2018   813'.54   C2016-903760-6

Book design by Susan Turner

Printed and bound in the United States of America

6 8 9 7

VINTAGE CANADA

Penguin
Random
House

For Kevin Ferreira,
whose ideas and actions make the world a better place,
and who taught me that we are all works in progress.
Welcome to the family.

stage one

Early Labor

Justice will not be served until those who are unaffected
are as outraged as those who are.
—Benjamin Franklin

Ruth

THE MIRACLE HAPPENED ON WEST SEVENTY-FOURTH STREET, IN THE HOME where Mama worked. It was a big brownstone encircled by a wrought-iron fence, and overlooking either side of the ornate door were gargoyles, their granite faces carved from my nightmares. They terrified me, so I didn't mind the fact that we always entered through the less-impressive side door, whose keys Mama kept on a ribbon in her purse.

Mama had been working for Sam Hallowell and his family since before my sister and I were born. You may not have recognized his name, but you would have known him the minute he said hello. He had been the unmistakable voice in the mid-1960s who announced before every show: *The following program is brought to you in living color on NBC!* In 1976, when the miracle happened, he was the network's head of programming. The doorbell beneath those gargoyles was the famously pitched three-note chime everyone associates with NBC. Sometimes, when I came to work with my mother, I'd sneak outside and push the button and hum along.

The reason we were with Mama that day was because it was a snow day. School was canceled, but we were too little to stay alone in our apartment while Mama went to work—which she did, through snow and sleet and probably also earthquakes and Armageddon. She muttered, stuffing us into our snowsuits and boots, that it didn't matter if she had to cross a blizzard to do it, but God forbid Ms. Mina had to spread the peanut butter on her own sandwich bread. In fact the only time I remember Mama taking time off work was twenty-five years later, when she had a double hip replacement, generously paid for by the Hallowells. She stayed home for a week, and even after that, when it didn't quite heal right and she insisted on returning to work, Mina found her tasks to do that kept her off her feet. But when I was little, during school vacations and bouts of fever and snow days like this one, Mama would take us with her on the B train downtown.

Mr. Hallowell was away in California that week, which happened often, and which meant that Ms. Mina and Christina needed Mama even more. So did Rachel and I, but we were better at taking care of ourselves, I suppose, than Ms. Mina was.

When we finally emerged at Seventy-second Street, the world was white. It was not just that Central Park was caught in a snow globe. The faces of the men and women shuddering through the storm to get to work looked nothing like mine, or like my cousins' or neighbors'.

I had not been into any Manhattan homes except for the Hallowells', so I didn't know how extraordinary it was for one family to live, alone, in this huge building. But I remember thinking it made no sense that Rachel and I had to put our snowsuits and boots into the tiny, cramped closet in the kitchen, when there were plenty of empty hooks and open spaces in the main entry, where Christina's and Ms. Mina's coats were hanging. Mama tucked away her coat, too, and her lucky scarf—the soft one that smelled like her, and that Rachel and I fought to wear around our house because it felt like petting a guinea pig or a bunny under your fingers. I waited for Mama to move through the dark rooms like Tinker Bell, alighting on a switch or a handle or a knob so that the sleeping beast of a house was gradually brought to life.

"You two be quiet," Mama told us, "and I'll make you some of Ms. Mina's hot chocolate."

It was imported from Paris, and it tasted like heaven. So as Mama tied on her white apron, I took a piece of paper from a kitchen drawer and a packet of crayons I'd brought from home and silently started to sketch. I made a house as big as this one. I put a family inside: me, Mama, Rachel. I tried to draw snow, but I couldn't. The flakes I'd made with the white crayon were invisible on the paper. The only way to see them was to tilt the paper sideways toward the chandelier light, so I could make out the shimmer where the crayon had been.

"Can we play with Christina?" Rachel asked. Christina was six, falling neatly between the ages of Rachel and me. Christina had the biggest bedroom I had ever seen and more toys than anyone I knew. When she was home and we came to work with our mother, we played school with her and her teddy bears, drank water out of real miniature china teacups, and braided the corn-silk hair of her dolls. Unless she had a friend over, in which case we stayed in the kitchen and colored.

But before Mama could answer, there was a scream so piercing and so ragged that it stabbed me in the chest. I knew it did the same to Mama, because she nearly dropped the pot of water she was carrying to the sink. "Stay here," she said, her voice already trailing behind her as she ran upstairs.

Rachel was the first one out of her chair; she wasn't one to follow instructions. I was drawn in her wake, a balloon tied to her wrist. My hand skimmed over the banister of the curved staircase, not touching.

Ms. Mina's bedroom door was wide open, and she was twisting on the bed in a sinkhole of satin sheets. The round of her belly rose like a moon; the shining whites of her eyes made me think of merry-go-round horses, frozen in flight. "It's too early, Lou," she gasped.

"Tell that to this baby," Mama replied. She was holding the telephone receiver. Ms. Mina held her other hand in a death grip. "You stop pushing, now," she said. "The ambulance'll be here any minute."

I wondered how fast an ambulance could get here in all that snow. "Mommy?"

It wasn't until I heard Christina's voice that I realized the noise had woken her up. She stood between Rachel and me. "You three, go to Miss Christina's room," Mama ordered, with steel in her voice. "*Now.*"

But we remained rooted to the spot as Mama quickly forgot about us, lost in a world made of Ms. Mina's pain and fear, trying to be the map that she could follow out of it. I watched the cords stand out on Ms. Mina's neck as she groaned; I saw Mama kneel on the bed between her legs and push her gown over her knees. I watched the pink lips between Ms. Mina's legs purse and swell and part. There was the round knob of a head, a knot of shoulder, a gush of blood and fluid, and suddenly, a baby was cradled in Mama's palms.

"Look at you," she said, with love written over her face. "Weren't you in a hurry to get into this world?"

Two things happened at once: the doorbell rang, and Christina started to cry. "Oh, honey," Ms. Mina crooned, not scary anymore but still sweaty and red-faced. She held out her hand, but Christina was too terrified by what she had seen, and instead she burrowed closer to me. Rachel, ever practical, went to answer the front door. She returned with two paramedics, who swooped in and took over, so that what Mama had done for Ms. Mina became like everything else she did for the Hallowells: seamless and invisible.

The Hallowells named the baby Louis, after Mama. He was fine, even though he was almost a full month early, a casualty of the barometric pressure dropping with the storm, which caused a PROM—a premature rupture of membranes. Of course, I didn't know that back then. I only knew that on a snowy day in Manhattan I had seen the very start of someone. I'd been with that baby before anyone or anything in this world had a chance to disappoint him.

The experience of watching Louis being born affected us all differently. Christina had her baby via surrogate. Rachel had five. Me, I became a labor and delivery nurse.

When I tell people this story, they assume the miracle I am referring to during that long-ago blizzard was the birth of a baby. True, that was astonishing. But that day I witnessed a greater wonder. As Christina held my hand and Ms. Mina held Mama's, there was a moment—one heartbeat, one breath—where all the differences in schooling and money and skin color evaporated like mirages in a desert. Where everyone was equal, and it was just one woman, helping another.

That miracle, I've spent thirty-nine years waiting to see again.

stage one
Active Labor

Not everything that is faced can be changed.
But nothing can be changed until it is faced.
—James Baldwin

Ruth

THE MOST BEAUTIFUL BABY I EVER SAW WAS BORN WITHOUT A FACE.

From the neck down, he was perfect: ten fingers, ten toes, chubby belly. But where his ear should have been, there was a twist of lips and a single tooth. Instead of a face there was a swirling eddy of skin with no features.

His mother—my patient—was a thirty-year-old gravida 1 para 1 who had received prenatal care including an ultrasound, but the baby had been positioned in a way that the facial deformity hadn't been visible. The spine, the heart, the organs had all looked fine, so no one was expecting this. Maybe for that very reason, she chose to deliver at Mercy–West Haven, our little cottage hospital, and not Yale–New Haven, which is better equipped for emergencies. She came in full term, and labored for sixteen hours before she delivered. The doctor lifted the baby, and there was nothing but silence. Buzzy, white silence.

"Is he all right?" the mother asked, panicking. "Why isn't he crying?"

I had a student nurse shadowing me, and she screamed.

"Get out," I said tightly, shoving her from the room. Then I took the newborn from the obstetrician and placed him on the warmer, wiping the vernix from his limbs. The OB did a quick exam, silently met my gaze, and turned back to the parents, who by now knew something was terribly wrong. In soft words, the doctor said their child had profound birth defects that were incompatible with life.

On a birth pavilion, Death is a more common patient than you'd think. When we have anencephalies or fetal deaths, we know that the parents still have to bond with and mourn for that baby. This infant— alive, for however long that might be—was still this couple's son.

So I cleaned him and swaddled him, the way I would any other newborn, while the conversation behind me between the parents and the doctor stopped and started like a car choking through the winter. *Why? How? What if you . . . ? How long until . . . ?* Questions no one ever wants to ask, and no one ever wants to answer.

The mother was still crying when I settled the baby in the crook of her elbow. His tiny hands windmilled. She smiled down at him, her heart in her eyes. "Ian," she whispered. "Ian Michael Barnes."

She wore an expression I've only seen in paintings in museums, of a love and a grief so fierce that they forged together to create some new, raw emotion.

I turned to the father. "Would you like to hold your son?"

He looked like he was about to be sick. "I can't," he muttered and bolted from the room.

I followed him, but was intercepted by the nurse in training, who was apologetic and upset. "I'm sorry," she said. "It's just . . . it was a *monster*."

"It *is* a *baby*," I corrected, and I pushed past her.

I cornered the father in the parents' lounge. "Your wife and your son need you."

"That's not my son," he said. "That . . . thing . . ."

"Is not going to be on this earth for very long. Which means you'd better give him all the love you had stored up for his lifetime right now." I waited until he looked me in the eye, and then I turned on my heel. I did not have to glance back to know he was following me.

When we entered the hospital room, his wife was still nuzzling the infant, her lips pressed to the smooth canvas of his brow. I took the tiny bundle from her arms, and handed the baby to her husband. He sucked in his breath and then drew back the blanket from the spot where the baby's face should have been.

I've thought about my actions, you know. If I did the right thing by forcing the father to confront his dying baby, if it was my place as a nurse. Had my supervisor asked me at the time, I would have said that I'd been trained to provide closure for grieving parents. If this man didn't acknowledge that something truly horrible had happened—or worse, if he kept pretending for the rest of his life that it never *had*—a hole would open up inside him. Tiny at first, that pit would wear away, bigger and bigger, until one day when he wasn't expecting it he would realize he was completely hollow.

When the father started to cry, the sobs shook his body, like a hurricane bends a tree. He sank down beside his wife on the hospital bed, and she put one hand on her husband's back and one on the crown of the baby's head.

They took turns holding their son for ten hours. That mother, she even tried to let him nurse. I could not stop staring—not because it was ugly or wrong, but because it was the most remarkable thing I'd ever seen. It felt like looking into the face of the sun: once I turned away, I was blind to everything else.

At one point, I took that stupid nursing student into the room with me, ostensibly to check the mother's vitals, but really to make her see with her own eyes how love has nothing to do with what you're looking at, and everything to do with who's looking.

When the infant died, it was peaceful. We made casts of the newborn's hand and foot for the parents to keep. I heard that this same couple came back two years later and delivered a healthy daughter, though I wasn't on duty when it happened.

It just goes to show you: every baby is born beautiful.

It's what we project on them that makes them ugly.

RIGHT AFTER I GAVE BIRTH to Edison, seventeen years ago at this very hospital, I wasn't worried about the health of my baby, or how I was going to juggle being a single parent while my husband was overseas, or how my life was going to change now that I was a mother.

I was worried about my hair.

The last thing you're thinking about when you're in labor is what you look like, but if you're like me, it's the first thing that crosses your mind once that baby's come. The sweat that mats the hair of all my white patients to their foreheads instead made my roots curl up and pull away from the scalp. Brushing my hair around my head in a swirl like an ice cream cone and wrapping it in a scarf each night was what kept it straight the next day when I took it down. But what white nurse knew that, or understood that the little complimentary bottle of shampoo provided by the hospital auxiliary league was only going to make my hair even frizzier? I was sure that when my well-meaning colleagues came in to meet Edison, they would be shocked into stupor at the sight of the mess going on atop my head.

In the end, I wound up wrapping it in a towel, and told visitors I'd just had a shower.

I know nurses who work on surgical floors who tell me about men wheeled out of surgery who insist on taping their toupees into place in the recovery room before their spouses join them. And I can't tell you the number of times a patient who has spent the night grunting and screaming and pushing out a baby with her husband at her side will kick her spouse out of the room postdelivery so I can help her put on a pretty nightgown and robe.

I understand the need people have to put a certain face on for the rest of the world. Which is why—when I first arrive for my shift at 6:40 A.M.—I don't even go into the staff room, where we will shortly receive the night's update from the charge nurse. Instead I slip down the hall to the patient I'd been with yesterday, before my shift ended. Her name was Jessie; she was a tiny little thing who had come into the pavilion looking more like a campaigning First Lady than a woman in active labor: her hair was perfectly coiffed, her face airbrushed with makeup, even her maternity clothes were fitted and stylish. That's a dead giveaway, since by forty weeks of pregnancy most mothers-to-be would be happy to wear a pup tent. I scanned her chart—G1, now

P1—and grinned. The last thing I'd said to Jessie before I turned her care over to a colleague and went home for the night was that the next time I saw her, she'd have a baby, and sure enough, I have a new patient. While I've been sleeping, Jessie's delivered a healthy seven-pound, six-ounce girl.

I open the door to find Jessie dozing. The baby lies swaddled in the bassinet beside the bed; Jessie's husband is sprawled in a chair, snoring. Jessie stirs when I walk in, and I immediately put a finger to my lips. *Quiet.*

From my purse, I pull a compact mirror and a red lipstick.

Part of labor is conversation; it's the distraction that makes the pain ebb and it's the glue that bonds a nurse to her patient. What other situation can you think of where one medical professional spends up to twelve hours consulting with a single person? As a result, the connection we build with these women is fierce and fast. I know things about them, in a mere matter of hours, that their own closest friends don't always know: how she met her partner at a bar when she'd had too much to drink; how her father didn't live long enough to see this grandchild; how she worries about being a mom because she hated babysitting as a teenager. Last night, in the dragon hours of Jessie's labor, when she was teary and exhausted and snapping at her husband, I'd suggested that he go to the cafeteria to get a cup of coffee. As soon as he left, the air in the room was easier to breathe, and she fell back against those awful plastic pillows we have in the birthing pavilion. "What if this baby changes everything?" she sobbed. She confessed that she never went anywhere without her "game face" on, that her husband had never even seen her without mascara; and now here he was watching her body contort itself inside out, and how would he ever look at her the same way again?

Listen, I had told her. *You let* me *worry about that.*

I'd like to think my taking that one straw off her back was what gave her the strength to make it to transition.

It's funny. When I tell people I've been a labor and delivery nurse for more than twenty years, they're impressed by the fact that I have assisted in cesareans, that I can start an IV in my sleep, that I can tell the difference between a decel in the fetal heart rate that is normal and one that requires intervention. But for me, being an L & D nurse is all about knowing your patient, and what she needs. A back rub. An epidural. A little Maybelline.

Jessie glances at her husband, still dead to the world. Then she takes the lipstick from my hand. "Thank you," she whispers, and our eyes connect. I hold the mirror as she once again reinvents herself.

ON THURSDAYS, MY SHIFT GOES from 7:00 A.M. till 7:00 P.M. At Mercy–West Haven, during the day, we usually have two nurses on the birthing pavilion—three if we're swimming in human resources that day. As I walk through the pavilion, I note idly how many of our delivery suites are occupied—it's three, right now, a nice slow start to the day. Marie, the charge nurse, is already in the room where we have our morning meeting when I come inside, but Corinne—the second nurse on shift with me—is missing. "What's it going to be today?" Marie asks, as she flips through the morning paper.

"Flat tire," I reply. This guessing game is a routine: *What excuse will Corinne use today for being late?* It's a beautiful fall day in October, so she can't blame the weather.

"That was last week. I'm going with the flu."

"Speaking of which," I say. "How's Ella?" Marie's eight-year-old had caught the stomach bug that's been going around.

"Back in school today, thank God," Marie replies. "Now Dave's got it. I figure I have twenty-four hours before I'm down for the count." She looks up from the Regional section of the paper. "I saw Edison's name in here again," she says.

My son has made the Highest Honors list for every semester of his high school career. But just like I tell him, that's no reason to boast. "There are a lot of bright kids in this town," I demur.

"Still," Marie says. "For a boy like Edison to be so successful . . . well. You should be proud, is all. I can only hope Ella turns out to be that good a student."

A boy like Edison. I know what she is saying, even if she's careful not to spell it out. There are not many Black kids in the high school, and as far as I know, Edison is the only one on the Highest Honors list. Comments like this feel like paper cuts, but I've worked with Marie for over ten years now, so I try to ignore the sting. I know she doesn't really mean anything by it. She's a friend, after all—she came to my house with her family for Easter supper last year, along with some of the other nurses, and we've gone out for cocktails or movie nights and once a girls' weekend at a spa. Still, Marie has no idea how often I have to just take a deep breath, and move on. White people don't mean half the offensive things that come out of their mouths, and so I try not to let myself get rubbed the wrong way.

"Maybe you should hope that Ella makes it through the school day without going to the nurse's office again," I reply, and Marie laughs.

"You're right. First things first."

Corinne explodes into the room. "Sorry I'm late," she says, and Marie and I exchange a look. Corinne's fifteen years younger than I am, and there's always some emergency—a carburetor that's dead, a fight with her boyfriend, a crash on 95N. Corinne is one of those people for whom life is just the space between crises. She takes off her coat and manages to knock over a potted plant that died months ago, which no one has bothered to replace. "Dammit," she mutters, righting the pot and sweeping the soil back inside. She dusts off her palms on her scrubs, and then sits down with her hands folded. "I'm really sorry, Marie. The stupid tire I replaced last week has a leak or something; I had to drive here the whole way going thirty."

Marie reaches into her pocket and pulls out a dollar, which she flicks across the table at me. I laugh.

"All right," Marie says. "Floor report. Room two is a couplet. Jessica Myers, G one P one at forty weeks and two days. She had a vaginal delivery this morning at three A.M., uncomplicated, without pain meds. Baby girl is breast-feeding well; she's peed but hasn't pooped yet."

"I'll take her," Corinne and I say in unison.

Everyone wants the patient who's already delivered; it's the easier job. "I had her during active labor," I point out.

"Right," Marie says. "Ruth, she's yours." She pushes her reading glasses up on her nose. "Room three is Thea McVaughn, G one P zero at forty-one weeks and three days, she's in active labor at four centimeters dilated, membranes intact. Fetal heart rate tracing looks good on the monitor, the baby's active. She's requested an epidural and her IV fluid bolus is infusing."

"Has Anesthesia been paged?" Corinne asks.

"Yes."

"I've got her."

We only take one active labor patient at a time, if we can help it, which means that the third patient—the last one this morning—will be mine. "Room five is a recovery. Brittany Bauer is a G one P one at thirty-nine weeks and one day; had an epidural and a vaginal delivery at five-thirty A.M. Baby's a boy; they want a circ. Mom was a GDM A one; the baby is on Q three hour blood sugars for twenty-four hours. The mom really wants to breast-feed. They're still skin to skin."

A recovery is still a lot of work—a one-to-one nurse-patient relationship. True, the labor's finished, but there is still tidying up to be done, a physical assessment of the newborn, and a stack of paperwork. "Got it," I say, and I push away from the table to go find Lucille, the night nurse, who was with Brittany during the delivery.

She finds me first, in the staff restroom, washing my hands. "Tag, you're it," she says, handing me Brittany Bauer's file. "Twenty-six-year-old G one, now P one, delivered vaginally this morning at five-thirty over an intact perineum. She's O positive, rubella immune, Hep B and HIV negative, GBS negative. Gestational diabetic, diet controlled, otherwise uncomplicated. She still has an IV in her left forearm. I DC'd the epidural, but she hasn't been out of bed yet, so ask her if she has to get up and pee. Her bleeding's been good, her fundus is firm at U."

I open the file and scan the notes, committing the details to memory. "Davis," I read. "That's the baby?"

"Yeah. His vital signs have been normal, but his one-hour blood sugar was forty, so we've got him trying to nurse. He's done a little bit on each side, but he's kind of spitty and sleepy and he hasn't done a whole lot of eating."

"Did he get his eyes and thighs?"

"Yeah, and he's peed, but hasn't pooped. I haven't done the bath or the newborn assessment yet."

"No problem," I say. "Is that it?"

"The dad's name is Turk," Lucille replies, hesitating. "There's something just a little . . . off about him."

"Like Creeper Dad?" I ask. Last year, we had a father who was flirting with the nursing student in the room during his wife's delivery. When she wound up having a C-section, instead of standing behind the drape near his wife's head, he strolled across the OR and said to the nursing student, *Is it hot in here, or is it just you?*

"Not like that," Lucille says. "He's appropriate with the mom. He's just . . . sketchy. I can't put my finger on it."

I've always thought that if I wasn't an L & D nurse, I'd make a great fake psychic. We are skilled at reading our patients so that we know what they need moments before they realize it. And we are also gifted when it comes to sensing strange vibes. Just last month my radar went off when a mentally challenged patient came in with an older Ukrainian woman who had befriended her at the grocery store where she worked. There was something weird about the dynamic between them, and I followed my hunch and called the police. Turned out the Ukrainian woman had served time in Kentucky for stealing the baby of a woman with Down syndrome.

So as I walk into Brittany Bauer's room for the first time, I am not worried. I'm thinking: *I've got this.*

I knock softly and push open the door. "I'm Ruth," I say. "I'm going to be your nurse today." I walk right up to Brittany, and smile down at the baby cradled in her arms. "Isn't he a sweetie! What's his name?" I ask, although I already know. It's a means to start a conversation, to connect with the patient.

Brittany doesn't answer. She looks at her husband, a hulking guy who's sitting on the edge of his chair. He's got military-short hair and he's bouncing the heel of one boot like he can't quite stay still. I get what Lucille saw in him. Turk Bauer makes me think of a power line that's snapped during a storm, and lies across the road just waiting for something to brush against it so it can shoot sparks.

It doesn't matter if you're shy or modest—nobody who's just had a baby stays quiet for long. They *want* to share this life-changing moment. They *want* to relive the labor, the birth, the beauty of their baby. But Brittany, well, it's almost like she needs his permission to speak. *Domestic abuse?* I wonder.

"Davis," she chokes out. "His name is Davis."

"Well, hello, Davis," I murmur, moving closer to the bed. "Would you mind if I take a listen to his heart and lungs and check his temperature?"

Her arms clamp tighter on the newborn, pulling him closer.

"I can do it right here," I say. "You don't have to let go of him."

You have to cut a new parent a little bit of slack, especially one who's already been told her baby's blood sugar is too low. So I tuck the thermometer under Davis's armpit, and get a normal reading. I look at the whorls of his hair—a patch of white can signify hearing loss; an alternating hair pattern can flag metabolic issues. I press my stethoscope against the baby's back, listening to his lungs. I slide my hand between him and his mother, listening to his heart.

Whoosh.

It's so faint that I think it's a mistake.

I listen again, trying to make sure it wasn't a fluke, but that slight whir is there behind the backbeat of the pulse.

Turk stands up so that he is towering over me; he folds his arms.

Nerves look different on fathers. They get combative, sometimes. As if they could bluster away whatever's wrong.

"I hear a very slight murmur," I say delicately. "But it could be nothing. This early, there are still parts of the heart that are developing. Even if it *is* a murmur, it could disappear in a few days. Still, I'll make a note of it; I'll have the pediatrician take a listen." While I'm talking, trying to be as calm as possible, I do another blood sugar. It's an Accu-Chek, which means we get instant results—and this time, he's at fifty-two. "Now, *this* is great news," I say, trying to give the Bauers something positive to hold on to. "His sugar is much better." I walk to the sink and run warm water, fill a plastic bowl, and set it on the warmer. "Davis is definitely perking up, and he'll probably start eating really soon. Why don't I get him cleaned up, and fire him up a little bit, and we can try nursing again?"

I reach down and scoop the baby up. Turning my back to the parents, I place Davis on the warmer and begin my exam. I can hear Brittany and Turk whispering fiercely as I check the fontanels on the baby's head for the suture lines, to make sure the bones aren't overriding each other. The parents are worried, and that's normal. A lot of patients don't like to take the nurse's opinion on any medical issue; they need to hear it from the doctor to believe it—even though L & D nurses are often the ones who first notice a quirk or a symptom. Their pediatrician is Atkins; I will page her after I'm done with the exam, and have her listen to the baby's heart.

But right now, my attention is on Davis. I look for facial bruising, hematoma, or abnormal shaping of the skull. I check the palmar creases in his tiny hands, and the set of his ears relative to his eyes. I measure the circumference of his head and the length of his squirming body. I check for clefts in the mouth and the ears. I palpate the clavicles and put my pinkie in his mouth to check his sucking reflex. I study the rise and fall of the tiny bellows of his chest, to make sure his breathing isn't labored. Press his belly to make sure it's soft, check his fingers and toes, scan for rashes or lesions or birthmarks. I make sure his testicles have descended and scan for hypospadias, making sure that the urethra is where it's supposed to be. Then I gently turn him over and scan the base of the spine for dimples or hair tufts or any other indicator of neural tube defect.

I realize that the whispering behind me has stopped. But instead of feeling more comfortable, it feels ominous. *What do they think I'm doing wrong?*

By the time I flip him back over, Davis's eyes are starting to drift shut. Babies usually get sleepy a couple of hours after delivery, which is one reason to do the bath now—it will wake him up long enough to try to feed again. There is a stack of wipes on the warmer; with practiced, sure strokes I dip one into the warm water and wipe the baby down from head to toe. Then I diaper him, swiftly wrap him up in a blanket like a burrito, and rinse his hair under the sink with some Johnson's baby shampoo. The last thing I do is put an ID band on him that will match the ones his parents have, and fasten a tiny electronic security bracelet on his ankle, which will set off an alarm if the baby gets too close to any of the exits.

I can feel the parents' eyes, hot on my back. I turn, a smile fastened on my face. "There," I say, handing the infant to Brittany again. "Clean as a whistle. Now, let's see if we can get him to nurse."

I reach down to help position the baby, but Brittany flinches.

"Get away from her," Turk Bauer says. "I want to talk to your boss."

They are the first words he has spoken to me in the twenty minutes I've been in this room with him and his family, and they carry an undercurrent of discontent. I'm pretty sure he doesn't want to tell Marie what a stellar job I've done. But I nod tightly and step out of the room, replaying every word and gesture I have made since introducing myself to Brittany Bauer. I walk to the nurses' desk and find Marie filling out a chart. "We've got a problem in Five," I say, trying to keep my voice even. "The father wants to see you."

"What happened?" Marie asks.

"Absolutely nothing," I reply, and I know it's true. I'm a good nurse. Sometimes a great one. I took care of that infant the way I would have taken care of any newborn on this pavilion. "I told them I heard what sounded like a murmur, and that I'd contact the pediatrician. And I bathed the baby and did his exam."

I must be doing a pretty awful job of hiding my feelings, though, because Marie looks at me sympathetically. "Maybe they're worried about the baby's heart," she says.

I am just a step behind her as we walk inside, so I can clearly see the relief on the faces of the parents when they see Marie. "I understand that you wanted to talk to me, Mr. Bauer?" she says.

"That nurse," Turk says. "I don't want her touching my son again."

I can feel heat spreading from the collar of my scrubs up into my scalp. No one likes to be called out in front of her supervisor.

Marie draws herself upright, her spine stiffening. "I can assure you that Ruth is one of the best nurses we have, Mr. Bauer. If there's a formal complaint—"

"I don't want her or anyone who looks like her touching my son," the father interrupts, and he folds his arms across his chest. He's pushed up his sleeves while I was out of the room. Running from wrist to elbow on one arm is the tattoo of a Confederate flag.

Marie stops talking.

For a moment, I honestly don't understand. And then it hits me with the force of a blow: they don't have a problem with what I've done.

Just with who I am.

Turk

THE FIRST NIGGER I EVER MET KILLED MY OLDER BROTHER. I SAT BETWEEN my parents in a Vermont courtroom, wearing a stiff-collared shirt choking me, while men in suits argued and pointed at diagrams of cars and tire skids. I was eleven and Tanner sixteen. He'd just got his driver's license two months before. To celebrate, my mother baked him a cake decorated with a Fruit Roll-Up highway and one of my old Matchbox cars. The guy who killed him was from Massachusetts and was older than my father. His skin was darker than the wood of the witness box, and his teeth were nearly electric by contrast. I couldn't stop staring.

The jury couldn't reach a verdict—hung, they called it—and so this man was free to go. My mother completely lost it, shrieking, babbling about her baby and justice. The murderer shook hands with his lawyer and then turned around, walking toward us, so that we were only separated by a railing. "Mrs. Bauer," he said. "I am so sorry for your loss."

As if he had nothing to do with it.

My mother stopped sobbing, pursed her lips, and spit.

* * *

BRIT AND ME, WE'VE BEEN waiting forever for this moment.

I'm driving with one hand on the steering wheel of the pickup and the other one on the bench seat between us; she clenches it every time a contraction hits her. I can tell it hurts like a bitch, but Brit just narrows her eyes and sets her jaw. It's not a surprise—I mean, I've seen her knock out the teeth of a beaner who dented her car at the Stop & Shop with a runaway cart—but I don't think she's ever been quite so beautiful to me as she is right now, strong and silent.

I steal glimpses at her profile when we idle at a red light. We have been married for two years, but I still can't believe that Brit is mine. She's the prettiest girl I've ever seen, for one, and in the Movement, she's about as close to royalty as you can get. Her dark hair snakes in a curly rope down her back; her cheeks are flushed. She's puffing, little breaths, like she's running a marathon. Suddenly she turns, her eyes bright and blue, like the middle of a flame. "No one said it would be this hard," she pants.

I squeeze her hand, which is something, because she's already squeezing mine to the point of pain. "This warrior," I tell her, "is going to be just as strong as its mom." For years, I was taught that God needs soldiers. That we are the angels of this race war, and without us, the world would become Sodom and Gomorrah all over again. Francis— Brit's legendary dad—would stand up and preach to all the fresh cuts the need to increase our numbers, so that we could fight back. But now that Brit and I are here, in this moment, about to bring a baby into the world, I'm filled with equal parts triumph and terror. Because as hard as I've tried, this place is still a cesspool. Right now, my baby is perfect. But from the moment it arrives, it's bound to be tainted.

"Turk!" Brittany cries.

Wildly, I take a left-hand turn, having nearly missed the hospital entrance. "What do you think of Thor?" I ask, turning the conversation to baby names, desperate to distract Brit from the pain. One of the guys I know from Twitter just had a kid and named him Loki. Some of the older crews were big into Norse mythology, and even though they've broken up into smaller cells by now, old habits die hard.

"Or Batman or Green Lantern?" Brittany snaps. "I'm not naming my kid after a comic book character." She winces through another contraction. "And what if it's a girl?"

"Wonder Woman," I suggest. "After her mother."

AFTER MY BROTHER DIED, EVERYTHING fell apart. It was like that trial had ripped off the outside layer of skin, and what was left of my family was just a lot of blood and guts with nothing to hold it together anymore. My father split and went to live in a condo where everything was green—the walls, the carpet, the toilet, the stove—and every time I visited, I couldn't help but feel queasy. My mother started drinking—a glass of wine with lunch and then the whole bottle. She lost her job as a paraprofessional at the elementary school when she passed out on the playground and her charge—a kid with Down syndrome—fell off the monkey bars and broke her wrist. A week later we put everything we owned into a U-Haul and moved in with my grandfather.

Gramps was a vet who had never stopped fighting a war. I didn't know him all that well, because he'd never liked my dad, but now that that obstacle was out of the way, he took it upon himself to raise me the way he thought I should have been raised all along. My parents, he said, had been too soft on me, and I was a sissy. He was going to toughen me up. He'd wake me up at dawn on weekends and drag me into the woods for what he called Basic Training. I learned how to tell poisonous berries apart from the ones you could eat. I was able to identify scat so I could track animals. I could tell time by the position of the sun. It was sort of like Boy Scouts, except that my grandfather's lessons were punctuated by stories of the gooks he fought in Vietnam, of jungles that would swallow you if you let them, of the smell of a man being burned alive.

One weekend he decided to take me camping. The fact that it was only six degrees outside and that snow was predicted did not matter. We drove to the edge of the Northeast Kingdom, close to the Canadian border. I went to the bathroom, and when I came back out my grandfather was gone.

His truck, which had been parked at a pump, was missing. The only hints that he'd been there at all were the impressions of the tire tracks in the snow. He'd left with my backpack, my sleeping bag, and the tent. I went into the gas station again and asked the attendant if she knew what had happened to the guy in the blue truck, but she just shook her head. "Comment?" she said, pretending like she didn't even speak English even though she was still technically in Vermont.

I had my coat, but no hat or mittens—they were still in the truck. I counted sixty-seven cents in my pocket. I waited until another customer pulled into the gas station and then, when the cashier was occupied, I shoplifted a pair of gloves and a hunter-orange hat and a bottle of soda.

It took me five hours to track my grandfather—a combination of racking my brain to remember what he'd been yammering on about in terms of directions that morning when I was half asleep, and walking down the highway looking for clues—like the wrapper from the tobacco he liked to chew, and one of my mittens. By the time I found his truck pulled off on the side of the road and could follow his footprints through the snow into the woods, I wasn't shivering anymore. I was a furnace. Anger, it turns out, is a renewable source of fuel.

He was bent over a campfire when I stepped into the clearing. Without saying a word, I walked up and shoved him so that he nearly fell into the burning embers. "You son of a bitch," I yelled. "You can't just walk away from me."

"Why not? If I don't make a man out of you, who the hell will?" he said.

Even though he was twice as big as me, I grabbed him by the collar of his jacket and hauled him upright. I drew back my fist and tried to punch him, but he grabbed my hand before the blow could land.

"You want to fight?" my grandfather said, backing away and circling me.

My father had taught me how to punch someone. Thumb on the outside of your fist, and twist the wrist at the very end of the throw. It was all talk, though; I'd never hit someone in my life.

Now, I drew back my fist and shot it forward like an arrow, only to have my grandfather twist my arm behind my back. His breath was hot in my ear. "Did your pansy-ass father teach you that?" I struggled, but he had me pinned. "You want to know how to fight? Or do you want to know how to *win*?"

I gritted my teeth. "I . . . want . . . to win," I ground out.

Gradually he relaxed his grip, keeping one hand clamped on my left shoulder.

"You're small, so you come in real low. Then you'll be blinding me with your body, and I'm expecting you to bring the punch up. If I duck, my fist will hit you in the face, which means I'll stay upright, and leave myself wide open. The last thing I'll be expecting is for you to come up over the shoulder like this."

He raised his right fist, looping it up and over in a dizzy arc that stopped a breath before it kissed my cheekbone. Then he let go of me and took a step back. "Go on."

I just stared at him.

This is what it feels like to beat someone up: like a rubber band stretched so tight it aches, and starts to shake. And then when you throw that punch, when you let go of the elastic, the snap is electric. You're on fire, and you didn't even realize you were combustible.

Blood sprayed from my grandfather's nose onto the snow; it coated his smile. "That's my boy," he said.

EVERY TIME BRIT GETS UP during labor, the contractions get so bad that the nurse—a redhead named Lucille—tells her to lie back down. But when she does, the contractions stop, and so Lucille tells her to take a walk. It's a vicious circle, and it's been seven hours already, and I'm starting to wonder if my kid is going to be a teenager before he decides to come into this world.

Not that I'm saying any of that to Brit.

I've held her steady while an anesthesiologist put in an epidural—something that Brit begged for, which totally surprised me, since we had planned to do a natural birth without drugs. Anglos like us stay away from them; the vast majority of people in the Movement look down on addicts. I whispered to her as she bent over the bed, the doctor feeling along her spine, asking if this was a good idea. *When* you *have the baby*, Brit said, *you get to decide.*

And I have to admit, whatever they've got pumping through her veins has really helped. She's tethered to the bed, but she's not writhing anymore. She told me that she can't feel anything below her belly button. That if she wasn't married to me she'd propose to the anesthesiologist.

Lucille comes in and checks the printout from the machine that's hooked up to Brit, which measures the baby's heartbeat. "You're doing great," she says, although I bet she says that to everyone. I tune out as she talks to Brit—not because I don't care, but because there's just some mechanical stuff you don't want to think about if you ever want to see your wife as sexy again—and then I hear Lucille tell Brit that it's time to push.

Brit's eyes lock on mine. "Babe?" she says, but the next word jams up in her throat, and she can't say what she wants to.

I realize that she is scared. This fearless woman is actually afraid of what comes next. I thread my fingers through hers. "I'm right here," I tell her, although I'm just as terrified.

What if this changes everything between me and Brit?

What if this baby shows up and I don't feel anything at all for it?

What if I turn out to be a lousy role model? A lousy father?

"The next time you feel a contraction," Lucille says, "I want you to bear down." She looks up at me. "Dad, get behind her, and when she has the contraction, you help her sit up so she can push."

I'm grateful for the direction. *This* I can do. As Brit's face reddens, as her body arcs like a bow, I cup her shoulders in my hands. She makes a low, guttural noise, like something in its last throes of life. "Deep breath in," Lucille coaches. "You're at the top of the contraction . . . now bring your chin to your chest for me and push right down into your bottom . . ."

Then, with a gasp, Brit goes limp, shrugging away from me as if she can't stand having my hands on her. "Get off me," she says.

Lucille beckons me closer. "She doesn't mean it."

"Like hell I don't," Brit spits out, another contraction rising.

Lucille arches her eyebrows at me. "Stand up here," she suggests. "I'm going to hold Brit's left leg and you're going to hold the right . . ."

It's a marathon, not a sprint. An hour later, Brit's hair is matted to her forehead; her braid is tangled. Her fingernails have cut little moons in the back of my hand, and she's not even making sense when she talks anymore. I don't know how much more of this either of us can take. But then Lucille's shoulders square during one long contraction, and the look on her face changes. "Hang on a minute," Lucille says, and she pages the doctor. "I want you to take some slow breaths, Brit . . . and get ready to be a mom."

It's only a couple of minutes before the obstetrician bursts into the room and snaps on a pair of latex gloves, but trying to help Brit to *not* push feels like being told to hold back a tidal wave with a single sandbag. "Hello, Mrs. Bauer," the doctor says. "Let's have a baby." He crouches down on a stool as Brit's body tenses up again. My elbow is hooked around her knee so that she can strain against it, and as I look down, the brow of our baby rises like a moon in the valley of her legs.

It's blue. Where there was nothing a breath ago, there is now a perfectly round head the size of a softball, and it's blue.

Panicked, I look at Brit's face, but her eyes are screwed shut with the force of the work she's doing. Anger, which always seems to be on a low simmer in my blood, starts to boil over. *They're trying to pull one over on us. They're lying. These goddamned—*

And then the baby cries. In a rush of blood and fluid, it slips into this world, screaming and punching at the air with tiny fists, pinking up. They put my baby—*my son*—on Brit's chest and rub him with a cloth. She's sobbing, and so am I. Brit's gaze is focused on the baby. "Look at what we made, Turk."

"He's perfect," I whisper against her skin. "*You're* perfect." She cups her hand around our newborn's head, like we are an electrical circuit that's now complete. Like we could power the world.

WHEN I WAS FIFTEEN, MY grandfather dropped like a stone in the shower and died from a heart attack. I reacted the way I reacted to everything those days—by getting into trouble. No one seemed to know what to do with me—not my mom, who had faded so much sometimes she blended into the walls and I walked right past her without realizing she was in the room; and not my dad, who lived in Brattleboro now and sold cars at a Honda dealership.

I met Raine Tesco when I was staying with my dad for a month the summer after my freshman year of high school. My dad's friend Greg ran an alternative coffeehouse (What did that even mean? That they served tea?) and had offered me a part-time job. Technically I wasn't old enough to work, so Greg was paying me under the table to do things like reorganize the stockroom and run errands. Raine was a barista with a sleeve of tattoos who chain-smoked out back during all his breaks. He had a six-pound Chihuahua named Meat that he'd taught to puff on a cigarette, too.

Raine was the first person who really *got* me. The first time I saw him out back, when I went to put the trash in the dumpster, he offered me a smoke—even though I was only a kid. I pretended I knew what I was doing, and when I coughed my lungs out he didn't make fun of me. "Must suck to be you, man," he said, and I nodded. "I mean, your dad?" He screwed up his face and did a perfect imitation of my father, ordering a medium half-caf no-foam nonfat soy latte.

Every time I went to visit my dad, Raine made time to see me. I'd talk to him about how unfair it was to get detention for whaling on a kid who had called my mom a drunk. He'd say that the problem wasn't me but my teachers, who didn't realize how much potential I had and how smart I was. He gave me books to read, like *The Turner Diaries*, to show me I wasn't the only guy who felt like there was a conspiracy of people keeping him down. He'd give me CDs to take home, white power bands with beats that sounded like a hammer pounding nails. We'd drive around in his car and he'd say things like how the heads of all the major networks had Jewish last names like Moonves and Zucker and were feeding us all the news, so that we'd believe whatever they wanted us to believe. What he talked about were the things that people might have thought about, but never were brave enough to say in public.

If anyone felt it was strange that a twenty-year-old might want to hang out with a fifteen-year-old kid, no one commented. Probably my parents were relieved to know that when I was with Raine, I wasn't actively beating anyone up or cutting school or getting into trouble. So when he invited me to a festival with some friends, I jumped at the chance to go. "Are there, like, bands there?" I asked, figuring that it was one of the music gatherings that dotted the Vermont countryside in July.

"Yeah, but it's more like summer camp," Raine explained. "I told everyone you're coming. They're psyched to meet you."

No one was *ever* psyched to meet me, so I was pretty pumped. That Saturday, I packed up a knapsack and a sleeping bag and sat in the passenger seat with Meat the Chihuahua in my lap while Raine picked up three friends—all of whom knew me by name, as if Raine had really been talking about me after all. They were all wearing black shirts with a logo over the chest: NADS. "What's that stand for?" I asked.

"North American Death Squad," Raine said. "It's kind of our thing."

I wanted one of those T-shirts so bad. "So, like, how do you get to be part of it?" I asked, as casually as I could manage.

One of the other guys laughed. "You get asked," he said.

I decided at that moment I was going to do whatever it took to get an invitation.

We drove for about an hour and then Raine got off an exit, turning left at a handwritten sign on a stick that said simply IE. There were more signs like this, indicating turns through cornfields and past sagging barns and even through a field of milling cows. As we crested a ridge, I saw about a hundred cars parked in a muddy field.

It looked like a carnival. There was a stage, and a band playing so loud my heart thumped like a backbeat. There were families milling around eating corn dogs and fried dough, toddlers balanced on their fathers' shoulders wearing T-shirts that said I'M THE WHITE CHILD YOU'RE SECURING THE RACE FOR! Meat wove around my feet on his leash, getting tangled as he scarfed down bits of popcorn that had been dropped. A guy clapped Raine on the shoulder and gave him a big reunion-style hello, leaving me to wander a few feet away toward a shooting range.

A fat man with eyebrows crawling like caterpillars across his brow grinned at me. "You want to give it a go, boy?"

There was a kid about my age firing at a target that was pinned up against a stump pile. He handed the semiautomatic Browning to the old man and then went to retrieve his bull's-eye. It was a profile of a man with an exaggerated, hooked nose. "Looks like you killed that Jew, Gunther," the man said, grinning. Then he scooped Meat up in his arms and pointed to a table. "I'll hold the pooch," he told me. "You pick the one you want."

There were stacks of targets: more Jewish profiles, but also black ones, with giant lips and sloping foreheads. There was Martin Luther King, Jr., in a bull's-eye with words printed across the top: MY DREAM DID COME TRUE.

For a moment I felt sick to my stomach. The pictures reminded me of political cartoons we had been studying in history class, gross exaggerations that led to world wars. I wondered what sorts of companies manufactured targets like this, because they sure as hell weren't being sold in places like Wal-Mart's hunting aisle. It was as if there was a whole secret society I'd never known about, and I'd just been whispered the password for admission.

I snagged a target with a bushy Afro bursting through the borders of the bull's-eye. The man affixed it to a clothesline. "Can't even tell it's a silhouette," he said with a snicker. He put Meat on the table to sniff at the targets as he zipped mine back to the edge of the stump pile. "You know how to handle a weapon?" he asked.

I'd taken shots with my grandpa's handgun, but I'd never used anything like this. I listened to the man explain how the gun worked; then I put on the headphones and goggles for protection, tucked the stock against my shoulder, squinted, and squeezed the trigger. There was a volley of shots, like a coughing fit. The sound drew Raine's attention, and he clapped, impressed, as the target zipped back to me with three clean shots in the forehead. "Look at you," he said. "A natural."

Raine folded the target and tucked it into his back pocket, so he

could show his friends later how good a marksman I was. I took Meat's
leash again, and we walked across the meeting grounds. On the stage,
a man was grandstanding. His presence was so commanding that his
voice became a magnet, and I found myself being pulled to see him
more clearly. "I want to tell you all a little story," the man said. "There
was a nigger in New York City, homeless, of course. He was walking
through Central Park and several people heard him ranting, saying
that he would punch a White man in his sleep. But these people, they
didn't realize we are fighting a war. That we are protecting our race. So
they did not act. They ignored the threats as the raving of a crazy fool.
And what happened? This beast of the field approached a White
Anglo—a man like you, maybe, or me, who was doing nothing but living the life God intended him to live—a man who cared for his ninety-
year-old mother. This beast of the field punched this man, who fell
down, struck his head on the pavement, and died. This White man,
who had only been taking a walk in the park, suffered a fatal injury. Yet,
I ask you—what happened to the nigger? Well, my brothers and sisters . . . *absolutely nothing*."

I thought of my brother's killer, walking free out of a courtroom. I
watched the people around me nod and clap, and thought: *I am not
alone.*

"Who *is* he?" I asked.

"Francis Mitchum," Raine murmured. "He's one of the old guard.
But he's, like, mythic." He said the speaker's name the way a pious man
spoke of God—part whisper, part prayer. "You see the spiderweb on
his elbow? You can't get that tat until you've killed someone. For every
kill, you get a fly inked." Raine paused. "Mitchum, he's got *ten*."

"Why do niggers never get charged with hate crimes?" Francis
Mitchum asked, a rhetorical question. "Why are they being given a
free pass? They would not even be domesticated, if not for the help of
Whites. Look at where they came from, in Africa. There's no civilized
government. They're all murdering each other in the Sudan. The
Hutus are killing the Tutsis. And they're doing it in our country too.
The gangs in our cities—that's just tribal warfare among niggers. And
now, they're coming after Anglos. *Because they know they can get away*

with it." His voice rose as he looked out at the crowd. "Killing a nigger is equal to killing a deer." Then he paused. "Actually, I take that back. At least you can *eat* venison."

Many years later, I realized that the first time I went to Invisible Empire camp—the first time I heard Francis Mitchum speak—Brit must have been there, too, traveling with her father. I liked to think that maybe she was standing on the other side of that stage, listening to him hypnotize the crowd. That maybe we had bumped into each other at the cotton candy stand, or stood side by side when sparks from the cross lighting shot into the night sky.

That we were meant to be.

FOR AN HOUR, BRIT AND I toss out names like baseball pitches: Robert, Ajax, Will. Garth, Erik, Odin. Every time I think I've come up with something strong and Aryan, Brit remembers a kid in her class with that name who ate paste or who threw up in his tuba. Every time she suggests a name she likes, it reminds me of some asshole I've crossed paths with.

When it finally comes to me, with the subtlety of a lightning strike, I look down into my son's sleeping face and whisper it: Davis. The last name of the president of the Confederacy.

Brit turns the word over in her mouth. "It's different."

"Different is good."

"Davis, but not Jefferson," she clarifies.

"No, because then he'll be Jeff."

"And Jeff's a guy who smokes dope and lives in his mother's basement," Brit adds.

"But Davis," I say, "well, Davis is the kid other kids look up to."

"Not Dave. Or Davy or David."

"He'll beat up anyone who calls him that by mistake," I promise.

I touch the edge of the baby's blanket, because I don't want to wake him. "Davis," I say, testing it. His tiny hands flare, like he already knows his name.

"We should celebrate," Brit whispers.

I smile down at her. "You think they sell champagne in the cafeteria?"

"You know what I *really* want? A chocolate milkshake."

"I thought the cravings were supposed to happen *before* the birth . . ."

She laughs. "I'm pretty sure I get to play the hormone card for at least another three months . . ."

I get to my feet, wondering if the cafeteria is even open at 4:00 A.M. But I don't really want to leave. I mean, Davis just *got* here. "What if I miss something?" I ask. "You know, like a milestone."

"It's not like he's going to get up and walk or say his first word," Brit answers. "If you miss anything it's going to be his first poop, and actually, that's something you *want* to avoid." She looks up at me with those blue eyes that are sometimes as dark as the sea, and sometimes as pale as glass, and that always can get me to do anything. "It's just five minutes," she says.

"Five minutes." I look at the baby one more time, feeling like my boots are stuck in pitch. I want to stay here and count his fingers again, and those impossibly tiny nails. I want to watch his shoulders rise and fall as he breathes. I want to see his lips purse up, like he's kissing someone in his dreams. It's crazy to look at him, flesh and blood, and know that Brit and I were able to build something real and solid out of a material as blurry and intangible as love.

"Whipped cream and a cherry," Brit adds, breaking my reverie. "If they've got it."

Reluctantly I slip into the hallway, past the nurses' station, down an elevator. The cafeteria is open, staffed by a woman in a hairnet who is doing a word-search puzzle. "Do you sell milkshakes?" I ask.

She glances up. "Nope."

"How about ice cream?"

"Yeah, but we're out. Delivery truck comes in the morning."

She doesn't seem inclined to help me, and focuses her attention on her puzzle again. "I just had a baby," I blurt out.

"Wow," she says flatly. "A medical miracle, in my very own checkout line."

"Well, my *wife* had a baby," I correct. "And she wants a milkshake."

"I want a winning lottery ticket and Benedict Cumberbatch's undying love, but I had to settle for this glamorous life instead." She looks at me as if I'm wasting her time, as if there are a hundred people waiting in line behind me. "You want my advice? Get her candy. Everyone likes chocolate." She reaches blindly behind her and pulls down a box of Ghirardelli squares. I flip it over, scanning the label.

"Is that all you have?"

"The Ghirardelli's on sale."

I flip it over and see the OU symbol—the mark that proves it's kosher, that you're paying the Jewish mafia a tax. I put it back on the shelf and set a pack of Skittles down on the counter instead, with two bucks. "You can keep the change," I tell her.

JUST AFTER SEVEN, THE DOOR opens, and just like that I'm on full alert.

Since Davis arrived, Lucille's been in twice—to check on Brit and the baby, and to see how he was nursing. But this—this isn't Lucille.

"I'm Ruth," she announces. "I'm going to be your nurse today."

All I can think is: *Over my dead body.*

It takes every ounce of willpower for me to not shove her away from my wife, my son. But security is only a buzzer away, and if they throw me out of the hospital, what good does that do us? If I can't be here to protect my family, then I've already lost.

So instead, I perch on the edge of the chair, every muscle in my body poised to react.

Brit grabs Davis so tightly I think he's going to start screaming. "Isn't he a sweetie!" the black nurse says. "What's his name?"

My wife looks at me, a question in her eyes. She doesn't want to have a conversation with this nurse any more than she'd have a conversation with a goat or any other animal. But like me, she's aware that Whites have become the minority in this country and that we're always under attack; we have to blend in.

I jerk my chin once, so infinitesimally I wonder if Brit will even see it. "His name is Davis," she says tightly.

The nurse moves closer to us, saying something about examining Davis, and Brit recoils. "You don't have to let go of him," she concedes.

Her hands start moving over my son, like some kind of crazy witch doctor. She presses the stethoscope against his back and then in the space between him and Brit. She says something about Davis's heart, and I can barely even hear it, because of the blood rushing in my own ears.

Then she picks him up.

Brit and I are so shocked that she just took our baby away—just over to the warmer for a bath, but still—that for a beat neither of us can speak.

I take a step toward her, where she's bent over my boy, but Brit grabs the tail of my shirt. *Don't make a scene.*

Am I supposed to just stand here?

Do you want her to know you're pissed off and take it out on him?

I want Lucille back. What happened to Lucille?

I don't know. Maybe she left.

How can she do that, when her patient is still here?

I have no idea, Turk, I don't run this hospital.

I watch the black nurse like a hawk while she wipes Davis down and washes his hair and wraps him up in a blanket again. She puts a little electronic bracelet on his ankle—like the ones you sometimes see on prisoners who've been released on probation. As if he's already being punished by the system.

I am staring so hard at the black nurse that I wouldn't be surprised if she goes up in flames. She smiles at me, but it doesn't quite reach her eyes. "Clean as a whistle," she announces. "Now, let's see if we can get him to nurse."

She goes to pull aside the neck of Brit's hospital johnny, and I'm done. "Get away from her," I say, my voice low and true as an arrow. "I want to talk to your boss."

A YEAR AFTER I WENT to Invisible Empire camp, Raine asked me if I'd like to be part of the North American Death Squad. It was not enough to just believe what Raine believed in, about Whites being a master race. It was not enough to have read *Mein Kampf* three times. To be one of them, truly, I had to prove myself, and Raine promised me I'd know where and when the right moment came to pass.

One night when I was staying at my dad's, I woke up to hear banging on my bedroom window. I wasn't really worried about them waking up the household; my father was out at a business dinner in Boston, not due back till after midnight. As soon as I threw up the sash, Raine and two of the guys spilled inside, dressed in ninja black. Raine immediately tackled me onto the floor, forearm against my throat. "Rule number one," he said, "don't open the door if you don't know who's going to come inside." He waited until I was seeing stars and then let me go. "Rule number two: take no prisoners."

"I don't understand," I said.

"Tonight, Turk," he told me, "we are custodians. We are going to clean Vermont of its filth."

I found a pair of black sweats and a screen-printed sweatshirt I wore inside out, so that it was black, too. Since I didn't have a black knit cap, Raine let me wear his, and he pulled his hair back in a pony-tail. We drove in Raine's car, passing a bottle of Jägermeister back and forth and blasting punk through the speakers, to Dummerston.

I hadn't heard of the Rainbow Cattle Company, but as soon as we got there, I understood what kind of place this was. There were men holding hands as they walked from the parking lot into the bar, and every time the door opened there was a flash of a brightly lit stage and a drag queen lip-synching. "Whatever you do, don't bend down," Raine told me and snickered.

"What are we doing here?" I asked, not sure why he'd dragged me to a gay bar.

Just then two men walked out, their arms slung around each other. "This," Raine said, and he jumped on one of the guys, slamming his head against the ground. His date started to run in the other direction but was tackled by one of Raine's friends.

The door opened again, and another pair of men stumbled out into the night. Their heads were pressed together as they laughed at some private joke. One reached into his pocket for a set of keys, and as he turned toward the parking lot, his face was lit by the glow of a passing car.

I should have put the pieces together earlier—the electric razor in the medicine cabinet, when my dad always used a blade; the detour my father made to stop for coffee every day to and from work at Greg's store; the way he had left my mother all those years ago without explanation; the fact that my grandfather had never liked him. I tugged my black cap down lower and yanked up the fleece neck warmer Raine had given me, so that I wouldn't be recognized.

Panting, Raine delivered another kick to his victim and then let the guy scurry into the night. He straightened, smiled at me, and cocked his head, waiting for me to take the lead. Which is how I realized that even if I'd been totally clueless, Raine had known about my father all along.

When I was six, the boiler in our house exploded at a time that no one was home. I remember asking the insurance adjuster who came to assess the damage what went wrong. He said something about safety valves and corrosion, and then he rocked back on his heels and said that when there's too much steam, and a structure is not strong enough to hold it, something like this is bound to happen. For sixteen years, I'd been building up steam, because I wasn't my dead brother and never would be; because I couldn't keep my parents together; because I wasn't the grandson my grandfather had wanted; because I was too stupid or angry or weird. When I think back on that moment, it's white hot: grabbing my father by the throat and smacking his forehead against the pavement; wrenching his arm up behind his back and kicking him in the back till he spit out blood. Flipping his limp body over, and calling him a faggot, as I drove my fist into his face again and again. Struggling against Raine as he dragged me to safety when the sirens grew louder and blue and red lights flooded the parking lot.

The story spread, the way stories do, and as it did, it swelled and morphed: the newest member of the North American Death Squad—namely, *me*—had jumped six guys at once. I had a lead pipe in one hand

and a knife in the other. I ripped off a guy's ear with my teeth and swallowed the lobe.

None of that, of course, was true. But this was: I had beaten my own father up so badly that he was hospitalized, and had to be fed through a straw for months.

And for that, I became mythic.

"WE WANT THE OTHER NURSE back," I tell Mary or Marie, whatever the charge nurse's name is. "The one who was here last night."

She asks the black nurse to leave, so that it's just us. I've pushed down my sleeves again, but her eyes still flicker to my forearm.

"I can assure you that Ruth has more than twenty years of experience here," she says.

"I think you and I both know I'm not objecting to her experience," I reply.

"We can't remove a provider from care because of race. It's discriminatory."

"If I asked for a female OB instead of a male one, would that be discriminatory?" Brit asks. "Or a doctor instead of a medical student? You make those allowances all the time."

"That's different," the nurse says.

"How, exactly?" I ask. "From what I can tell, you're in a customer service business, and I'm the customer. And you do what makes the customer feel comfortable." I stand up and take a deep breath, towering over her, intimidating by design. "I can't imagine how upsetting it would be to all those other moms and dads here if, you know, things got out of control. If instead of this nice, calm conversation we're having, our voices were raised. If the other patients started to think that maybe *their* rights would be ignored too."

The nurse presses her lips together. "Are you threatening me, Mr. Bauer?"

"I don't think that's necessary," I answer. "Do you?"

There is a hierarchy to hate, and it's different for everyone. Personally, I hate spics more than I hate Asians, I hate Jews more than *that*, and at the very top of the chart, I despise blacks. But even more than any of these groups, the people you always hate the most are antiracist White folks. Because they are turncoats.

For a moment, I wait to see whether Marie is one of them.

A muscle jumps in her throat. "I'm sure we can find a mutually agreeable solution," she murmurs. "I will put a note on Davis's file, stating your . . . wishes."

"I think that's a good plan," I reply.

When she huffs out of the room, Brit starts to laugh. "Baby, you are something when you're fierce. But you know this means they're going to spit in my Jell-O before they serve it to me."

I reach into the bassinet and lift Davis into my embrace. He is so small he barely stretches the length of my forearm. "I'll bring you waffles from home instead," I tell Brit. Then I lower my lips to my son's brow, and whisper against his skin, a secret for just us. "And you," I promise. "You, I'll protect for the rest of my life."

A COUPLE OF YEARS AFTER I became involved in the White Power Movement, when I was running NADS in Connecticut, my mother's liver finally quit on her. I went back home to settle the estate and sell my grandfather's house. As I was sorting through her belongings, I found the transcripts of my brother's trial. Why she had them, I don't know; she must have gone out of her way to get them at some point. But I sat on the wooden floor of the living room, surrounded by boxes that would go to Goodwill and into the trash dumpster, and I read them— every page.

Much of the testimony was new to me, as if I hadn't lived through every minute of it. I couldn't tell you if I was too young to remember, or if I'd intentionally forgotten, but the evidence focused on the median line of the road and toxicology screens. Not the defendant's—but my brother's. It was *Tanner's* car that had drifted into oncoming traffic, because he was high. It was in all the diagrams of the tire skids: the proof of how a man on trial for negligent homicide had done his best to avoid a car that had veered into his lane. How the jury could not say, without a doubt, that the car accident was solely the defendant's fault.

I sat for a long time with the transcript in my lap. Reading. Rereading.

But this is how I see it: if that nigger hadn't been driving that night, my brother wouldn't be dead.

Ruth

IN TWENTY YEARS, I'VE BEEN FIRED ONCE BY A PATIENT, AND IT WAS FOR two hours. She screamed bloody murder and threw a vase of flowers at my head while in the throes of labor. But she hired me back when I brought her drugs.

After Marie asks me to step outside, I stand in the hall for a moment, shaking my head. "What was that about?" Corinne asks, looking up from a chart at the nurses' station.

"Just a real winner of a dad," I deadpan.

Corinne winces. "Worse than Vasectomy Guy?"

Once, I had a patient in labor whose husband had gotten a vasectomy two days before. Every time my patient complained about pain, he complained, too. At one point, he called me into the bathroom and pulled down his pants to show me his inflamed scrotum, as my patient huffed and puffed. *I told him he should call the doctor,* she said.

But Turk Bauer is not silly and selfish; based on the way he brandished that Confederate flag tattoo, I'm guessing he is not too fond of people of color. "Worse than that."

"Well." Corinne shrugs. "Marie's good at talking people off the ledge. I'm sure she can fix whatever the problem is."

Not unless she can make me white, I think. "I'm going to run to the cafeteria for five minutes. Cover for me?"

"If you bring me Twizzlers," Corinne says.

In the cafeteria I stand for several minutes in front of the coffee bar, thinking about the tattoo on Turk Bauer's arm. I don't have a problem with white people. I live in a white community; I have white friends; I send my son to a predominantly white school. I treat them the way I want to be treated—based on their individual merits as human beings, not on their skin tone.

But then again, the white people I work with and eat lunch with and who teach my son are not overtly prejudiced.

I grab Twizzlers for Corinne and a cup of coffee for myself. I carry my cup to the condiment island, where there's milk, sugar, Splenda. There's an elderly woman fussing with the top of the cream pitcher, trying to get it open. Her purse sits on the counter, but as I approach, she picks up the handbag and anchors it to her side, crossing her arm over the strap.

"Oh, that pitcher can be tricky," I say. "Can I help?"

She thanks me and smiles when I hand her back the cream.

I'm sure she doesn't even realize she moved her purse when I got closer.

But *I* did.

Shake it off, Ruth, I tell myself. I'm not the kind of person who sees the bad in everyone; that's my sister, Adisa. I get on the elevator and head back to my floor. When I arrive, I toss Corinne her Twizzlers and walk toward Brittany Bauer's door. Her chart and little Davis's chart sit outside; I grab the baby's to make sure that the pediatrician will be flagged about the potential heart murmur. But when I open the folder, there's a hot-pink Post-it on the paperwork.

NO AFRICAN AMERICAN PERSONNEL
TO CARE FOR THIS PATIENT.

My face floods with heat. Marie is not at the charge nurse's desk; I start to methodically search through the ward until I find her talking to one of the pediatricians in the nursery. "Marie," I say, pasting a smile on my face. "Do you have a minute?"

She follows me back toward the nurses' station, but I really don't want to have this conversation in public. Instead, I duck into the break room. "Are you kidding me?"

She doesn't pretend to misunderstand. "Ruth, it's nothing. Think of it the way you'd think of a family's religious preferences dictating patient care."

"You can't possibly be equating this with a religious preference."

"It's just a formality. The father is a hothead; this just seemed the smoothest way to get him to calm down before he did something extreme."

"*This* isn't extreme?" I ask.

"Look," Marie says. "If anything, I'm doing you a favor. So you don't have to deal with that guy anymore. Honestly, this isn't about *you*, Ruth."

"Really," I say flatly. "How many other African American personnel are on this ward?"

We both know the answer to that. A big, fat zero.

I look her square in the eye. "You don't want me to touch that baby?" I say. "Fine. Done."

Then I slam the door behind me so hard that it rattles.

ONCE, RELIGION GOT TANGLED UP in my care of a newborn. A Muslim couple came into the hospital to have their baby, and the father explained that he had to be the first person to speak to the newborn. When he told me this, I explained that I would do everything I could to honor his request, but that if there were any complications with the birth, my first priority was to make sure that the baby was saved—which required communication, and meant that silence in the delivery room was not likely or possible.

I gave the couple some privacy while they discussed this, and finally the father summoned me back. "If there are complications," he told me, "I hope Allah would understand."

As it turned out, his wife had a textbook delivery. Just before the baby was born, I reminded the pediatrician of the patient request, and the doctor stopped calling the arrival of the head, right shoulder, left, like a football play-by-play. The only sound in the room was the baby's cry. I took the newborn, slippery as a minnow, and placed him in a blanket in his father's arms. The man bent close to the tiny head of his son, and whispered to him in Arabic. Then he placed the baby into his wife's arms, and the room exploded with noise again.

Sometime later that day, when I came in to check on my two patients, I found them asleep. The father stood over the bassinet, staring at his child as if he didn't quite understand how this had happened. It was a look I saw often on the faces of fathers, for whom pregnancy wasn't real until this very moment. A mother has nine months to get used to sharing the space where her heart is; for a father it comes on sudden, like a storm that changes the landscape forever. "What a beautiful boy you have," I said, and he swallowed. There are just some feelings, I've learned, for which we never invented the right words. I hesitated, then asked what had been on my mind since the delivery. "If it's not rude of me to ask, would you tell me what you whispered to your son?"

"The adhan," the father explained. *"God is great; there is no God but Allah. Muhammad is the messenger of Allah."* He looked up at me and smiled. "In Islam, we want the first words a child hears to be a prayer."

It seemed absolutely fitting, given the miracle that every baby is.

The difference between the Muslim father's request and the request made by Turk Bauer was like the difference between day and night.

Between love and hate.

IT'S A BUSY AFTERNOON, so I don't have time to talk to Corinne about the new patient she's inherited until we are both pulling on our coats and walking to the elevator. "What was that all about?" Corinne asks.

"Marie took me off the case because I'm Black," I tell her.

Corinne wrinkles her nose. "That doesn't sound like Marie."

I turn to her, my hands stilling on the lapels of my coat. "So I'm a liar?"

Corinne puts her hand on my arm. "Of course not. I'm just sure there's something else going on."

It's wrong to take out my frustration on Corinne, who has to deal with that awful family now. It's wrong for me to be angry at her, when I'm really angry at Marie. Corinne, she's always been my partner in crime, not my adversary. But I feel like I could talk till I'm blue in the face and she wouldn't really understand what this feels like.

Maybe I should talk till I'm blue in the face. Maybe then I'd be acceptable to the Bauers.

"Whatever," I say. "That baby means nothing to me."

Corinne tilts her head. "You want to grab a glass of wine before we head home?"

I let my shoulders relax. "I can't. Edison's waiting."

The elevator dings, and the doors open. It's packed, because it's end of shift. Staring back at me is a sea of blank white faces.

Normally I don't even think about that. But suddenly, it's all I can see.

I'm tired of being the only Black nurse on the birthing pavilion.

I'm tired of pretending that doesn't matter.

I'm tired.

"You know what," I say to Corinne. "I think I'm going to just take the stairs."

WHEN I WAS FIVE, I couldn't blend. Although I'd been reading since age three—the result of my mother's diligent schooling each night when she came home from work—if I came across the word *tree* I pronounced it "ree." Even my last name, Brooks, became "rooks." Mama went to a bookstore and got a book on consonant blends and tutored me for a year. Then she had me tested for a gifted program, and instead of going to school in Harlem—where we lived—my sister and I rode the bus with her for an hour and a half every morning to a public school on the Upper West Side with a mostly Jewish student population. She'd drop me off at my classroom door, and then she'd take the subway to work at the Hallowells'.

My sister, Rachel, was not the student I was, though, and the bus trip was draining for all of us. So for second grade, we moved back to our old school in Harlem. I spent a year being dulled at all my bright edges, which devastated Mama. When she told her boss, Ms. Mina got me an interview at Dalton. It was the private school her daughter, Christina, attended, and they were looking for diversity. I received a full scholarship, stayed at the top of my class, received prizes at every assembly, and worked like mad to reward my mama's faith in me. While Rachel made friends with kids in our neighborhood, I knew no one. I didn't really fit in at Dalton, and I definitely didn't fit in in Harlem. As it turned out, I was a straight-A student who still couldn't blend.

There were a few students who invited me to their houses—girls who said things like "You don't talk like you're Black!" or "I don't think of you that way!" Of course, none of those girls ever came to visit me in Harlem. There was always a conflicting dance class, a family commitment, too much homework. Sometimes I imagined them, with their silky blond hair and braces, walking past the check casher on the corner of the street where I lived. It was like picturing a polar bear in the tropics, and I never let myself think on it long enough to wonder if that was how they saw me, at Dalton.

When I got into Cornell, and many others from my school didn't, I couldn't help but hear the whispers. *It's because she's Black.* Never mind that I had a 3.87 average, that I'd done well on my SATs. Never mind that I could not afford to go to Cornell, and would instead be taking the full ride offered me by SUNY Plattsburgh. "Baby," my mama said, "it's not easy for a Black girl to want. You have to show them you're not a Black girl. You're Ruth Brooks." She would squeeze my hand. "You are going to get everything good that's coming to you—not because you beg for it, and not because of what color you are. Because you deserve it."

I know I wouldn't have become a nurse if my mama hadn't worked so hard to put me smack in the middle of the path of a good education. I also know that I decided long ago to try to circumvent some of the problems I had, when it came to my own child. So when Edison was two, my husband and I made the choice to move to a white neighborhood with better schools, even though that meant we would be one of the only families of color in the area. We left our apartment near the railroad tracks in New Haven, and after having multiple listings "disappear" when the realtor found out what we looked like, we finally found a tiny place in the more affluent community of East End. I enrolled Edison in a preschool there, so that he started at the same time as all the other kids, and no one could see him as an outsider. He was one of them, from the start. When he wanted to have his friends over for a sleepover, no parent could say it was too dangerous an area for their kid to visit. It was, after all, their neighborhood, too.

And it worked. My, how it worked. It took me advocating for him at first—making sure that he had teachers who noticed his intelligence as well as his skin color—but as a result, Edison is in the top three of his class. He's a National Merit Scholar. He is going to college and he will be anything he wants to be.

I've spent my life making sure of it.

When I get home from work, Edison is doing his homework at the kitchen table. "Hey, baby," I say, leaning down to kiss the top of his head. I can only do that now when he's seated. I still remember the moment I realized he was taller than me; how strange it felt to reach my arms up instead of down, to know that someone I'd been supporting his whole life was in a position to support me.

He doesn't glance up. "How was work?"

I paste a smile on my face. "You know. Same old."

I shrug off my coat, pick up Edison's jacket from where it's been slung on the back of the couch, and hang them both in the closet. "I'm not running a cleaning service here—"

"Then leave it where it was!" Edison explodes. "Why does everything have to be my fault?" He shoves away from the table so fast that he nearly knocks over his chair. Leaving his computer and his open notebook behind, he storms out of the kitchen. I hear the door of his bedroom slam.

This is not my boy. My boy is the one who carries groceries up three flights of stairs for old Mrs. Laska, without her even having to ask. My boy is the one who always holds open the door for a lady, who says please and thank you, who still keeps in his nightstand every birthday card I've ever written him.

Sometimes a new mother turns to me, a shrieking infant in her arms, and asks me how she's supposed to know what her baby needs. In a lot of ways, having a teenager isn't all that different from having a newborn. You learn to read the reactions, because they're incapable of saying exactly what it is that's causing pain.

So although all I want to do is go into Edison's room and gather him up close and rock him back and forth the way I used to when he was little and hurting, I take a deep breath and go into the kitchen instead. Edison has left me dinner, a plate covered with foil. He can make exactly three dishes: macaroni and cheese, fried eggs, and Sloppy Joes. The rest of the week he heats up casseroles I make on my days off. Tonight's is an enchilada pie, but Edison's also cooked up some peas, because I taught him years ago a plate's not a meal unless there's more than one color on it.

I pour myself some wine from a bottle I got from Marie last Christmas. It tastes sour, but I force myself to sip it until I can feel the knots in my shoulders relax, until I can close my eyes and not see Turk Bauer's face.

After ten minutes pass, I knock softly on the door of Edison's room. It's been his since he was thirteen; I sleep on the pullout couch in the living room. I turn the knob and find him lying on his bed, his arms behind his head. With his T-shirt stretched over his shoulders and his chin tilted up, I see so much of his daddy in him that for a moment, I feel like I've fallen through time.

I sit down beside him on the mattress. "Are we gonna talk about it, or are we gonna pretend nothing's wrong?" I ask.

Edison's mouth twists. "Do I really get a choice?"

"No," I say, smiling a little. "Is this about the calculus test?"

He frowns. "The calc test? That was no big deal; I got a ninety-six. It's just that I got into it with Bryce today."

Bryce has been Edison's closest friend since fifth grade. His mother is a family court judge and his father is a Yale classics professor. In their living room is a glass case, like the kind you'd find at a museum, housing a bona fide Grecian urn. They've taken Edison on vacation to Gstaad and Santorini.

It feels good to have Edison hand me this burden, to wallow in someone else's difficulties for a while. This is what's so upsetting to me about the incident at the hospital: I'm known as the fixer, the one who figures out a solution. I'm not the problem. I'm *never* the problem.

"I'm sure it'll blow over," I tell Edison, patting his arm. "You two are like brothers."

He rolls onto his side and pulls the pillow over his head.

"Hey," I say. "Hey." I tug at the pillow and realize that there's one single streak, left by a tear, darkening the skin of his temple. "Baby," I murmur. "What happened?"

"I told him I was going to ask Whitney to homecoming."

"Whitney . . ." I repeat, trying to place the girl from the tangle of Edison's friends.

"Bryce's sister," he says.

I have a brief flash of a girl with strawberry-blond braids I met years ago when picking Edison up from a playdate. "The chubby one with braces?"

"Yeah. She doesn't have braces anymore. And she's *definitely* not chubby. She's got . . ." Edison's eyes soften, and I imagine what my son is seeing.

"You don't have to finish that sentence," I say quickly.

"Well, she's amazing. She's a sophomore now. I mean, I've known her forever, but lately when I look at her it's not just as Bryce's little sister, you know? I had this whole thing planned, where one of my buddies would be waiting outside her classroom after each period, holding a note. The first note was going to say WILL. The second was going to say YOU. Then GO, TO, HOMECOMING, and WITH. And then at the end of school, I'd be waiting with the ME sign, so she'd finally know who was asking."

"This is a thing now?" I interrupt. "You don't just ask a girl to the homecoming dance . . . you have to produce a whole Broadway event to make it happen?"

"What? Mama, that's not the point. The point is that I asked Bryce to be the one who brought her the HOMECOMING note and he freaked out."

I draw in my breath. "Well," I say, carefully picking through my words, "it's sometimes hard for a guy to see his little sister as anyone's potential girlfriend, no matter how close he is to the person who wants to date her."

Edison rolls his eyes. "That's not it."

"Bryce may just need time to get used to the idea. Maybe he was surprised that you'd think of his sister, you know, that way. Because you *are* like family."

"The problem is . . . I'm *not*." My son sits up, his long legs dangling over the edge of the bed. "Bryce laughed. He said, 'Dude. It's one thing for *us* to hang out. But you and Whit? My parents would shit a brick.'" His gaze slides away. "Sorry about the language."

"That's okay, baby," I said. "Go on."

"So I asked him why. It didn't make any sense to me. I mean, I've been to *Greece* with his family. And he said, 'No offense, but my parents would *not* be cool with my sister dating a Black guy.' Like it's okay to have a Black friend who comes on family vacations but it's not okay for that friend to get involved with your daughter."

I have worked so hard to keep Edison from feeling this line being drawn, it never occurred to me that when it happened—which, I guess, was inevitable—it would burn even more, because he had never seen it coming.

I reach for my son's hand and squeeze it. "You and Whitney would not be the first couple to find yourselves on opposite sides of a mountain," I say. "Romeo and Juliet, Anna Karenina and Vronsky. Maria and Tony. Jack and Rose."

Edison looks at me in horror. "You do realize that in every example you just gave me, at least one of them dies?"

"What I'm *trying* to say is that if Whitney sees how special you are, she'll want to be with you. And if she doesn't, she's not worth the fight."

I put my arm around his shoulders; Edison leans into me. "That doesn't make it suck any less."

"Language," I say automatically. "And no, it doesn't."

Not for the first time, I wish Wesley were still alive. I wish he hadn't gone back on that second tour of duty in Afghanistan; I wish that he hadn't been driving in the convoy when the IED exploded; I wish that he had gotten to know Edison not just as a child but as a teen and now a young man. I wish he were here to tell his son that when a girl makes your blood rush it's just the first time of many.

I wish he were here, period.

If only you could see what we made, I think silently. *He's the best of both of us.*

"Whatever happened to Tommy?" I ask abruptly.

"Tommy Phipps?" Edison frowns. "I think he got busted for dealing heroin behind the school last year. He's in juvie."

"Do you remember in nursery school, when that little delinquent said you looked like burnt toast?"

A slow smile stretches across Edison's face. "Yeah."

It was the first time a child had mentioned to Edison that he was different from everyone else in his class—and had done so in a way that also made it seem bad. Burnt. Charred. Ruined.

Before that maybe Edison had noticed, maybe he hadn't. But that was the first time I had the Talk with my son about skin color.

"You remember what I told you?"

"That my skin was brown because I had more melanin than anyone else in the school."

"Right. Because everyone knows it's better to have *more* of something than *less*. And melanin protects your skin from damage from the sun, and helps make your eyesight better, and Tommy Phipps would always be lacking. So actually, you were the lucky one."

Slowly, like water on parched pavement, the smile evaporates from Edison's face. "I don't feel so lucky now," he says.

As LITTLE GIRLS, MY OLDER sister and I looked nothing alike. Rachel was the color of fresh-brewed coffee, just like Mama. Me, I was poured from the same pot, but with so much milk added, you couldn't even taste the flavor anymore.

The fact that I was lighter got me privileges I didn't understand, privileges that drove Rachel crazy. Tellers at banks gave me lollipops, and then, as an afterthought, offered one to my sister. Teachers called me the pretty Brooks sister, the good Brooks sister. During class portraits, I would be moved up to the front row; Rachel got hidden in the back.

Rachel told me that my real father was white. That I wasn't really part of our family. Then, Rachel and I got into it one day and started yelling at each other and I said something about going to live with my real daddy. That night my mama sat me down and showed me pictures of my father, who was also Rachel's father—a man with light brown skin like mine—holding me as a newborn. The date on the photo was a full year before he left all three of us for good.

Rachel and I grew up as different as two sisters could be. I'm short, and she's tall as a queen. I was an avid student; she was naturally smarter than I was, but hated school. She embraced what she referred to as her "ethnic roots" in her twenties, legally changed her name to Adisa, and started wearing her hair in its natural kinky state. Although a lot of ethnic names are Swahili, *Adisa* comes from the Yoruba language, which she'll tell you is West African—"where our ancestors *actually* came from when they were brought here as slaves." It means, *One who is clear*. See, even her name judges the rest of us for not knowing the truths that she does.

Now, Adisa lives near the train tracks in New Haven in a neighborhood where drug deals go down in broad daylight and young men shoot at each other throughout the night; she has five kids, and she and the father of her children have minimum-wage jobs and barely scrape by. I love my sister to death, but I don't understand the choices she's made any more than she can understand mine.

I've wondered, you know. If my drive to become a nurse, to want more, to achieve more for Edison all came from the fact that even between two little Black sisters, I had a head start. I've wondered if the reason Rachel turned herself into Adisa was because feeding that fire inside herself was exactly what she needed to believe she had a chance to catch up.

ON FRIDAY, MY DAY OFF, I have an appointment at the nail salon with Adisa. We sit side by side, our hands under the UV drying vents. Adisa looks at the bottle of my chosen OPI nail color and shakes her head. "I can't believe you picked a polish called Juice Bar Hopping," she says. "That's got to be the whitest color ever."

"It's orange," I point out.

"I meant the name, Ruth, the *name*. You ever see a brotha in a juice bar? No. Because nobody goes to a bar to drink juice. Just like nobody asks for a sippy cup full of tequila."

I roll my eyes. "Really? I just told you all about getting barred from a patient's care and you want to talk about what color I'm putting on my nails?"

"I'm talking about what color you chose to live your life, girl," Adisa says. "What happened to you happens to the rest of us every day. Every *hour*. You're just so used to playing by their rules you forgot you got skin in the game." She smirks. "Well. Lighter skin, but still."

"What's that supposed to mean?"

She shrugs. "When was the last time you told someone Mama still works as a domestic?"

"She hardly works now. You know that. She's basically a charity Mina contributes to."

"You didn't answer my question."

I scowl. "I don't know when I mentioned it last. Is that the first thing *you* bring up in conversation? Plus, it doesn't matter what color I am. I'm good at my job. I didn't deserve to be taken off that case."

"And I don't deserve to be living in Church Street South, but it's going to take more than me to change two hundred years of history."

My sister likes to play the victim. We've had some pretty heated exchanges about that before. If you don't want to be seen as a stereotype, then the way I see it, don't *be* one. But to my sister, that means playing a white man's game, and being who *they* want her to be, instead of being unapologetically herself. Adisa says the word *assimilation* with so much venom that you'd think anyone who chooses it—like I did—is swallowing poison.

It's also very like my sister to take a problem *I* have and turn it into her own rant.

"None of what happened at the hospital is your fault," my sister says, surprising me. I figured she'd say I had this coming to me, because I've been pretending to be someone I'm not and somewhere along the pretending, I forgot the truth. "It's their world, Ruth. We just live in it. It's like if you up and moved to Japan. You could choose to ignore the customs and never learn the language, but you're going to get along a lot easier if you do, right? Same thing here. Every time you turn on the TV or the radio you see and hear about white people going to high school and college, eating dinner, getting engaged, drinking their pinot noir. You learn how they live their lives, and you speak their language well enough to blend in with them. But how many white people you know who go out of their way to see Tyler Perry movies so they can learn how to act around Black people?"

"That's not the point—"

"No, the point is you can *do as the Romans do* all you want, but it don't mean the Emperor will let you into his palace."

"White people do not run the world, Adisa," I argue. "There are plenty of successful people of color." I name the first three that pop into my head. "Colin Powell, Cory Booker, Beyoncé—"

"—and ain't none of them dark, like me," Adisa counters. "You know what they say: the deeper you go into the projects, the darker the skin."

"Clarence Thomas," I pronounce. "He's darker than you and he's on the Supreme Court."

My sister laughs. "Ruth, he's so conservative he probably *bleeds* white."

My phone dings, and I carefully extract it from my purse so I don't mess up my nails.

"Edison?" Adisa asks immediately. Say what you will about her, but she loves my son as much as I do.

"No. It's Lucille from work." Just seeing her name pop up on my phone makes my mouth go dry; she was the nurse during the delivery of Davis Bauer. But this isn't about that family at all. Lucille's got a stomach bug; she needs someone to fill in for her tonight. She's willing to trade me, so that instead of working all day Saturday, I can leave at eleven. It means pulling a double shift, but I'm already thinking of what I could do with that time on Saturday. Edison needs a new winter coat this year—I swear he's grown four inches over the summer. I could treat him to lunch, after shopping. Maybe there's even a movie coming out that Edison and I could go see. It's been hitting me hard lately—the realization that getting my son to a point where he's accepted to college also means that I will be left alone. "They want me to come in to work tonight."

"Who's they? The Nazis?"

"No, another nurse who's sick."

"Another *white* nurse," Adisa clarifies.

I don't even respond.

Adisa leans back in her chair. "Seems to me they're not in a position to be asking you for favors."

I am about to defend Lucille, who had absolutely nothing to do with Marie's decision to put a Post-it note on the baby's file, when the nail technician interrupts us, checking our fingers to see if the polish is dry. "Okay," she says. "All done."

Adisa waggles her fingers, a shocking shade of hot pink. "Why do we keep coming here? I hate this salon," she says, her voice low. "They don't look me in the eye and they won't put my change right in my hand. It's like they think my Black is gonna rub off on them."

"They're Korean," I point out. "Did you ever think that maybe, in their culture, neither of those things are polite?"

Adisa raises a brow. "All right, Ruth," she says. "You just keep telling yourself it's not about you."

NOT TEN MINUTES INTO MY unscheduled shift, I'm already sorry I said yes. There's a storm crackling outside, one the weathermen didn't see coming, and the barometric pressure's tanked—which leads to early ruptured membranes, to women going into premature labor, to patients who are writhing in the halls because we don't have enough space for them. I'm running around like a chicken with its head cut off, which is a good thing, because it keeps me from thinking about Turk and Brittany Bauer and their baby.

But not so much that I don't casually check the chart when I first come on duty. I tell myself that I just want to make sure that someone—someone *white*—has scheduled that consult with a pediatric cardiologist before the baby is discharged. And yes, there it is in the schedule, along with a record of Corinne doing the baby's heel stick on Friday afternoon to draw blood for the state newborn screening. But then someone calls my name and I find myself pulled into the orbit of a laboring woman, who is being wheeled up from Emergency. Her partner looks terrified, the kind of man who is used to being able to fix things who has come to the sudden realization that this is outside his wheelhouse. "I'm Ruth," I say to the woman, who seems to have telescoped further into herself with each subsequent contraction. "I'm going to be here with you the whole time."

Her name is Eliza and her contractions are four minutes apart, according to her husband, George. This is their first pregnancy. I get my patient settled in the last birthing room we have available and take a urine sample, then hook her up to the monitor, scanning the gravestone printout. I grab her vitals and start asking questions: *How strong are the contractions? Where are you feeling them—the front or the back? Are you leaking any fluid? Are you bleeding? How's the baby moving?*

"If you're ready, Eliza," I say, "I'm going to check your cervix." I put on a pair of gloves and move to the foot of the bed, touch her knee.

An expression flickers across her face that gives me pause.

Now, most laboring women will do anything to get that baby out of them. There's fear about getting through childbirth, yes, but that's different from the fear of being touched. And that's what I'm reading all over Eliza's face.

A dozen questions jockey their way to the tip of my tongue. Eliza changed in the bathroom with her husband's help, so I didn't see if she had any bruises that might flag an abusive relationship. I glance at George. He looks like an ordinary father-to-be—nervous, out of place—not like a guy with anger management issues.

Then again, Turk Bauer looked pretty normal to me until he rolled up his sleeves.

Shaking my head to clear it, I turn to George and pin a smile over my instincts. "Would you mind going to the kitchenette and getting some ice chips for Eliza?" I say. "It'd be a tremendous help."

Never mind that's a nurse's job—George looks supremely relieved to be given a task. The minute he's out of the room I turn to Eliza. "Is everything all right?" I ask, looking her in the eye. "Is there something you need to tell me that you couldn't say with George in the room?"

She shakes her head, and then bursts into tears.

I strip off my gloves—the cervical exam can wait—and reach for her hand. "Eliza, you can talk to me."

"The reason I got pregnant is because I was raped," she sobs. "George doesn't even know it happened. He's so happy about this baby . . . I couldn't tell him it might not be his."

The story comes out, whispered, in the middle of the night, when Eliza has stalled at seven centimeters dilated, and George has gone to get a snack from the cafeteria. Labor is like that—a shared trauma bond, an accelerant that makes relationships stronger. And so even though I am little more than a stranger to Eliza, she pours out her soul to me, as if she has fallen overboard and I am the only glimpse of land on the horizon. She was on a business trip, celebrating the close of a deal with an important, elusive client. The client invited her out to dinner with some others and bought her a drink, and the next thing Eliza remembered was waking up in his hotel room, and feeling sore all over.

When she finishes, we both sit, letting the words settle. "I couldn't tell George," Eliza says, her hands bunched on the rough hospital linens. "He would have gone to my boss, and believe me, they wouldn't risk losing this deal just because of something that happened to me. The best-case scenario is that I would have been given a severance package to keep my mouth shut."

"So nobody knows?"

"*You* do," she says. Eliza looks at me. "What if I can't love the baby? What if every time I look at her, I see what happened?"

"Maybe you should get DNA testing," I tell her.

"What good would it do?"

"Well," I say, "you'd *know*."

She shakes her head. "And then what?"

It is a good question, one that I feel all the way to my own core. Is it better not knowing the ugly truth, and pretending it doesn't exist? Or is it better to confront it, even though that knowledge may be a weight you carry around forever?

I am about to give her my opinion when Eliza is seized by another contraction. Suddenly, we are both in the trenches again, fighting for a life.

It takes three hours, and then Eliza pushes her daughter into the world. Eliza starts crying, like many new mothers do, but I know it's not for the same reasons. The OB hands the newborn to me, and I stare down into the angry ocean of that baby's eyes. It doesn't matter how she was conceived. It just matters that she made it here.

"Eliza," I say, settling the baby on her chest, "here's your daughter."

Even as George reaches over his wife's shoulder to stroke the newborn's mottled thigh, Eliza won't look at the baby. I lift the baby up, hold her closer to Eliza's face. "Eliza," I say, more firmly. "Your daughter."

She drags her gaze toward the baby in my hands. Sees what I see: the blue eyes of her husband. The identical nose. The cleft that matches the one in his chin. This baby might as well be a tiny clone of George.

All the tension fades from Eliza's shoulders. Her arms close around her daughter, holding the child so close there is no room for *but what if*. "Hello, baby," she whispers.

This family, they'll make their own reality.

I just wish it were that easy for the rest of us.

BY NINE THE NEXT MORNING, it feels like the entirety of New Haven has come to the hospital to give birth. I have been mainlining coffee, running back and forth among three postpartum patients, and praying fervently in between that we don't get another woman in active labor before I leave here at eleven. In addition to Eliza's delivery, I had two more patients last night—a G3 P3 who, truth be told, could have had that baby on her own and nearly did—and a G4 P1 who had an emergency C-section. Her baby, only twenty-seven weeks, is in the NICU.

When Corinne comes on duty at seven, I'm in the OR with the emergency C-section, so we don't cross paths until it's 9:00 A.M. and I'm in the nursery. "I heard you pulled a double," she says, wheeling a bassinet into the room. "What are you doing in here?"

The nursery used to be where the babies were kept while mothers got a decent night's sleep, before they stayed twenty-four/seven in their mothers' hospital rooms. So now, it's used mostly for storage, and for routine procedures like circumcisions, which no parent wants to watch. "Hiding," I tell Corinne, pulling a granola bar out of my pocket and devouring it in two bites.

She laughs. "What the *hell* is going on today? Did I miss the memo for the Apocalypse or something?"

"Tell me about it." I glance at the infant for the first time, and feel a shudder run down my spine. BABY BOY BAUER, the card on the bassinet reads. Without even meaning to, I take a step backward.

"How's he doing?" I ask. "Is he eating any better?"

"His sugar's up but he's still logy," Corinne answers. "He hasn't nursed for the past two hours because Atkins is going to do the circ."

As if Corinne has conjured the pediatrician, Dr. Atkins comes into the nursery. "Right on schedule," she says, seeing the bassinet. "The anesthesia's had enough time to kick in and I've already talked to the parents. Ruth, did you give the baby sweeties?"

Sweeties are a little bit of sugar water, rubbed on the babies' gums to soothe and distract them from the discomfort. I would have given the baby sweeties before a circ, if I were his nurse.

"I'm not taking care of this patient anymore," I say stiffly.

Dr. Atkins raises a brow and opens the patient file. I see the Post-it note, and as she reads it, an uncomfortable silence swells, sucking up all the air in the room.

Corinne clears her throat. "I gave him sweeties about five minutes ago."

"Great," Dr. Atkins says. "Then let's get started."

I stand for a moment, watching as Corinne unwraps the baby and prepares him for this routine procedure. Dr. Atkins turns to me. There's sympathy in her eyes, and that's the last thing I want to see. I don't need pity just because of a stupid decision Marie made. I don't need pity because of the color of my skin.

So I make a joke of it. "Maybe while you're at it," I suggest, "you can sterilize him."

THERE ARE FEW THINGS SCARIER than a stat C-section. The air becomes electric once the doctor makes that call, and conversation becomes parsed and vital: *I've got the IV; can you get the bed? Someone grab the med box and book the case.* You tell the patient that something is wrong, and that we have to move fast. A page gets sent from the hospital operator to anyone on the team who's outside the building, while you and the charge nurse take the patient to the OR. While the charge nurse rips the instruments from their sterilized paper bag and turns on the anesthesia equipment, you get the patient onto the table, prep the belly, get the drapes up and ready. The minute the doctor and the anesthesiologist run through the door, the cut is made, the baby's out. It takes less than twenty minutes. At big hospitals, like Yale–New Haven, they can do it in seven.

Twenty minutes after Davis Bauer has his circumcision, another of

Corinne's patients has her water break. A loop of umbilical cord spools out between her legs, and Corinne is paged from the nursery, an emergency. "Monitor the baby for me," she says, as she rushes into the woman's room. A moment later I see Marie at the head of the patient's bed, wheeling it with an orderly into the elevator. Corinne is crouched on the bed between the patient's legs, her gloved hand in the shadows, trying to keep the umbilical cord inside.

Monitor the baby for me. She means that she wants me to watch over Davis Bauer. It is protocol that a circumcised baby has to be checked routinely to make sure that he's not bleeding. With both Marie and Corinne in the thick of a stat C-section, there is literally no one else to do it.

I step into the nursery, where Davis is sleeping off the morning trauma.

It will only be twenty minutes till Corinne comes back, I tell myself, or until Marie relieves me.

I fold my arms and stare down at the newborn. Babies are such blank slates. They don't come into this world with the assumptions their parents have made, or the promises their church will give, or the ability to sort people into groups they like and don't like. They don't come into this world with anything, really, except a need for comfort. And they will take it from anyone, without judging the giver.

I wonder how long it takes before the polish given by nature gets worn off by nurture.

When I look down at the bassinet again, Davis Bauer has stopped breathing.

I lean closer, certain that I'm just missing the rise and fall of his tiny chest. But from this angle, I can see how his skin is tinged blue.

Immediately I reach for him, pressing my stethoscope against his heart, tapping his heels, unwrapping his swaddling blanket. Lots of babies have sleep apnea, but if you move them around a bit, change the position from the back to the belly or the side, respiration begins again automatically.

Then my head catches up to my hands: *No African American personnel to care for this patient.*

Glancing over my shoulder at the door of the nursery, I angle my body so that if someone were to come inside, they'd only see my back. They wouldn't see what I'm doing.

Is stimulating the baby the same as resuscitating him? Is touching the baby technically caring for him?

Could I lose my job over this?

Does it matter if I'm splitting hairs?

Does anything matter if this baby starts breathing again?

My thoughts whip quickly into a hurricane: it has to be a respiratory arrest; newborns never have cardiac events. A baby might not breathe for three to four minutes, and still have a heart rate of 100, because its normal heart rate is 150 . . . which means even if blood isn't reaching the brain, it's perfusing the rest of the body and as soon as you can get the baby oxygenated that heart rate will come up. For this reason, it's less important to do chest compressions on an infant than to breathe for them. In this, it's the opposite of the way you'd care for an adult patient.

But even when I shove aside my doubts and try everything short of medical interaction, he doesn't resume breathing. Normally, I'd grab a pulse ox probe to get a monitor on his oxygenation and heart rate. I'd find an oxygen mask. I'd make calls.

What am I supposed to do?

What am I not *supposed to do?*

Any moment now, Corinne or Marie might walk into the nursery. They'd see me interfering with this infant, and then what?

Sweat runs down my spine as I hastily wrap the baby up in his swaddling blanket again. I stare at his tiny body. My pulse throbs in my eardrums, a metronome of failure.

I'm not sure if three minutes have passed, or only thirty seconds, when I hear Marie's voice behind me. "Ruth," she says, "what are you doing?"

"Nothing," I respond, paralyzed. "I'm doing nothing."

She looks over my shoulder, sees the blue skin of the baby's cheek, and for a hot beat meets my gaze. "Get me an Ambu bag," Marie orders. She unwraps the baby, taps his little feet, turns him over.

Does exactly what I did.

Marie fits the pediatric face mask over Davis's nose and mouth and starts to squeeze the bag, inflating his lungs. "Call the code . . ."

I follow her order; dial 1500 into the nursery phone. "Code blue in the neonatal nursery," I say, and I imagine the team being pulled from their regular jobs in the hospital—an anesthesiologist, an intensive care nurse, a recording nurse, a nursing assistant from a different floor. And Dr. Atkins, the pediatrician who saw this baby only minutes ago.

"Start compressions," Marie tells me.

This time I don't waver. With two fingers, I push down on the baby's chest, two hundred compressions per minute. As the crash cart is jostled into the nursery, I reach with my spare hand for the leads and affix the electrodes to the baby so that we can see the results of my efforts on the cardiac monitor. Suddenly the tiny nursery is jammed with people, all jockeying for a spot in front of a patient who is only nineteen inches long. "I'm trying to intubate here," the anesthesiologist yells at an ICU nurse who's attempting to find a scalp vein.

"Well, I can't get an antecubital line," she argues.

"I'm in," the anesthesiologist says, and he falls back to let the nurse have better access. She prods, and I push harder with my fingers, hoping to make a vein—any vein—stand out in stark relief.

The anesthesiologist stares at the monitor. "Stop compressions," he calls, and I raise my hands like I've been caught in the middle of a crime.

We all look at the screen, but the baby's rhythm is 80.

"Compressions aren't effective," he says, so I press down harder on the rib cage. It's such a fine line. There are no abdominal muscles protecting the organs beneath that little pouch of belly; bear down a bit too much or a tad off center and I might rupture the infant's liver.

"The baby isn't pinking," Marie says. "Is the oxygen even on?"

"Can someone get blood gases?" the anesthesiologist asks, his question tangling with hers over the baby's body.

The ICU nurse reaches into baby's groin for a pulse, trying to stick the femoral artery for a blood sample to see if the baby's acidotic. A runner—another member of the code team—rushes the vial off to the lab. But by the time we get the results in a half hour, it won't matter. By then, this baby will be breathing again.

Or he won't.

"Dammit, why don't we have a line yet?"

"You want to try?" the ICU nurse says. "Be my guest."

"Stop compressions," the anesthesiologist orders, and I do. The heart rate on the monitor reads 90.

"Get me some atropine." A syringe is handed to the doctor, who pulls off the tip, removes the Ambu bag, and squirts the drug down the tube into the baby's lungs. Then he continues to bag, pushing oxygen and atropine through the bronchi, the mucous membranes.

In the middle of a crisis, time is viscous. You swim through it so slowly you cannot tell if you're living or reliving each awful moment. You can see your hands doing the work, ministering, as if they do not belong to you. You hear voices climbing a ladder of panic, and it all becomes one deafening, discordant note.

"What about cannulating the umbilicus?" the ICU nurse asks.

"It's been too long since birth," Marie replies.

This is going downhill fast. Instinctively, I press harder.

"You're being too aggressive," the anesthesiologist tells me. "Lighten up."

But what breaks my rhythm is the scream. Brittany Bauer has entered the room and is wailing. She's being held back by the recording nurse as she fights to get closer to the baby. Her husband—immobile, stunned—stares at my fingers pushing against his son's chest.

"What's happening to him?" Brittany cries.

I don't know who let them in here. But then again, there was nobody available to keep them out. Labor & Delivery has been overworked and understaffed since last night. Corinne is still in the OR with her stat C-section, and Marie is here with me. The Bauers would have heard the emergency calls. They would have seen medical personnel rushing toward the nursery, where their newborn was supposed to be sleeping off the anesthesia from a routine procedure.

I would have run there, too.

The door flies open, and Dr. Atkins, the pediatrician, immediately shoves her way to the head of the bassinet. "What's going on?"

There is no answer, and I realize I am the one who is supposed to reply.

"I was here with the baby," I say, my syllables accented in rhythm to the compressions I am still doing. "His color was ashen and respirations had ceased. We stimulated him, but there was no gasping or spontaneous breath, so we began CPR."

"How long have you been at it?" Dr. Atkins asks.

"Fifteen minutes."

"Okay, Ruth, please stop for a sec . . ." Dr. Atkins looks at the cardiac monitor. The heart rate, now, is 40.

"Tombstones," Marie murmurs.

It's the term we use when we see wide QRS complexes on the cardiogram—the right side of the heart is responding too slowly to the left side of the heart; there's no cardiac output.

There's no hope.

A few seconds later, the heartbeat stops completely. "I'm calling it," Dr. Atkins says. She takes a deep breath—this is never easy, but it's even worse when it's a newborn—then tugs the Ambu bag off the tube and tosses it into the trash. "Time?"

We all look up at the clock.

"No," Brittany gasps, falling to her knees. "Please don't stop. Please don't give up."

"I'm so sorry, Mrs. Bauer," the pediatrician says. "But there's nothing we can do for your son. He's gone."

Turk wrenches away from his wife and grabs the Ambu out of the trash. He shoves the anesthesiologist out of the way and tries to affix it again to Davis's breathing tube. "Show me how," he begs. "I'll take over. You don't have to quit."

"Please—"

"I can get him to breathe. I know I can . . ."

Dr. Atkins puts her hand on his shoulder, and Turk collapses into himself, an implosion of grief. "There is no way you can bring Davis back," she says, and he covers his face and starts to sob.

"Time?" Dr. Atkins repeats.

Part of the protocol of death is that everyone in the room consents to the moment it occurs. "Ten oh four," Marie says, and we all murmur, a somber chorus: *I agree*.

I step back, staring at my hands. My fingers are cramped from performing the compressions. My own heart hurts.

Marie takes the baby's temperature, a cool 95. By now Turk is anchored to his wife's side, holding her upright. Their faces are blank, numb with disbelief. Dr. Atkins is talking softly to them, trying to explain the impossible.

Corinne walks into the nursery. "Ruth? What the hell happened?"

Marie tucks Davis's blanket tight around him and slips the little stocking cap back on his head. The only evidence of the trauma he's suffered is a small tube, like a little straw, coming out of his pursed mouth. She cradles the baby in her arms, as if tenderness still counts. She hands him to his mother.

"Excuse me," I say to Corinne, when maybe what I really mean is *Forgive me*. I push past her and skirt the grieving parents and the dead baby and barely make it to the restroom before I am violently ill. I press my forehead to the cool porcelain lip of the toilet and close my eyes, and even then I can still feel it: the give of the rippled rib cage under my fingers, the whoosh of his blood in my own ears, the acid truth on my tongue: had I not hesitated, that baby might still be alive.

I HAD A PATIENT ONCE, a teenage girl, whose baby was born dead due to class 3 placental abruption. The placenta had peeled away from the uterine lining and the baby had no oxygen; the severity of the bleeding meant we almost lost the mother as well as the newborn. The baby was sent to our morgue pending autopsy—which is automatic in Connecticut for the death of a neonate. Twelve hours later, the girl's grandmother arrived from Ohio. She wanted to hold her great-grandchild, just once.

I went down to the morgue, to where the dead babies are kept in an ordinary Amana refrigerator, stacked on the shelves in tiny body bags. I took the baby out and slipped him from the bag, stared for a minute at his perfect little features. He looked like a doll. He looked like he was sleeping.

I just couldn't find it in myself to hand this woman an ice-cold baby, so I wrapped him up again and went to the emergency room for some heated blankets. In the morgue, I swaddled the baby in them, one after another, trying to take the chill from his skin. I took one of the knit caps we usually put on newborns to cover the peak of his head, mottled purple with settled blood.

We have a policy, if a newborn dies: we never take him away from the mother. If that grieving woman wants to hold her baby for twenty-four hours, to sleep with him tucked against her heart, to brush his hair and bathe him and have all the moments with her child she will never get to have, we make it happen. We wait until the mother is ready to let go.

That grandmother, she held her great-grandson for the entire afternoon. Then she put the infant back into my arms. I put a towel over my shoulder, as if I were nursing him, and got into the elevator, taking him down to the basement level of the hospital, where our morgue is located.

You'd think that the hardest part of an experience like this is the moment the mother gives you her child, but it's not. Because at that moment, it's still a child, to her. The hardest part is taking off the little knit hat, the swaddling blanket, the diaper. Zipping him into the body bag. Closing the refrigerator door.

AN HOUR LATER I AM in the staff room, taking my coat from the locker, when Marie pokes her head inside. "You're still here? Good. Got a minute?"

I nod, sitting down across from her at the table. Someone has tossed a handful of hard candy on it. I take a piece and unwrap it, let the butterscotch bleed onto my tongue. I hope it will keep me from saying what I shouldn't say.

"What a morning," Marie sighs.

"What a night," I answer.

"That's right, you pulled a double." She shakes her head. "That poor family."

"It's horrible." I may not agree with their beliefs, but that doesn't mean I think they deserve to lose a baby.

"We had to sedate the mom," Marie tells me. "The baby's gone downstairs."

Wisely, she does not mention the father to me.

Marie flattens a form on the table. "This is obviously just protocol. I need to write up what officially happened when Davis Bauer went into respiratory arrest. You were in the nursery?"

"I was covering for Corinne," I reply. My voice is steady, soft, even though every syllable feels as dangerous as a blade at my throat. "She got called to the OR unexpectedly. The Bauer baby had his circ at nine, and couldn't be left unattended. Since you were at the stat C, too, I was the only body even available to stand in for observation."

Marie's pen scratches across the form; none of this is anything she doesn't know or expect. "When did you notice that the infant had stopped breathing?"

I curl my tongue around the candy. Tuck it high in my cheek. "A moment before you arrived," I say.

Marie starts to speak, and then bites her lip. She taps the pen twice, then puts it down with a definitive click. "A moment," she repeats, as if she is weighing the scope and size of that word. "Ruth . . . when I came in, you were just *standing* there."

"I was doing what I was supposed to do," I correct. "I wasn't touching that baby." I get up from the table, buttoning my coat, hoping she cannot see that my hands are shaking. "Is there anything else?"

"It's been a tough day," Marie says. "Get some rest."

I nod and leave the break room. Instead of taking the elevator to street level, though, I plunge to the bowels of the hospital. In the over-exposed fluorescent fixtures of the morgue, I blink, letting my eyes adjust. I wonder why clarity is always so damn white.

He's the only dead baby there. His limbs are still pliable, his skin hasn't taken on a chill. There's mottling in his cheeks and feet, but that is the only clue that he is anything other than what he seems to be at first glance: someone's beloved.

I lean against a steel gurney, cradling him in my arms. I hold him the way I would have, if I'd been allowed to. I whisper his name and pray for his soul. I welcome him into this broken world and, in the same breath, say goodbye.

Kennedy

IT'S BEEN QUITE THE MORNING.

First, we all overslept because I thought Micah had set his alarm and he thought I had set my alarm. Then our four-year-old, Violet, refused to eat a bowl of Cheerios and sobbed until Micah agreed to fry an egg for her, at which point she was so far gone down the path of nuclear meltdown that she burst into tears again when the plate was set down. "I want a fuckin' knife!" she screamed, and it was quite possibly the only thing that could have stopped both Micah and me in our frenetic tracks.

"Did she say what I think she said?" Micah asked.

Violet wailed again—this time more clearly. "I want a fork and knife!"

I burst out laughing, which made Micah give me a withering look. "How many times have I told you to stop swearing?" he says. "You think it's funny that our four-year-old sounds like a sailor?"

"Technically she wasn't. Technically, you misheard it."

"Don't lawyer me," Micah muttered.

"Don't lecture me," I said.

So by the time we left—Micah taking Violet to preschool before he went to perform six back-to-back surgeries; me, driving in the opposite direction to my office—the only family member in a good mood was Violet, who had breakfast with *all* her utensils and was wearing her fancy sequined Mary Janes because neither of her parents had the energy to fight her about that, too.

An hour later, my day has gone from bad to worse. Because although I went to law school at Columbia, graduated in the top 5 percent of my class, spent three years clerking for a federal judge, today my boss—the head of the New Haven Judicial District of the Division of Public Defender Services in the state of Connecticut—has sent me to negotiate about bras.

Warden Al Wojecwicz, the director of corrections at the New Haven facility, is sitting in a stuffy conference room with me, his deputy director, and a lawyer from the private sector, Arthur Wang. I'm the only woman in the room, mind you. This convening of what I've come to call the Itty Bitty Titty Committee has been precipitated by the fact that two months ago, female lawyers were barred from entering the prison if we were wearing underwire bras. We kept setting off the metal detectors.

The prison wouldn't settle for a pat-down, insisting on a strip search, which was illegal and time-consuming. Ever resourceful, we started going into the ladies' room and leaving our underwear there, so that we could go in and visit our clients. But then the prison said we couldn't go inside braless.

Al rubs his temples. "Ms. McQuarrie, you have to understand, this is just about minimizing risk."

"Warden," I reply, "they let you go inside with *keys*. What do you think I'm going to do? Bust someone out of jail with a foundation garment?"

The deputy warden cannot meet my gaze. He clears his throat. "I went to Target and looked at the bras they have for sale there—"

My eyebrows shoot up to my hairline, and I turn to Al. "You sent him to do field research?"

Before he can answer, Arthur leans back in his chair. "You know, it does beg the question of whether the entire clothing policy should be under review," he muses. "Last year I was trying to see a client last-minute, before I headed out for vacation. I was wearing sandals, and was told I couldn't enter the prison with them. But the only other shoes I had were golf cleats, which were perfectly acceptable."

"Cleats," I repeat. "The shoes with actual *spikes* on the bottom? Why would you send someone in with cleats but not flip-flops?"

The warden and the deputy exchange a glance. "Well, because of the toe-lickers," says the deputy.

"You're afraid that someone is going to suck our toes?"

"Yes," the deputy says, deadpan. "Trust me, it's for your own protection. It's like a conjugal visit with your foot."

For just a heartbeat I picture the life I could have had if I'd joined a sterile corporate law firm, on the partner track. I imagine meeting my clients in paneled wood conference rooms, instead of repurposed storage closets that smell like bleach and pee. I imagine shaking the hand of a client whose hand isn't trembling—from meth withdrawal or abject terror at a justice system he doesn't trust.

But there are always trade-offs. When I met Micah, he was a fellow in ophthalmology at Yale–New Haven. He examined me and said I had the most beautiful colobomas he'd ever seen. On our first date I told him I really did believe justice was blind, and he said that was only because he hadn't had a chance to operate yet. If I hadn't married Micah, I would have probably followed the rest of the law review staff to sleek chrome offices in big cities. Instead, he went into practice, and I stopped clerking to give birth to Violet. When I was ready to go back to work, Micah was the one who reminded me of the sort of law I used to champion. Thanks to his salary, I was able to practice it. *I'll make the money*, Micah used to tell me. *You make the difference*. As a public defender I was never going to get rich, but I'd be able to look at myself in the mirror.

And since we live in a country where justice is supposed to be meted out equally, no matter how much money you have or what age you are or what your race or gender or ethnicity is, shouldn't public defenders be just as smart and aggressive and creative as any attorney for hire?

So I flatten my hands on the table. "You know, Warden, I don't play golf. But I do wear a bra. You know who else does? My friend Harriet Strong, who's a staff attorney for the ACLU. We went to law school together, and we try to have lunch once a month. I think she'd be fascinated to hear about this meeting, considering Connecticut prohibits discrimination based on sexual orientation and gender identity, and given that only female lawyers or those lawyers identifying as female would even be wearing bras when visiting clients in this facility. Which means that your policy is infringing on attorneys' rights *and* is preventing us from providing counsel. I'm also pretty sure Harriet would love to talk to the Women's Bar Association of Connecticut to see how many other female lawyers have complained. In other words, this falls smack into the category of *You are fucked if this gets out in the press.* So the next time I come to see a client, I am going to take my thirty-four C Le Mystère demi-cup with me, and—pardon the metaphor—I am going to assume there will not be any fallout. Would I be assuming correctly?"

The warden's mouth tightens. "I'm confident we can revisit the underwire ban."

"Good," I say, gathering my briefcase. "Thanks for your time, but I have to get to court."

I sail out of the little room, Arthur at my heels. As soon as we are outside the prison, in the blinding sunlight, he grins. "Remind me not to wind up opposite you in court."

I shake my head. "Do you *really* play golf?"

"I do when it means sucking up to a judge," he says. "Are you *really* a thirty-four C?"

"You'll never know, Arthur," I laugh, and we head to our separate cars in the parking lot, off to minister to two very different worlds.

* * *

MY HUSBAND AND I DO not sext. Instead our phone conversations con-
sist of a roll call of nationalities: Vietnamese. Ethiopian. Mexican.
Greek. As in "Where should we get takeout from tonight?" But when
I get out of my meeting at the jail, there is a message waiting for me
from Micah: *Sorry I was an asshole this morning.*

I grin, and text him back. *No wonder our kid curses.*

Date 2nite? Micah writes.

My thumbs fly over my phone. *U had me at asshole*, I type. *Indian?*

I vindalook forward to it, Micah responds.

See, this is why I can't ever stay mad at him.

MY MOTHER, WHO GREW UP in North Carolina on the debutante circuit,
believes there is nothing a little cuticle softener and eye cream can't fix.
To this end, she is always trying to get me to *take care of myself*, which
is code for *try to make an effort to look nice*, which is completely ridiculous, given that I have a small child and about a hundred needy clients
at any given moment, all of whom deserve my time more than the
hairdresser who could put highlights in my hair.

Last year, for my birthday, my mother gave me a gift I have consciously avoided until today: a gift certificate to a day spa for a ninety-
minute massage. I can do a lot in ninety minutes. File one or two briefs,
argue a motion, make and feed Violet breakfast, even (if I'm going to
be honest) squeeze in a rollicking romp in the sheets with Micah. If I
have ninety minutes, the last thing I want to do is spend it naked on a
table while some stranger rubs oil all over me.

But, as my mother points out, it's expiring in a week, and I haven't
used it yet. So—because she knows I'm too busy to take care of details
like this, she has taken the liberty of booking me into Spa-ht On, a day
spa catering to the busy professional woman, or so it says on the logo.
I sit in the waiting room until I am called, wondering if they really
thought that name through. Spa-ht on? Or Spat on?

Either one sounds unpalatable to me.

I stress about whether or not I am supposed to wear panties under my robe, and then struggle to figure out how to open my locker and secure it. Maybe this is the grand plan—clients are so frustrated by the time they get to the massage that they cannot help but leave in a better state than they started. "I'm Clarice," my therapist tells me, in a voice as soft as a Tibetan gong. "I'm just going to step out while you get comfortable."

The room is dark, lit with candles. There is some insipid music playing. I shrug off my robe and slippers and climb under the sheet, fitting my face into the little hole in the massage table. A few moments later, there is a soft knock. "Are we ready?"

I don't know. *Are* we?

"Now, you just relax," Clarice says.

I try. I mean, I really do. I close my eyes for about thirty seconds. Then I blink them open and stare at her feet in their sensible sneakers through the face hole of the massage table. Her firm hands begin to run the length of my spine. "Have you worked here a long time?" I ask.

"Three years."

"I bet there are some clients you walk in and see and wish you didn't have to touch," I muse. "I mean, like back hair? Ugh."

She doesn't answer. Her feet shift on the floor. I wonder if she's thinking that I'm one of those clients, now.

Does she really see my body like a doctor would—a slab to be worked upon? Or is she seeing the cellulite in my ass and the roll of fat that I usually hide under my bra strap and thinking that the yoga mom she rubbed down last hour was in much better shape?

Clarice, wasn't that the name of the girl from *Silence of the Lambs*?

"Fava beans and a nice Chianti," I murmur.

"I beg your pardon?"

"Sorry," I mutter, my chin mashed into the massage table. "Hard to talk in this contraption." I can feel my nose getting stuffy. When I lie facedown like this too long, that happens. And then I have to mouth-breathe and I think that the therapist is listening and sometimes I even drool through the hole. More reasons I don't like massages.

"Sometimes I think about what would happen if I got into a car crash and was stuck upside down like that," I say. "Not in the car, you know, but at the hospital in one of those neck braces that get screwed into your skull so that your vertebrae don't shift? What if the doctors flipped me onto my belly, and I got congested like I am right now and couldn't tell them? Or if I was in that kind of coma where you're awake but trapped inside your body and you can't talk, and you desperately need to blow your nose." My head is pounding now, from being in this position. "It doesn't even have to be that complicated. What if I live to a hundred and five and I'm in a rest home and I get a cold and no one thinks to get me a few drops of Afrin?"

Clarice's feet move away from my range of view, and then I feel cool air on my legs as she begins to massage my left calf. "My mother got me this treatment for my birthday," I say.

"That's nice . . ."

"She is a big fan of moisturizing. She actually said that it wouldn't kill me to not have dinosaur hide for skin if I wanted my husband to stick around. I pointed out that if lotion was what was keeping my marriage intact I had a much bigger problem than whether or not I had time to schedule a massage . . ."

"Ms. McQuarrie?" the therapist says. "I don't think I've ever had a client who needed a massage quite as much as you do."

For some reason, this makes me proud.

"And at the risk of losing my tip, I also don't think I've ever had a client who was so bad at getting a massage."

This makes me even prouder. "Thanks," I say.

"Maybe you could just try . . . to relax. Stop talking. Clear your mind."

I close my eyes again. And start going over my to-do list in my head.

"For what it's worth," I murmur, "I'm bad at yoga too."

ON DAYS WHEN I work late and Micah is still at the hospital, my mother picks Violet up from school. It's a win-win-win—I don't have to pay for a sitter, my mother gets time with her only grandchild, and Violet adores her. No one throws a tea party like my mom, who insists on using her old wedding china and linen napkins and pouring sweet tea from the pot. I know, when I come home, that Violet will have been bathed, read to, and tucked in. There will be leftover lemon drops or oatmeal raisin cookies from the afternoon's tea party, still warm inside a Tupperware. My kitchen will be cleaner than I left it that morning.

My mother also drives Micah crazy. "Ava means well," he is fond of saying. "But so did Joseph McCarthy." He says that my mother is a bulldozer dressed as a southern belle. In a way, this is true. My mother has a way of getting what she wants before you consciously realize you've been played.

"Hi," I say, dropping my briefcase on the couch as Violet launches herself into my arms.

"I finger-painted," Violet announces, holding her palms up to me. They are still slightly blue. "I couldn't take the picture home yet because it's still wet."

"Hey, sugar," my mother says, coming out of the kitchen. "How was your day?" Her voice always makes me think of heliotrope and a convertible ride and the sun beating on the crown of your head.

"Oh, the usual," I tell her. "I didn't have a client try to kill me today, so that was a plus." Last week, a man I was representing in an aggravated assault charge tried to strangle me at the defense table when the judge set bail unusually high. I'm still not sure if my client was angry, or planting a seed for an insanity defense. If it was the latter, I sort of have to give him props for thinking ahead.

"Kennedy, not in front of the C-H-I-L-D. Vi, honey, can you go get Grandma's purse?" I set Violet on her feet, and she sprints into the mudroom. "You know when you say things like that it makes me want to get a prescription for Xanax," my mother sighs. "I thought that you were going to start looking for a real job when Violet went to school."

"A, I do have a real job, and B, you're already taking Xanax, so that's a specious threat."

"Must you argue *everything*?"

"Yeah. I'm a lawyer." I realize then that my mother is wearing her coat. "Are you cold?"

"I told you I couldn't stay late tonight. Darla and I are going to that counterdance to meet some silver foxes."

"Contra dance," I correct. "Number one, ew. Number two, you never told me."

"I did. Last week. You just chose not to listen, sugar." Violet comes into the room again and hands her her purse. "That's a good girl," she says. "Give me a kiss now."

Violet throws her arms around my mother. "But you can't go," I say. "I have a date."

"Kennedy, you're married. If anyone needs a date, it's me. And Darla and I have big plans for just that."

She sails out the door and I sit down on the couch. "Mommy," Violet says, "can we have pizza?"

I look at the sequined shoes on her feet. "I've got a better idea," I tell her.

"WELL!" MICAH SAYS, WHEN HE sees me sitting at the table of the Indian restaurant with Violet, who has never been anywhere fancier than a Chili's. "This is a surprise."

"Our babysitter skipped town," I tell him, and I glance sidelong at Violet. "And we are skating the thin edge of DEFCON Four, so I already ordered."

Violet is coloring on the paper tablecloth. "Daddy," she announces, "I want pizza."

"But you love Indian food, Vi," Micah says.

"No I don't. I want pizza," she insists.

Just then, the waiter comes over with our food. "Perfect timing," I murmur. "See, honey?"

Violet turns her face up to the waiter, her blue eyes wide as she stares at his Sikh turban. "How come he's wearing a towel?"

"Don't be rude, sweetie," I reply. "That's called a turban, and that's what some Indian people wear."

She furrows her brow. "But he doesn't look like Pocahontas."

I want the floor to open up and swallow me, but instead, I paste a smile on my face. "I'm so sorry," I tell the waiter, who is now unloading our dishes as quickly as he can. "Violet . . . look, your favorite. Chicken tikka masala." I spoon some onto her plate, trying to distract her until the waiter goes away.

"Oh my God," I whisper to Micah. "What if he thinks we're horrible parents? Or horrible *people*?"

"Blame Disney."

"Maybe I should have said something different?"

Micah takes a spoonful of vindaloo and puts it on his plate. "Yeah," he says. "You could have picked Italian."

Turk

I'M STANDING IN THE MIDDLE OF THE NURSERY MY SON IS NEVER GOING to use.

My fists are like two anvils at my sides; I want to swing them. I want to punch holes in the plaster. I want the whole fucking room to come tumbling down.

Suddenly there is a firm hand on my shoulder. "You ready?"

Francis Mitchum—my father-in-law—stands behind me.

This is his duplex—Brit and I live on one side, and he lives on the other. Francis crosses the room and yanks down the Peter Rabbit curtains. Then he pours paint into a little tray and begins to roll the walls white again, washing away the pale yellow that Brit and I brushed onto the walls less than a month ago. The first coat doesn't quite cover the paint beneath, so the color peeks through, like something trapped under ice. With a deep breath I lie down under the crib. I lift the Allen wrench and begin to loosen the bolts that I had so carefully tightened, because I didn't want to be the reason anything bad happened to my son.

Who knew there didn't *have* to be a reason?

I left Brit sleeping off a sedative, which was an improvement over the way she was this morning at the hospital. I'd thought nothing could be worse than the crying that wouldn't stop, the sound of her breaking into pieces. But then, at about 4:00 A.M., all of that stopped. Brit didn't make a sound. She just stared, blank, at the wall. She wouldn't answer when I called her name; she wouldn't even look at me. The doctors gave her medicine to make her sleep. Sleep, they told me, was the best way for a body to heal.

Me, I hadn't slept, not a wink. But I knew it wasn't sleep that was going to make me feel better. That was going to take some wilding, a moment of destruction. I needed to pound out the pain inside me, give it a home someplace else.

With one last turn of the wrench, the crib collapses, the heavy mattress landing on my chest. Francis turns at the sound of the crash. "You all right there?"

"Yeah," I say, the wind knocked out of me. It hurts, but this is a kind of hurt I understand. I'll have a bruise; it will fade. I slide myself out from the tangle of wood and kick at it with my boot. "Probably a piece of crap anyway."

Francis frowns. "What are you going to do with it?"

I can't keep it. I know that Brit and I might have another baby one day, if we're lucky, but putting this crib back into a nursery would be like making our new child sleep with a ghost.

When I don't answer, Francis wipes his hands clean with a rag and begins to gather up the pieces of wood. "The Aryan Women's League will take it," he says. Brit had gone to a few of their meetings. They were a bunch of former skinchicks who went to WIC with fake IDs and got baby formula for free, bilking the system to bring formula to women whose men were serving time for fighting for the cause.

Francis isn't much to look at now. He runs the drywall crew I work for, has a decent rating on Angie's List, and votes Tea Party. (Old skinheads don't die. They used to join the KKK, but now they join the Tea Party. Don't believe me? Go listen to an old Klan speaker and compare it to a speech by a Tea Party Patriot. Instead of saying *Jew*, they now say *Federal government*. Instead of saying *Fags*, they say *Social ilk of our country*. Instead of saying *Nigger*, they say *Welfare*.) But in the eighties and nineties, he was a legend. His White Alliance Army had as much clout as Tom Metzger's White Aryan Resistance, Matt Hale's World Church of the Creator, William Luther Pierce's National Alliance, and Richard Butler's Aryan Nations. Back then he was raising Brit on his own, and his terror squad would roam the streets of New Haven with tack hammers, broken hockey sticks, blackjacks, lead pipes—beating up niggers and faggots and Jews while Brit, still a baby, napped in the car.

But when things began to change in the mid-nineties—when the government cracked down on skinhead crews—leaders like Francis found themselves strung up by their own brass balls, headed to prison. Francis understood that if you don't want to break, you have to bend. He was the guy who changed the structure of the White Power Movement from an organization to small cells of friends with common political leanings. He told us to grow our hair out. To go to college. To join the military. To blend in. With my help, he created and ran a website and message board. *We aren't crews anymore*, he'd tell me over and over. *We are pockets of discontent within the system.*

And as it turned out, it was even more terrifying to people to know we walked and lived among them unseen.

I think about the Aryan Women's League taking the crib. The changing table that I got at a garage sale and sanded down. The baby clothes that Brit picked through at Goodwill, that are folded up in the dresser. The baby powder and shampoo and bottles. I think about some other baby, some *live* baby, using it.

I stand up so fast I get dizzy, and find myself staring into a mirror with little balloons painted on its frame. I'd come home from work to find Brit at the table with a brush in her hand, and I teased her about becoming Martha Stewart. She said the only thing she had in common with Martha Stewart was a record, but she was laughing. She painted a balloon on my cheek and then I kissed her, and for that one moment, holding her in my arms with the unborn baby balanced between us, everything was perfect.

Now my eyes are ringed with dark circles; my beard's started to grow in; my hair is matted. I look like I'm on the run from something.

"Fuck this," I whisper, and I slam out of the nursery into the bath-room.

There, I find my electric razor. I plug it in and in one clean swoop mow a clear trail down the center of my head. I buzz each side, letting tufts of hair fall on my shoulders and into the sink. Like magic, as the hair falls away, a picture is revealed right on the crown of my head, just above the hairline: a thick black swastika, with my initials and Brit's forming its knotted center.

I'd gotten it when she said yes, she'd marry me.

I had been twenty-one, and pretty shitfaced at the time.

When I came to show Brit this testament to my love, she didn't even have a chance to comment before Francis walked up and smacked me hard on the back of the head. "Are you as stupid as you look?" he asked. "What part of *undercover* don't you understand?"

"It's my secret," I told him, and I smiled at Brit. "*Our* secret. When my hair grows in no one will know it's there, but us."

"And what if you go bald?" Francis asked.

He could tell, from the expression on my face, that I hadn't thought about that.

Francis didn't let me out of his house for the next two weeks, until all you could see was a dark shadow under my buzz cut that sort of looked like mange.

Now, I take a straightedge and some shaving cream and finish the job. I run my hand over my smooth head. It feels lighter. I notice the movement of air behind my ears.

I walk back into the nursery, which isn't a nursery anymore. The crib is gone, and the rest of the furniture is stacked in the hall. Every-thing else is in boxes, thanks to Francis. Before Brit is discharged this afternoon, I will haul back in a bed frame and a nightstand, and she will see it as the guest room it was a few months ago.

I stare at Francis, daring him to challenge me. His eyes trace the lines of my tattoo, like he is feeling for a scar. "I get it, boy," he says softly. "You're going to war."

*   *   *

THERE'S NOTHING WORSE THAN LEAVING a hospital without the baby you went in to have. Brit's in the wheelchair (hospital protocol) being driven by an orderly (more hospital protocol). I have been relegated to bringing up the rear, a stocking cap pulled low on my forehead. Brit keeps her eyes on her hands, folded in her lap. Is it just me, or is everyone staring at us? Are they wondering what's the medical issue with the woman who doesn't have a bald head or a cast or anything else visibly wrong?

Francis has already pulled the SUV up to the horseshoe driveway of the hospital. A security guard opens the back door as I help Brit out of the chair. I'm surprised by how light she feels, and I wonder if she will just float away from me once her hands stop gripping the arms of the wheelchair.

For a moment, pure panic crosses over her face. I realize she's recoiling from the dark cave of the backseat, as if there might be a monster hiding inside.

Or a car seat.

I slide my arm around her waist. "Baby," I whisper. "It's okay."

Her spine stiffens, and she steels herself before ducking into the car. When she realizes that she is not sitting next to an empty baby carrier, every muscle relaxes, and Brit leans back against the seat with her eyes closed.

I slip into the front seat. Francis catches my eye and raises his brows. "How are you feeling, ladybug?" he asks, using the term of endearment he used to call her as a child.

She doesn't answer. Just shakes her head, as one fat tear snakes down her cheek.

Francis revs the engine and peels out of the hospital driveway, as if he could outrun everything that happened there.

Somewhere, in a freezer in the basement, is my child. Or maybe by now he's gone, carved open like a Thanksgiving turkey on the coroner's table.

I could tell him what happened. I could tell him the Horrible Thing I see every time I close my eyes: that black bitch beating on my son's chest.

She was alone with Davis. I overheard the other nurses talking about it, in the hallway. She was alone, when she wasn't supposed to be. Who knows what happened, when no one was looking?

I glance back at Brit. When I look in her eyes, they're empty.

What if the worst thing isn't that I've lost my child? What if it's that I've also lost my wife?

AFTER HIGH SCHOOL, I MOVED to Hartford and got a job at Colt's Manufacturing. I took a few classes at the community college there, but the liberal shit those professors dished out made me so sick I quit. I didn't stop hanging around the college, though. My first recruit was a skateboarder, a skinny kid with long hair who cut in front of a black dude in line at the student café. The nigger shoved him, and Yorkey shoved him back and said, "If you hate it here so much, go back to Africa." The food fight that ensued was epic, and it ended with me reaching out a hand to Yorkey and pulling him from the fray. "You know," I told him as we stood outside smoking, "you don't have to be the victim."

Then I handed him a copy of *The Final Call*, the Nation of Islam newsletter that I'd planted on bulletin boards all over the campus. "You see this?" I said, starting to walk, knowing he'd follow. "You want to tell me why no one's marching into the black student union and arresting them for hate speech? For that matter, how come there's not a *White* student union?"

Yorkey snorted. "Because," he said, "*that* would be *discrimination*."

I looked at him as if he was Einstein. "Exactly."

After that, it was easy. We'd find the kids who were bullied by jocks and interfere, so that they knew they had protectors. We invited them to hang out with us after classes, and as we drove, I'd plug in a playlist of Skrewdriver, No Remorse, Berzerker, Centurion. White Power bands that sounded like a demon growling, that made you want to mess with the world.

I made them believe they had worth, simply because of the color they were born. When they complained about anything on campus, from the registration process to the food, I reminded them that the president of the school was a Jew, and that it was all part of a bigger plan by the Zionist Occupation Government to suppress us. I taught them "Us" meant "White."

I took their weed and molly and tossed it in the dumpster, because addicts snitched. I made them over in my image. "I've got a great pair of Doc Martens," I told Yorkey. "They're just your size. But there's no way I'm passing them on to a guy with greasy hair in a man bun." The next day, he showed up with his hair neatly trimmed, his scruff shaved. Before long, I'd created my own wilding squad: the newly minted Hartford division of NADS.

I wager I taught the students at that school more than any hotshot professor. I showed them the elemental differences between the races. I proved that if you're not the predator, you're the prey.

I WAKE IN A POOL of sweat, fighting my way out of a bad dream. Immediately, I feel across the covers for Brit, but there's no one there.

I swing my legs over the side of the bed and start moving, fighting through the dark like it's a crowd. I might as well be sleepwalking, the way I'm drawn to the room that Francis and I worked so hard to re-paint before Brit was released from the hospital.

She is standing in the doorway, her hands bracing her, like she needs help staying upright. The moon's coming through the window, so she's trapped in her own shadow. As my eyes adjust to the night, I try to see what she sees: the old armchair with a doily over its top; the iron frame of the twin guest bed. The walls, white again. I can still smell the fresh paint.

I clear my throat. "We thought it would help," I say, my voice small.

She pivots, but only halfway, so that for a second it looks like she's made out of light. "What if it never happened?" Brit whispers. "What if it was just a nightmare?"

She's wearing one of my flannel shirts—that's what she likes to sleep in—and her hands are splayed over her belly.

"Brit," I say, taking a step toward her.

"What if no one remembers him?"

I pull her into my arms, feel the hot circle of her breath on my chest. It's like fire. "Baby," I vow, "I'm not going to let anyone forget."

I HAVE ONE SUIT. ACTUALLY, Francis and I have one suit that we share. There's just not much of a need for fancy clothing when you work drywall during the day and run a White Power website at night. But the next afternoon, I put on the suit—black, pinstripes, the kind of thing I imagine Al Capone would have looked really sharp in—and a white shirt and a tie, and Brit and I drive back to the hospital to meet with Carla Luongo, the lawyer in Risk Management who has agreed to see us.

But when I come out of the bathroom freshly shaved, the tattoo on the back of my head stark and unmistakable, I am surprised to find Brit curled on the bed in my flannel shirt and sweatpants. "Baby," I say. "We have a meeting with the lawyer, remember?" I've told her this a half hour ago. There's no way she forgot.

Her eyes roll toward me like they are ball bearings, loose in her head. Her tongue pushes words around her mouth like they're food. "Don't . . . wanna . . . go . . . back."

She turns away from me, pulling up the covers, and that's when I see the bottle on the nightstand: the sleeping pills that the doctor gave her to help her transition. I take a deep breath and then haul my wife upright. She feels like a sandbag, heavy and immobile. *Shower*, I think, but that would require me to get in with her, and we don't have time. Instead, I take the glass of water on the bedside table and throw it in her face. She sputters, but it gets her to sit up on her own. I pull off her pajamas and grab the first things I can find in her drawer that look decent—a pair of black pants and a sweater that buttons up the front. As I am dressing her, I have a sudden flash of myself doing this same thing to my baby, and I wind up yanking so hard on Brit's arm that she yelps and I kiss her on the wrist. "Sorry, baby," I murmur, and more gently, I pull a comb through her hair and do my best to bunch it together into a ponytail. I stuff her feet into a pair of little black shoes that might actually be bedroom slippers and then haul her into my arms, and out to the car.

By the time we reach the hospital, she is near catatonic. "Just stay awake," I beg her, anchoring her to my side as we walk in. "For Davis."

Maybe that gets through to her, because as we are ushered into the lawyer's office, her eyes open a fraction wider.

Carla Luongo is a spic, just like I guessed from her name. She sits down on a chair and offers us a couch. I watch her nearly swallow her tongue when I take off my wool hat. Good. Let her know who she's dealing with, right up front.

Brit leans against me. "My wife," I explain, "is still not feeling well."

The lawyer nods sympathetically. "Mr. and Mrs. Bauer, let me first just say how sorry I am for your loss."

I don't respond.

"I'm sure you have questions," she says.

I lean forward. "I don't have questions. I know what happened. That black nurse killed my son. I saw her with my own eyes, beating at his chest. I told her supervisor I didn't want her touching my baby, and what happened? My worst fear came true."

"I'm sure you realize that Ms. Jefferson was only doing her job . . ."

"Oh, yeah? Was it also her job to go against what her boss ordered? It was all in Davis's file."

The lawyer stands so that she can grab a file on her desk. It's got the little colored confetti of stickers on the side that is some secret code, I imagine. She opens it, and even from here I can see the Post-it note. Her nostrils flare, but she doesn't comment.

"That nurse wasn't supposed to be taking care of my son," I say, "and she was left alone with him."

Carla Luongo looks at me. "How do you know that, Mr. Bauer?"

"Because your staff can't keep their voices down. I heard her say she was covering for the other nurse. The day before, she was screaming her head off, just because I made a request to take her off my son's case. And what happened? She was pounding on my baby. I *watched* her," I say, tears springing to my eyes. I wipe them away, feeling foolish, feeling weak. "You know what? Fuck this. I'm going to take this hospital to the bank. You killed my son; you're going to pay for it."

Honestly, I have no idea how the legal system works; I've done my best to stay away from getting caught by the cops. But I've watched enough TV infomercials to believe that if you can get cash in a class-action lawsuit for having some lung disease brought about by asbestos, you most certainly have a bone to pick if your baby dies when he's supposed to be receiving choice medical care.

I grab my suit jacket in one fist and half-drag Brit to the office door. I've just managed to open it when I hear the lawyer's voice behind me. "Mr. Bauer," she asks. "Why would you sue the hospital?"

"You're kidding, right?"

She takes a step forward, gently but firmly closing the door of her office again. "Why would you sue the *hospital,*" she repeats, "when everything suggests that Ruth Jefferson was the individual who killed your baby?"

ABOUT A YEAR INTO MY running the Hartford NADS crew, we had a steady income. I was able to lift guns from Colt's by forging inventory, and then sell them on the street. Mostly, we sold to blacks, because they were just going to kill each other with them anyway, and also because they paid three times more for a weapon than the Italians would. Yorkey and I ran the operation, and one night we were on our way home from a deal when a cop car pulled up behind me, its lights flashing.

Yorkey nearly shit a brick. "Fuck, man. What do we do?"

"We pull over," I told him. It wasn't like we had the stolen gun in the car anymore. As far as the police were concerned, Yorkey and I were headed back from a party at a buddy's apartment. But when the cops asked us to step out of the car, Yorkey was sweating like a coal miner. He looked like he was guilty as sin, which is probably why the police searched the car. I waited, because I knew I had nothing to hide.

Apparently, Yorkey couldn't say the same thing. That gun hadn't been the only deal going down that night. While I was negotiating, Yorkey had bought himself an eight ball of meth.

But because it was in *my* glove compartment, I went down for it.

The thing about doing time is that it was a world I understood, where everyone was separated by race. My sentence for possession was six months, and I planned to spend every minute planning my revenge. Yorkey had used before he became part of NADS; it was part of the skater culture. But my squad, they didn't touch drugs. And they sure as hell didn't squirrel them away in my glove compartment.

In prison, the black gangs have everyone outnumbered, so sometimes the Latinos and the White gangs will band together. But in jail, you just basically try to keep your head straight and keep out of trouble. I knew that if there was anyone in the White Power Movement who happened to be in doing time, they would find me sooner or later—but I was hoping that the niggers wouldn't find me first.

I took to keeping my nose buried in a Bible. I needed God in my life, because I had a public defender, and when you have a public defender, you'd better hope that God's on your side, too. But I wasn't reading the parts of Scripture I'd read before, when I was learning the doctrines of Christian Identity theology. Instead, I found myself dog-earing the pages about suffering, and salvation, and hope. I fasted, because I read something about it in the Bible. And during my fast God told me to surround myself with other people like me.

So the next day, I showed up at the jail Bible study group.

I was the only guy there who wasn't black.

At first we just stared at each other. Then, the dude running the meeting jerked his chin at a kid who couldn't have been much older than me, and he made a space next to himself. We all held hands, and when I held his, it was soft, like my father's hands used to be. I have no idea why that popped into my head, but that's what I was thinking when they started to say the Lord's Prayer, and then suddenly I was saying it along with them.

I went to Bible study every day. When we finished reading Scripture, we'd say *Amen*, and then Big Ike, who ran the group, would ask,

"Who's got court tomorrow?" Usually, someone would say they had a preliminary hearing or that the arresting officer was testifying or something like that, and Big Ike would say, "All right, then, let's pray that the officer don't throw you under no bus," and he'd find a passage in the Bible about redemption.

Twinkie was the black kid who was my age. We talked a lot about girls, and how we missed hooking up with them. But believe it or not, we talked more about the food we craved on the outside. Me, I would have committed a felony for Taco Bell; Twinkie only wanted Chef Boyardee. Somehow, it didn't matter so much what color his skin was. Had I met him on the streets of Hartford, I would have kicked his ass. But in jail, it was different. We'd team up when we played Spades, cheating with hand signals and eye rolls that we made up in private, because no one expected the White Power guy and the black kid to be working together.

One day, I was sitting in the common room with a bunch of White guys when a gang shooting came in on the midday news. The anchor on the TV was talking about how the bullets sprayed, how many people had been hit by accident. "That's why if we ever go at it with the gangs," I said, "we win. They don't go target shooting like us. They don't know how to hold weapons, look at that death grip. Typical nigger bullshit."

Twink wasn't sitting with us, but I could see him across the room. His eyes sort of skated over me, and then back to whatever he was doing. Later that day, we were playing cards for cigarettes, and I gave him a sign to come back in diamonds, because I was cutting diamond spades. Instead, he threw clubs, and we lost. As we were walking out of the common room, I turned on him. "What the hell, dude? I gave you a sign."

He looked right at me. "Guess it's just typical nigger bullshit," he said.

I thought: *Shit, I hurt his feelings.* Then: *So what?*

It's not like I stopped using that word. But I'll admit, sometimes when I said it, it stuck in my throat like a fish bone before I could cough it free.

* * *

FRANCIS FINDS ME JUST AS I put my boot through the front window of our duplex, pushing out the old casing so that it explodes onto the porch in a rain of splinters and glass. He folds his arms, raises a brow.

"Sill's rotted out," I explain. "And I didn't have a pry bar."

With a gaping hole in the wall, the cold air rushes into the house. It feels good, because I'm on fire.

"So this has nothing to do with your meeting," Francis says, in a way that suggests it has *everything* to do with the last half hour I've spent at the local police department. It was my next stop after the hospital. I'd dropped off Brit, who crawled back into bed, and drove straight there.

My meeting, really, was not even a meeting. Just me sitting across from a fat cop named MacDougall who filed my complaint against Ruth Jefferson. "He said he'd do a little research," I mutter. "Which means I'll never hear from him again."

"What did you tell him?"

"That that bitch killed my baby."

MacDougall didn't know anything about my son, or what had happened at the hospital, so I had to tell the whole sorry story over again. MacDougall asked me what I wanted from him, as if it wasn't evident.

"I want to bury my son," I told him. "And I want her to pay for what she did."

The cop asked if, maybe, I was just overcome with grief. If I had misinterpreted what I saw. "She wasn't just doing CPR," I told MacDougall. "She was hurting my baby. Even one of the other doctors told her to lighten up."

I said she had it in for me. Immediately the cop glanced at my tattoos. "No kidding," he said.

"It's a fucking hate crime, that's what it is," I tell Francis now. "But God forbid anyone stand up for the Anglos, even though we're a minority now."

My father-in-law falls into place beside me, ripping a piece of flashing out of the window cavity with his bare hands. "You're preaching to the choir, Turk," he says.

Francis may not have talked publicly about White Power in years, but I happen to know that in a locked storage facility three miles away from here, he is stockpiling weapons for the racial holy war. "I hope you're planning on sealing this up," he says, and I pretend he isn't talking about the window.

Just then my cellphone rings. I fish it out of my pocket but don't recognize the number on the screen. "Hello?"

"Mr. Bauer? This is Sergeant MacDougall. I spoke with you earlier today?"

I curl my hand around the phone and turn away, forging a wall of privacy with my back.

"I wanted to let you know that I had a chance to talk to Risk Management at the hospital, as well as to the medical examiner. Carla Luongo corroborated your story. The ME was able to tell me that your son died due to hypoglycemic seizure, which led to respiratory and then cardiac arrest."

"So what does that mean?"

"Well," he says, "the death certificate's been released to the hospital. You can bury your son."

I close my eyes, and for a moment, I can't even find a response.

"Okay," I manage.

"There's one more thing, Mr. Bauer," MacDougall adds. "The medical examiner confirmed that there was bruising on your son's rib cage."

My whole future hinges on the breath between that sentence and his next.

"There's evidence that Ruth Jefferson may have been at fault in the death of your son. And that it could have been a racially motivated incident," MacDougall says. "I'm putting in a call to the district attorney's office."

"Thank you," I say gruffly, and I hang up the phone. Then my knees give out, and I land heavily in front of the damaged sill. I can feel

Francis's hand on my shoulder. Even though there's no barrier between me and the outside, I struggle to breathe.

"I'm sorry, Turk," Francis says, misinterpreting my response.

"Don't be." I pull myself up and run to the dark bedroom where Brit is hibernating beneath a mound of covers. I throw open the curtains and let the sun flood the room. I watch her roll over, wincing, squinting, and I take her hand.

I can't give her our baby. But I can give her the next best thing.

Justice.

WHILE I HAD BEEN PLOTTING my revenge against Yorkey during my six months in jail, he had been busy, too. He'd allied himself with a group of bikers called the Pagans. They were hulking thugs who were, I assumed, somehow involved with meth, like him. And they were more than delighted to have his back, if it meant they could take down the leader of the Hartford NADS. Street cred like that went a long way.

I spent my first day out of jail trying to round up the old members of my crew, but they all knew what was about to go down, and they all had an excuse. "I gave up everything for you," I said, when I had exhausted even the freshest cut in the squad. "And this is how you repay me?"

But the last thing I was going to do was let anyone think going to jail had dulled my edges. So that night, I went to the pizza place that used to be the unofficial headquarters of my crew, and waited until I heard the growl of a dozen bikes pull up. I threw down my jacket, cracked my knuckles, and walked out to the alley behind the restaurant.

Yorkey, the son of a bitch, was hiding behind a wall of muscle. Seriously, the smallest Pagan was about six-five and three hundred pounds.

I may have been smaller, but I was fast. And none of those guys had grown up ducking from my grandfather's fists.

I wish I could tell you what happened that night, but all I have to go on is what I've heard from others. How I ran like a freaking berserker at the biggest guy, and revved up my arm so that my punch caught him square in the mouth and knocked out his entire front row of teeth. How I lifted one dude off his feet and sent him like a cannon-ball into the others. How I kicked a biker so hard in his kidney he allegedly pissed red for a month. How blood ran in the alley like rain on pavement.

All I know is I had nothing left to lose but my reputation, and that's enough ammunition to power a war. I don't remember any of it, except waking up the next morning in the pizza joint, with a bag of ice on my broken hand and one eye swollen shut.

I don't remember any of it, but word spread. I don't remember any of it, but once again, I was the stuff of legend.

ON THE DAY I BURY my son, the sun is shining. The wind's coming from the west, and it has teeth. I stand in front of the tiny hole in the ground.

I don't know who organized this whole funeral. Someone had to call to get a plot, to let people know there would be a service. I assume it was Francis, who now stands at the front of the casket, reading a verse from Scripture: "'For this child I prayed, and the Lord hath given me my petition which I asked of him,'" Francis recites. "'Therefore also I have lent him to the Lord; as long as he liveth he shall be lent to the Lord. And he worshiped the Lord there.'"

There are guys from the drywall crew here, and some of Brit's friends in the Movement. But there are also people I don't know, who have come to pay their respects to Francis. One of them is Tom Metzger, the man who founded the White Aryan Resistance. He's seventy-eight now, a loner like Francis.

When Brit starts sobbing during the reading of the psalm, I reach out to her, but she pulls away. Instead, she turns to Metzger, who she called Uncle Tommy when she was growing up. He puts an arm around her, and I try not to feel the absence of her as a slap.

I've heard plenty of platitudes today: *He's in a better place; he's a fallen soldier; time heals all wounds.* What no one told me about grief is how lonely it is. No matter who else is mourning, you're in your own little cell. Even when people try to comfort you, you're aware that now there is a barrier between you and them, made of the horrible thing that happened, that keeps you isolated. I had thought that, at the very least, Brit and I would hurt together, but she can barely stand to look at me. I wonder if it's for the same reason I have avoided *her*: because I look at her eyes and I see them in Davis's face; because I notice the dimple in her chin and think that my son had it, too. She—who used to be everything I ever wanted—is a constant memory now of everything I've lost.

I focus my attention on the casket being lowered into the ground. I keep my eyes extra wide, because if I do that, the tears won't spill over, and I won't look like a pussy.

I start making a list in my head, of all the things I will never get to do with my son: *see him smile for the first time. Celebrate his first Christmas. Get him a BB gun. Give him advice to ask a girl out.* Milestones. But the road of parenthood, for me, has been wiped clean of landmarks.

Suddenly Francis is standing in front of me with the shovel. I swallow hard, take it, and become the first person to start to bury my child. After pushing a scoop of dirt into the rip in the ground, I jam the shovel into the earth again. Tom Metzger helps Brit lift it, her hands shaking, and do her part.

I know I'm supposed to stand vigil while everyone else here helps to put Davis underground. But I'm too busy fighting the urge to dive into that tiny pit. To shovel the dirt out with my bare hands. To lift the casket, to pry it open, to save my baby. I'm holding myself in check so hard that my body is vibrating with the effort.

And then, something happens that diffuses all that tension, that twists the escape valve so that the steam inside me disappears. Brit's hand slips into mine. Her eyes are still vacant with drugs and pain; her body is angled away from me, but she definitely reached out. She definitely needed me.

For the first time in a week, I start to think that, maybe, we will survive.

*   *   *

WHEN FRANCIS MITCHUM SUMMONS YOU, you go.

In the aftermath of my rout of the Pagans, I received a handwritten note from Francis, telling me that he'd heard the rumors, and wanted to see if they were true. He invited me to meet him the following Saturday in New Haven, and included an address. I was a little surprised to drive there and find it smack in the middle of a subdivision, but I assumed it was a gathering of his squad when I saw all the cars parked out front. When I rang the doorbell, no one answered, but I could hear activity in the backyard, so I edged around the side of the house and let myself in through the unlocked fence.

Almost immediately, I was run down by a swarm of kids. They were probably about five years old, not that I had too much experience with humans of that size. They were racing toward a woman who was holding a baseball bat, trying to direct the unruly group into some form of a line. "It's my birthday," one little boy said. "So I get to go first!" He grabbed for the bat and began to swing it at a piñata: a papier-mâché nigger hanging from a noose.

Well, at least I knew I was in the right place.

I turned in the other direction, and came face-to-face with a girl who was holding stars in her hands. She had long curly hair, and her eyes were the palest shade of blue I'd ever seen.

I'd been hit a hundred times before, but never like that. I couldn't remember the word *hello*.

"Well," she said, "you're a little old for games, but you can have a turn if you want."

I just stared at her, confused, until I realized that she was referring to the hook-nosed profile poster taped up on the side of the house. I wanted to play, yes, but Pin the Star on the Jew wasn't what I had in mind.

"I'm looking for Francis Mitchum," I said. "He asked me to meet him here?"

She looked at me, her eyes narrowing. "You must be Turk," she said. "He's expecting you." She turned on her heel and walked into the house with the easy grace of someone who is used to having people follow in her wake.

We passed a few women in the kitchen, who were bouncing from fridge to cabinets and back like popcorn kernels on a hot griddle, exploding one at a time with commands: *Get the plates! Don't forget the ice cream!* There were more kids inside, but they were older—preteen, I was guessing, because they reminded me of me not that long ago—held in thrall by the man who stood in front of them. Francis Mitchum was shorter than I remembered, but then, I'd last seen him on a podium. His silver hair was lush and swept back from his face, and he was lecturing on Christian Identity theology. "The snake," he explained, "has sex with Eve." The kids looked around at each other when he said the word *sex*, as if hearing it spoken out loud so casually was their welcome into the sanctum of adulthood. "Why else would God say she couldn't eat an apple? They're in a garden, for Pete's sake. The apple is a symbol, and the downfall of man is getting laid. The Devil comes to Eve in the form of a snake, and she's tricked into messing around, and she gets pregnant. But then she goes back to Adam and tricks *him* into having sex. She has Cain, who's born with the mark of the Devil on him—a 666, a Star of David. That's right, Cain is the first Jew. But she also gives birth to Abel, who's Adam's kid. And Cain kills Abel because he's jealous, and he's the seed of Satan."

"You believe in this bullshit?" asked the beautiful girl beside me. Her voice was as even as a seam. It felt like a trick.

Some White Power folks were Christian Identity followers, and some weren't. Raine was. Francis was. I was. We believed that we were the *real* House of Israel, God's chosen ones. The Jews were impostors, and would be wiped out during the race war.

I grinned. "When I was about their age, I was starving and I stole a hot dog at a gas station. I didn't care so much about stealing, but for two weeks I was convinced God was going to smite me for eating pork."

When she met my gaze, it felt like the space between the moment you turned on a stove's pilot light, and the moment it was blue and burning. It felt like the possibility of an explosion.

"Daddy," she announced. "Your guest is here."

Daddy?

Francis Mitchum glanced at me, turning his attention away from the clot of preteens he'd been talking to, who were staring at me, too.

He stepped over the tangle of adolescent limbs and clapped me on the shoulder. "Turk Bauer. It's good of you to come."

"It's an honor to be asked," I replied.

"I see you've already met Brittany," Francis said.

Brittany. "Not officially." I held out my hand. "Hi."

"Hi," Brit repeated, laughing. She held on a moment too long, but not enough for anyone to notice.

Except Mitchum, who—I assumed—did not miss much. "Walk with me a bit?" he said, and I fell into step beside him as we returned to the backyard.

We chatted about the weather (late start to spring this year) and the drive from Hartford to New Haven (too much construction on I-91S). When we reached a corner of the yard, near an apple tree, Mitchum sat down on a lawn chair and gestured for me to do the same. From here, we had a bird's-eye view of the piñata game. The birthday boy was up to bat again, but so far, no candy had been spilled. "That's my godson," Mitchum said.

"I was wondering why I got invited to a kids' party."

"I like talking to the next generation," he admitted. "Makes me still feel relevant."

"Oh, I don't know about that, sir. I'd say you're still pretty relevant."

"Now, *you*," Mitchum said. "You've made quite a name for yourself lately."

I just nodded. I wasn't sure why Francis Mitchum had wanted to meet me.

"I hear your brother was killed by a nigger," he said. "And your father's a flamer—"

My head swung up, cheeks hot. "He's not my father anymore."

"Take it easy, boy. None of us can pick our parents. It's what we choose to make of them that's important." He looked at me. "When was the last time you saw him?"

"When I was beating him unconscious."

Again, I felt like I was being given a quiz, and I must have answered correctly, because Mitchum kept talking. "You've started your own crew, and by many accounts, you're the best recruiter on the East Coast. You took the rap for your second in command, and then taught him a lesson as soon as you got out of jail."

"Just doing what needed to be done."

"Well," Mitchum answered, "there aren't too many like you, nowadays. I thought honor was a commodity that was going extinct."

Just then, one of the other little boys snapped the neck off the piñata, and the candy cascaded onto the grass. The kids fell on it, grabbing up sweets in their fists.

The birthday boy's mother came out of the kitchen carrying a platter of cupcakes. "Happy birthday to you," she started to sing, and the children crowded around the picnic table.

Brittany stepped out onto the porch. Her fingers were blue with icing.

"Back when I was running a squad," Mitchum said, "no one in the Movement would have been caught dead being a junkie. Now, for the love of God, Aryan boys are teaming up with redskins on reservations to *make* meth somewhere the feds can't intervene."

Happy birthday to you!

"They're not teaming up," I told Mitchum. "They're banding together against common enemies: the Mexicans and the blacks. I'm not defending what they're doing, but I understand why they might be unlikely allies."

Happy birthday, dear Jackson!

Mitchum narrowed his gaze. "Unlikely allies," he repeated. "For example, an old guy with experience . . . and a young guy with the biggest balls I've ever seen. A man who knows the former generation of Anglos, and one who could lead the next. A fellow who grew up on the streets . . . and one who grew up with technology. Why, that could be quite a pairing."

Happy birthday to you!

Across the yard, Brit caught my eye and blushed.

"I'm listening," I said.

* * *

AFTER THE FUNERAL, EVERYONE COMES back to the house. There are casseroles and pies and platters, none of which I eat. People keep telling me they're sorry for our loss, as if they had something to do with it. Francis and Tom sit outside on the porch, which still has some shards of glass on it from my window project, and drink the bottle of whiskey Tom's brought.

Brit sits on a couch like the middle of a flower, surrounded by the petals of her friends. When someone she doesn't know well comes too near, they close around her. Eventually, they leave, saying things like *Call me if you need me* and *Every day it'll get a little easier*. In other words: lies.

I am just walking the last guest out when a car pulls up. The door opens, and MacDougall, the cop who took my complaint, gets out. He walks up the steps to where I am standing, his hands in his pockets. "I don't have any information for you yet," he says bluntly. "I came to pay my respects."

I feel Brit come up behind me like a shadow. "Babe, this is the officer who's going to help us."

"When?" she asks.

"Well, ma'am, investigations into these things take time . . ."

"These things," Brit repeats. "These *things*." She shoves past me, so that she is toe-to-toe with the cop. "My son is not a *thing*. *Was*," she corrects, her voice snagging. "*Was* not a thing."

Then she turns on her heel and disappears into the belly of the house. I look at the cop. "It's been a tough day."

"I understand. As soon as the prosecutor contacts me I'll be in—"

He doesn't finish his sentence, however, before the sound of a crash fills all the space behind me. "I have to go," I tell him, but I'm already closing the door in his face.

There's another crash before I reach the kitchen. As soon as I step inside, a casserole dish flies by my face, striking the wall behind me. "Brit," I cry out, moving toward her, and she wings a glass at my head. It glances off my brow, and for a moment, I see stars.

"Is this supposed to make me feel better?" Brit screams. "I fucking hate mac and cheese."

"Baby." I grasp her by the shoulders. "They were trying to be nice."

"I don't want them to be nice," she says, tears streaming down her face now. "I don't want their pity. I don't want anything, except that bitch who killed my baby."

I fold my arms around her, even though she stays stiff in them. "This isn't over yet."

She shoves at me so hard and so unexpectedly that I stumble backward. "It should be," she says, with so much venom in her words that I am paralyzed. "It *would* be, if you were a real man."

A muscle ticks in my jaw and I ball my hands into fists, but I don't react. Francis, who's entered the room at some point, comes up behind Brit and slips an arm around her waist. "Come on now, ladybug. Let's get you upstairs." He leads her out of the kitchen.

I know what she's saying: that a warrior isn't much of a warrior when he's fighting behind a computer. True, going underground with our movement was Francis's idea, and it's been a brilliant and insidious plan—but Brit's right. There's a big difference between the instant gratification that comes from landing a punch and the delayed pride that comes from spreading fear through the Internet.

I grab the car keys off the kitchen counter, and a moment later I'm cruising downtown, near the railroad tracks. I think, for a heartbeat, about finding that black nurse's address. I have the technological expertise to do it in less than two minutes.

Which is about as long as it would take the cops to point a finger at me if anything happened to her or her property.

Instead, I park under a railroad overpass and get out of the car. My heart's pounding, my adrenaline is high. It's been so long since I've been wilding that I've forgotten the high of it, unlike anything that alcohol or sports or even falling in love can produce.

The first person that gets in my way is unconscious. Homeless, he's drunk or drugged or asleep on a cardboard pallet under a mountain of plastic bags. He's not even black. He's just . . . easy.

I grab him by the throat, and he startles from one nightmare into another. "What are you looking at?" I scream into his face, even though I have him pinned by the neck, so that he couldn't be looking at anything *but* me. "What the fuck is your problem?"

Then I head-butt him in the mouth, so that I knock his teeth loose. I throw him back on the pavement, hearing a satisfying crack as his skull meets the ground.

With every blow, I can breathe a little easier. It has been years since I did this, but it feels like yesterday—my fists have a muscle memory. I pound this stranger into someone who will never be recognized, since it's the only way to remember who I am.

Ruth

WHEN YOU ARE A NURSE, YOU KNOW BETTER THAN MOST ANYONE ELSE that life goes on. There are good days and there are bad days. There are patients who stay with you, and those you can't wait to forget. But there is always another mother in labor, or delivering, who drives you forward. There is always a new crop of tiny humans who haven't even written the first sentence in the story of their lives. The process of birth is such an assembly line, in fact, that it always surprises me when I am forced to stop and look twice—like when a baby I helped deliver seemingly yesterday is suddenly my patient, about to have her own child. Or when the phone rings, and the hospital lawyer asks if I could just come in to *talk*.

I am not sure that I have ever conversed with Carla Luongo. In fact I'm not sure that I knew the hospital lawyer—pardon me, *risk management liaison*—was named Carla Luongo. But then I've never been in trouble before. I've never been a risk that needs to be managed.

It's been two weeks since Davis Bauer's death—fourteen days of me going in to work and doing my business hanging IVs and telling women to push and teaching them how to get a newborn to latch on. But more important, it's been fourteen nights when I've awakened with a start, reliving not that infant's death but the moments before. Playing them in slow motion and reversing them and erasing the edges of the narrative in my head so that I start to believe what I've told myself. What I've told others.

What I tell Carla Luongo, on the phone, when she calls.

"I'd be happy to meet with you," I say, when what I really mean is: *Am I in trouble?*

"Terrific," she replies. "How does ten o'clock sound?"

Today my shift begins at eleven, so I tell her that's fine. I scribble down the floor number where her office is just as Edison walks into the kitchen. He crosses, opens the fridge, and takes the orange juice from inside. He looks like he's about to drink right from the bottle, but I raise one eyebrow and he thinks otherwise.

"Ruth?" Carla Luongo says into my ear. "Are you still there?"

"Yes. Sorry."

"See you soon, then?"

"Looking forward to it," I say brightly and hang up.

Edison sits down and piles a heap of cereal into a bowl. "Were you talking to someone white?"

"What kind of question is that?"

He shrugs and pours the milk into the bowl, curling his answer around the spoon he tucks into his mouth. "Your voice changes."

CARLA LUONGO HAS A RUN in her hose. I should be thinking of many other things, including why this interview is even necessary, but I find myself focusing on the tear in her panty hose and thinking that if she were anyone else—anyone I considered a *friend*—I would quietly tell her to spare her any embarrassment.

The thing is, even though Carla keeps telling me she is on my side (there are sides?) and that this is a formality, I am finding it hard to believe her.

I have spent the past twenty minutes recounting in explicit detail how I wound up in the nursery alone with the Bauer baby. "So you were told not to touch the infant," the lawyer repeats.

"Yes," I say, for the twentieth time.

"And you didn't touch him until . . . How did you phrase it?" She clicks the cap of her pen.

"Until I was directed to by Marie, the charge nurse."

"And what did she say?"

"She asked me to start compressions." I sigh. "Look, you've written all this down. I can't tell you anything else I haven't already told you. And my shift's about to start. So are we about done here?"

The lawyer leans forward, her elbows balanced on her knees. "Did you have any interactions with the parents?"

"Briefly. Before I was removed from the baby's care."

"Were you angry?"

"I beg your pardon?"

"Were you angry? I mean, you were left to care for this infant, by yourself, when you'd already been given the directive to leave him alone."

"We were shorthanded. I knew it wouldn't be long till Corinne or Marie came back to relieve me," I reply, and then realize I haven't answered her question. "I wasn't angry."

"Yet Dr. Atkins says you made an offhand comment about sterilizing the baby," the lawyer says.

My jaw drops. "You spoke to the pediatrician?"

"It's my job to speak to everyone," she says.

I look up at her. "The parents obviously think I'm contaminated," I say. "It was just a stupid joke." One that would have meant nothing at all, if everything else hadn't happened. *If. If. If.*

"Were you keeping an eye on the baby? Were you even looking at him?"

I hesitate, and even in that breath, I can feel that this is the linchpin, the moment I will come back to and rub over in my mind until it is so smooth I can't remember every knot and groove and detail. I can't tell the lawyer that I disobeyed Marie's orders, because it could cost me my job. But I can't tell her that I tried to resuscitate the infant, either, because then those orders suddenly seem legitimate.

Since I touched that baby, and he died.

"The baby was fine," I say carefully. "And then I heard him gasp."

"What did you do?"

I look at her. "I followed orders. I was told not to do anything," I tell Carla Luongo. "So I didn't." I hesitate. "You know, another nurse in my situation might have looked at that note in the infant's file and found it . . . biased."

She knows what I'm implying: I could sue the hospital for discrimination. Or at least I want her to think I can, when in reality doing so would cost me money I don't have for a lawyer, as well as my friendships, and my job.

"Naturally," Carla says smoothly, "that's not the kind of team player we'd want on staff." In other words: *keep threatening to sue, and your career here is history.* She jots something down in her little black leather notebook and then stands up. "Well," she says. "Thanks for taking the time."

"No problem. You know where to find me."

"Oh yes," she says, and the whole way back to the birthing pavilion, I try to shake the sense that those two simple words could be a threat.

When I get back to my floor, however, I don't have time to wallow in self-doubt. Marie sees me step out of the elevator and grabs my arm with relief. "Ruth," she says. "Meet Virginia. Virginia, this is Ruth, one of our most experienced L and D nurses."

I look at the woman standing in front of me, wide-eyed as she watches a gurney being wheeled down the hallway for what must be a stat C-section. That's all I need to understand what's going on here. "Virginia," I say smoothly, "Marie's got a lot on her plate right now, so why don't you shadow me?"

Marie tosses me a silent thank-you and runs after the gurney. "So," I say to Virginia. "Nontraditional student?"

Unlike most of the baby-faced nursing candidates we get parading through here, Virginia is in her thirties. "Late start," she explains. "Or early, depending on how you look at it. I had my kids young, and wanted them out of the house before I started my official career. You probably think I'm crazy to be going back to school this old."

"Better late than never," I say. "Besides, being a mom ought to count as on-the-job training for L and D, don't you think?"

I intercept the nurse who's coming off duty and figure out which rooms I'm taking over: a couplet with a GDM G1 now P1 at forty weeks and four days who had a vaginal delivery at 5:00 A.M.; baby is on Q3 hour blood sugars for twenty-four hours; a G2 P1 at thirty-eight weeks and two days in active labor. "It's like alphabet soup," Virginia says.

"It's just shorthand," I laugh. "You get used to it. But I'll translate for you—we're taking over two rooms. One is a mom with gestational diabetes who delivered this morning and whose baby needs sugars every three hours. One is a woman in labor who already has one kid," I say, "so at least she's done this before. Just follow my lead."

With that, I push into her room. "Hello, Mrs. Braunstein," I say to the patient, who is holding on to her partner's hand in a death grip. "I hear you're a repeat customer. My name's Ruth, and this is Virginia. Virginia, it looks like Mr. Braunstein here could use a chair. Can you pull one closer?" I keep up a constant, calm chatter as I examine her strip and feel her belly. "Everything looks good."

"Doesn't *feel* good," the woman grits out.

"We can take care of that," I say smoothly.

Mrs. Braunstein turns to Virginia. "I want a water birth. That's on my plan."

Virginia nods tentatively. "Okay."

"Once we monitor you for twenty minutes or so, we'll see how the baby's doing, and if it's possible, we will definitely get you into the tub," I say.

"The other thing is that we don't want a circumcision, if it's a boy," Mrs. Braunstein says. "We're having a bris."

"Not a problem," I tell her. "I'll make a note in the file."

"I'm pretty sure I'm at about six centimeters," she says. "When I had Eli, I threw up just about then, and I'm starting to feel queasy now . . ."

I reach for the emesis basin and pass it to Virginia.

"Let's see if we can examine you before that happens," I suggest, and I slip on a pair of latex gloves, pulling up the sheet at the end of the bed.

Mrs. Braunstein turns to Virginia. "Are you sure that's a good idea?"

"Um." She turns to me. "Yes?"

I lower the sheet. "Mrs. Braunstein," I say. "Virginia's a nursing *student*. I've been in this business for twenty years. If you want, I'm sure she'd be delighted to add to her education by seeing how many centimeters you're dilated. But if you're in any sort of discomfort and just want to get that part of this over with, I'd be happy to accommodate you."

"Oh!" The patient turns bright red. "I just assumed . . ."

That she is in charge. Because even though Virginia is ten years younger than me, she is white.

I exhale, the same way I tell my imminent mothers to exhale, and—like them—with that breath, I let the frustration go. I put a gentle hand on Mrs. Braunstein's knee, and offer her a professional smile. "Let's just get this baby out," I suggest.

MY MAMA STILL WORKS FOR Mina Hallowell in her Upper West Side brownstone. Ever since Mr. Sam passed, it's Ms. Mina that my mom is supposed to be helping. Her daughter, Christina, lives nearby, but has her own life. Her son, Louis, lives in London with his husband, a director in the West End. Apparently I'm the only person who finds it ironic that Mama is three years *older* than the woman she's supposed to be assisting. Every time I've talked to my mama about retiring, though, she shrugs me off and says the Hallowells need her. I'd venture that my mama needs the Hallowells just as much, if only to feel like she still has a purpose.

My mother only has off on Sundays, and since I usually am asleep that day after a long Saturday-night shift, when I visit her it has to be at the brownstone instead. I don't visit very often, though. I tell myself it's because I have work or Edison or a thousand other reasons that take precedence, but in reality, it's because a little piece of me dies every time I walk inside and see my mama in that shapeless blue uniform, with a white apron wrapped around her hips. You'd think that after all this time, Ms. Mina would just tell Mama to dress the way she likes, but no. Maybe this is the reason why, when I *do* visit, I make a point of using the front entrance, with the doorman, instead of the servants' elevator in the back of the building. There is just some perverse part of me that likes knowing I will be announced like any other guest. That the name of the maid's daughter will be written down in a log.

Today when my mother lets me inside, she gives me a big hug. "Ruth! If this isn't the best surprise! I just knew today was going to be a good one."

"Really?" I say. "Why?"

"Well, I put on my heavy coat because the weather's turning, and wouldn't you know I found a twenty-dollar bill in the pocket left behind from last fall when I wore it. And I said to myself, *Lou, this is either a good omen, or else it's the start of Alzheimer's.*" She grins. "I chose the former."

I love the way her wrinkles have weathered her smile. I love seeing how age will look on my face, one day.

"Is my grandbaby here too?" she asks, looking behind me in the hall. "Did you bring him for another one of those college visits?"

"No, Mama, he's in classes now. You're gonna have to make do with just me."

"*Just* you," she teases. "As if that was never enough." She closes the door behind her as I unbutton my coat. She holds out her hand for it, but I reach into the closet instead for a hanger. The last thing I'm going to do is make my mama wait on me, too. I put my coat next to hers, and just for old times' sake, run my hand down the soft underbelly of Mama's lucky scarf before closing the closet door.

"Where's Ms. Mina?" I ask.

"Shopping, downtown, with Christina and the baby," she says.

"I don't want to interrupt you if you're busy —"

"For you, baby, I always have time. Come into the dining room. I'm just doing a little cleaning." She starts down the hallway, and I follow, carefully noticing the way she's favoring her right knee because of the bursitis in her left.

On the dining room table a white sheet is spread, and the strings of crystal that form the massive chandelier overhead are laying on it like trails of tears. A pungent bowl of ammonia solution sits in the center. My mother sits down and resumes her task of dipping each strand, then letting it air dry.

"How did you get those down?" I ask, eyeing the chandelier.

"Carefully," my mama replies.

I think about her balancing on the table, or a chair. "It's too dangerous for you to do that kind of stuff anymore—"

She waves me away. "I been doing this for fifty years," my mama says. "I could clean crystal in a coma."

"Well, keep climbing up to get them down from the chandelier and you might get your wish." I frown. "Did you go to the orthopedist whose name I gave you?"

"Ruth, stop babying me." She starts to fill in the space between us by asking about Edison's grades. She says that Adisa is worried about her sixteen-year-old dropping out of high school (something she failed to mention to me at the nail salon). As we talk, I help lift strands of crystal and dip them into the ammonia solution, feeling the liquid burn my skin, and pride—even more bitter—burn the back of my throat.

When my sister and I were little, Mama used to bring us here on Saturdays to work. She framed this as a big deal, a privilege—*not all kids are well behaved enough to shadow a parent at a job! If you're good, you get to push the button on the dumbwaiter that brings the dishes up from the dining room to the kitchen!* But what started as a treat soured quickly for me. True, sometimes we got to play with Christina and her Barbies, but when she had a friend over, Rachel and I were evicted to the kitchen or the laundry room, where Mama showed us how to iron cuffs and collars. At ten, I finally rebelled. "Maybe *you're* okay with this, but I don't want to be Ms. Mina's slave," I told my mother, loud enough to maybe be overheard, and she slapped me. "You do *not* use that word to describe an honest, paying job," my mama corrected. "The same job that put that sweater on your back and those shoes on your feet."

What I didn't realize at the time was that our apprenticeship had a higher purpose. We were learning the whole time—how to make hospital corners on a bed, how to get stains out of the grout, how to make a roux. My mama had been teaching us to be self-sufficient, so that we'd never be in the position Ms. Mina was in, unable to do things for ourselves.

We finish cleaning the crystal drops, and I stand on a chair while my mama hands them to me one by one to hang from the chandelier again. They are blinding in their beauty. "So," Mama says when we are nearly finished, "are you going to tell me what's wrong, or do I have to pry it loose?"

"Nothing's wrong. I was just missing you, that's all."

It's true. I came to Manhattan because I wanted to see her. I wanted to go somewhere where I knew I'd be valued.

"What happened at work, Ruth?"

When I was a child my mother's intuition was so uncanny it took me many years to realize she wasn't psychic. She didn't know the future; she just knew *me*.

"Usually you can't stop talking about a set of triplets or a father-in-law who punched out a new daddy in the waiting room. Today, you haven't mentioned the hospital at all."

I step down from the chair and fold my arms. The best lies are the ones that are wrapped around a core of truth. So although I conspicuously leave out any mention of Turk Bauer or the dead baby or Carla Luongo, I tell Mama about the nursing student and the patient who so easily assumed that she was the one in charge, instead of me. The words spill like a waterfall, with more force behind them than I expect. By the time I am finished, we are both sitting in the kitchen, and my mother has set a cup of tea down in front of me.

Mama purses her lips, as if she's weighing evidence. "Maybe you just imagined it."

I wonder if this is why I'm the way I am, the reason I tend to make excuses for everyone but myself and try so hard to fit in seamlessly. My mother modeled that behavior for years.

But what if she is right? Could I be overreacting? I replay the interaction in my head. It's not the same as the incident with Turk Bauer—Mrs. Braunstein didn't even mention the color of my skin. What if my mama's right and I'm the one who's being overly sensitive? What if *I'm* making the assumption that the patient's comments were made because Virginia's white and I'm not? Doesn't that make *me* the one who can't see past race?

Clear as a bell, I hear Adisa's voice in my head: *That's just what they want: for you to doubt yourself. As long as they can make you think you're not worthy, they still got you in chains.*

"I'm sure the lady didn't mean anything by it," Mama pronounces. *But it didn't make me feel any less small.*

I don't say it out loud, but I think it, and it sends a shiver down my spine. This isn't me. I don't accuse; I don't believe the majority of white people judge me because I'm Black or assume they are superior to me. I don't prowl the world looking for an excuse to pick a fight. I leave that to Adisa. Me, I do my best to fly under the radar. Sure, I know that racism exists and that people like Turk Bauer are waving that banner, but I don't judge all white folks by the historical actions of a few.

Or, rather, I never have before.

It's as if the little Post-it note on the patient file of Davis Bauer has nicked a vital artery, and I can't figure out how to stop the bleeding.

Suddenly we hear a jangle of keys and bluster as Ms. Mina and her daughter and grandson return to the brownstone. Mama hurries into the foyer to take their coats and their shopping bags, and I trail after her. Christina's eyes widen when she sees me, and she throws her arms around me while Mama peels the snowsuit off her four-year-old son, Felix. "Ruth!" she cries. "This is fate. Mom, wasn't I just talking to you about Ruth's son?"

Ms. Mina looks up at me. "She was indeed. Ruth, dear, aren't you just beautiful. Not a single wrinkle on that skin. I swear, you don't age."

Again, I hear Adisa in my head: *Black don't crack.* Very forcefully, I tamp down on that voice and gently fold tiny Ms. Mina into an embrace. "Neither do you, Ms. Mina," I say.

"Oh, go on with those lies." She pretends to wave away my words, and then smiles slyly. "No, seriously. Go on with them. I love hearing every one."

I try to signal to my mama. "I should probably be going—"

"Don't you cut your visit short on our account," Ms. Mina says, taking Felix from Mama's arms. "You stay as long as you want." She turns to Mama. "Lou, we'll take our tea in the gold room."

Christina grabs my hand. "Come with me," she says, and she drags me up the stairs to the bedroom where we used to play.

It's a shrine of sorts, with the same furniture she had as a child, but now there is a crib and a litter of toys on the floor. I step on something that nearly hobbles me, and Christina rolls her eyes. "Oh, God, Felix's Playmobil men. Crazy, right, to spend hundreds of dollars on something plastic? But you know Felix. He loves his pirates."

I crouch down, examining the intricate ship as Christina rummages through the closet. There is a captain in a red coat and a feathered black hat, and several pirates tangled in the plastic web of rigging. On the deck is a character with plastic skin that's an orange-brown, with a little silver collar around his neck.

Good lord, is this supposed to be a slave?

Yes, it's historically accurate. But still, it's a *toy.* Why *this* slice of the past? What's next—the Japanese POW internment camp play set? The Trail of Tears Lego? The Salem Witch Hunt game?

"I wanted to tell you before you read it in the paper," Christina says. "Larry's thinking of running for Congress."

"Wow," I answer. "How do you feel about that?"

She throws her arms around me. "*Thank you.* Do you realize you're the first friend I've told who doesn't act like this is the first step to the

White House or start talking about whether we should get a place in Bethesda or Arlington? You're the first person, period, who it occurred to that I might have a choice in the matter."

"Well, don't you? It seems like a pretty big disruption for the whole family."

"Yeah," Christina says. "I'm not sure I have the fortitude to be the wife of a politician."

I laugh. "You have the fortitude to run the country by yourself."

"That is *exactly* what I mean. Apparently I'm supposed to forget the fact that I graduated summa cum laude and instead I get to stand around holding my cute kid and smiling like the only thought I can hold in my head is what shade of lipstick matches my blouse," Christina sighs. "Promise me something? If I ever cut my hair into a bob that kind of looks like a helmet, you'll euthanize me?"

You see, I tell myself. *Here is proof.* I've known Christina my whole life. And yes, maybe there are differences between us—socioeconomic, political, racial—but that doesn't mean we can't connect, human to human, friend to friend.

"Sounds to me like you've already made up your mind," I point out.

She looks at me, hopeless. "I can't say no to him," Christina sighs. "That's why I fell for him in the first place."

"I know," I tell her. "But it could be worse."

"How?"

"Congressmen serve for two years," I point out. "Two years is a blink. Imagine if he'd set his heart on being a *senator*."

She shudders, then grins. "If he makes it to the White House," Christina says, "I'm hiring you as my chief of staff."

"Maybe surgeon general," I counter.

Christina links her arm through mine as we walk back to the gold room, where my mama is now setting out a tray of china and a teapot, a platter of homemade almond cookies. Felix sits on the floor, playing with a wooden train. "Mmm, Lou, I dream about these cookies," Christina says. She hugs my mama before reaching for one. "We are so lucky to have you as part of our family."

Family doesn't get a paycheck, I think.

I smile. But like anything you wear that doesn't fit, it pinches.

DURING ONE OF THOSE INDENTURED Servant Saturdays when I was playing hide-and-seek with Christina and Rachel, I took a wrong turn and found myself in a room that was off-limits. Mr. Hallowell's study was usually locked, but when I turned the knob, desperate to hide from the high-pitched squeal of Christina calling, "Ready or not, here I come . . ." I found myself stumbling inside the secret sanctum.

Rachel and I had spent a good deal of time imagining what might be behind that closed door. She thought it was a laboratory, with rows and rows of pickled body parts. I thought it was candy, because in my seven-year-old mind, that was the most valuable stash worth locking up. But when I landed on my hands and knees on the Oriental rug in Mr. Hallowell's study, the reality was pretty disappointing: there was a leather couch. Shelves and shelves of what looked like silver wheels. A portable movie screen. And feeding the film into the chattering teeth of a projector was Sam Hallowell himself.

I always thought Mr. Hallowell looked like a movie star, and Mama used to say he practically *was* one. As he turned around, pinning me with his gaze, I tried to come up with an excuse for why I had breached this forbidden territory but was distracted by the grainy picture, on the screen, of Tinker Bell lighting animated fireworks over a castle.

"This is all you've ever known," he said, and I realized that his speech was funny, that the words blurred into each other. He lifted a glass to his mouth and I heard the ice cubes clink. "You have no idea what it was like to see the world change in front of your eyes."

On the screen, a man I didn't recognize was speaking. "Color does brighten things up, doesn't it?" he said, as a black-and-white wall of photos behind him bloomed into all the shades of the rainbow.

"Walt Disney was a genius," Mr. Hallowell mused. He sat down on the couch and patted the seat beside him, and I scrambled over. A cartoon duck with glasses and a thick accent was sticking his hand in animated cans of paint and dumping the contents on the floor. *You mix them all together and they spell muddy . . . and then you got black,* the car-toon duck said, stirring the paint with his flippered foot so that it turned ebony. *That's exactly the way things were in the very beginning of time. Black. Man was completely in the dark about color. Why? Because he was stupid.*

Mr. Hallowell was close enough now for me to smell his breath—sour, like that of my uncle Isaiah, who'd missed Christmas last year because Mama said he had gone somewhere to dry out. "Christina and Louis and you and your sister, you don't know any different. For you it's always looked like this." He stood up suddenly and turned to me so that the projector shadowed his face, a dance of bright silhouettes. "The following program is brought to you in Living Color on NBC!" he boomed, spreading his arms so wide that the liquid in his glass sloshed over the side and onto the carpet. "What do you think, Ruth?" he asked.

I thought that I wanted him to move, so I could see what the duck was going to do next.

Mr. Hallowell's voice softened. "I used to say that before every program," he told me. "Until color TV was so common, no one needed reminding that it was a miracle. But before that—*before* that—I was the voice of the future. Me. Sam Hallowell. *The following program is brought to you in living color on NBC!*"

I didn't tell him to move over, so that I could see the cartoon. I sat with my hands in my lap, because I knew that sometimes when people spoke, it wasn't because they had something important to say. It was because they had a powerful need for someone to listen.

Late that night after my mama had brought us back home and tucked us into our beds, I had a nightmare. I opened my eyes and ev-erything was cast in shades of gray, like the man on the movie screen before he pinked up and the background exploded with color. I saw myself running through the brownstone, pulling at locked doors, until Mr. Hallowell's study opened. The film we had watched was ticking through the projector, but the picture was black and white now, too. I started screaming, and my mama rushed in and Rachel and Ms. Mina and Christina and even Mr. Hallowell, but when I told them my eyes weren't working and that all the color in the world had vanished, they laughed at me. *Ruth*, they said, *this is the way it always has been. Always will be.*

BY THE TIME MY TRAIN gets back to New Haven, Edison is already home and bent over the kitchen table doing his schoolwork. "Hey, baby," I say, dropping a kiss on the crown of his head as I walk in, and giving him an extra squeeze. "That's from Grandma Lou."

"Aren't you supposed to be at work?"

"I had a half hour before my shift starts, and I decided I'd rather spend it with you than in traffic."

His eyes flicker toward me. "You're gonna be late."

"You're worth it," I tell him. I grab an apple from a bowl in the middle of the kitchen table—I always keep something healthy there, because Edison will eat whatever's not nailed down—and take a bite, reaching for some of the papers spread out in front of my son. "Henry O. Flipper," I read. "Sounds like a leprechaun."

"He was the first African American graduate from West Point. Everyone in AP History has to teach a class profiling an American hero, and I'm trying to figure out what my lesson's going to be."

"Who else is in the running?"

Edison looks up. "Bill Pickett—a Black cowboy and rodeo star. And Christian Fleetwood, a Black Civil War soldier who won the Medal of Honor."

I glance at the grainy photos of each man. "I don't know any of these people."

"Yeah, that's the point," Edison says. "We get Rosa Parks and Dr. King and that's about it. You ever hear of a brotha named Lewis Latimer? He drew telephone parts for Alexander Graham Bell's patent applications, and worked as a draftsman and patent expert for Thomas Edison. But you didn't name me after him because you didn't know he existed. The only time people who look like us are making history, it's a footnote."

He says this without bitterness, the way he would announce that

we are out of ketchup or that his socks turned pink in the wash—as if
it is something he's not thrilled about, but can't get worked up over,
because it's unlikely to change the outcome at this particular moment.
I find myself thinking about Mrs. Braunstein and Virginia again. It
feels like a splinter my mind keeps getting caught on, and Edison just
pressed deep on it again. Have I really never noticed these things before? Or have I been very studiously keeping my eyes shut tight?

Edison glances at his watch. "Mama," he says, "you're gonna be
really late."

He's right. I tell him what he can heat up for dinner, what time he
should go to bed, what time my shift is over. Then I hurry to my car
and drive to the hospital. I take as many shortcuts as I can, but I'm still
ten minutes late. I take the stairs instead of waiting for the elevator,
and by the time I reach the birthing pavilion I am out of breath and
sweating. Marie is standing at the nurses' desk, as if she's waiting on
me. "I'm sorry," I say immediately. "I was in New York with my mother,
and then stuck in traffic, and—"

"Ruth . . . I can't let you work tonight."

I am dumbfounded. Corinne is late more than 50 percent of the
time, but I have a single transgression and I get punished for it?

"It won't happen again," I say.

"I can't let you work," Marie repeats, and I realize that she hasn't
met my gaze, not once. "I've been informed by HR that your license is
being suspended."

Suddenly, I am made of stone. "What?"

"I'm so sorry," she whispers. "Security will escort you out of the
building after you clear out your locker."

"Wait," I say, noticing the two goons who are hovering behind the
nurses' desk. "You're kidding me. Why is my license being suspended?
And how am I supposed to work if it is?"

Marie draws in her breath and turns to the security guards. They
step forward. "Ma'am?" one of them says, and he gestures toward the
break room, as if after twenty years I might not know the way.

* * *

THE LITTLE CARDBOARD BOX I carry out to the car has a toothbrush, toothpaste, a bottle of Advil, a cardigan sweater, and a collection of photos of Edison. That's all I kept in my locker at work. It sits in the backseat and keeps drawing my attention in the rearview mirror, surprising me, like a passenger I wasn't expecting.

I have not even pulled out of the parking lot before I call the union lawyer. It's 5:00 P.M., and the chances of him being at his desk are slim, so when he answers the phone I burst into tears. I tell him about Turk Bauer and the baby and he calms me down and says he will do some digging and call me back.

I should go home. I should make sure Edison is all right. But that will spark a conversation about why I'm not at work, and I'm not sure I can cope with that right now. If the union lawyer does his job, maybe I can even be reinstated before I'm supposed to work tomorrow night.

Then my phone rings. "Ruth?" Corinne says. "What the *fuck* is going on?"

I lean back against the driver's seat, closing my eyes. "I don't know," I admit.

"Hang on," she says, and I hear muffled noises. "I'm in the goddamned supply closet for privacy. I called you as soon as I heard."

"Heard what? I don't know anything, except that my license is apparently being suspended."

"Well, that bitchy hospital lawyer said something to Marie about professional misconduct—"

"Carla Luongo?"

"Who's she?"

"The bitchy hospital lawyer. She threw me under the bus," I say, bitter. Carla and I had each gotten a glimpse of the other's cards, and I'd thought that was enough for us to implicitly agree we both had aces. I just never expected her to play her hand so quickly. "That racist father must have threatened a lawsuit, and she sacrificed me to save the hospital."

There's a pause. It's so small that maybe if I wasn't listening for it, I might not have heard it. And then Corinne—my colleague, my friend—says, "I'm sure it wasn't intentional."

At Dalton, there was one table at lunch where all the Black kids sat, except me. Once, another scholarship student of color invited me to join them for lunch. I said thanks, but I usually spent that time tutoring a white friend who didn't understand trig. This was not the truth. The truth was that the Black table made my white friends nervous, because even if they'd sat down there with me, they would have been tolerated but not welcomed. In a world where they always fit in, the one place they *didn't* chafed hard.

The other truth was that if I sat with the other kids of color, I couldn't pretend I was different from them. When Mr. Adamson, my history teacher, started talking about Martin Luther King and kept looking at me, my white friends shrugged it off: *He didn't mean it that way.* At the Black table, if one student talked about Mr. Adamson staring at her during that same lesson, another African American student would validate the experience: *That totally happened to me, too.*

I so badly wanted to blend in in high school that I surrounded myself with people who could convince me that if I felt like I was being singled out because of the color of my skin, I was making things up, overthinking, being ridiculous.

There was no Black table in the cafeteria at the hospital. There were a handful of janitors of color, and one or two doctors, and me.

I want to ask Corinne when she was last Black, because then and only then would she have the right to tell me if Carla Luongo's actions were intentional or accidental. But instead I tell her I have to go, and I hang up while she is still responding. Then I drive out of the hospital where I've been hiding for two decades, underneath the highway that pulses with New York–bound traffic, like an artery. I pass a small tent city of homeless vets and a drug deal going down and park outside the projects where my sister lives. She answers the door with a toddler on her hip and a wooden spoon in her hand and an expression on her face that suggests she has been expecting me for years.

"WHY ARE YOU SURPRISED?" ADISA asks. "What did you think was going to happen, moving into Whiteville?"

"East End," I correct, and she just gives me a look.

We are sitting at her kitchen table. Given the sheer number of children she lives with, the apartment is remarkably clean. Pages from coloring books are taped to the wall, and there is a macaroni casserole in the oven. In the kitchen, Adisa's oldest, Tyana, is feeding the baby at her high chair. Two of the boys are playing Nintendo in the living room. Her other child is MIA.

"I hate to say I told you so . . ."

"No, you don't," I mutter. "You've been *waiting* to tell me that forever."

She shrugs, agreeing. "You're the one who kept saying, *Adisa, you don't know what you talking about. My skin color isn't even a factor.* And go figure, you're *not* just like one of them, are you?"

"You know, if I wanted to be a punching bag, I could have just stayed at the hospital." I bury my face in my hands. "What am I supposed to tell Edison?"

"The truth?" Adisa suggests. "There's no shame in it. It's not like you did anything wrong. It's better he learn earlier than his mama that he can run with the white crowd but it don't make him any less Black."

When Edison was younger, Adisa used to babysit him after school if I pulled an afternoon shift, until he begged to stay home alone. His cousins ribbed him for not being able to understand their slang, and when he did start to master it, his white friends in school looked at him like he had grown a second head. Even I was having trouble understanding my nephews, elbowing each other on the couch and laughing until Tyana whacked them both with a dish towel so that she could put the baby to sleep. (*Oh, we out chea,* I heard one of the boys say, and it took me a few minutes to realize that translated to *We're out here,* and that Tabari was teasing his brother for thinking he was all that because he won a round of the game.) Edison might not have fit in with the white kids in his school, but that at least he could blame on his skin. He didn't fit in with his cousins, either, and *they* looked like him.

Adisa folds her arms. "You need to find a lawyer and sue that damn hospital right back."

"That costs money," I groan. "I just want this all to go away."

My heart starts to hammer. I can't lose our home. I can't take my savings—all of which is Edison's college fund—and liquidate it just so that we can eat and pay the mortgage and buy gas. I can't ruin my son's opportunities just because mine blew up in my face.

Adisa must see that I'm on the verge of a total breakdown because she reaches for my hand. "Ruth," she says softly. "Your friends may have turned on you. But you know what the good thing is about having a sister? It's forever."

She locks her eyes on mine—hers are so dark that you can barely see the edge between iris and pupil. But they're steady, and she doesn't let go of me, and slowly, slowly, I let myself breathe.

WHEN I RETURN TO MY house at seven o'clock, Edison comes running to the front door. "What are you doing home?" he asks. "Is everything okay?"

I paste a smile onto my face. "I'm fine, baby. There was just a mix-up with the shifts, so Corinne and I went out to dinner at Olive Garden."

"Are there leftovers?"

God bless the teenage boy, who can't see past his own hunger pangs. "No," I tell him. "We shared an entrée."

"Well, that seems like a missed opportunity," he grumbles.

"Did you wind up writing about Latimer?"

He shakes his head. "No. I think I'm going to pick Anthony Johnson. First Black landowner," he says. "Way back in 1651."

"Wow," I reply. "That's impressive."

"Yeah, but there's kind of a hitch. See, he was a slave that came over to Virginia from England and worked on a tobacco plantation until it was attacked by Native Americans and everyone but five people there died. He and his wife, Mary, moved and claimed two hundred and fifty acres of land. The thing is, he owned slaves. And I don't know if I feel like being the one to tell that to the rest of my class, you know? Like it's something they can use against me someday in an argument." He shakes his head, lost in thought. "I mean, how could you *do* that, if you knew what it was like to be a slave yourself once?"

I think about all the things I've done to feel like I belong at the top—education, marriage, this home, keeping a barrier between myself and my sister. "I don't know," I say slowly. "In his world, the people with power owned other people. Maybe that's what he thought he needed to do to feel powerful too."

"That doesn't mean it was right," Edison points out.

I wrap my arms around his waist and hold him tight, pressing my face against his shoulder so he cannot see the tears in my eyes.

"What's that for?"

"Because," I murmur, "you make this world a better place."

Edison hugs me back. "Imagine what I could do if you'd brought me chicken parm."

Once he goes to bed, I sift through the mail. Bills, bills, and more bills, plus one slim envelope from the Department of Public Health, suspending my nursing license. I stare at it for five whole minutes, but the words don't materialize into anything other than what it is: the proof that this is not a nightmare I will wake up from, wondering at my own crazy imagination. Instead, I sit in the living room, my thoughts racing too fast for me to think about turning in. It's a mistake, that's all. I know it, and I just need to make everyone else see it, too. I'm a nurse. I heal people. I bring them comfort. I fix things. I can fix *this*.

My phone buzzes in my pocket. I glance at the number—it's the union lawyer calling me back. "Ruth," he says when I answer. "I hope it's not too late."

I almost laugh. As if I'm going to get any sleep tonight. "Why did the Department of Public Health take away my license?"

"Because of an allegation of possible negligence," he explains.

"But I didn't do anything wrong. I've worked there for twenty years. Can they still fire me?"

"You've got bigger problems than keeping your job. A criminal prosecution has been filed against you, Ruth. The State is holding you responsible for the death of that baby."

"I don't understand," I say, the sentence sharp as knives on my tongue.

"They already convened a grand jury. My advice is for you to hire a defense attorney. This is out of my league."

This is not real. This *can't* be real. "My supervisor said not to touch the infant, and I didn't, and now I'm being punished for it?"

"The State doesn't care what your supervisor said," the union lawyer replies. "The State just sees a dead baby. They're targeting you because they think you failed as a nurse."

"You're wrong." I shake my head in the darkness, and I say the words I've swallowed down my whole life. "They're targeting me because I'm Black."

In spite of all this, I fall asleep. I know this because when I first hear the jackhammer at 3:00 A.M. I think it is part of my dream—me, stuck in traffic, late for work, while a road crew creates a canyon between me and where I need to be. In my dream I honk the car horn. The jackhammer doesn't stop.

And then just like that I am bursting through the surface of consciousness, and the jackhammer of knocking detonates as the police break the door off its hinges and swarm into my living room, their guns drawn. "What are you doing?" I cry out. "What are you doing?"

"Ruth Jefferson?" one of them yells, and I can't find my voice, I can't speak at all, so I just jerk my chin: *Yes*. Immediately he pulls my arm behind my back and pushes me facedown onto the floor, his knee in the small of my back as he zips a plastic tie around my wrists. The others are overturning furniture, dumping drawers onto the floor, sweeping books off the shelves. "A grand jury has charged you with murder and involuntary manslaughter," the policeman says. "You're under arrest."

Another voice pierces through the tinny echo of these words. "Mama?" Edison asks. "What's going on?"

All eyes turn to the doorway of the bedroom. "Don't move!" shouts another cop, aiming his gun at my baby. "Hands in the air!"

I start to scream.

They are all over Edison, three of them wrestling him onto the ground. He is handcuffed like me. I see him straining toward me, panic lining every muscle of his neck, the whites of his eyes rolling as he tries to see if I am all right.

"Leave him be," I sob. "He has nothing to do with this!"

But they don't know that. All they see is a six-foot-tall black boy.

"Do what they say, Edison," I cry. "And call your aunt."

My joints crack as the policeman who is holding me down suddenly yanks me upright by my wrists, pulling my body in a way it doesn't want to go. The other policemen file behind, leaving the contents of my kitchen cabinets, my bookshelves, my drawers in heaps on the floor.

I am wide awake now, being dragged in my nightgown and slippers down my porch steps so that I stumble and scrape my knee on the pavement before I am pushed headfirst into the back of a police car. I pray to God that someone will remember to cut my son's hands loose. I pray to God that my neighbors, who have been awakened by the hullaballoo in our sleepy neighborhood at 3:00 A.M., and who stand in their doorways with their white faces reflecting the moon, will ask themselves one day why they remained dead silent, not a single one asking if there was anything they could do to help.

I HAVE BEEN TO THE police station before. I went when my car was side-swiped in the grocery store parking lot and the fool who did it just drove off. I held the hand of a patient who had been sexually assaulted and couldn't get the courage to tell the authorities. But now I am brought into the station the back way, where the bright fluorescent lights make me blink. I am handed off to another officer, just a boy really, who sits me down and asks me for my name, my address, my date of birth, my Social Security number. I speak so softly that a few times he has to ask me to be louder. Then I am led to what looks like a copy machine, except it's not. My fingers are rolled one by one across the glass surface and the prints appear on a screen. "Pretty awesome, right?" the boy says.

I wonder if my fingerprints are already in the system. When Edison was in kindergarten I had gone with him to a community safety day, to get him fingerprinted. He was scared, so I did it first. Back then, I believed that the worst thing that could ever happen was that he might be taken from me.

It never occurred to me that *I* might be taken from *him*.

I am then placed up against a cinder-block wall and photographed straight on, and in profile.

The young cop leads me to the only cell that our police department has, which is small and dark and freezing cold. There's a toilet in the corner, and a long-necked sink. "Excuse me," I say, clearing my throat as the door locks behind me. "How long do I stay here?"

He looks at me, not without sympathy. "As long as it takes," he says cryptically, and then he is gone.

I sit down on the bench. It is made of metal, and the chill goes right through my nightgown. I have to pee, but I am too embarrassed to do it here, in the open, because what if that's the moment they come for me?

I wonder if Edison has called Adisa, if even now she is trying to get me out of here. I wonder if Adisa has filled him in, told him about the baby that died. I wonder if my own boy blames me.

I have a sudden flash of myself just twelve hours ago, dipping strands of a crystal chandelier into an ammonia solution while classical music played in the Hallowells' brownstone. The incongruity makes me choke on a laugh. Or perhaps it is a sob. I can't tell anymore.

Maybe if Adisa can't get me out of here, the Hallowells can. They know people who know people. But my mama would have to be told what happened first, and although she would defend me to her death, I know there would be a part of her thinking, *How did it come to this? How did this girl, whose lucky life I broke my back for, wind up in a jail cell?*

And I wouldn't know the answer. On one side of the seesaw is my education. My nursing certification. My twenty years of service at the hospital. My neat little home. My spotless Toyota RAV4. My National Honor Society–inductee son. All these building blocks of my existence, and yet the only quality straddling the other side is so hulking and dense that it tips the balance every time: my brown skin.

Well.

I didn't do all this hard work for nothing. I can still use that fancy college degree and the years I've spent in the company of white people to turn this around, to make the policemen understand that this is a misunderstanding. Like them, I live in this town. Like them, I pay my taxes. They have so much more in common with me than with the angry bigot who started this debacle.

I have no idea how long it is until someone returns to the cell; I don't have a watch or a clock. But it's enough time for me to get that spark of hope burning in my chest again. So when I hear the tumblers click, I look up with a grateful smile.

"I'm going to take you for questioning," the young officer says. "I have to, um, you know." He gestures to my hands.

I stand up. "You must be exhausted," I tell him. "Staying awake all night."

He shrugs, but he also blushes. "Someone's gotta do it."

"I bet your mama's so proud of you. I know *I* would be. I think my son's only a couple of years younger than you." I hold my hands out in front of me, innocent and wide-eyed, as he glances down at my wrists.

"You know, I think we're okay without them," he says after a beat. He puts his hand on my arm, still firmly guiding me.

I hide my smile inside. I take this as a victory.

I am left alone in a room with a large mirror that I am sure is a window to another space on the other side of the wall. There is a tape recorder on the table, and a fan that is whirring overhead, although it is freezing here, too. I flex my hands on my lap, waiting. I don't stare at my reflection, because I know they are watching, and because of this I can only catch a glimpse of myself. In my nightgown, I might as well be a ghost.

When the door opens, two detectives enter—a bull of a man and a tiny sprite. "I'm Detective MacDougall," says the man. "And this is Detective Leong."

She smiles at me. I try to read into it. *You are a woman too*, I think, hoping for telepathy. *You are Asian American. You've been in my seat metaphorically, if not literally.*

"Can I get you some water, Mrs. Jefferson?" asks Detective Leong.

"That would be nice," I say.

While she goes to get me water, Detective MacDougall explains to me that I don't have to talk to them, but if I do, what I say might be used against me in court. Then again, he points out, if I have nothing to hide, maybe I'd like to give them my side of the story.

"Yes," I say, although I have watched enough cop shows to know that I am supposed to shut up. But that is fiction; this is real life. I didn't do anything illegal. And if I don't explain, how will anyone ever know that? If I don't explain, doesn't that just make me look like I'm guilty?

He asks if it's all right to turn on the tape recorder.

"Of course," I say. "And thank you. Thank you so much for being willing to hear me out. This is all a very big misunderstanding, I'm afraid."

By now Detective Leong is back. She hands me the water and I drink it all, a full eight-ounce glass. I did not know until I started how thirsty I was.

"Be that as it may, Ms. Jefferson," says MacDougall, "we have some pretty strong evidence to contradict what you're saying. You don't deny that you were present when Davis Bauer died?"

"No," I reply. "I was there. It was awful."

"What were you doing at the time?"

"I was part of the crash team. The baby became very ill, very fast. We did the best we could."

"Yet I just finished looking at photos from the medical examiner that suggest the child was physically abused—"

"Well, there you are," I blurt out. "I didn't touch that baby."

"You just said you were part of the crash team," MacDougall points out.

"But I didn't touch the baby until he started to code."

"At which point you started hammering on the baby's chest—"

My face flushes with heat. "What? No. I was doing CPR—"

"A bit too enthusiastically, according to eyewitnesses," the detective adds.

Who? I think, running through my brain to list all the people who were there with me. Who would have seen what I was doing and not recognized it for what it was: emergency medical care?

"Mrs. Jefferson," Detective Leong asks, "did you have any discussions with anyone in the hospital about your feelings for this baby and his family?"

"No. I was taken off the case, and that was that."

MacDougall narrows his eyes. "You didn't have a problem with Turk Bauer?"

I force myself to take a deep breath. "We didn't see eye to eye."

"Do you feel that way about all white people?"

"Some of my best friends are white." I meet his gaze squarely.

MacDougall stares at me for so long I can see his pupils shrink. I know he is waiting to see if I'll turn away first. Instead, I notch up my chin.

He pushes back from the table and stands up. "I have to make a call," he says, and he walks out of the room.

I take this as a victory, too.

Detective Leong sits on the edge of the table. Her badge is at her hip; it's shiny, like a new toy. "You must be so tired," she says, and I can hear in her voice the same game I was trying to play with the young cop in the holding cell.

"Nurses get used to working on very little sleep," I say evenly.

"And you've been a nurse for a while, right?"

"Twenty years."

She laughs. "God, I've been on the job for nine months. I can't imagine doing anything for that long. I guess it's not work if you love it, right?"

I nod, still wary. But if I have any chance of making these detectives understand that I'm being railroaded, it's going to be with her. "That's true. And I love what I do."

"You must have felt awful when you were told by your supervisor you couldn't take care of that baby anymore," she says. "Especially given your level of expertise."

"It wasn't the best day I've ever had, no."

"My first day on the job? I totaled a police car. Drove it into a highway barrier at a construction site. Seriously. I scored highest on the detective exam, but in the field, I was a joke. The other guys in my class still call me Crash. I mean, let's be honest, a female detective has to work twice as hard as the guys, but the only thing they remember me for is a simple mistake. I was so upset. I still *am*."

I look at her, the truth balanced on my tongue like a hard candy. *I wasn't supposed to touch the baby. But I did, even though I could have gotten in trouble. And it still wasn't enough.*

"Look, Ruth," the detective adds, "if this was an accident, now would be the time to say so. Maybe the hurt you were feeling got the best of you. It would be totally understandable, given the circumstances. Just tell me, and I'll do what I can to make this go down easier."

That is when I realize that she still thinks I'm at fault.

That she's not being nice to me by sharing her own story. She's being manipulative.

That those TV shows are right.

I swallow hard, so that honesty sits in the pit of my belly. Instead, I speak four short words in a voice I do not recognize. "I want a lawyer," I say.

stage one

Transition

The piano keys are black and white but they sound like
a million colors in your mind.

—María Cristina Mena

Kennedy

WHEN I ARRIVE AT THE OFFICE, ED GOURAKIS—ONE OF MY COL-
leagues—is spouting off about the new hire. One of our junior public
defenders left to have a baby and informed HR that she wasn't returning. I knew that Harry, our boss, had been interviewing, but it isn't
until Ed corners me at my cubicle that I realize a decision's been made.

"Did you meet him yet?" Ed asks.

"Meet who?"

"Howard. The newbie."

Ed is the kind of guy who went into public defense because he
could. In other words—he has a trust fund so large it doesn't matter
how shitty our salaries are. And yet, in spite of the fact that he's grown
up with every privilege possible, nothing is ever quite good enough.
The Starbucks across the street serves coffee that's too hot. There was
an accident on I-95N that made him twenty minutes late. The vending
machine at the courthouse stopped carrying Skittles.

"I literally walked in here four seconds ago. How could I have a
chance to meet anyone?"

"Well, he's clearly here to meet a diversity target. Just look for the puddles on the floor. This guy is so wet behind the ears he's leaving a trail."

"First, that metaphor didn't work. No one drips from their ears. Second, so what if he's young? I realize that it's hard for someone of your advanced age to remember . . . but you were young once too."

"There were," Ed says, lowering his voice, "more *deserving* candidates."

I rummage through the piles on my desk for the files I need. There is a stack of pink phone messages waiting for me that I patently ignore. "Sorry to hear your nephew wasn't picked," I murmur.

"Very funny, McQuarrie."

"Look, Ed, I've got a job to do. I don't have time for office gossip." I lean toward my screen and pretend to be incredibly absorbed by my first email, which happens to be a solicitation from Nordstrom Rack.

Eventually Ed realizes I'm not going to engage with him anymore, and he stomps into the break room, where, no doubt, the coffee will not be up to par and we will be out of his favorite flavor of creamer. I close my eyes and lean back in my chair.

Suddenly I hear a rustle on the other side of my cubicle and a tall, slim young black man stands up. He is wearing a cheap suit with a bow tie, and hipster glasses. He is very clearly the new hire for this office, and he has been sitting there, all along, listening to Ed's comments.

"Hashtag awkward," he says. "I'm Howard, in case there's any doubt in your mind."

I stretch my face so far into a smile that I imagine the puppets Violet watches on *Sesame Street*, whose jaws can drop on a hinge when they are overcome by emotion. "Howard," I repeat, jumping to my feet and immediately offering my hand to shake. "I'm Kennedy. It's *really* nice to meet you."

"Kennedy," he says. "Like John F.?"

I get asked that all the time. "Or Robert!" I say, although Howard was actually right. I might prefer to be named for the politician who did so much for civil rights, but in reality, my mother just had a crush on his ill-fated brother and the Camelot mythology.

I will do whatever it takes to make this poor kid realize that at least one person in this office is glad he's here. "So. Welcome!" I say brightly. "If you need anything, have any questions about the way we do things here—feel free to ask me."

"Great. Thanks."

"And maybe we can grab lunch?"

Howard nods. "I'd like that."

"Well. I have to get to court." I hesitate, and then address the elephant in the room. "Also, don't listen to Ed. Not everyone around here thinks the way he does." I smile at him. "For example, I think it's pretty amazing that you're giving back to your community."

Howard smiles back at me. "Thanks, but . . . I grew up in Darien."

Darien. One of the wealthiest towns in the state.

Then he sits down, invisible behind the partition that's between us.

I HAVEN'T EVEN HAD MY second cup of coffee yet and I've already hustled through far too much traffic and a tangle of reporters, leaving me to wonder what is going on in superior court in the courtroom where I'm *not*, since the only reason a TV crew might cover arraignments is to provide a sleep aid for insomniacs. So far we have gotten through three cases: a criminal violation of a restraining order with a defendant who did not speak English; a repeat offender with bleached hair and bags under her eyes who allegedly issued a bad check for twelve hundred dollars to buy a designer purse; and a man who was dumb enough to not just steal someone's identity and start using the credit cards and bank account but actually pick someone named Cathy and not think he was going to be caught.

Then again, as I often tell myself, if my clients were all smarter, my job would be obsolete.

The way it works in New Haven Superior Court on arraignment day is that one of us from the PD's office stands in for anyone who is brought before a judge and doesn't have a lawyer but needs one. It's like being trapped in a rotating door, and every time you step into the building, there's a whole new décor and layout and you're expected to know where you're headed and how to navigate there. Most of the time I meet my new clients at the defense table, at which point I have the span of a heartbeat to assimilate the facts of their arrest and try to get them out on bail.

Did I mention I hate arraignment day? It basically requires me to be Perry Mason with ESP, and even if I do a stellar job and manage to get personal recognizance bail for a defendant who otherwise would be locked up pending trial, chances are pretty good that I will not be the attorney litigating his case. The juicy ones that I'd *want* to take to trial will either be plucked out of my grasp by someone with more seniority at the office or transfer to a private (read: *paid*) lawyer.

That is surely going to be the trajectory for the next defendant.

"Next: the State versus Joseph Dawes Hawkins the Third," the clerk reads.

Joseph Dawes Hawkins is still so young that he has acne. He looks absolutely terrified, which is what a night in a jail will do to you when your experience with criminal behavior is limited to binge-watching *The Wire*. "Mr. Hawkins," the judge asks, "will you please identify yourself for the record?"

"Um. Joe Hawkins," the boy replies. His voice cracks.

"Where do you live?"

"One thirty-nine Grand Street, Westville."

The clerk reads the charge: drug trafficking.

I'm going to guess, based on the kid's expensive haircut and his wide-eyed response to the legal system, he was pushing something like Oxy, not meth or heroin. The judge enters an automatic plea of not guilty. "Joe, you've been charged with drug trafficking. Do you understand what that charge means?" The boy nods. "Do you have counsel present today?"

He glances over his shoulder at the gallery, goes a little paler, and then says, "No."

"Would you like to speak to the public defender?"

"Yeah, Your Honor," he says, and that's my cue.

Privacy is limited to the so-called cone of silence at the defense table. "I'm Kennedy McQuarrie," I say. "How old are you?"

"Eighteen. I'm a senior at Hopkins."

The private school. Of course he is. "How long have you lived in Connecticut?"

"Since I was two?"

"Is that a question or an answer?" I ask.

"Answer," he says, and he swallows. His Adam's apple is the size of a monkey's fist knot, which makes me think of sailing, which makes me think of Violet swearing.

"Are you working?"

He hesitates. "You mean besides selling the Oxy?"

"I didn't hear that," I reply immediately.

"Oh, I said—"

"*I didn't hear that.*"

He glances up, nods. "Got it. No. No, I don't work."

"Who do you live with?"

"My parents."

I am ticking off a checklist in my mind, peppering him with a barrage of questions. "Do your parents have the means to hire an attorney?" I ask finally.

He glances at my suit, which is from Target, and which has a stain on it from the milk that Violet upended in her cereal bowl this morning. "Yeah."

"Shut up and let me do the talking," I coach, and I turn to the bench. "Your Honor," I say, "young Joseph here is only just eighteen and this is his first offense. He's a senior in high school who lives with his mom and dad—a nursery school teacher and a bank president. His parents own their own home. We ask for Joseph to be released on his own recognizance."

The judge turns to my counterpart in this dance, the prosecutor who stands at the mirror image of the defense table. Her name is Odette Lawton, and she is about as jolly as the death penalty. Where most prosecutors and public defenders recognize that we are flip sides of the same shitty-state-pay-grade coin and can leave the animosity in the courtroom and socialize outside it, Odette keeps to herself. "What is the State looking for, Counselor?"

She glances up. Her hair is cropped close to her head and her eyes are so dark you can't see the pupils. She looks like she is well rested and has just had a facial; her makeup is flawless.

I stare down at my hands. The cuticles are bitten and either I have green finger paint underneath the nails or I am rotting from the inside out.

"This is a serious charge," Odette says. "Not only was a prescription narcotic found on Mr. Hawkins's person, but there was intent to sell. To turn him loose into the community would be a threat and a grievous mistake. The State requests that bail be set at ten thousand dollars with surety."

"Bail is set at ten thousand dollars," the judge repeats, and Joseph Dawes Hawkins III is lugged out of the courtroom by a bailiff.

Well, you can't win 'em all. The good news here is that Joseph's family can afford the bail—even if it means he will have to forfeit Christmas in Barbados. The better news is that I will never see Joseph Dawes Hawkins III again. His father may have wanted to teach him a lesson by not having the family attorney present from the get-go so Joey would have to sit in a cell overnight, but I'm sure it is only a matter of time before that same fancy lawyer calls my office and picks up Joey's case.

"The State versus Ruth Jefferson," I hear.

I glance up as a woman is led into the courtroom in chains, still wearing her nightgown, a scarf wrapped around her head. Her eyes scan the gallery wildly, and for the first time I realize that it's more crowded than usual for Tuesday arraignments. Packed, even.

"Would you please identify yourself for the record?" the judge asks.

"Ruth Jefferson," she says.

"Murderer," a woman screams. There is a buzz in the crowd that swells into a roar. Just then Ruth flinches. I see her turn her face into her shoulder and I realize that she is wiping off the saliva that someone has spit on her from over the gallery rail.

The bailiffs are already hauling the guy off—a hulking brute I can see only from the rear. On his scalp is a tattooed swastika, twined with letters.

The judge calls for order. Ruth Jefferson stands tall and keeps looking around for someone—or something—that she can't seem to find.

"Ruth Jefferson," the clerk reads, "you are charged with count one, murder; count two, negligent homicide."

I am so busy trying to figure out what the hell is going on here that I do not realize everyone is looking at me, and that this defendant has apparently told the judge that she needs a public defender.

Odette stands up. "This is a heinous criminal act involving a three-day-old infant, Your Honor. The defendant voiced her animosity and animus toward the parents of this child, and the State will show that she acted intentionally and deliberately, with malice aforethought, in reckless disregard of the newborn's safety, and that in fact at her hands the baby suffered trauma that led to death."

This woman killed a newborn? I'm running through scenarios in my head: Is she a nanny? Is this a shaken baby case? A SIDS death?

"This is crazy," Ruth Jefferson explodes.

I elbow her gently. "This is *not* the time."

"Let me talk to the judge," she insists.

"No," I tell her. "Let *me* talk to the judge *for* you." I turn to the bench. "Your Honor, may we have a moment?"

I lead her to the defense table, just a few steps from where we are standing. "I'm Kennedy McQuarrie. We'll talk about the details of your case later, but right now, I need to ask you some questions. How long have you lived here?"

"They put me in *chains*," she says, her voice dark and fierce. "These people came to my house in the middle of the night and handcuffed me. They handcuffed my *son*—"

"I understand that you're upset," I explain. "But we have about ten seconds for me to get to know you, so I can help you through this arraignment."

"You think you can know me in ten seconds?" she says.

I draw back. If this woman wants to sabotage her own arraignment it's not *my* fault.

"Ms. McQuarrie," the judge says. "Sometime before I get my AARP card, please . . ."

"Yes, Your Honor," I say, turning to him.

"The State recognizes the insidious and unpalatable nature of this crime," Odette says. She is staring right at Ruth. The dichotomy between these two black women is arresting: the prosecutor's sleek suit and spike heels and crisp tailored shirt standing in counterpoint to Ruth's rumpled nightgown and head scarf. It feels like more than a snapshot. It feels like a statement, like a case study for a course I don't remember enrolling in. "Given the magnitude of the charges, the State requests that the defendant be held without bail."

I can feel all the air rush out of Ruth's lungs.

"Your Honor," I say, and then I stop.

I have nothing to work with. I don't know what Ruth Jefferson does for a living. I don't know if she owns a house or if she moved to Connecticut yesterday. I don't know if she held a pillow over that baby's face until it stopped breathing or if she is rightfully angry about a trumped-up charge.

"Your Honor," I repeat, "the State has offered no proof for their specious claims. This is a very serious charge with virtually no evidence. In light of this I'd ask the court to set reasonable bail in the amount of twenty-five thousand dollars surety."

It's the best I can do, given the lack of information she's provided. My job is to get Ruth Jefferson through her arraignment, as efficiently and as fairly as possible. I glance up at the clock. There are probably about ten more clients after her.

Suddenly there is a tug on my sleeve. "You see that boy?" Ruth murmurs, and she looks at the gallery. Her gaze locks on a young man in the rear of the courtroom, who gets to his feet as if he is being drawn upright by a magnet. "That's my son," Ruth says, and then she turns to me. "Do you have kids?"

I think of Violet. I think of what it would be like if the biggest problem in your life was not watching your child getting frustrated but watching your child getting handcuffed.

"Your Honor," I say, "I'd like to retract what I just said."

"I beg your pardon, Counselor?"

"Before we discuss bail, I would like an opportunity to speak with my client."

The judge frowns. "You just *had* one."

"I would like an opportunity to speak with my client for more than ten seconds," I amend.

He rubs his hand over his face. "Fine," he concedes. "You can speak to your client at the recess and we'll revisit this matter at second call."

The bailiffs grab Ruth's arms. I can tell she has no idea what's going on. "I'm coming," I manage to tell her, and then she's dragged out of the courtroom, and before I know it, I'm speaking on behalf of a twenty-year-old who calls himself the symbol # ("Like Prince, but not," he tells me), who has spray-painted graffiti of a giant penis on a highway bridge and cannot understand why it's criminal mischief, and not art.

I HAVE TEN MORE ARRAIGNMENTS, and during all of them, I'm thinking about Ruth Jefferson. Thank God for the stenographers' union contract, which mandates a fifteen-minute pee break, during which I find my way into the dank, dirty guts of the courthouse to the holding cell where they've taken my client.

She looks up from the metal bunk where she's sitting, rubbing her wrists. She's no longer wearing the chains that she had in the courtroom, like any other defendant accused of murder would have, but it's almost as if she doesn't notice they're gone. "Where have you been?" she asks, her voice sharp.

"Doing my job," I reply.

Ruth meets my eye. "That's all I was doing, too," she says. "I'm a nurse."

I start to piece together the puzzle: something must have gone south during Ruth's care of the infant, something that the prosecution believes was not an accident. "I need to get some information from you. If you don't want to be locked up pending trial, you and I need to work together."

For a long moment Ruth is silent, and it surprises me. Most people in her situation would grab on to the lifeline offered by a public defender. This woman, however, feels like she's trying to determine if I'm going to measure up.

It's a pretty disturbing feeling, I must admit. My clients don't tend to be judgmental; they're people who are used to being judged . . . and found lacking.

Finally she nods.

"Okay," I say, letting out a breath I did not realize I'd been holding. "How old are you?"

"Forty-four."

"Are you married?"

"No," Ruth says. "My husband died in Afghanistan, during his second deployment. An IED went off. It was ten years ago."

"Your son—is he your only child?" I ask.

"Yes. Edison's in high school," she says. "He's applying to college right now. Those animals came into my house and handcuffed a straight-A student."

"We'll get to that in a second," I promise. "You have a nursing degree?"

"I went to SUNY Plattsburgh and then to Yale Nursing School."

"Are you employed?"

"I worked at Mercy–West Haven Hospital for twenty years, on the birthing pavilion. But yesterday, they took my job away from me."

I make a note on a legal pad. "What source of income do you have now?"

She shakes her head. "My husband's military death benefits, I suppose."

"Do you own your own home?"

"A townhouse in East End."

That's the area where Micah and I live. It's an affluent white neighborhood. The black faces I see there are usually passing through in their cars. Violence is rare, and when a mugging or a carjacking does happen, the online comments section of the *New Haven Independent* is full of East End folks lamenting how the "elements" from poor neighborhoods like Dixwell and Newhallville are finding their way into our perfect hamlet.

By "elements," of course, they mean black people.

"You look surprised," Ruth remarks.

"No," I reply quickly. "It just happens to be where I live, too, and I've never seen you around."

"I keep a pretty low profile," she says dryly.

I clear my throat. "Do you have relatives in Connecticut?"

"My sister, Adisa. She's the one who's sitting with Edison. She lives in Church Street South."

It's a low-income apartment complex in the Hill neighborhood, between Union Station and the Yale medical district. Something like 97 percent of the kids live in poverty, and I've had my share of clients from there. It's only a handful of miles away from East End, and yet it's another world: kids selling drugs for their older brothers, older brothers selling drugs because there aren't any jobs, girls turning tricks, gang shootings every night. I wonder how Ruth wound up living so differently from her sister.

"Are your parents still alive?"

"My mother works on the Upper West Side of Manhattan." Ruth's eyes slide away from mine. "You remember Sam Hallowell?"

"The TV network guy? Didn't he die?"

"Yes. But she's still the family maid."

I open the folder with Ruth's name on it, which has the indictment that was handed down by the grand jury and that precipitated her arrest. I hadn't had time to scan anything more than the charges before this moment, but now I skim with that superpower that PDs have, where certain words leap off the page and lodge into our consciousness. "Who's Davis Bauer?"

Ruth's voice gets softer. "A baby," she says, "who died."

"Tell me what happened."

Ruth begins to weave a story. For every thick black fact she spins, there's a silver flicker of shame. She tells me about the parents and the supervisor's sticky note and the circumcision and the emergency C-section and the newborn's seizure. She says that the man with the swastika tattoo who spit at her in the courtroom was the baby's father. Threads knot around us, like the silk from a cocoon.

". . . and the next thing I knew," Ruth says, "the baby was dead."

I glance down at the police statement. "You never touched him?" I clarify.

She stares at me for a long moment, as if she is trying to figure out if I can be trusted. Then she shakes her head. "Not until the charge nurse told me to start compressions."

I lean forward. "If I can get you out of here, so you can go home to your son, you'll have to post a percentage of the bail amount. Do you have any money saved up?"

Her shoulders square. "Edison's college fund, but I won't touch that."

"Would you be willing to put your home up?"

"What does that even mean?"

"You let the State put a lien on it," I explain.

"And then what? If I lose the trial does that mean Edison won't have anywhere to live?"

"No. This is only a measure to make sure you're not going to skip town if they let you leave."

Ruth takes a deep breath. "Okay. But you have to do me a favor. You have to tell my son that I'm all right."

I nod, and then she nods.

In that moment, we're not black and white, or attorney and accused. We're not separated by what I know about the legal system and what she has yet to learn. We are just two mothers, sitting side by side.

THIS TIME, AS I WALK through the gallery of the courtroom, I feel like I've put on corrective lenses. I notice onlookers I didn't pay attention to before. They may not be tattooed like the baby's father, but they are white. Only a few are wearing Doc Martens; the rest are in sneakers. Are they skinheads, too? Some hold signs with Davis's name on them, some wear powder-blue ribbons pinned to their shirts in solidarity. How did I miss this the first time I came into the courtroom? Have they assembled to support the Bauer family?

I think about Ruth walking down the street in East End and wonder how many other residents questioned what she was doing there, even if they never said it to her face. *How incredibly easy it is to hide behind white skin*, I think, looking at these probable supremacists. The benefit of the doubt is in your favor. You're not suspicious.

The few black faces in the room stand out in harsh counterpoint. I walk up to the boy Ruth acknowledged earlier, who immediately stands. "Edison?" I say. "My name is Kennedy."

He is taller than I am by nearly a foot, but he still has the face of a baby. "Is my mama all right?"

"She's fine, and she sent me out here to tell you so."

"Well, you took your sweet time," says the woman beside him. She has long braids shot through with red, and her skin is much darker than Ruth's. She is drinking a Coke, although there's no food or drink allowed in the courtroom, and when she sees me looking at the can she raises an eyebrow as if she is daring me to say something.

"You must be Ruth's sister."

"Why? Because I'm the only nigga in this room other than her son?"

I reel backward at the word she uses, which I am sure is exactly the reaction she's going for. If Ruth seemed judgmental or prickly, then her sister is a porcupine with an anger management problem. "No," I say, in the same tone I use with Violet when I try to reason with her. "First of all, you're not the only . . . person of color . . . here. And second, your sister told me you were with Edison."

"Can you get her out?" Edison asks.

I focus my attention on him. "I'm going to try my hardest."

"Can I see her?"

"Not right now."

The door leading to chambers opens and the clerk enters, telling us to rise as he announces the judge's return.

"I have to go," I tell him.

Ruth's sister fixes her gaze on me. "Do your job, white girl," she says.

The judge takes the bench and re-calls Ruth's case. Ruth is brought up from the bowels of the building again, and takes a spot beside me. She gives me a questioning look, and I nod: *He's all right.*

"Ms. McQuarrie," the judge sighs. "Have you had ample time to speak with your client?"

"Yes, Your Honor. Just days ago Ruth Jefferson was a nurse at Mercy–West Haven Hospital, caring for women in labor and their newborns as she has for the past twenty years. When a medical emergency occurred involving a baby, Ruth worked with the rest of the hospital personnel trying to save the child's life. Tragically, it was not meant to be. In the pending investigation surrounding what happened, Ruth was suspended from her job. She is a college graduate; her son is an honor student. Her husband is a military hero who gave his life for our country in Afghanistan. She has family in the community, and equity in the house she lives in. I ask the court to set reasonable bail. My client is not a flight risk; she has no prior record; she's willing to abide by any particular conditions the court wants to set on her bail. This is a very defendable case."

I've painted Ruth as an upstanding American citizen who has been misunderstood. Just about the only thing I don't do is take out an American flag and start waving it around.

The judge turns to Ruth. "How much equity are we talking about?"

"I beg your pardon?"

"What's the value of the mortgage on your house?" I ask.

"A hundred thousand dollars," Ruth replies.

The judge nods. "I'm going to set bail at one hundred thousand dollars. As a condition of the bail, I'll accept the house being posted. Next case?"

The white supremacist supporters in the gallery start booing. I am not sure they'd be happy with any verdict short of a public lynching. The judge calls for order and bangs his gavel. "Clear them out," he finally says, and bailiffs begin to move through the aisles.

"What happens now?" Ruth asks.

"You're getting out."

"Thank God. How long will it take?"

I glance up. "A couple of days."

A bailiff takes Ruth's arm to bring her back to the holding cell. As she is being led away, that curtain behind her eyes slips, and for the first time I see panic.

It's not like it is on TV and in the movies; you don't just walk out of the courthouse free. There are papers to be procured and bondsmen to be dealt with. I know that because I'm a public defender. Most of my clients know that because they tend to be repeat offenders.

But Ruth, she's not like most of my clients.

She's not *even* one of my clients, when you get down to it.

I've been with the public defender's office now for almost four years, and I've moved out of misdemeanors. I've done so many burglary cases and criminal mischief and identity theft and bad checks that at this point, I could probably argue them in my sleep. But this is a murder case, a high-profile trial that will be plucked out of my hands as soon as the court date is set. It will go to someone in my office who has more experience than I do, or who plays golf with my boss, or who has a penis.

In the long run, I won't be Ruth's lawyer. But right now, I still am, and I can help her.

I wing a silent thank-you to the white supremacists who've created this uproar. Then I run down the central aisle of the gallery to Edison and his aunt. "Listen. You need to get a certified copy of Ruth's house deed," I tell her sister. "And a certified copy of the tax assessment, and a copy of your sister's most recent mortgage payment, which shows what the current payoff is, and you need to bring that to the clerk's office—"

I realize that Ruth's sister is staring at me like I've suddenly started to speak Hungarian. But then again, she lives in Church Street South; she does not own her own place. This might as well be a foreign language to her.

Then I realize that Edison is writing down everything I've said on the back of a receipt from his wallet. "I'll figure it out," he promises.

I give him my card. "This is my cell number. If you have any questions, you can call me. But I won't be the one trying your mother's case. Someone else from my office will be in touch with you after she gets out."

This admission snaps Ruth's sister back into action. "So that's it? You put up her house to get her out of jail, so your good deed is done now? I guess since my sister's black, she obviously did the crime and you'd rather not get your hands dirty, right?"

This is ridiculous on so many levels, not the least of which is that the majority of my clients are African American. But before I can explain the hierarchy of politics in the public defender's office, Edison intercedes. "Auntie, chill out." Then he turns to me. "I'm sorry."

"No," I tell him. "*I* am."

WHEN I FINALLY GET HOME that night, my mother is sitting with her stocking feet tucked beneath her, watching Disney Junior on television, a glass of white wine in her hand. She has had a glass of white wine every night for as long as I can remember. When I was little, she called it her medicine. Beside her on the couch is Violet, curled on her side, fast asleep. "I didn't have the heart to move her," my mother says.

I sit down gingerly beside my daughter, take the bottle of wine that's on the coffee table, and drink from its neck. My mother's eyebrows arch. "That bad?" she asks.

"You have no idea." I stroke Violet's hair. "You must have tired her out today."

"Well." My mother hesitates. "We had a little bit of a blowup at dinner."

"Was it the fish sticks? She won't eat them since going on her Little Mermaid kick."

"No, she ate them, and you'll be delighted to know that Ariel has left the building. In fact, that was what got her all hot and bothered. We started watching *Princess and the Frog*, and Violet informed me that she wants to be Tiana for Halloween."

"Thank God," I say. "She was dead set on wearing a shell bikini top a week ago, and the only way that was going to happen was if it was over her long underwear."

My mother raises her brows. "Kennedy," she says. "Don't you think Violet would be happier as Cinderella? Or Rapunzel? Or even that new one with the white hair who makes everything ice over?"

"Elsa?" I fill in. "Why?"

"Don't make me say it out loud, sugar," my mother replies.

"You mean because Tiana's black?" I say. Immediately, I think of Ruth Jefferson, of the white supremacists booing in the gallery.

"I don't think Violet is making a statement about equality as much as she is about frogs. She told me she's going to ask for one as a pet for Christmas and kiss it and see what happens."

"She's not getting a frog for Christmas. But if she wants to be Tiana for Halloween I'll buy her the costume."

"I will *sew* her the costume," my mother corrects. "No grandbaby of mine is going trick-or-treating in a store-bought piece of trash that would probably go up in flames if she walked past a jack-o'-lantern." I don't fight her on this. I can't even sew a seam. I have a pair of work trousers in my closet that are hemmed with superglue.

"Terrific. I'm glad you can overcome your resistance in order to make Violet's dream come true."

My mother lifts her chin a notch. "I did not tell you this so you could scold me, Kennedy. Just because I grew up in the South doesn't make me prejudiced."

"Mom," I point out. "You had a black *nanny*."

"And I adored Beattie like she was family," my mother says.

"Except . . . she wasn't."

My mother pours more wine into her glass. "Kennedy," she sighs. "It's just a silly costume. Not a cause."

Suddenly I'm so incredibly tired. It's not just the pace of my job or the overwhelming number of cases I have that wears me down. It's wondering if anything I do actually makes a difference.

"Once," my mother says, her voice soft, "when I was about Violet's age, and Beattie wasn't looking, I tried to drink out of the colored water fountain at the park. I stepped up on the cement block and turned the knob. I was expecting something extraordinary. I was expecting *rainbows*. But you know—it was just like everyone else's water." She meets my gaze. "Violet would make the most beautiful little Cinderella."

"Mom . . ."

"I'm just saying. It took how many years for Disney to give all those little black girls their own princess? You think it's right for Violet to want something they've been waiting on forever?"

"*Mom!*"

She lifts her hands in concession. "Fine. Tiana. Done."

I lift the bottle of wine, tilt it up, and drink down every last drop.

AFTER MY MOTHER LEAVES, I fall asleep on the couch with Violet, and when I wake up, *The Lion King* is being aired on Disney Junior. I blink just in time to see the death of Mufasa playing out on-screen. He is being trampled by the water buffalo just as Micah walks in, pulling off the garrote of his tie with one hand. "Hey," I say. "I didn't hear you drive up."

"Because I am a ninja ingeniously masquerading as an ophthalmological surgeon." He leans down and kisses me, smiles at Violet, who is softly snoring. "My day was full of glaucoma and vitreous fluid. How was yours?"

"Considerably less gross," I say.

"Did Crazy Sharon come back?"

Crazy Sharon is a repeat offender, a stalker who has a thing for Peter Salovey, the president of Yale University. She leaves him flowers, love notes, and once, underwear. I've done six arraignments with her, and Salovey has been president only since 2013.

"No," I say, and I tell him about Ruth, and Edison, and the skinheads in the gallery.

"Really?" Micah is most interested in the last. "Like, with suspenders and flight jackets and the boots and everything?"

"Number one, no, and number two, should I be scared that you know all that?" I move my feet on the coffee table so he can sit down opposite me. "In fact, they looked just like us. It's pretty terrifying. I mean, what if your next-door neighbor was a white supremacist and you didn't know it?"

"I'm going to go out on a limb and say that Mrs. Greenblatt is not a skinhead," Micah says. As he talks, he gently lifts Violet into his arms.

"It's all a moot point anyway. It's too big a case for me to be assigned," I tell him, climbing the stairs to our daughter's bedroom. And then I add, "Ruth Jefferson lives in East End."

"Hunh," Micah replies. He settles Vi into her bed and pulls up her covers, dropping a kiss on her forehead.

"What's that supposed to mean?" I ask, combative, even though I had the same sort of reaction.

"It's not supposed to mean *anything*," Micah says. "It was just a response."

"What you really mean, but you're too polite to say, is that there aren't black families in East End."

"I guess. Maybe."

I follow him into our room and unzip my skirt, peel off my panty hose. When I'm wearing the T-shirt and boxers I usually sleep in, I go into the bathroom to brush my teeth beside Micah. I spit, wipe my mouth on the back of my hand. "Did you know that in *The Lion King*, the hyenas—the bad guys—all speak in either black or Latino slang? And that the little cubs are told not to go where the hyenas live?"

He looks at me, amused.

"Do you realize that Scar, the villain, is darker than Mufasa?"

"Kennedy." Micah puts his hands on my shoulders, leans down, and kisses me. "There is a *slight* chance you're overthinking this."

That's the moment I know I'm going to move heaven and earth to be Ruth's public defender.

Turk

I'M GUESSING THIS LAWYER'S PRETTY DECENT, GIVEN HOW SWANKY HIS office is. The walls aren't painted, they're paneled. The glass of water his secretary gets me is a heavy crystal tumbler. Even the air smells rich, like the perfume of a lady who would normally shy away from me on a public street.

I'm wearing again today the jacket Francis and I share, and I've ironed my pants. I have a wool cap pulled low on my head, and I keep twirling my wedding ring around and around on my finger. I could pass for any ordinary Joe who wants to sue someone, instead of a guy who would normally skirt the legal system and take justice into his own hands.

Suddenly Roarke Matthews is standing in front of me. His suit is ironed with knife-edge pleats, his shoes are buffed to a high gloss. He looks like a soap opera star, except that his nose is a little off-kilter, like he broke it playing football in high school. He holds out a hand to greet me. "Mr. Bauer," he says, "why don't you come with me?"

He leads me into an even more imposing office, this one full of black leather and chrome, and gestures to a spot on the love seat. "Let me say again how sorry I am for your loss," Matthews says, like everyone else does these days. The words have gotten so ordinary in fact that they feel like rain; I hardly even notice them anymore. "On the phone, we talked about the possibility of filing a civil suit—"

"Whatever it's called," I interrupt. "I just want someone to pay for this."

"Ah," Matthews says. "And that is why I asked you to come in here. You see, it's quite complicated."

"What's so complicated? You sue the nurse. She's the one who did this."

Matthews hesitates. "You could sue Ruth Jefferson," he agrees. "But let's be realistic—she doesn't have a pot to piss in. As you know, there's a criminal prosecution under way that the State has undertaken. That means that if you file a civil suit simultaneously, Ms. Jefferson would ask for a stay of all discovery, so she couldn't incriminate herself during the pending criminal prosecution. And the fact that you've filed a civil suit against her can be used against you in cross-examination during the criminal lawsuit."

"I don't understand."

"The defense will make you out to be a gold digger with a grudge," Matthews says bluntly.

I sit back, my hands on my knees. "So that's it? I don't have a case?"

"I never said that," the lawyer replies. "I just think you've chosen the wrong target. Unlike Ms. Jefferson, the hospital *does* have deep pockets. Moreover, they have an obligation to supervise their staff, and they are responsible for the nurse's actions or inactions. That's who I would recommend filing the lawsuit against. Now, we'd still name Ruth Jefferson—you never know, right now she has nothing, but tomorrow she could win the lottery or receive an inheritance." He raises a brow. "And then, Mr. Bauer, you might not just get justice—you might get a very handsome payout."

I nod, imagining this. I think about being able to tell Brit how I'm going to do right by Davis. "So what do we do to get started?"

"Now?" Matthews says. "Nothing. Not until the criminal lawsuit is over. The civil suit will still be viable when it's done, and that way, it can't be used to incriminate your character." He leans back, spreading his hands. "Come back to me when the trial's over," Matthews says. "I'm not going anywhere."

AT FIRST I DIDN'T BELIEVE Francis when he said that the new wave of Anglo supremacy would be a war fought not with fists but with ideas, spread subversively and anonymously through the Internet. But all the same, I was smart enough not to tell him he was a crazy old coot. For one thing, he was still one of the legends of the Movement. And more importantly, he was the father of the girl I couldn't get my mind off.

Brit Mitchum was beautiful, but in a way that knocked me off my feet. She had the softest skin I'd ever touched, and pale blue eyes that she ringed with dark eyeliner. Unlike other skinchicks, she didn't buzz her hair at the crown and let wispy bangs frame her face and the back of her neck. Instead, Brit had thick hair that spilled down to the middle of her back. Sometimes she braided it, and the braid was as thick as my wrist. I thought a lot about what it would feel like to have those curls hanging over my face like a curtain as she kissed me.

But the last thing I was going to do was make a move on a girl whose father could have my spine snapped by making a single phone call. So instead, I went to visit, often. I pretended to have a question for Francis, who liked seeing me because it gave him a chance to talk up his idea for an Anglo website. I helped him change the oil in his truck and fixed a leaky garbage disposal for him. I made myself useful, but when it came to Brit, I worshipped from afar.

So I was pretty blown away when one day she came out to a chopping block where I was splitting wood for Francis. "So," she says, "are the rumors true?"

"What rumors?" I asked.

"They say you took down a whole motorcycle gang and that you killed your own father."

"In that case, no," I said.

"Then you're just a little pussy like the other guys who like to pretend they're big bad Anglos so they can bask in my daddy's glow?"

Shocked, I looked up at her, and saw her mouth twitch. I raised the ax over my head, flexed my muscles, and sent the ax hurtling into the piece of wood, which cleaved neatly. "I like to think I fall somewhere between the two extremes," I said.

"Maybe I want to see for myself." She took a step closer. "Next time your crew goes on the hunt."

I laughed. "There is no way I'm taking Francis Mitchum's daughter out with my guys."

"Why not?"

"Because you're Francis Mitchum's daughter."

"That's not an answer."

Hell, yes, it was, even if she couldn't see it.

"My father's been taking me out with his crew my whole life."

Somehow I found that hard to believe. (Later I found out it was true, but he left Brit buckled into her car seat, sound asleep, in the back of his truck.) "You're not tough enough to run with my crew," I said, just to get her off my back.

When she didn't reply, I figured that was that. I lifted the ax again, and started the downswing, only to have Brit dart, lightning-fast, into the path of the blade. Immediately I let go of the shaft, feeling the ax spin out of my hands to wedge itself deeply in the ground about six inches away from her. "Jesus fucking Christ," I shouted. "What is *wrong* with you?"

"Not tough enough?" she replied.

"Thursday," I told her. "After dark."

EVERY NIGHT, I HEAR MY son cry.

The sound wakes me up, which is how I know he's a ghost. Brit never hears him, but then she is still floating in a haze of sleeping pills and Oxy left over from when I busted my knee. I get out of bed and take a piss and follow the noise, which gets louder and louder and louder, and then disappears when I reach the living room. There's no one there, just the computer screen, green and glaring at me.

I sit down on the couch and I drink a six-pack and still I can hear my boy crying.

My father-in-law gives me almost two weeks of grieving, and then starts dumping out all the beer in the house. One night, Francis comes to find me when I'm sitting on the living room couch, my head in my hands, trying to drown out the baby's sobs. I think for a minute he's going to deck me—he may be an old dude, but he could still take me—but instead, he yanks the laptop from its power cord and throws it at me. "Get even," he says simply, and he walks back into his side of the duplex.

For a long time, I just sit there, the computer pressed up next to me, like a girl who's begging for a dance.

I can't say I reach for it. More like, it makes its way back home to me.

With the touch of a key, a webpage loads. I haven't been here since before Brit had the baby.

When Francis and I teamed up to create our website, I read manuals on coding and metadata while Francis fed me the material we would post. We called our site LONEWOLF, because that was what we all had to become.

This was no longer the eighties. We were losing our best men to the prison system. The old guard was getting too old to curb-stomp and wield nunchucks. The fresh cuts were too plugged in to get excited about a KKK rally where a bunch of ancient yahoos sat around drinking and talking about the good ol' days. They didn't want to hear an old wives' tale, like that black people stank when their hair got wet. They wanted statistics they could take back to their lefty teachers and relatives who got tangled in knots when they said *we* were the real victims of discrimination in this country.

So we gave them what they asked for.

We posted the truth: that the U.S. Census Bureau said Whites would be a minority by 2043. That 40 percent of black people who were on welfare *could* work, but didn't. That the fact that the Zionist

Occupation Government was taking over our nation could be traced right to Alan Greenspan at the Federal Reserve.

Lonewolf.org quickly became something bigger than itself. We were the younger, hipper alternative. The fresh edge of rebellion.

Now, my hands move across the keyboard while I log in as the administrator. Part of the reason for running this site is the anonymity, the ability to hide behind what I believe. We are all anonymous here, and we are also all brothers. This is my army of nameless, faceless friends.

But today all that is about to change.

Many of you know me by my blog posts, and have responded with your own comments. Like me, you are a True Patriot. Like me, you wanted to follow an idea, not a person. But today, I am going to step into the light, because I want you to know me. I want you to know what happened *to me.*

My name is Turk Bauer, I type. *And I am going to tell you the story of my son.*

After I hit the post button, I watch the story of my son's short, brave life hover on the computer screen. I want to believe that if he had to die, it was for a cause. It was for *our* cause.

I do not drink that night, and I do not fall back asleep. Instead, I watch the numerical counter at the top of the header, which marks each page view.

1 reader.

6 readers.

37 readers.

409 readers.

By the time the sun comes up, more than thirteen thousand people know Davis's name.

I make coffee, and scroll through the comments section as I drink my first cup.

I'm so sorry for your loss.

Your boy was a race warrior.

Goddamned blue gum shouldn't have been allowed to work in a White hospital anyhow.

I've made a donation in your son's name to the American Freedom Party.

But one of them stops me cold:

Romans 12:19, it read. *Dearly beloved, avenge not yourselves, but rather give place unto wrath: for it is written, Vengeance is mine; I will repay, saith the Lord.*

THE THURSDAY AFTER BRIT DODGED my ax, I had dinner with her and her father. We were well into dessert before Brit looked up, as if she'd just remembered something she needed to tell us. "I hit a nigger with my car today," she announced.

Francis reared back in his seat. "Well, what was he doing in front of your car?"

"I have no idea. Walking, I guess. But he dented the front fender."

"I can take a look at it," I said. "I've done some bodywork."

A smile played around Brit's mouth. "I bet you have."

I turned thirty shades of red while Brit told her dad that she'd convinced me to take her to see a movie after dinner, some chick flick. Francis clapped me on the back. "Better you than me, son," he said, and then we were in my car, about to make a night of it.

Brit was like a live wire, buzzing in the passenger seat. She couldn't stop talking; she couldn't stop asking questions: Where were we going? Who would we target? Had I been there before?

The way I figured it, either tonight went well and that earned me Brit's undying respect, or tonight went poorly and her father broke my neck for putting her in danger.

I took her to an abandoned parking lot near a hot dog stand that was pretty popular with faggots, who sometimes met here to hook up in the bushes behind. (Seriously, though, could there be any greater cliché than gay guys meeting at a wiener stand? They deserved to be beaten up for that alone.) I had thought about messing up some coons, but they were basically animals and could be pretty strong in a fight, whereas even Brit could pound a pansy.

"Are the other guys meeting us here?" she asked.

"There are no other guys," I admitted. "I used to have a crew, but after one of them turned on me, I realized I like working alone. That's how the rumor started about the bikers. The only reason I took down a whole gang by myself is because I can't trust anyone else."

"I get it," Brit said. "It sucks to be abandoned by the people who are supposed to support you."

I glanced at her. "Somehow I think you've lived a pretty privileged life."

"Yeah, except for the part where my mother up and left me behind when I was a baby, like I was just . . . trash."

I knew Francis didn't have a wife, but I didn't know what had happened. "Man, that sucks. I'm sorry."

To my surprise, Brit wasn't upset. She was furious. "*I'm* not." Her eyes burned like coals in a fire. "Daddy said she ran off with a nigger."

Just then, two men walked up to the hot dog stand to order. They got their dogs, and walked over to a half-broken picnic table.

"You ready?" I asked Brit.

"I was born ready."

I hid my smile; was I ever that brave? We got out of my car and sauntered across the street, as if we were going to grab a bite, too. But instead, I stopped at the picnic table and smiled pleasantly. "Hey. Either of you limp wrists got a cigarette?"

They exchanged a glance. I *love* that glance. It's the same one you see on an animal when it realizes it's been cornered. "Let's just go," the blond one said to the short, skinny dude.

"See, that doesn't work for me," I said, stepping closer. "Because I'll still know you're out there." I grabbed Blondie by the throat and punched his lights out.

He went down like a stone. I turned to watch Brit, who had jumped on the skinny guy's back and was riding him like a nightmare. Her fingernails raked across his cheek, and as he stumbled to the ground she started kicking him in the kidneys, then straddled him, lifted his head, and smashed it back down on the pavement.

I had fought beside women before. There's a common misconception that skinchicks are subservient, barefoot, and pregnant most of the time. But if you're going to be a skinhead girl, you have to be a tough bitch. Brit might not have gotten her hands dirty before, but she was a natural.

When she was pounding on a slack, unconscious body, I hauled her upright. "Come on," I urged, and together we ran to the car.

We drove to a hill that offered a great view of planes taking off and landing at Tweed airport. The runway lights winked at us as we sat on the hood of the car, Brit swimming in adrenaline. "God," she yelled, tipping her throat to the night sky. "That was unfuckingbelievable. It felt like . . . like . . ."

She couldn't find the word, but I could. I knew what it was like to have so much bottled up inside that you had to explode. I knew what it was like to cause pain, for a few seconds, instead of feeling it. The source of Brit's restlessness might be different from mine, but she had been reined in all the same, and she'd just found the breach in the fence. "It feels like freedom," I said.

"Yes," she breathed, staring at me. "Do you ever feel like you don't belong in your own skin? Like you were meant to be someone else?"

All the time, I thought. But instead of saying that, I leaned over and kissed her.

She spun so that she was sitting on me, facing me. She kissed me harder, biting my lip, devouring. Her hands were under the tail of my shirt, fumbling with the buttons of my jeans. "Hey," I said, trying to grab her wrists. "There's no rush."

"Yes there is," she whispered into my neck.

She was on fire, and if you get too close to a fire, you go up in flames, too. So I let her slip beneath my zipper, I helped her hike up her skirt and rip off her panties. Brit lowered herself onto me, and I moved inside her like the start of something.

ON THE MORNING OF THE arraignment, I get dressed while Brit is still sleeping in the pajamas she's worn for the past four days. I eat a bowl of cereal and I prepare myself for war.

At the courthouse are about twenty friends I didn't know I had.

They are loyal followers of LONEWOLF, frequent posters on my site, men and women who read about Davis and wanted to do more than just type their sympathy. Like me, they don't look the way most people would expect a skinhead to look. No one is bald, except me. They're all wearing ordinary clothing. Some have tiny sun-wheel pins on their collars. Many wear a baby-blue ribbon for Davis. Some pat my shoulder or call me by name. Others just nod, the tiniest inclination of their heads, to let me know they are here for me as I pass down the aisle.

Just then a nigger comes up to me. I nearly shove her away when she starts talking—a knee-jerk reaction—and then I realize I know her voice, and that she's the prosecutor.

I have talked to Odette Lawton on the phone, but she didn't sound black. This feels like a slap, like some kind of conspiracy.

Maybe this is a good thing. It's no surprise that the liberals who run the court system have it out for Anglos, and there's no way we could ever get a fair trial because of it. They'll make this about *me* instead of that nurse. But if the lawyer who's on my side is black, well, then I can't possibly be prejudiced, can I?

They'll never have to know what I'm *really* thinking.

Someone reads the judge's name—DuPont—which doesn't sound like some Jew name, which is a good start. Then I sit through four other defendants before they call the name Ruth Jefferson.

The courtroom sizzles like a griddle. People start booing, and raising up signs with my son's face on them—a picture I uploaded to the website, the only one I have of him. Then the nurse is brought in, wearing a nightgown and shackles on her wrists. She is looking around the gallery. I wonder if she's trying to find me.

I decide to make it easy for her.

In one swift movement, I'm on my feet and leaning over the low railing that separates us from the lawyers and the stenographer. I take a deep breath and hurl a gob of spit that smacks the bitch on the side of the face.

I can tell the second she recognizes me.

Instantly I am flanked by bailiffs who drag me out of the courtroom, but that's okay, too. Because even as I'm pulled away, the nurse will see the swastika snaking down the back of my scalp.

It's okay to lose a battle, when you are in it to win the war.

THE TWO MEATHEAD BAILIFFS DUMP me outside the heavy doors of the courthouse. "Don't think about coming back in," one warns, and then they disappear inside.

I rest my hands on my knees, catching my breath. I may not have access to the courtroom, but this is a free country, as far as I know. They can't keep me from staying here and watching Ruth Jefferson get carted to jail.

Resolved, I look up, and that's when I see them: the vans, with satellite dishes. The reporters smoothing their skinny skirts and testing their microphones. The media that has come to report on this case.

The lawyer said they needed a grieving parent, not an angry parent? I can give them that.

But first, I pull out my cellphone and call Francis at home. "Get Brit out of bed, and park her in front of the television." I glance at the news vans. "Channel Four."

Then I take a cap out of my pocket, the one I wore into the courthouse this morning so I wouldn't draw attention to my tattoo until I wanted to. I center it on my head.

I think about Davis, because that's all I need to make tears come to my eyes.

"You saw that, right?" I approach a slant reporter I've seen on NBC. "You saw me get thrown out of that building?"

She glances at me. "Uh, yeah. Sorry, but we're here to cover a different story."

"I know," I say. "But I'm the father of the dead baby."

I tell the reporter that Brit and I had been so excited about our first baby. I say I'd never seen anything as perfect as his tiny hands, his nose, which looked just like Brit's. I say that my wife is still so upset over what happened to Davis that she can't get out of bed, can't even be here today at court.

I say it is a tragedy for someone who has taken a vow to heal to intentionally kill a helpless infant, just because she is upset at being removed from a patient's care. "I understand that we didn't see eye to eye," I say, looking at the reporter. "But that doesn't mean my son deserved to die."

"What do you hope the outcome will be, Mr. Bauer?" she asks.

"I want my son back," I tell her. "But that isn't going to happen."

Then I excuse myself. Truth is, I'm starting to choke up, thinking about Davis. And I'm not going to be broadcast blubbering like a girl.

I duck away from the other reporters, who are now falling all over each other to speak to me, but they get distracted as the doors to the courthouse open and Odette Lawton exits. She starts talking about how this is a heinous crime, how the State will make sure that justice is done. I slip along the side of the building, past where a janitor is smoking a cigarette, to a loading dock in the back. This, I know, leads to a lower-level door, which leads to the holding cells.

I can't get inside; there are guards posted. But I stand at a distance, huddled against the wind, until a van pulls out with the words YORK CORRECTIONAL INSTITUTION printed on its side. That's the only prison for women in the state, in Niantic. It's where the nurse must be headed.

At the last minute, I step into its path, so that the driver has to swerve.

I know, inside that van, Ruth Jefferson will be jolted by that motion. That she'll look out the window to see what caused it.

That the last thing she sees before prison will be me.

AFTER I TOOK BRIT WILDING, I became a regular visitor in her home, and I pretty much ran the website from Francis's living room. On LONEWOLF we hosted discussions: tax forums that pitted Joe Legal, the White worker, against Jose, the Illegal Job Thief; threads about why our economy was being ruined by Obama; an online book club; a section for creative writing and poetry—which included a three-hundred-page alternate ending to the Civil War. There was a section for Anglo women to connect with each other, and another for teens, which helped them navigate situations like what to do when a friend said he was gay (end the friendship immediately, or explain that no one is born that way and the trend will vanish eventually). There were opinion topics (*Which is worse: a White gay or a straight black? Which universities are the most anti-White?*). Our most popular thread was the one about forming a White Nationalist K–12 school. We had over a million posts there.

But we also had a section of the site where we gave suggestions of what people could do individually or within their cells if they wanted to take action, without promoting outright violence. Mostly, we found ways to get minorities all twisted up believing that there was an army of us in their midst, when in reality, it was just one or two people.

Francis and I practiced what we preached. We adopted a stretch of highway in a mostly black area, and posted a sign that said it was being maintained by the KKK. One night, we drove to the Jewish Community Center in West Hartford. During Friday night services, we slipped a flyer under the windshield wiper of each car in the parking lot: a photo of Adolf Hitler in full *sieg heil*, and underneath it in bold letters: THE HOLOCAUST WAS A HOAX. On the back were bullets of facts:

Zyklon B was a delousing agent; for it to be used as a gas would have required huge amounts and airtight chambers, neither of which were present at the camps.

There were no remains of mass murders at the camps. Where were the bone and teeth fragments? Where were the piles of ashes?

American incinerators burn one body in eight hours, but two crematoria in Auschwitz burned 25,000 bodies a day? Impossible.

The Red Cross inspected the camps every three months and made plenty of complaints—none of which mentioned gasing millions of Jews.

The liberal Jewish media has perpetuated this myth to advance their agenda.

By the next morning, the *Hartford Courant* would run an article about the neo-Nazi element that was infiltrating this community. Parents would be worried for their children. Everyone would be on edge.

That was exactly how we liked it. We didn't have to terrorize anyone as long as we could scare the shit out of them.

"Well," Francis said, as we were driving back to the duplex. "That was a good night's work."

I nodded, but I kept my eyes on the road. Francis had a thing about that—he wouldn't let me drive with the radio on, for example, in case I got too easily distracted.

"I got a question for you, Turk," he said. I waited for him to ask me how we could get top placement for LONEWOLF in a Google search, or if we could stream podcasts, but instead he turned to me. "When are you going to make an honest woman out of my daughter?"

I nearly swallowed my tongue. "I, um, I would be honored to do that."

He looked at me, appraising. "Good. Do it soon."

As it turned out, it took a while. I wanted it to be perfect, so I asked around on LONEWOLF for suggestions. One guy had gotten all decked out in full SS regalia to propose. Another took his beloved to the site of their first real date, but I didn't think a hot dog stand with gay guys blowing each other in the woods was a terrific setting. Several posters got into a vehement fight about whether or not an engagement ring was necessary, since Jews ran the diamond industry.

In the end, I decided to just tell her how I felt. So one day I picked her up and drove back to my place. "Really?" she said. "*You're* going to cook?"

"I thought maybe we could do it together," I suggested as we walked into the kitchen. I turned away because I thought for sure she would see how terrified I was.

"What are we having?"

"Well, don't be disappointed." I held out a container of hummus. On top, I had written: *There are no words to tell you hummus I love you.*

She laughed. "Cute."

I handed her an ear of corn and mimed shucking it. She pulled down the husk and a note fell out: *I think you're amaizing.*

Grinning, she held out her hand for more.

I gave her a bottle of ketchup, with a sticker on the back: *I love you from my head tomatoes.*

"That's pushing it," Brit said, smiling.

"I was limited by the season." I passed her a stick of margarine. *You're my butter half.*

Then I opened the fridge.

On the top shelf were four zucchini propped up to form the letter *M*, three carrots creating an *A*, two curved bananas: *r*, *r*, and a piece of gingerroot: *Y.*

On the next shelf was a cellophane-wrapped package of chopped meat that I'd shaped into the letters *ME.*

On the bottom shelf was a squash with Brit's name carved into it.

Brit covered her mouth with her hand as I dropped to my knee. I handed her a ring box. Inside was a blue topaz, which was exactly the color of her eyes. "Say yes," I begged.

She slipped the ring onto her hand as I stood. "I was kind of expecting a Hefty twist tie after all that," Brit said, and she threw her arms around me.

We kissed, and I hiked her up on the counter. She wrapped her legs around me. I thought about spending the rest of my life with Brit. I thought about our kids; how they would look just like her; how they'd have a father who was a million times better than mine had been.

An hour later, when we lay in each other's arms on the kitchen floor, on a pile of our clothes, I gathered Brit close. "I'm assuming that's a yes," I said.

Her eyes lit up, and she ran to the fridge, returning a few seconds later. "Yes," she said. "But first you have to promise me something. We . . ." She dropped a melon into my hands.

Cantaloupe.

* * *

WHEN I COME BACK FROM court and walk into the house, the television is still on. Francis meets me at the door, and I look at him, a question on my lips. Before I can ask, though, I see that Brit is sitting in the living room on the floor, her face inches away from the screen. The midday news is on, and there is Odette Lawton talking to reporters.

Brit turns, and for the first time since our son was born, for the first time in weeks, she smiles. "Baby," she says, bright and beautiful and mine again. "Baby, you're a *star*."

Ruth

THEY PUT ME IN CHAINS.

Just like that, they shackle my hands in front of me, as if that doesn't send two hundred years of history running through my veins like an electric current. As if I can't feel my great-great-grandmother and her mother standing on an auction block. They put me in chains, and my son—who I've told, every day since he was born, *You are more than the color of your skin*—my son watches.

It is more humiliating than being in public in my nightgown, than having to urinate without privacy in the holding cell, than being spit at by Turk Bauer, than having a stranger speak for me in front of a judge.

She had asked me if I touched the baby, and I'd lied to her. Not because I thought, at this point, that I still had a job to save, but because I just couldn't think through fast enough what the right answer would be, the one that might set me free. And because I didn't trust this stranger sitting across from me, when I was nothing more to her than the other twenty clients she would see today.

I listen to this lawyer—Kennedy something, I have already forgotten her last name—volley back and forth with another lawyer. The prosecutor, who's a woman of color, does not even make eye contact with me. I wonder if this is because she feels nothing but contempt for me, an alleged criminal . . . or because she knows if she wants to be taken seriously, she has to widen the canyon between us.

True to her word, Kennedy gets me bail. Just like that, I want to hug this woman, thank her. "What happens now?" I ask, as the people in the courtroom hear the decision, and become a living, breathing thing.

"You're getting out," she tells me.

"Thank God. How long will it take?"

I am expecting minutes. An hour, at the most. There must be paperwork, which I can then lock away to prove that this was all a misunderstanding.

"A couple of days," Kennedy says. Then a beefy guard has my arm and firmly pushes me back to the rabbit warren of holding cells in the basement of this godforsaken building.

I wait in the same cell I was taken to during the recess in court. I count all the cinder blocks in the wall: 360. I count them again. I think about that spider of a tattoo on Turk Bauer's head, and how I hadn't believed he could possibly be worse than he already was, but I was wrong. I don't know how much time passes before Kennedy comes. "What is going *on*?" I explode. "I can't stay here for days!"

She talks about mortgage deeds and percentages, numbers that swim in my head. "I know you're worried about your son. I'm sure your sister will keep an eye on him."

A sob swells like a song in my throat. I think about my sister's home, where her boys talk back to their dad when he tells them to take out the trash. Where dinner is not a conversation but take-out Chinese with the television blaring. I think about Edison texting me at work, things like *Reading* Lolita *4 AP Eng. Nabokov = srsly messed up dude.*

"So I stay here?" I ask.

"You'll be taken to the prison."

"Prison?" A chill runs down my spine. "But I thought I got bail?"

"You did. But the wheels of justice move exceedingly slow, and you have to stay until the bail is processed."

Suddenly a guard I haven't seen before appears at the door of the cell. "Coffee klatch is over, ladies," he says.

Kennedy looks at me, her words fast and fierce like bullets. "Don't talk about your charges. People are going to try to work a deal by prying information out of you. Don't trust anyone."

Including you? I wonder.

The guard opens the door of the cell and tells me to hold out my arms. There are those shackles and chains again. "Is that really necessary?" Kennedy asks.

"I don't make the rules," the guard says.

I am led down another hallway to a loading dock, where a van is waiting. Inside is another woman in chains. She's wearing a tight dress and glitter eyeliner and has a weave that reaches halfway down her back. "You like what you see?" she asks, and I immediately avert my eyes.

The sheriff climbs into the front seat of the van and starts the engine.

"Officer," the woman calls. "I'm a girl who loves her jewelry, but these bracelets are cramping my style."

When he doesn't respond, she rolls her eyes. "I'm Liza," she says. "Liza Lott."

I can't help it; I laugh. "That's really your name?"

"It better be, since I picked it. I like it so much better than . . . Bruce." She purses her lips, staring at me, waiting for my reaction. My eyes move from her large manicured hands to her stunning face. If she's expecting me to be shocked, she has another thing coming. I'm a nurse. I have literally seen it all, including a trans man who became pregnant when his wife was infertile, and a woman with two vaginas.

I meet her gaze, refusing to be intimidated. "I'm Ruth."

"You get your Subway sandwich, Ruth?"

"What?"

"The food, sugar. It's so much better at court than in jail, am I right?"

I shake my head. "I've never done this before."

"Me, I should have a punch card. You know, the kind where you get a free coffee or a tiny tube of mascara at your tenth visit." She grins. "What are you in for?"

"I wish I knew," I say, before I can remember not to.

"What the fuck, girl? You were in the courtroom, you were arraigned," Liza replies. "You didn't hear what you were charged with?"

I turn away, focusing on the scenery out the window. "My lawyer told me I shouldn't talk to anyone about that."

"Well." She sniffs. "Pardon me, Your Majesty."

In the rearview mirror, the sheriff's eyes appear, sharp and blue. "She's in for murder," he says, and none of us speak for the rest of the ride.

WHEN I APPLIED TO YALE Nursing School, Mama asked her pastor to say an extra prayer for me, in the hope that God could sway the admissions committee if my transcript from college could not. I remember being mortified as I sat in church beside her, as the congregation lifted their spirits and their voices heavenward on my behalf. There were people dying of cancer, infertile couples hoping for a baby, war in third world countries—in other words, so many more important things the Lord had to do with His time. But Mama said I was equally important, at least to our congregation. I was their success story, the college graduate who was going on to Make a Difference.

On the day before classes were supposed to start, Mama took me out to dinner. "You're destined to do small great things," she told me. "Just like Dr. King said." She was referring to one of her favorite quotes: *If I cannot do great things, I can do small things in a great way.* "But," she continued, "don't forget where you came from." I didn't really understand what she meant. I was one of a dozen kids from our neighborhood who had gone to college, and only a handful of those were destined for graduate school. I knew she was proud of me; I knew she felt like her hard work to set me on a different path had paid off. Given that she'd been pushing me out of the nest since I was little, why would she want me to carry around the twigs that had built it? Couldn't I fly further without them?

I took classes in anatomy and physiology, in pharmacology and principles of nursing, but I planned my schedule so that I was always home for dinner, to tell my mama about my day. It didn't matter that my commute to and from the city was two hours each way. I knew that if Mama hadn't spent thirty years scrubbing the floors at Ms. Mina's house, I wouldn't be on that train at all.

"Tell me everything," Mama would say, spooning whatever she'd cooked onto my plate. I passed along the remarkable things I learned— that half the population carries the MRSA germs in their nose; that nitroglycerin can cause you to have a bowel movement if it makes contact with your skin; that you are taller in the morning than the evening, by nearly a half inch, because of the fluid between your spinal discs. But there were things I didn't tell her, too.

Though I may have been at one of the finest nursing schools in the country, that mattered only on campus. At Yale, other nursing students asked to see my meticulous notes or to have me join their study group. During clinical rotations at the hospital, teachers praised my expertise. But when the day was over, I'd walk into a convenience store to buy a Coke and the owner would follow me around to make sure I didn't shoplift. I'd sit on the train as elderly white women walked by without making eye contact, even though there was an empty seat beside me.

A month into my tenure at nursing school, I bought a Yale travel mug. My mother assumed it was because I had to leave before dawn in order to catch the train to New Haven every day, and she'd get up and make me a fresh cup of coffee each morning to fill it. But it wasn't caffeine I needed; it was a ticket into a different world. I would settle the mug on my lap every time I got on the train, with the word YALE purposefully turned so other passengers could read it as they boarded. It was a flag, a sign saying: *I'm one of you.*

THE WOMEN'S PRISON, IT TURNS OUT, is a good hour's drive from New Haven. After we arrive, Liza and I are shuttled into a holding cell that looks exactly the same as the one I was in at the courthouse, only more crowded. There are fifteen other women already inside. There are no seats, so I slide down a wall and sit on the floor between two women. One has her hands laced in front of her and is praying under her breath in Spanish. The other is biting her cuticles.

Liza leans against the bars and begins to weave her long hair into a fishtail braid. "Excuse me," I say quietly. "Do you know if they'll let me make a phone call?"

She glances up at me. "Oh, *now* you wanna talk to me."

"I'm sorry. I don't mean to be rude. I . . . I'm new to all of this."

She snaps a rubber band at the end of her braid. "Sure, you get a phone call. Right after they serve you your caviar and give you a nice massage."

I am shocked by this. Isn't a phone call a basic right for prisoners? "That's not what it's like in the movies," I murmur.

Liza places her hands under her breasts and plumps them. "Don't believe everything you see."

A female guard opens the door to the cell. The praying woman gets up, her eyes full of hope, but the officer motions to Liza instead. "Good God, Liza. You back again?"

"Don't you know nothing about economics? It's all supply and demand. I ain't in this business by myself, Officer. If there weren't such a demand for my services, the supply would just dry up."

The guard laughs. "Now there's an image," she says, and she takes Liza by the arm to lead her out.

One by one we are plucked from the cell. No one who leaves comes back. To distract myself I start making lists of what I must remember to tell Adisa one day when I can look back on this and laugh: that the food we are given, during our multihour wait, is so unidentifiable that I can't tell if it's a vegetable or a meat; that the inmate who was mopping the floor when we were marched inside looked exactly like my second-grade teacher; that although I am embarrassed by my nightgown, there is a woman in the holding cell with me who is wearing the kind of mascot costume you see at high school football games. Then finally the same officer who took Liza away opens the door and calls my name.

I smile at her, trying to be as obedient as possible. I read her name tag: GATES. "Officer Gates," I say, when we are out of earshot of the other women in the cell, "I know you're just doing your job, but I'm actually being released on bail. The thing is, I need to get in touch with my son—"

"Save it for your counselor, inmate." She takes another mug shot of me, and rolls my fingerprints again. She fills out a form that asks everything from my name and address and gender to my HIV status and substance abuse history. Then she leads me into a room slightly bigger than a closet that has nothing inside but a chair.

"Strip," she announces. "Put your clothes on the chair."

I stare at her.

"*Strip*," she repeats.

She folds her arms and leans against the door. If the first freedom you lose in prison is privacy, the second is dignity. I turn my back and pull my nightgown over my head. I fold it up carefully and set it on the chair. I step out of my panties, and fold them, too. I put my slippers on top of the pile.

As a nurse you learn how to make a patient comfortable during moments that would otherwise be humiliating—how to drape the spread legs of a woman in labor, or draw a johnny over a bare bottom. When a laboring mother defecates because of the pressure of the baby's head, you clean it up briskly and say it happens to everyone. You take any embarrassing situation and you do what you can to make it less so. As I stand shivering, naked, I wonder if this guard's job is the absolute opposite of mine. If she wants nothing more than to make me feel shame.

I decide I'm not going to give her the satisfaction.

"Open your mouth," the officer says, and I stick out my tongue like I would at the doctor's office.

"Lean forward and show me what's behind your ears."

I do as I'm told, although I can't imagine what anyone could hide behind her ears. I am instructed to flip my hair, and to spread my toes and to lift up my feet so she can see the bottoms.

"Squat," the guard says, "and cough three times."

I imagine what a woman might be able to smuggle into jail, given the remarkable flexibility of the female anatomy. I think about how, when I was a student nurse, I had to practice to figure out the width of a dilated cervix. One centimeter was an opening the size of a fingertip. Two and a half centimeters were the second and third fingers, slipped into an opening the size of the neck of a bottle of nail polish remover. Four centimeters of dilation were those same fingers, spread in the neck of a forty-ounce bottle of Sweet Baby Ray's barbecue sauce. Five centimeters was the opening of a fifty-ounce Heinz ketchup bottle. Seven centimeters: a plastic shaker of Kraft Parmesan cheese.

"Spread the cheeks."

A few times, I have helped deliver the baby of a survivor of sexual assault. It makes perfect sense that, during childbirth, memories of abuse might be triggered. A body in labor is a body in stress, and for a rape survivor, that can lead to a survival reflex that physiologically slows down or stops the progress. In these cases, it's even more important for the L & D room to be a safe space. For the woman to be listened to. For her to feel like she has a say in what happens to her.

I may not have much say here, but I still can make the choice to not be a victim. The whole point of this examination is to make me feel lesser than, like an animal. To make me ashamed of my nakedness.

But I have spent twenty years seeing how beautiful women are— not because of how they look, but because of what their bodies can withstand.

So I stand up and face the officer, daring her to look away from my smooth brown skin, the dark rings of my nipples, the swell of my belly, the thatch of hair between my legs. She hands me the orange scrubs that are designed to conform me, and the ID tag with my inmate number, meant to define me as part of a group, instead of an individual. I stare at her until she meets my eye. "My name," I say, "is Ruth."

FIFTH GRADE, BREAKFAST. MY NOSE was buried in a book, and I was reading facts aloud. "There were twins who were born eighty-seven days apart," I announced.

Rachel sat across from me, picking at her cornflakes. "Then they weren't twins, stupid."

"Mama," I yelled automatically. "Rachel called me stupid." I turned the page. "Sigurd the Mighty was killed by a dead man he beheaded. He tied the guy's head to his saddle and was scraped by a tooth and got an infection and died."

My mother hurried into the kitchen. "Rachel, don't call your sister stupid. And Ruth, stop reading vile things while everyone's trying to eat."

Reluctantly, I closed the book, but not before letting my eyes light on a final fact: there was a family in Kentucky that, for generations, had been born with blue skin. It was a result of inbreeding and genetics. *Cool*, I thought, holding out the flat of my hand and turning it over.

"Ruth!" my mother said sharply, which was enough to let me know it was not the first time she'd called my name. "Go change your shirt."

"Why?" I asked, before I remembered I wasn't supposed to talk back.

My mother yanked at my uniform blouse, which had a stain the size of a dime near my ribs. I scowled. "Mama, no one's even going to see it once I put my sweater on."

"And if you take that sweater off?" she asked. "You don't go to school with a stain on your shirt, because if you do, people aren't going to judge you for being sloppy. They're going to judge you for being Black."

I knew better than to cross Mama when she got like this. So I took the book and ran to the room I shared with Rachel to find a clean white shirt. As I buttoned it, my gaze drifted toward the trivia book where it had fallen open on my bed.

The loneliest creature on earth is a whale that has spent more than twenty years calling out for a mate, I read, *but whose voice is so different from those of other whales that none of them ever respond.*

IN THE BEDROLL I AM given are sheets, a blanket, shampoo, soap, toothpaste, and a toothbrush. I am entrusted to the custody of another inmate, who tells me important things: that from now on, all my personal hygiene items have to be purchased from the commissary, that if I want to watch *Judge Judy* in the rec room I have to get there early for a good seat; that halal meals are the only edible ones so I might want to say I'm Muslim; that someone named Wig gives the best tattoos, because her ink is mixed with urine, which means it's more permanent.

As we pass by the cells I notice that two inmates occupy each one, and that the majority of the prisoners are Black, and that the officers are not. There is a part of me that feels the way I used to when my mother made my sister take me out with her friends in our neighborhood. The girls would make fun of me for being an Oreo—black on the outside, white on the inside. I'd wind up getting very quiet out of fear that I was going to make a fool of myself. What if a woman like that is my roommate? What could we possibly have in common?

The fact that we're both in prison, for one.

I turn the corner, and the inmate sweeps her arm in a grand gesture. "Home sweet home," she announces, and I peek inside to find a white woman sitting on a bunk.

I put my bedroll on the empty mattress and begin to pull free the sheets and blanket.

"Did I say you could sleep there?" the woman asks.

I freeze. "I . . . uh, no."

"You know what happened to my last roommate?" She has frizzy red hair and eyes that do not quite look out in the same direction. I shake my head. She comes closer, until she is a breath away. "Neither does anyone else," she whispers. Then she bursts out laughing. "Sorry, I'm just messing with your head. My name's Wanda."

My heart is beating in the back of my throat. "Ruth," I manage. I gesture to the empty mattress. "So this is . . ."

"Yeah, whatever. I don't give a shit, as long as you stay out of my stuff."

I jerk my head, agreeing, and make the bed as Wanda watches. "You from around here?"

"East End."

"I'm from Bantam. You ever been there?" I shake my head. "No one's ever been to Bantam. This your first time?"

I glance up, confused. "In Bantam?"

"In *prison*."

"Yes, but I won't be here for long. I'm waiting for my bail to clear."

Wanda laughs. "Okay, then."

Slowly, I turn. "What?"

"I've been waiting for the same thing. Going on three weeks now."

Three weeks. I feel my knees buckle, and I sink to the mattress. Three weeks? I tell myself that my situation is not Wanda's. But all the same: *three weeks*.

"So what are you in for?" she asks.

"Nothing."

"It's amazing how nobody in here did anything illegal." Wanda lies back on her bunk, stretching her arms up over her head. "*They* say I killed my husband. *I* say he ran into my knife." She looks at me. "It was an accident. You know, like the way he broke my arm and gave me a black eye and pushed me down the stairs and those were accidents too."

There are stones in her voice. I wonder if, in time, mine will sound that way, too. I think of Kennedy, telling me to keep to myself.

I think of Turk Bauer and picture the tattoo I saw in the courtroom, blazing across his shaved scalp. I wonder if he has spent time in prison. If this means we, too, have something in common.

Then I picture his baby, curled in my arms in the morgue, cold and blue as granite.

"I don't believe in accidents," I say, and I leave it at that.

THE COUNSELOR, OFFICER RAMIREZ, is a man with a face as round and soft as a donut, who is slurping his soup. He keeps spilling on his shirt, and I try not to look every time it happens. "Ruth Jefferson," he says, reading my file. "You had a question about visitation?"

"Yes," I reply. "My son, Edison. I need to get in touch with him, so that he knows how to get together the papers we need for bail. He's only seventeen."

Ramirez rummages in his desk. He takes out a magazine—*Guns & Ammo*—and a stack of flyers about depression, and then hands me a form. "Write down the name and address of the people you want on the visitor list."

"And then what?"

"Then I mail it out and when they sign it and send it back, the form gets approved and you're good to go."

"But that could take weeks."

"About ten days, usually," Ramirez says. *Slurrrrp.*

Tears flood into my eyes. This is like a nightmare, the kind where someone shakes your shoulder as you are telling yourself this is a dream, and says, *This isn't a dream.* "I can't leave him alone that long."

"I can contact child protective services—"

"No!" I blurt out. "Don't."

Something makes him put down his spoon and look at me, not unkindly. "There's always the warden. He can grant you a courtesy visit for two adult visitors before the official application is processed. But given that your son is seventeen, he'd have to come in the company of another adult."

Adisa, I think. And then, immediately, I remember why she'll never be approved by the warden for a visit: she has a record, thanks to a forged rent check five years back.

I push the form back across the desk to him. The walls feel like the shutter of a camera closing. "Thank you anyway," I manage, and I walk back to my cell.

Wanda is sitting on her bunk, nibbling on a Twix bar. She takes one look at me, then breaks off a tiny piece and offers it.

I take it in my hand and close my fist around it. The chocolate starts to melt.

"No phone call?" Wanda asks, and I shake my head. I sit on my bunk, and then turn away from her, so that I am facing the wall.

"It's time for *Judge Judy*," she says. "You want to watch?"

When I don't respond, I hear Wanda pad out of our cell, presumably toward the rec room. I lick the candy from my hand and then press my palms together and talk to the only slice of hope I have left. *God*, I pray, *please, please be listening*.

WHEN I WAS LITTLE, I used to have sleepovers with Christina at her brownstone. We would unroll our sleeping bags in the living room and Sam Hallowell would run a movie projector with old cartoons that he must have gotten when he was a television executive. This was, back then, a big deal—there were no VCRs or video on demand; a private screening was a treat reserved for movie stars—and, I guess, their children. Although I was skittish about being away from home for the night, this was the next best thing: Mama would run the bath for us and get me into my pajamas and make a treat of hot cocoa and cookies before she left; and by the time we woke up, she was already back and making us pancakes.

Whatever differences there were between Christina and me grew more indelible as we got older. It was harder to pretend that it didn't matter my mama worked for hers; or that I had to work after school while she became a striker for the soccer team; or that the clothes I wore on Casual Fridays used to belong to Christina. It wasn't that she was unfriendly to me. The barricade was built with my own suspicions, one brick of embarrassment at a time. Christina's friends were all blond, pretty, athletic, fanning around her like the matching spokes of a snowflake; if I didn't hang around their edges, I told myself, it was because I didn't want Christina to feel like she *had* to include me. The real reason I distanced myself, though, was because it hurt less to step away than to risk that inevitable moment where I would become an afterthought.

The only problem with dissociating myself from Christina was that I didn't have many other friends. There was a Pakistani exchange student, and a girl with cataracts that I tutored in math, but what we had in common was the fact that we didn't really fit in anywhere else. There was a cluster of other Black kids, but their upbringing was still a world away from mine—with their parents who were stockbrokers and fencing lessons and summer cottages on Nantucket. There was Rachel—who was eighteen now and pregnant with her first child. She probably needed a friend, but even when we were face-to-face across the kitchen table, I couldn't think of a single thing to say to her, because the things she wanted out of her life were so different from what I hoped for in my own, and because—honestly—I was a little scared that if I started hanging around with her, all the stereotypes she'd wrapped herself in would rub off like shoe polish and make it even harder to fit in seamlessly in the halls of Dalton.

So maybe that's why, when Christina invited me to a slumber party she was having one Friday, I said yes before I could remember to stop myself. I said yes, and hoped that she would prove me gloriously wrong. In the company of all these new friends of hers, I wanted to share our inside jokes about the time Christina and I made helmets out of tinfoil and hid in the dumbwaiter pretending it was a spaceship to the moon; or when Ms. Mina's dog, Fergus, pooped on her bed and we used white paint to cover the stain, certain no one would ever notice. I wanted to be the only one who knew which kitchen cabinet held the snacks and where the extra bedding was kept and the names of each of Christina's old stuffed animals. I wanted everyone else to know that Christina and I had been friends even longer than they had.

Christina had invited two other sophomores—Misty, who claimed to be dyslexic to get accommodations on homework, but who seemed to have no trouble reading aloud from the stack of *Cosmo* magazines that Christina had brought onto the roof deck; and Kiera, who was obsessed with Rob Lowe and her own thigh gap. We had all stretched towels out on the teak deck. Christina turned up the radio as a Dire Straits song came on and started singing all the lyrics by heart. I thought of how we used to play Ms. Mina's records—all original Broadway cast recordings—and dance around pretending to be Cinderella or Eva Perón or Maria von Trapp.

From my bag, I pulled out a bottle of sunscreen. The other girls had rubbed themselves with baby oil, as if they were steaks on a grill, but the last thing I wanted was to be darker. I noticed Kiera looking at me. "Can you *tan*?"

"Um, yeah," I said, but I was spared going into detail by Misty interrupting.

"This is so awesome," she said. "The British invasion." She twisted the magazine so that we could look at the models, each one twiggier than the last, draped in next season's clothes with Union Jacks and gold-buttoned red coats that made me think of Michael Jackson.

Christina sank down beside me, pointing. "Linda Evangelista is, like, perfect."

"Ugh, really? She looks like a Nazi. Cindy Crawford is so *natural*," Kiera countered. I peered at the photographs. "My sister's going to London this summer," Kiera added. "Backpacking through Europe. I made my dad promise, in writing, that when I was eighteen I could go too."

"Backpacking?" Misty shuddered. "Why?"

"Because it's romantic, duh. Just think about it. Eurail passes. Hostels. Meeting hot guys."

"I think the Savoy is pretty romantic too," Misty said. "And they have *showers*."

Kiera rolled her eyes. "Back me up, Ruth. No one in a romance novel ever meets in the lobby of the Savoy. They bump into each other on a train platform or accidentally pick up each other's backpacks, right?"

"Sounds like fate," I said, but what I was thinking was that there was no way I couldn't work for a summer, not if I planned to go to college.

Christina flopped onto her belly on the towel. "I'm starving. We need snacks." She looked up at me. "Ruth, could you go get us something to eat?"

Mama smiled when I came into the kitchen, which smelled like heaven. A rack of cookies was cooling, another sheet was just going into the oven. She held out the mixing spoon and let me lick the dough. "How are things up in Saint-Tropez?"

"Everyone's hungry," I told her. "Christina wants food."

"Oh, she does, does she? Then how come she isn't the one standing in my kitchen asking?"

I opened my mouth to reply, but couldn't find the answer. Why *had* she asked me? Why had I *gone*?

My mama's mouth drew tight. "Why are you here, baby?"

I looked down between my bare feet. "I told you—we're hungry."

"Ruth," she repeated. "Why are you here?"

This time I couldn't pretend to misunderstand. "Because," I said, so quietly that I could barely hear it, so quietly I was hoping my mother couldn't either, "I don't have anywhere else to go."

"That is *not* true," she insisted. "When you're ready for us, we'll be waiting on you."

I grabbed a plate and began to stack cookies on it. I didn't know what my mother meant and I didn't really want to know. I avoided her the rest of the afternoon, and when she left for the night, we were already locked inside Christina's bedroom, playing Depeche Mode and dancing on the mattress. I listened to the other girls confess their secret crushes and pretended I had one myself, so I could be part of the conversation. When Kiera brought out a flask filled with vodka ("It has the least calories, you know, if you want to get drunk"), I acted like it was no big deal, even though my heart was racing. I didn't drink, because Mama would have killed me, and because I knew I had to stay in control. Every night, before bedtime, I lotioned my skin and rubbed cocoa butter into my knees and heels and elbows to keep from being ashy; I brushed my hair around my head to encourage growth and wrapped it in a scarf. Mama did this, and so did Rachel, but I was pretty sure those rituals would be foreign to everyone at this sleepover, even Christina. I didn't want to answer questions, or stick out any more than I already did, so my plan was to be the last girl in the bathroom and to stay there until everyone had fallen asleep . . . and then to wake up before dawn and fix my hair before anyone else was stirring.

So I stayed awake as Misty recounted in painstaking detail what it was like to give a blow job and Kiera got sick in the bathroom. I let everyone brush their teeth before me, and waited long enough to hear snoring before I emerged in the pitch dark.

We were sleeping wedged like sardines, four of us in Christina's queen-size bed. I lifted the covers and slipped in beside Christina, smelling the familiar peach shampoo she had used forever. I thought she was asleep, but she rolled over and looked at me.

My scarf was wrapped around my head, red as a wound, the ends trailing down my back. I saw Christina's eyes flicker to it, and then back to mine. She did not mention the wrap. "I'm glad you're here," Christina whispered, and for a brief, blessed moment, so was I.

LATE THAT NIGHT, AS WANDA's snore whistles through the bunk, I lie awake. Every half hour a CO comes by with a flashlight, making sure that everyone is asleep. When he does, I close my eyes, pretending. I wonder if it gets easier to sleep with the sounds of a hundred women around you. I wonder if it gets easier, period.

During one of these circuits, the flashlight bounces with the CO's footsteps and then stops at our cell. Immediately Wanda sits, scowls. "Get up," the CO says.

"What the hell?" Wanda challenges. "Now you're tossing cells at midnight? You ever hear of prisoners' rights—"

"Not you." The officer jerks his head toward me. "Her."

At that, Wanda holds up her hands, backing off. She may have been willing to share a Twix with me, but now I am on my own.

My knees shake as I stand and walk to the open cell door. "Where are you taking me?"

The CO doesn't respond, just steers me down the catwalk. He stops at a doorway, buzzes the control desk, and there is a grating buzz as a lock is released. We step into an air lock and wait for the door to close behind us before the next door magically opens.

In silence he leads me to a small room that looks like a closet. He hands me a paper grocery bag.

I peek inside to see my nightgown and my slippers. I yank the scrubs off my body, starting to fold them out of habit, and then leave them in a pile on the floor. I pull on my old clothes, my old life.

The CO is waiting when I open the door again. This time he takes me past the cell where I was kept waiting when I first arrived, which has only two women in it now, both curled on the floor asleep, and reeking of alcohol and vomit. Then suddenly we are outside, crossing a fence with a necklace of barbed wire.

I turn to him, panicking. "I don't have any money," I say. I know we are an hour or so away from New Haven, and I don't have bus fare or a phone or even proper clothing.

The CO jerks his head into the distance, and that's when I notice that the dark is moving, a shadow against a moonless night. The silhouette morphs until I see the outline of a car, and a person inside, who gets out and starts running toward me. "Mama," Edison says, his face buried in my neck, "let's go home."

Kennedy

THERE ARE TWO TYPES OF PEOPLE WHO BECOME PUBLIC DEFENDERS: those who believe they can save the world, and those who know damn well they can't. The former are starry-eyed law school grads convinced they can make a difference. The latter are those of us who have worked in the system and know the problems are so much bigger than we are or the clients we represent. Once a bleeding heart calluses into realism, victories become individual ones: being able to reunite a mom who's gone through rehab with her kid, who was put in foster care; winning a motion to suppress evidence of a former addiction that might color the odds for a current client; being able to juggle hundreds of cases and triage those that need more than a meet 'em and plead 'em. As it turns out, public defenders are less Superman and more Sisyphus, and there's no small number of lawyers who wind up crushed under the weight of the infinite caseloads and the crappy hours and the shitty pay. To this end, we learn quickly that if we're going to keep a tiny bit of our lives sacrosanct, we don't bring our work home with us.

Which is why, when I dream of Ruth Jefferson for two consecutive nights, I know I'm in trouble.

In the first dream, Ruth and I are having an attorney-client meeting. I ask her the standard set of questions I'd ask of any client, but every time she speaks, it is in a language I don't understand. It's not even a language I recognize. Embarrassed, I have to keep asking her to repeat herself. Finally she opens her mouth, and a flock of blue butterflies pours out.

The second night I dream that Ruth has invited me over to dinner. It is the most sumptuous table, with enough food for a football team, and each dish is more delicious than the last. I drink one glass of water, and then another, and a third, and the pitcher is empty. I ask if I can get a refill, and Ruth looks horrified. "I thought you knew," she says, and when I glance up I realize that we are locked inside a prison cell.

I wake up, dying of thirst. Rolling onto my side, I reach for the glass of water I keep on my nightstand and take a long, cool drink. I feel Micah's arm slide around my waist and pull me against him. He kisses my neck; his hand slides up my pajama shirt.

"What would you do if I went to prison?" I blurt out.

Micah's eyes open. "I'm pretty sure since you're my wife, and over eighteen, this is legal."

"No." I roll to face him. "What if I did something . . . and got convicted?"

"That's kind of hot." Micah grins. "Lawyer in prison. Okay, I'll play. What did you do? Say public indecency. *Please* say public indecency." He pulls me flush against him.

"Seriously. What would happen to Violet? How would you explain it to her?"

"K, is this your way of telling me that you actually, finally *did* kill your boss?"

"It's a hypothetical."

"In that case, could we revisit the question in about fifteen minutes?" His eyes darken, and he kisses me.

WHILE MICAH SHAVES, I TRY to pin my hair into a bun. "Going to court today?" he asks.

His face is still flushed; so is mine. "This afternoon. How did you know?"

"You don't stick needles into your head unless you're going to court."

"They're bobby pins, and that's because I'm trying to look professional," I say.

"You're too sexy to look professional."

I laugh. "Let's hope my clients don't feel the same way." I spear a flyaway hair into submission and lean my hip against the sink. "I'm thinking of asking Harry to give me a felony."

"Great idea," Micah says with mild sarcasm. "I mean, since you already have five hundred open cases, you should definitely take on one that requires even more time and energy."

It's true. Being a public defender means I have nearly ten times as many cases as are recommended by the ABA, and that, on average, I have less than an hour to prepare each case that goes to trial. Most of the time I am working, I do not eat lunch, or take a bathroom break.

"If it makes you feel any better, he probably won't give it to me."

Micah clatters his razor against the porcelain. When we were first married, I used to stare at the tiny hairs that dried in the bowl of the sink with wonder, thinking that I might read in them our future the way a psychic would read tea leaves. "Does this sudden ambition have anything to do with the question about you going to prison?"

"Maybe?" I admit.

"Well, I'd much rather you take his case than join him behind bars."

"Her," I correct. "It's Ruth Jefferson. That nurse. I just can't shake her story."

Even when a client has done something unlawful, I can find sympathy. I can acknowledge a bad choice was made, but still believe in justice, as long as everyone has equal access to the system—which is exactly why I do what I do.

But with Ruth, there's something that doesn't quite add up.

Suddenly Violet comes charging into the bathroom. Micah tightens the towel around his waist, and I tie my robe. "Mommy, Daddy," she says. "Today I match Minnie."

She clutches a stuffed Minnie Mouse, and indeed, she has managed to pull on a polka-dotted skirt, yellow sneakers, a red bikini top, and long white tea gloves from the dress-up bin. I look at her, wondering how I am going to explain that she can't wear a bikini to school.

"Minnie's a fallen woman," Micah points out. "I mean, it's been seventy years. Mickey ought to put a ring on it."

"What's a fallen woman?" Violet asks.

I kiss Micah. "I'm going to kill you," I say pleasantly.

"Ah," he replies. "So *that's* why you're going to prison."

AT THE OFFICE, WE HAVE a television—a tiny screen that sits between the coffee machine and the can opener. It's a professional necessity, because of the press coverage our clients sometimes get. But in the mornings, before court is even in session, it's usually tuned to *Good Morning America*. Ed has an obsession with Lara Spencer's wardrobe, and to me, George Stephanopoulos is the perfect balance of hard-hitting reporter and eye candy. We sit through a round of hypothetical polls pitting presidential candidates against one another while Howard makes a fresh pot of coffee, and Ed recounts dinner with his in-laws. His mother-in-law still calls him by the name of his wife's ex, even though they've been married for nine years. "So this time," Ed says, "she asked me how much toilet paper I use."

"What did you tell her?"

"Just enough," Ed replies.

"Why did she even want to know?"

"She said they're trying to *cut back*," Ed answered. "That they're on a *fixed income*. Mind you, they go to Foxwoods three out of four weekends a month, but now we're rationing the Charmin?"

"Well, that's crap," I say, grinning. "See what I did there?"

Robin Roberts is interviewing a portly, middle-aged redhead whose poem was accepted for a highly literary anthology—but only after he submitted it with a Japanese pseudonym. "It was rejected thirty-five times," the man says. "So I thought maybe I'd be noticed more if my name was more . . ."

"Colorful?" Roberts supplies.

Ed snorts. "Slow news day."

Behind me, Howard drops a spoon. It clatters into the sink.

"Why is this even a thing?" Ed asks.

"Because it's a lie," I say. "He's a white insurance adjuster who co-opted someone else's culture so he could get fifteen minutes of fame."

"If that were all it took, wouldn't hundreds of poems by Japanese poets get published every year? Clearly what he wrote was good. How come no one's talking about that?"

Harry Blatt, my boss, blusters through the break room, his coat a tornado around his legs. "I hate rain," he announces. "Why didn't I move to Arizona?" With that greeting, he grabs a cup of coffee and holes himself up in his office.

I follow him, knocking softly on the closed door.

Harry is still hanging up his drenched coat when I enter. "What?" he asks.

"You remember that case I arraigned—Ruth Jefferson?"

"Prostitution?"

"No, she's the nurse from Mercy–West Haven. Can I take it?"

He settles behind his desk. "Right. The dead baby."

When he doesn't say anything else, I stumble to fill the void. "I've been practicing for five years, almost. And I feel really connected to this one. I'd like the opportunity to try it."

"It's a murder," Harry says.

"I know. But I really, really think I'm the right public defender for this case," I say. "And you're going to have to give me a felony sooner or later." I smile. "So I'm suggesting sooner."

Harry grunts. Which is better than a no. "Well, it would be good to have another go-to lawyer for the big cases. But since you're a rookie, I'll have Ed second-chair it with you."

I'd rather have a Neanderthal sitting at the table with me.

Oh, wait.

"I can do it myself," I tell Harry. It isn't until he finally nods that I realize I've been holding my breath.

* * *

I count the hours and the arraignments I have to slog through before I'm free to drive to the women's prison. As I sit in traffic, I run over opening conversations in my mind that will allow Ruth to have confidence in me as her attorney. I may not have tried a murder before, but I've done dozens of drug and assault and domestic jury trials. "This isn't my first rodeo," I say out loud to the rearview mirror, and then roll my eyes.

"It's an honor to represent you."

Nope. Sounds like a publicist meeting Meryl Streep.

I take a deep breath. "Hello," I try. "I'm Kennedy."

Ten minutes later, I park, shrug on a mantle of false confidence, and stride into the building. A CO with a belly that makes him look ten months pregnant sizes me up. "Visiting hours are over," he says.

"I'm here to see my client. Ruth Jefferson?"

The officer scans his computer. "Well, you're out of luck."

"I beg your pardon?"

"She was released two days ago," he says.

My cheeks flame. I can only imagine how stupid I look, losing track of my own client. "Yes! Of course!" I pretend that I knew this all along, that I was only testing him.

I can still hear him snickering as the door of the prison closes behind me.

A couple of days after I send a formal letter to Ruth's house—the address of which I have from the bail posting—she comes to the office. I am headed to the copy machine when the door opens and she walks in, nervous and hesitant, as if this cannot possibly be the right place. With the bare bones and the stacks of boxes and paper, we look more like a company that is either setting up shop or closing its doors than a functional legal office.

"Ruth! Hello!" I hold out my hand. "Kennedy McQuarrie," I say.

"I remember."

She is taller than I am, and stands with remarkable posture. I think, absently, that my mother would be impressed.

"You got my letter," I say, the obvious. "I'm glad you're here, be-cause we've got a lot to talk about." I look around, wondering where I am going to put her. My cubicle is barely big enough for me. The break room is too informal. There's Harry's office, but he's in it. Ed is using the one client meeting room we have to take a deposition. "Would you like to grab a bite? There's a Panera around the corner. Do you eat . . ."

"Food?" she finishes. "Yes."

I pay for her soup and salad, and pick a booth in the back. We talk about the rain, and how we needed it, and when the weather might turn. "Please," I say, gesturing to her food. "Go ahead."

I pick up my sandwich and take a bite just as Ruth bows her head and says, "Lord, we thank you for our food, furnishing our bodies for Christ's sake."

My mouth is still full as I say *Amen*.

"So you're a churchgoer," I add, after I swallow.

Ruth looks up at me. "Is that a problem?"

"Not at all. In fact, it's good to know, because it's something that can help a jury like you."

For the first time, I really look at Ruth carefully. The last time I saw her, after all, her hair was wrapped and she was wearing a night-gown. Now, she is dressed conservatively in a striped blouse and navy skirt, with shiny patent flats that are rubbed raw in one small spot each at the heels. Her hair is straight, pulled into a knot at the base of her neck. Her skin is lighter than I remember, almost the same color as the coffee milk that my mother used to let me drink when I was little.

Nerves manifest differently in different people. Me, I get talkative. Micah gets pensive. My mother gets snobbish. And Ruth, apparently, gets stiff. Which is something else I file away, because jurors who see that can misinterpret it as anger or haughtiness.

"I know it's hard," I say, lowering my voice for privacy, "but I need you to be a hundred percent honest with me. Even though I'm a stranger. I mean, hopefully, I won't be one for long. But it's important to realize that nothing you say to me can be used against you. It's com-pletely client-privileged."

Ruth puts her fork down carefully, and nods. "All right."

I take a small notebook out of my purse. "Well, first, do you prefer the term *black* or *African American* or *people of color*?"

Ruth stares at me. "People of color," she says after a moment.

I write this down. Underline it. "I just want you to feel comfortable. Frankly, I don't even *see* color. I mean, the only race that matters is the *human* one, right?"

Her lips press together tightly.

I clear my throat, breaking the knot of silence. "Remind me again where you went to school?"

"SUNY Plattsburgh, and then Yale Nursing School."

"Impressive," I murmur, scribbling this down.

"Ms. McQuarrie," she says.

"Kennedy."

"Kennedy . . . I can't go back to prison." Ruth looks into my eyes, and for a moment, I can see right down into the heart of her. "I've got my boy, and there's no one else who can raise him to be the man I know he's going to be."

"I know. Listen, I'm going to do my best. I have a lot of experience in cases with people like you."

That mask freezes her features again. "People like me?"

"People accused of serious crimes," I explain.

"But I didn't do anything."

"I believe you. However, we still have to convince a jury. So we have to go back to the basics to figure out why you've been charged."

"I'd think that's pretty obvious," Ruth says quietly. "That baby's father didn't want me near his son."

"The white supremacist? He has nothing to do with your case."

Ruth blinks. "I don't understand how that's possible."

"He isn't the one who indicted you. None of that matters."

She looks at me as if I'm crazy. "But I'm the only nurse of color on the birthing pavilion."

"To the State, it doesn't matter if you're black or white or blue or green. To them, you had a legal duty to take care of an infant under your charge. Just because your boss said don't touch the baby doesn't mean you get a free pass to stand there and do nothing." I lean forward. "The State doesn't even have to specify what the degree of murder is. They can argue multiple theories—contradictory theories. It's like shooting fish in a bucket—if they hit any of them, you're in trouble. If the State can show implied malice because you were so mad at being taken off the baby's case, and suggest that you premeditated the death, the jury can convict you of murder. Even if we told the jury it was an accident, you'd be admitting to a breach in duty of care and criminal negligence with reckless and wanton disregard for the safety of the baby—you'd basically be giving them negligent homicide on a silver platter. In either of those scenarios, you're going to prison. And in either of those scenarios it doesn't matter what color your skin is."

She draws in her breath. "Do you really believe that if I was white, I'd be sitting here with you right now?"

There is no way you can look at a case that has, at its core, a nurse who is the only employee of color in the department, a white supremacist father, and a knee-jerk decision by a hospital administrator . . . and not assume that race played a factor.

But.

Any public defender who tells you justice is blind is telling you a big fat lie. Watch the news coverage of trials that have racial overtones, and what will stick out profoundly is the way attorneys and judges and juries go out of their way to say this *isn't* about race, even though it clearly is. Any public defender will also tell you that even though the majority of our clients are people of color, you can't play the race card during a trial.

That's because it's sure suicide in a courtroom to bring up race. You don't know what your jury is thinking. Or can't be certain of what your judge believes. In fact, the easiest way to lose a case that has a racially motivated incident at its core is to actually call it what it is. Instead, you find something else for the jury to hang their hat on. Some shred of evidence that can clear your client of blame, and allow those twelve men and women to go home still pretending that the world we live in is an equal one.

"No," I admit. "I believe it's too risky to bring up in court." I lean forward. "I'm not saying you weren't discriminated against, Ruth. I'm saying that this is not the time or place to address it."

"Then when *is*?" she asks, her voice hot. "If no one ever talks about race in court, how is anything ever supposed to change?"

I don't have the answer to that. The wheels of systemic justice are slow; but fortunately, there's a little more oil in the machinery for personal justice, which throws cash at the victims to remove some of the indignity. "You file a civil lawsuit. I can't do it for you, but I can call around and find you someone who works with employment discrimination."

"But I can't afford a lawyer—"

"They'll take your case on contingency. They'll get a third of whatever payout you win," I explain. "To be honest, with that Post-it note, I think you'd be able to get compensatory damages for the salary you lost, as well as punitive damages for the idiotic decision your employer made."

Her jaw drops. "You mean I'd get money?"

"I wouldn't be surprised if it was a couple million," I admit.

Ruth Jefferson is speechless.

"You've got one hundred and eighty days to file an EEOC complaint."

"And then what?"

"Then, the EEOC will sit on it until the criminal trial is finished."

"Why?"

"Because assigning a guilty verdict against a plaintiff is significant," I say frankly. "It will change how your civil lawyer will draw up the complaint for you. A guilty finding is admissible as evidence, and would hurt your civil case."

She turns this over in her mind. "Which is why you don't want to talk about discrimination during *this* trial," Ruth says. "So that guilty verdict won't come to pass." She folds her hands in her lap, silent. She shakes her head once, and then closes her eyes.

"You were kept from doing your job," I say softly. "Don't keep me from doing mine."

Ruth takes a deep breath, opens her eyes, and meets my gaze. "All right," she says. "What do you want to know?"

Ruth

THE MORNING AFTER I AM RELEASED FROM JAIL I WAKE UP AND STARE AT the same old crack in the ceiling that I always say I'll patch and never get around to doing. I feel the bar from the pullout couch digging into my back and give thanks for it. I close my eyes and listen to the sweet harmony of the garbage trucks on our street.

In my nightgown (a fresh one; I will donate the one I wore to the arraignment to Goodwill at the first opportunity) I start a pot of coffee and pad down the hall to Edison's bedroom. My boy rests like the dead; even when I turn the knob and slip inside and sit down on the edge of the mattress, he doesn't stir.

When Edison was little, my husband and I would watch him sleep. Sometimes Wesley would put his hand on Edison's back, and we'd measure the rise and fall of his lungs. The science of creating another human is remarkable, and no matter how many times I've learned about cells and mitosis and neural tubes and all the rest that goes into forming a baby, I can't help but think there's a dash of miracle involved, too.

Edison rumbles deep in his chest, and he rubs his eyes. "Mama?" he says, sitting up, instantly awake. "What's wrong?"

"Nothing," I tell him. "Everything is right in the world."

He exhales, then looks at his clock. "I have to get ready for school."

I know, from our conversation in the car last night on the drive home, that Edison missed a whole day of classes in order to post bail for me, learning more about mortgages and real estate than I probably know myself. "I'll call the school secretary. To explain about yesterday."

But we both know there's a difference between *Please excuse Edison for being absent; he had a stomach bug* and *Please excuse Edison for being absent; he was bailing his mother out of jail.* Edison shakes his head. "That's okay. I'll just talk to my teachers."

He doesn't meet my eye, and I feel a seismic shift between us.

"Thank you," I say quietly. "Again."

"You don't have to thank me, Mama," he murmurs.

"No, I do." I realize, to my shock, that all the tears I managed to keep inside during the last twenty-four hours are suddenly swimming in my eyes.

"Hey," Edison says, and he reaches out to hug me.

"I'm sorry," I say, hiccuping against his shoulder. "I don't know why I'm falling apart *now*."

"It's going to be okay."

I feel it again, that movement of the earth beneath my feet, the resettling of my bones against the backdrop of my soul. It takes me a second to realize that for the first time in our lives, Edison is the one comforting me, instead of the other way around.

I used to wonder if a mother could see the shift when her child became an adult. I wondered if it was clinical, like at the onset of puberty; or emotional, like the first time his heart was broken; or temporal, like the moment he said *I do*. I used to wonder if maybe it was a critical mass of life experiences—graduation, first job, first baby—that tipped the balance; if it was the sort of thing you noticed immediately when you saw it, like a port-wine stain of sudden gravitas, or if it crept up slowly, like age in a mirror.

Now I know: adulthood is a line drawn in the sand. At some point, your child will be standing on the other side.

I thought he'd wander. I thought the line might shift.

I never expected that something I did would be the thing that pushed him over it.

It takes me a long time to figure out what to wear to the public defender's office. For twenty-five years I've dressed in scrubs; my nice clothing is reserved for church. But somehow a floral dress with a lace collar and kitten heels don't seem right for a business meeting. In the back of my closet I find a navy skirt I wore to parent-teacher night at Edison's school, and pair it with a striped blouse my mama bought me for Christmas from Talbots that still has the tags on. I rummage past my collection of Dansko clogs—the saviors of nurses everywhere—and find a pair of flats that are a little worse for the wear, but that match.

When I arrive at the address on the letterhead, I'm sure I've got the wrong place. There's no one at the front desk—in fact, there isn't a front desk. There are cubicles and towers of boxes that form a maze, as if the employees are mice and this is all part of some grand scientific test. I take a few steps inside and suddenly hear my name.

"Ruth! Hello! Kennedy McQuarrie!"

As if I could possibly have forgotten her. I nod, and shake her hand, because she's holding out her own. I don't really understand why she *is* my lawyer. She told me flat out, at the arraignment, that wouldn't be the case.

She starts chattering, so much that I can't get a word in edgewise. But that's okay, because I'm nervous as all get-out. I don't have the money for a private lawyer, at least not without liquidating everything I've saved for Edison's education, and I would go to prison for life before I let that happen. Still, just because everyone *can* have a lawyer in this country doesn't mean all lawyers are the *same*. On TV the people who have private attorneys get acquitted, and the ones with public defenders pretend that there isn't a difference.

Ms. McQuarrie suggests we go somewhere for lunch, even though I'm too anxious to eat. I start to take out my wallet after we order, but she insists on paying. At first, I bristle—ever since I was little, and started wearing Christina's hand-me-downs, I haven't wanted to be someone's charity case. But before I can complain I check myself. What if this is what she does with all her clients, just to build up rapport? What if she's trying to make me like her as much as I want her to like me?

After we sit down with our trays, out of habit, I say grace. Mind you, I'm used to doing that when other people don't. Corinne's an atheist who's always joking about the Spaghetti Monster in the Sky when she hears me pray or sees me bow my head over my bag lunch. So I'm not surprised when I find Ms. McQuarrie staring at me as I finish. "So you're a churchgoer," she says.

"Is that a problem?" Maybe she knows something I don't, like that juries are more likely to convict people who believe in God.

"Not at all. In fact, it's good to know, because it's something that can help a jury like you."

Hearing her say that, I look into my lap. Am I so naturally unlikable that she needs to find things that will sway people in my favor?

"First," she says, "do you prefer the term *Black* or *African American* or *people of color*?"

What I prefer, I think, is *Ruth*. But I swallow my response and say, "People of color."

Once, at work, an orderly named Dave went off on a rant about that term. "It's not like I don't have color," he'd said, holding out his pasty arms. "I'm not see-through, right? But I guess *people of* more *color* hasn't caught on." Then he had noticed me in the break room, and had gone red to his hairline. "Sorry, Ruth. But you know, I hardly think of you as Black."

My lawyer is still talking. "I don't even *see* color," she tells me. "I mean, the only race that matters is the *human* one, right?"

It's easy to believe *we're all in this together* when you're not the one who was dragged out of your home by the police. But I know that when white people say things like that, they are doing it because they think it's the right thing to say, not because they realize how glib they sound. A couple of years ago, Adisa went ballistic when *#alllivesmatter* took over Twitter as a response to the activists who were holding signs that said BLACK LIVES MATTER. "What they're really saying is *white* lives matter," Adisa told me. "And that Black folks better remember that before we get too bold for our own good."

Ms. McQuarrie coughs lightly, and I realize my mind's been wandering. I force my eyes to her face, smile tightly. "Remind me again where you went to school?" she asks.

I feel like this is a test. "SUNY Plattsburgh, and then Yale Nursing School."

"Impressive."

What is? That I'm college educated? That I went to Yale? Is this what Edison will face for the rest of his life, too?

Edison.

"Ms. McQuarrie," I begin.

"Kennedy."

"Kennedy." The familiarity sits uncomfortably on my tongue. "I can't go back to prison." I think of how, when Edison was a toddler, he'd put on Wesley's shoes and shuffle around in them. Edison will have a lifetime to see the magic he used to believe in as a child be methodically erased, one confrontation at a time. I don't want him to have to face that any sooner than necessary. "I've got my boy, and there's no one else who can raise him to be the man I know he's going to be."

Ms. McQuarrie—*Kennedy*—leans forward. "I'm going to do my best. I have a lot of experience in cases with people like you."

Another label. "People like me?"

"People accused of serious crimes."

Immediately, I am on the defensive. "But I didn't do anything."

"I believe you. However, we still have to convince a jury. So we have to go back to the basics to figure out why you've been charged."

I look at her carefully, trying to give her the benefit of the doubt. This is the only case on my radar, but maybe she is juggling hundreds. Maybe she honestly *has* forgotten the skinhead with the tattoo who spit on me in the courtroom. "I'd think that's pretty obvious. That baby's father didn't want me near his son."

"The white supremacist? He has nothing to do with your case."

For a moment, I'm speechless. I was removed from the care of a patient because of the color of my skin, and then penalized for following those directions when the same patient went into distress. How on earth could the two not be related? "But I'm the only nurse of color on the birthing pavilion."

"To the State, it doesn't matter if you're Black or white or blue or green," Kennedy explains. "To them you had a legal duty to take care of an infant under your charge." She starts listing all the ways the jury can find a reason to convict me. Each feels like a brick being mortared into place, trapping me in this hole. I realize that I have made a grave mistake: I had assumed that justice was truly just, that jurors would assume I was innocent until proven guilty. But prejudice is exactly the opposite: judging before the evidence exists.

I don't stand a chance.

"Do you really believe that if I was white," I say quietly, "I'd be sitting here with you right now?"

She shakes her head. "No. I believe it's too risky to bring up in court."

So we are supposed to win a case by pretending the reason it happened doesn't exist? It seems dishonest, oblivious. Like saying a patient died of an infected hangnail, without mentioning that he had Type 1 diabetes.

"If no one ever talks about race in court," I say, "how is anything ever supposed to change?"

She folds her hands on the table between us. "You file a civil lawsuit. I can't do it for you, but I can call around and find you someone who works with employment discrimination." She explains, in legalese, what that means for me.

The damages she mentions are more than I ever imagined in my wildest dreams.

But there is a catch. There's always a catch. The lawsuit that might net me this payout, that might help me hire a private lawyer who might actually be willing to admit that race is what landed me in court in the first place, can't be filed until *this* lawsuit wraps up. In other words, if I'm found guilty now, I can kiss that future money goodbye.

Suddenly I realize that Kennedy's refusal to mention race in court may not be ignorant. It's the very opposite. It's because she is aware of exactly what I have to do in order to get what I deserve.

I might as well be blind and lost, and Kennedy McQuarrie is the only one with a map. So I look her in the eye. "What do you want to know?" I say.

Kennedy

WHEN I COME HOME THE NIGHT AFTER MY FIRST MEETING WITH RUTH, Micah is working late and my mother is watching Violet. The house smells of oregano and freshly baked dough. "Is it my lucky day?" I call out, shuffling off the heaviness of my job as Violet gets up from the table where she's coloring and makes a beeline for me. "Is there home-made pizza for dinner?"

I swing my daughter up in my arms. She is clutching a violent red crayon in one small fist. "I made you one. Guess what it is."

My mother comes out of the kitchen holding an amoebic blob on a plate. "Oh, clearly it's an . . . alie—" I catch my mother's eye, and she shakes her head. Behind Violet's back she puts her hands up and bares her teeth. "Dinosaur," I correct. "I mean, obviously."

Violet smiles widely. "But he's sick." She points to the oregano spotting the cheese. "That's why he has a rash."

"Is it chicken pox?" I ask, as I take a bite.

"No," she says. "He has a reptile dysfunction."

I nearly spit out the pizza. Immediately I drop Violet to her feet. As she runs back to the table to continue coloring, I raise a brow. "What were you watching?" I calmly ask my mother.

She knows that the only television we let Violet watch is *Sesame Street* or Disney Junior. But from the studied wash of innocence on my mother's face I know she's hiding something. "Nothing."

I pivot, staring at the blank TV screen. On a hunch, I pick the remote up from the couch and turn it on.

Wallace Mercy is grandstanding in all his glory, outside City Hall in Manhattan. His wild white hair stands on end, like he's been electrocuted. His fist is raised in solidarity with whatever apparent injustice he's currently championing. "My brothers and sisters! I ask you: when did the word *misunderstanding* become synonymous with *racial profiling*? We demand an apology from the New York City police commissioner, for the shame and inconvenience suffered by this celebrated athlete—" The Fox news logo runs beneath the slightly familiar face of a handsome dark-skinned man.

Fox News. A channel that Micah and I do not generally watch. A channel that would easily be the home of multiple ads about erectile dysfunction.

"You let Violet watch this?"

"Of course not," my mother says. "I just turned it on during her naptime."

Violet looks up from her coloring. "The Five-o-Meter!"

I shoot my mother the Look of Death. "You're watching *The Five* with my four-year-old daughter."

She throws up her hands. "All right, fine, yes, sometimes I do. It's the news, for goodness' sake. It's not like I'm putting on P-O-R-N. Besides, did you even hear about this? It's a simple misunderstanding and that ridiculous fake reverend is shooting his mouth off again all because the police were trying to do their job."

I look at Violet. "Honey," I say, "why don't you go pick out the pajamas you want to wear, and two books for bedtime?"

She runs upstairs and I turn back to the television. "If you want to watch Wallace Mercy, at least put on MSNBC," I say.

"I don't want to watch Wallace. In fact I don't think he's doing Malik Thaddon any good by taking on his cause."

Malik Thaddon, *that's* why he looks familiar. He won the U.S. Open a few years back. "What happened?"

"He walked out of his hotel and was grabbed by four policemen. Apparently it was a case of mistaken identity."

Ava settles beside me on the couch as the camera zooms in on Wallace Mercy's verbal tantrum. The cords in his neck stand out and there is a throbbing vein at his temple; this man is a heart attack waiting to happen. "You know," my mother says. "If they weren't so *angry* all the time, maybe more people would listen to them."

I don't have to ask who *they* are.

I take another bite of my dinosaur pizza. "How about we go back to only turning the television on to a channel that doesn't have commercials with side effects?"

My mother folds her arms. "I would think of all people you'd want your child to be a student of the world, Kennedy."

"She's a baby, Mom. Violet doesn't need to think that the police might grab *her* one day."

"Oh, please. Violet was coloring. All that went right over her head. The only thing she even remarked on was Wallace Mercy's extremely poor choice of hairdo."

I press my fingers to the corners of my eyes. "Okay. I'm tired. Let's just table this conversation."

My mother takes my empty plate and stands up, clearly miffed. "Far be it from me to see myself as more than just the hired help."

She disappears into the kitchen, and I go to put Vi to bed. She has picked a book about a mouse with a mouthful of a name none of her friends can pronounce, and *Go, Dog. Go!* which is the title I hate more than anything else in her library. I climb into bed with her and drop a kiss on the crown of her head. She smells like strawberry bubble bath and Johnson's shampoo, exactly like my own childhood. As I start to read aloud, I make a mental note to thank my mother for bathing Violet and feeding her and loving her as fiercely as I do, even if she *did* expose her to Wallace Mercy's righteous wrath.

In that moment, my mind drifts to Ruth. *Violet doesn't need to think that the police might grab her one day,* I had said to my mother.

But honestly, the odds of my child being a victim of mistaken identity are considerably smaller than, say, Ruth's.

"Mommy!" Violet demands, and I realize I've inadvertently stopped reading, lost in thought.

" 'Do you like my hat?' " I read aloud. " 'I do not.' "

Ruth

Adisa says I need to treat myself, so she offers to buy me lunch. We go to a little bistro that bakes its own bread, and that serves portions so large you always wind up taking home half. It's busy, so Adisa and I sit at the bar.

I have been spending more time with my sister, which is both comforting and strange. Before, I was almost always working when I wasn't with Edison; now my schedule is empty.

"This is nice and all," Adisa says to me, "but have you given any thought to how you gonna pay for your own lunch down the road?"

I think about what Kennedy said yesterday about filing a civil suit. It's money, but it's money I cannot count on yet—maybe never. "I'm a little more concerned with feeding my son," I admit.

She narrows her glance. "How much cushion you have?"

There's no point lying to her. "About three months."

"You know if things get tight, you can ask me for help, right?"

At that, I can't help but smile. "Seriously? I had to give *you* a loan last month."

Adisa grins. "I said you can ask me for help. I didn't say I'd be able to provide it." She shrugs. "Besides, you know there's an answer."

What I have learned this week is that I am overqualified for nearly every entry-level administrative job in New Haven, including all open secretarial and receptionist positions. My sister believes I should file for unemployment. But I see that as dishonest, since once this is settled, I plan to go back to work. Getting a part-time job is another alternative, but I'm qualified as a nurse, and my license is suspended. So instead, I've avoided the conversation.

"All I know is that when Tyana's boyfriend got busted for larceny and went to trial, the court date wasn't for eight months," Adisa says. "Which puts you five months in the hole. What advice did that skinny white lawyer give you?"

"Her name is Kennedy, and we were too busy trying to figure out how I won't go to prison to discuss how I can support myself while I'm waiting for a trial date."

Adisa snorts. "Yeah, because that kind of detail probably never occurs to someone like her."

"You met her *once*," I point out. "You know nothing about her."

"I know that people who become public defenders are doing it because morals are more important to them than money, or else they would be off making partner in the big city. Which means Miz Kennedy either has a trust fund or a sugar daddy."

"She got me out on bail."

"Correction: your *son* got you out on bail."

I shoot Adisa a glare and turn my attention to the bartender, who is polishing glasses.

Adisa rolls her eyes. "You don't want to talk, that's fine." She looks up at the television over the bar, on which an infomercial is playing. "Hey," she says to the bartender. "Can we watch something else?"

"Be my guest," he says and hands her a remote control.

A minute later, Adisa is flipping through the cable stations. She stops when she hears a familiar gospel jingle: *Lord, Lord, Lord, have Mercy!* And then, the camera cuts tight to Wallace Mercy, the activist. Today he is lambasting a Texas school district that had a young Muslim boy arrested after he brought a homemade clock to school to show his science teacher and it was mistakenly identified as a bomb. "Ahmed," Wallace says, "if you are listening, I want to tell you something. I want to say to all the black and brown children out there, who are afraid that they too might be misunderstood because of the color of their skin . . ."

I am pretty sure Wallace Mercy used to be a preacher, but I don't think he ever got the memo that said he doesn't need to shout when he's miked on a television set.

"I want to say that I too was once thought to be less than I was, because of how I looked. And I am not going to lie—sometimes, when the Devil is whispering doubt into my ear, I still think those people were right. But most of the time, I think, *I have shown all of those bullies up*. I have succeeded in spite of them. And . . . *so will you*."

Adisa gasps. "Oh my God, Ruth, that's what you need. Wallace Mercy."

"I am one hundred percent sure that Wallace Mercy is the *last* thing I need."

"What are you talking about? Your kind of story is exactly what he lives for. Job discrimination because of race? He'll eat it up. He'll make sure everyone in the country knows you were wronged."

On the television, Wallace is shaking a fist. "Does he have to be so mad all the time?"

Adisa laughs. "Well, hell, girl. *I'm* mad all the time. I'm exhausted, just from being Black all day," she says. "At least he gives people like us a voice."

"A loud one."

"Exactly. Damn, Ruth, you been drinking the Kool-Aid. You been swimming with the sharks for so long, you've forgotten you're krill."

"What?"

"Don't sharks eat krill?"

"They eat *people*."

"This is what I'm telling you!" Adisa sighs. "White folks have spent years giving Black folks their freedom on paper, but deep down they still expect us to say *yes, massuh*, and be quiet and grateful for what we got. If we speak our minds we can lose our jobs, our homes, even our lives. Wallace is the man who gets to be angry for us. If it weren't for him, white folks would never know the stupid shit they do upsets us, and Black folks would get madder and madder because they can't risk talking back. Wallace Mercy is what keeps the powder keg in this country from blowing up."

"Well, that's all very well and good, but I'm not on trial because I'm Black. I'm on trial because a baby died when I was on duty."

Adisa smirks. "Who told you that? Your lily-white lawyer? Of course she don't think this is about race. She don't think about race, period. She don't *have* to."

"Okay, well, when you get your law degree, you can advise me about this case. Until then, I'm going to take her word for it." I hesitate. "You know, for someone who hates being stereotyped, you sure as hell do it a lot yourself."

My sister holds up her hands, a surrender. "Okay, Ruth. You're right. I'm wrong."

"I'm just saying—so far, Kennedy McQuarrie is doing her job."

"Her job is to rescue you so she can feel good about herself," Adisa says. "It's called a white knight for a reason." She narrows her gaze at me. "And you know what's on the other end of that color spectrum."

I don't give her the satisfaction of a response. But we both know the answer.

Black. The color of the villain.

I HAVE ONLY BEEN TO Christina's Manhattan home once, just after she married Larry Sawyer. It was to drop off a wedding gift, and the whole experience had been awkward. Christina and Larry had a destination wedding in Turks and Caicos, and Christina had said over and over how sorry she was that she couldn't invite *all* of her friends down there but instead had to limit the guest list. When she opened my present—a set of linen tea towels, screen-printed with the hand-written recipes of my mother's cookies and cakes and pies she loved most—she burst into tears and hugged me, saying that it was the most personal, thoughtful gift she'd received, and that she would use them every day.

Now, more than ten years later, I wonder if she ever used her kitchen, much less the tea towels. The granite countertops gleam, and in a blue glass bowl there are fresh apples that look like they've been polished. There is no evidence that a four-year-old lives anywhere nearby. I have an itch to open the double Viking oven, just to see if there's a single crumb or grease stain.

"Please," Christina says, gesturing to one of the kitchen chairs. "Sit."

I do, startled to find that there is soft music coming out of the wall behind me.

"It's a speaker," she says, laughing at my face. "It's hidden."

I wonder what it would be like to live in a place that feels like it is constantly part of a photo shoot. The Christina I used to know left a trail of destruction from the foyer to the kitchen the moment she came home from school—dropping her coat and book bag and kicking off her shoes. Just then, a woman appears so silently she might as well have emerged from the wall as well. She sets a plate of chicken salad down in front of me, and one in front of Christina.

"Thanks, Rosa," Christina says, and I realize that she probably still drops her coat and her bags and her shoes when she comes into her house. But Rosa is her Lou. It's just a different person now who's picking up after her.

The maid slips away again, and Christina starts talking about a hospital fundraiser and how Bradley Cooper agreed to come and then backed out at the last minute because of strep throat, and then *Us Weekly* photographed him that same night in a dive bar in Chelsea with his girlfriend. She is chattering so much about a topic I care nothing about that before I even finish half my salad, I realize why she's invited me here.

"So," I interrupt. "Did you hear about it from my mom?"

Her face falls. "No. Larry. Now that he's filed the paperwork to run for office, we have the news on twenty-four/seven." She bites her lower lip. "Was it awful?"

A laugh bubbles up in my throat. "What part of it?"

"Well, all of it. Getting fired. Being arrested." Her eyes grow wide. "Did you have to go to jail? Was it like *Orange Is the New Black*?"

"Yeah, without the sex." I look at her. "It wasn't my fault, Christina. You have to believe me."

She reaches across the table and grabs my hand. "I do. I do, Ruth. I hope you know that. I wanted to help you, you know. I told Larry to hire someone from his old firm to represent you."

I freeze. I try to see this as a gesture of friendship, but it feels like I'm a problem to solve. "I . . . I couldn't accept that . . ."

"Well, before you go thinking I'm your fairy godmother, Larry shot me down. He feels as badly as I do, honestly, but with his candidacy, it's just not a good time to be connected to something scandalous."

Scandalous. I taste the word, bite into it like a berry, feel it burst.

"We had a huge fight about it. I mean, like, I made him move into the second bedroom and everything. It's not like he's going for the neo-Nazi vote. But it's not that simple, I guess. Race relations are a mess right now, with the police commissioner under fire and everything, and Larry needs to stay as far away from that as possible or it could cost him the election." She shakes her head. "I am so sorry, Ruth."

My jaw feels too tight. "Is this why you had me over here?" I ask. "To tell me you can't be associated with me anymore?"

What had I been stupid enough to think? That this was a social visit? That for the first time in a decade Christina had suddenly decided she wanted me to drop in for lunch? Or had I known all along that if I came here, it was because I was hoping for a miracle in the form of the Hallowells—even if I was too proud to admit it?

For a long moment, we just stare at each other. "No," Christina says. "I needed to see you with my own eyes. I wanted to make sure you were . . . you know . . . all right."

Pride is an evil dragon; it sleeps underneath your heart and then roars when you need silence.

"Well, you can check this off your good deed list," I say bitterly. "I'm doing *just* fine."

"Ruth—"

I hold up my hand. "Don't, Christina, okay? Just . . . don't."

I try to feel through the chain of our history for the snag, the mend in the links, where we went from being two girls who knew everything about each other—favorite ice cream flavor, favorite New Kids on the Block member, celebrity crush—to two women who knew nothing about how the other lived. Had we drifted apart, or had our closeness been the ruse? Was our familiarity due to friendship, or geography?

"I'm sorry," Christina says, her voice tiny.

"I am too," I whisper.

Suddenly she bolts from the table and comes back a moment later, emptying the contents of her bag. Sunglasses and keys and lipsticks and receipts scatter the surface of the table; Advil tablets, loose in the bottom of her bag, spill like candy. She opens her wallet and takes a thick wad of bills and presses it into my hand. "Take this," Christina says. "Just between the two of us."

When our hands brush, there's an electric shock. I jump up, as if it were a bolt of lightning. "No," I say, backing away. This is a line, and if I cross it, everything changes between Christina and me. Maybe we have never been equals, but at least I've been able to pretend. If I take this money, I can't go on fooling myself.

"I can't."

Christina is fierce, folding my fingers around the money. "Just do it," she says. Then she looks up at me as if all is well in the world, as if nothing has changed, as if I have not just become a beggar at her feet, a charity, a cause. "There's dessert," Christina says. "Rosa?"

I trip over my chair in my hurry to escape. "I'm not really very hungry." I avert my glance. "I have to go."

I grab my coat and my purse from the rack in the foyer and hurry out the door, closing it tight behind me. I push the elevator button over and over, as if that might make it come faster.

And I count the bills. Five hundred and fifty-six dollars.

The elevator dings.

I hurry toward the welcome mat outside Christina's door and slip all the money beneath it.

This morning I told Edison we couldn't drive the car anymore. The registration has expired and I can't afford to renew it. Selling it will be my last resort, but in the meantime, while I try to save enough to cover the state and federal fees and the gas, we will take the bus.

I get into the elevator and close my eyes until I reach ground level. I run down Central Park West until I cannot catch my breath, until I know I will not change my mind.

THE BUILDING ON HUMPHREY STREET looks like any other government building: a square, cement, bureaucratic block. The welfare office is packed, every cracked plastic seat filled with someone who is bent over a clipboard. Adisa walks me up to the counter. She's working now—making minimum wage as a part-time cashier—but she's been in and out of this office a half dozen times when she was between jobs, and knows the ropes. "My sister needs to apply for assistance," she announces, as if that statement doesn't make me die a little inside.

The secretary looks to be Edison's age. She has long, swinging earrings shaped like tacos. "Fill this out," she says, and she hands me a clipboard with an application.

Since there is nowhere to sit, we lean against the wall. While Adisa searches for a pen in her cavernous shoulder bag, I glance at the women balancing clipboards and toddlers on their knees, at the men who reek of booze and sweat, at a woman with a long gray braid who is holding a doll and singing to herself. About half the room is Caucasian—mothers wiping the noses of their children in wads of tissues, and nervous men in collared shirts who tap their pens against their legs as they read each line on the form. Adisa sees me glancing at them. "Two-thirds of welfare goes to white folks," she says. "Go figure."

I have never been so grateful for my sister.

I fill out the first few queries: name, address, number of dependents.

Income, I read.

I start to put down my annual salary, and then cross it out. "Write zero dollars," Adisa says.

"I get a little bit from Wesley's—"

"Write zero dollars," Adisa repeats. "I know people who got rejected for SNAP because they had *cars* that were worth too much. You're going to screw the system the way the system screwed you."

When I don't start writing, she takes the application, fills in the blanks, and returns it to the secretary.

An hour passes, and not a single person is called from the waiting room. "How long does this take?" I whisper to my sister.

"However long they feel like making you wait," Adisa replies. "Half the reason these people can't get a job is because they're too busy sitting here waiting on benefits to go apply anywhere."

It's nearly three o'clock—four hours after we've arrived—before a caseworker comes to the door. "Ruby Jefferson?" she says.

I stand up. "Ruth?"

She glances at the paperwork. "Maybe," she concedes.

Adisa and I follow her down a hallway to a cubicle and sit. "I'm going to ask you some questions," she says in a monotone. "Are you still employed?"

"It's complicated . . . I was suspended."

"What's that mean?"

"I'm a nurse, but my license has been put on hold until an impending lawsuit is over." I say these words in a rush, like they are being purged from the core of me.

"It don't matter," Adisa says. "Imma break it down fuh you. She don't got no job and she don't got no money." I stare at my sister; I had been hoping that maybe the caseworker and I could find some common ground, that she might recognize me not as a typical governmental assistance applicant but as someone middle-class who has gotten a bum deal. Adisa, on the other hand, has whipped out the Ebonics, pushing as far away from my tactic as possible.

The caseworker shoves her glasses up her nose. "What about your son's college fund?"

"It's a five twenty-nine," I say. "You can only use it for education."

"She need medical," Adisa interrupts.

The woman glances at me. "What are you paying right now for COBRA?"

"Eleven hundred a month," I answer, flushing. "But I won't be able to afford that by next month."

The woman nods, noncommittal. "Get rid of your COBRA payment. You qualify for Obamacare."

"Oh, no, you don't understand. I don't want to get *rid* of my coverage; I want to just get temporary funding," I explain. "That's the health insurance that comes from the hospital. I'm going to get my job back eventually—"

Adisa rounds on me. "And in the meantime what if Edison breaks his leg?"

"Adisa—"

"You think you O. J. Simpson? You gonna get off and walk away? News flash, Ruth. You ain't O.J. You fa sho ain't Oprah. You ain't Kerry Washington. They get passes from white people because they famous. You just another nigga who's going down."

I am sure that the caseworker can see the steam rising from my hair. My fingers are clenched so tightly into fists that I can feel myself drawing blood. I'm not quite sure what precipitated this transformation into full-on gangsta, but I'm going to kill my sister.

Hell, I've already been indicted for homicide.

The caseworker glances from Adisa to me and then down at the paperwork. She clears her throat. "Well," she says, all too happy to get rid of us, "you qualify for medical, SNAP, and cash assistance. You'll be hearing from us."

Adisa hooks her arm through mine and pulls me up from my chair. "Thank you," I murmur, as my sister drags me from the cubicle.

"Now, that wasn't so bad, was it?" she says, when we are out of earshot, standing next to a potted plant near the elevator bank. She is suddenly back to her normal self.

I round on her. "What the hell was that? You were a total asshole."

"An asshole who got you the money you need," Adisa points out. "You can thank me later."

MY TRAINER IS A GIRL named Nahndi, and I am old enough to be her mother. "So basically there are five stations," she tells me. "Cashier, headset, coffee headset, presenter, and runner. I mean, there are people on table too, of course, they're the ones who are making the food . . ."

I trail her, tugging at my uniform, which has an itchy tag at the neck. I am working an eight-hour shift, which means I get a thirty-minute break and a free meal and minimum wage. After exhausting all the temp agency office job positions, I'd applied to McDonald's. I said I'd taken time off from work to be a mom. I didn't even mention the word *nurse*. I just wanted to be hired, so that I could give up some of the benefits I'd received at the unemployment office. For my own sanity I needed to believe that I could still, at least in part, take care of myself and my son.

When the manager called to offer me the job, he asked if I could start immediately, since they were short-staffed. So I left a note for Edison on the kitchen counter saying I had a surprise for him, and caught a bus downtown.

"The fry hopper is where the fries are loaded. There are three basket sizes to use, depending on how busy we are," Nahndi says. "There's a timer here you push when you drop the basket. But at two-forty, you need to shake it so the fries don't just become one giant blob, okay?"

I nod, watching the line worker—a college student named Mike—do everything she is saying. "Once the timer goes off, you hold the basket over the vat and let the oil drain for about ten seconds. And then dump them into the fry station—watch out, that's hot—and salt them."

"Unless it's a no-salt fry order," Mike says.

"We'll worry about that later," Nahndi replies. "The salt dispenser puts the same amount on every batch. Then you toss with the fry scoop and press a timer. All those fries need to be sold in five minutes, and if they're not, they get dumped out."

I nod. It's a lot to process. I had a thousand things to remember as a nurse, but after twenty years, that was muscle memory. This is all new.

Mike lets me try the fry station. I am surprised at how heavy the basket is when it's dripping. My hands are slippery in their plastic gloves. I can feel the oil settling through my hairnet. "That's great!" Nahndi says.

I learn how to bag properly, how many minutes each food item can sit in a warming basket before being discarded, which cleaners are used on which surfaces, how to tell the manager you need more quarters, how to push the medium-size button on the register before you push the button for Number 1 meal, or else the customer won't get fries with his order. Nahndi has the patience of a saint when I forget ranch dipping sauce or grab a McDouble instead of a double cheeseburger (they're identical, except for one extra slice of cheese). She feels confident enough, after an hour, to put me on table, assembling the food.

I have never been one to shy away from scut work. God knows, in nursing you have your share of holding emesis basins and changing soiled sheets. What I always would tell myself was that after an episode like that, the patient was even more uncomfortable—physically, or emotionally, or both—than I was. My job was to make things better as professionally as possible.

So getting a job as a fast-food worker really doesn't bother me. I'm not here for the glory. I'm here for the paycheck, as meager as it might be.

I take a deep breath and grab the three-part bun and set the pieces in their spots in the toaster. Meanwhile, I open a Big Mac box. This is easier said than done while wearing plastic gloves. The top part of the bun is sesame-seed down in the top of the box; the middle piece sits balanced on top of that; the bottom part is bottom-side down in the bottom half of the box. Two squirts of Big Mac sauce from the giant metal sauce gun go on each side; shredded lettuce and minced onions are sprinkled on top of that. The middle piece gets two strategically located pickles (they should be "dating, not mating," said Nahndi). The bottom gets a slice of American cheese. Then I reach into the warmer for two 10:1 patties, and place one on the top and one on the bottom. Lift the middle piece and place on the bottom part, place the top of the bun on *that*, and the box is closed and given to a runner for bagging or counter service.

It's not delivering a baby, but I feel the same flush of a job well done.

Six hours into my shift, my feet hurt and I reek of oil. I've cleaned the bathrooms twice—including once after a four-year-old got sick all over the floor. I have just started working as a runner to Nahndi's cashier when a woman orders a twenty-piece McNuggets. I check the box myself before putting it on a tray, and like I've been taught, I call her order number and tell her to have a nice day as I am handing it over. She sits down ten feet away from me and eats every last piece of chicken. Then suddenly, she is back at the counter. "This box was empty," she tells Nahndi. "I paid for *nothing*."

"I'm so sorry," Nahndi says. "We'll get you a new one."

I sidle closer, lowering my voice. "I checked that box myself. I watched her eat all twenty of those nuggets."

"I know," Nahndi whispers back. "She does this all the time."

The manager on duty, a cadaverous man with a soul patch, approaches. "Everything all right here?"

"Just fine," Nahndi says. She takes the new box of nuggets out of my hand and passes it to the customer, who carries it out to the parking lot. The manager goes back to the presenter position, handing out food at the drive-through.

"You've got to be kidding me," I mutter.

"If you let it get under your skin, you won't make it through a single shift." Nahndi turns her attention toward a high-spirited group of kids who surf through the door on the wave of their own laughter. "After-school rush," she warns. "Get your game face on."

I turn back to the screen, waiting for the next order to magically appear.

"Welcome to McDonald's," Nahndi says. "Can I take your order?"

I hope it's not a shake. That's the one machine I don't feel confident running yet, and Nahndi already told me a story about how, her first week, she forgot to put in the pins and the milk exploded all over her and onto the floor.

"Um, I'll take a Big Mac meal," I hear. "Dude, what do you want?"

"I left my wallet at home . . ."

I spin around, because I know that voice. Standing in front of the counter is Edison's friend Bryce, and beside him, hands jammed into the pockets of his jacket, is my son.

I can see the absolute horror in Edison's eyes as he scans my hairnet, my uniform, my new life. So instead of smiling at him, or saying hello, I turn my back again before Bryce can recognize me, too. Before I have to hear Edison make yet another excuse for the situation I've put him in.

EDISON IS NOT HOME WHEN I arrive, strip off my uniform, and shower away the smell of grease. I text him, but he doesn't answer. So instead, I cook dinner, pretending that nothing is wrong. By the time he finally comes home, I have just put a casserole on the table. "It's hot," I tell him, but he goes straight to his bedroom. I think he is still upset about my new job, but a moment later he appears, holding a giant Mason jar full of coins, as well as a checkbook. He tosses these on the table. "Two thousand three hundred and eighty-six," Edison announces. "And there's got to be a couple hundred more in the jar."

"That's money for college," I say.

"We need it now. I've got the whole spring and summer to work; I can make more."

I know how scrupulously Edison has saved his earnings from the grocery store where he's worked since he was sixteen. It was always understood that he'd chip in for his education, and between scholarships and FAFSA and the 529 plan we started for him as a baby, I would swing the rest of the tuition. The thought of taking money that is earmarked for college makes me feel sick. "Edison, no."

His face crumples. "Mama, I can't. I can't let you work at McDonald's when I have money we could use. You got any idea how that makes me feel?"

"First, that isn't money, that's your future. Second, there's no shame in a good honest day's work. Even if it's making French fries." I squeeze his hand. "And it's only for a little while, till this is all cleared up and I can work at the hospital again."

"If I drop track I can get more shifts at the Stop and Shop."

"You're not dropping track."

"I don't care about a dumb sport."

"And I don't care about anything but *you*," I tell him. I sit down across from him. "Baby, let me do this. Please." I feel my eyes fill with tears. "If you asked me who Ruth Jefferson was a month ago, I would have said she's a good nurse, and she's a good mother. But now I have people telling me I wasn't a good nurse. And if I can't put a casserole on the table and clothes on your back—then I have to second-guess myself as a mother, too. If you don't let me do this . . . if you don't let me take care of you . . . then I don't know who I'm supposed to be anymore."

He folds his arms tight across his chest, looks away from me. "Everyone knows. I hear them whispering and then they stop when I get close."

"The students?"

"Teachers, too," he admits.

I bristle. "That's inexcusable."

"No, it's not like that. They're going out of their way, you know? Like giving me extra time for papers and saying that they know things are rough at home right now . . . and every time one of them is like that—so *nice*, and *understanding*—I feel like I want to hit something, because it's even worse than when people pretend they don't know you missed school because your mother was in jail." He grimaces. "That test I failed? It wasn't because I didn't know the stuff. It was because I cut class, after Mr. Herman cornered me and asked if there was anything he could do to help."

"Oh, Edison—"

"I don't want their help," he explodes. "I don't want to be someone who *needs* their help. I want to be just like everyone else, you know, not a special case. And then I get mad at myself because I'm whining like I'm the only one with problems when you might . . . when you . . ." He breaks off, rubbing his palms against his knees.

"Don't say it," I say, folding him into my arms. "Don't even think it." I pull away and frame his beautiful face. "We *don't* need their help. We'll get through this. You believe me, right?"

He looks at me, really looks at me, like a pilgrim searches the night sky for meaning. "I don't know."

"Well, I do," I say firmly. "Now, eat what's on your plate. Because I am sure as hell not going to McDonald's if it gets cold."

Edison picks up his fork, grateful for the distraction. And I try not to think about the fact that for the first time in my life, I've lied to my son.

A WEEK LATER I AM rushing around, trying to find my uniform visor, when the doorbell rings. Standing on my porch, to my shock, is Wallace Mercy—wiry white shock of hair, three-piece suit, pocket watch, and all. "Oh, my," I say. The words are puffs of breath, dry in the desert of my disbelief.

"My sister," he booms. "My name is Wallace Mercy."

I giggle. I actually *giggle*. Because, really, who *doesn't* know that?

I glance around to see if he is being followed by an entourage, by cameras. But the only sign of his renown is a sleek black town car pulled up to the curb with its flashers on, and a driver in the front seat. "I wonder if I might take a moment of your time?"

The closest brush with fame I've had is when a late-night-TV-show host's pregnant wife got into a car accident near the hospital and was put on the ward for twenty-four hours of monitoring. Although she turned out to be perfectly fine, my role segued from healthcare provider to publicist, holding back the crowd of reporters who threatened to overrun the ward. It figures that now, the only other time in my life I've met a celebrity, I am wearing a polyester uniform. "Of course." I usher him through the door, silently thanking God that I already made my pullout bed back into a couch. "Can I get you something to drink?"

"Coffee would be a blessing," he says.

As I turn on the Keurig, I'm thinking that Adisa would die if she were here. I wonder if it would be rude to take a selfie with Wallace Mercy and send it to her. "You have a lovely home," he tells me, and he looks at the photos on my mantel. "This your boy? I've heard he's something else."

From whom? I think. "Do you take milk? Sugar?"

"Both," Wallace Mercy says. He takes the mug and gestures to the couch. "May I?" I nod, and he motions so that I will sit down on the chair beside him. "Miz Jefferson, do you know why I'm here?"

"Honestly, I can't even quite believe you *are* here, much less figure out why."

He smiles. He has the most even white teeth I have ever seen, stark against the darkness of his skin. I realize that up close, he is younger than I expected. "I have come to tell you that you are not alone."

Confused, I tilt my head. "That's very kind, but I already have a pastor—"

"But your community is much bigger than just your church. My sister, this is not the first time our people have been targeted. We may not have the power yet, but what we have is each other."

My mouth rounds as I start to put the pieces together. It's like Adisa said: my case is just another apple box for him to stand on, to get noticed. "It's very kind of you to come here, but I don't think my story is one that would be particularly interesting to you."

"On the contrary. May I be so bold as to ask you a question? When you were singled out and asked to not interfere with the care of a white baby, did any of your colleagues come to your defense?"

I think about Corinne, squirming when I complained about Marie's unjust directive, and then defending Carla Luongo. "My friend knew I was upset."

"Did she go to bat for you? Would she risk her job for you?"

"I would hardly have asked her to do that," I say, getting annoyed.

"What color skin does your colleague have?" Wallace asks bluntly.

"The fact that I'm Black was never an issue in my relationship with my colleagues."

"Not until they needed a scapegoat. What I am trying to say, Ruth—may I call you that?—is that *we* stand with you. Your Black brothers and sisters *will* go to bat for you. They *will* risk their jobs for you. They will march on your behalf and they will create a roar that cannot be ignored."

I stand up. "Thank you for your . . . interest in my case. But this is something that I'd have to discuss with my lawyer, and no matter what—"

"What color skin does your lawyer have?" Wallace interrupts.

"What difference does it make?" I challenge. "How can you ever expect to be treated well by white people if you're constantly picking them over for flaws?"

He smiles, as if he's heard this before. "You've heard of Trayvon Martin, I assume?"

Of course I have. The boy's death had hit me hard. Not just because he was about Edison's age but because, like my son, he was an honor student who had been doing nothing wrong, except being Black.

"Do you know that during that trial, the judge—the white judge—banned the term *racial profiling* from being used in the courtroom?" Wallace says. "She wanted to make sure that the jury knew the case was not about race, but about murder."

His words punch through me, arrows. They are almost verbatim what Kennedy told me about my own case.

"Trayvon was a good kid, a smart boy. You are a respected nurse. The reason that judge didn't want to bring up race—the same reason your lawyer is skirting it like it's the plague—is because Black people like you and Trayvon are supposed to be the exceptions. You are the very definition of when bad things happen to good people. Because that is the only way white gatekeepers can make excuses for their behavior." He leans forward, his mug clasped in his hands. "But what if that's not the truth? What if you and Trayvon aren't the exceptions . . . but the rule? What if injustice is the *standard*?"

"All I want is to do my job, live my life, raise my boy. I don't need your help."

"You may not need it," he says, "but apparently there are a lot of people out there who want to help you, just the same. I mentioned your case last week, briefly, on my show." He shifts, reaching into the inside breast pocket of his suit and pulling out a small manila envelope. Then he stands and passes it to me. "Good luck, sister. I'll be praying for you."

As soon as the door closes behind him, I open the seal and dump out the contents. Inside are bills: tens, twenties, fifties. There are also dozens of checks, written out to me, from strangers. I read the addresses on them: Tulsa, Oklahoma. Chicago. South Bend. Olympia, Washington. At the bottom of the pile is Wallace Mercy's business card.

I gather everything into the envelope, tuck it into an empty vase on a shelf in the living room, and then see it: my missing visor, resting on the cable box.

It feels like a crossroads.

I settle the visor on my head, grab my wallet and my coat, and head out the door to my shift.

I KEEP MY FAVORITE PICTURE of Wesley and me on the mantel of my house. We were at our wedding, and his cousin snapped it when we weren't looking. In the photo, we are standing in the lobby of the elegant hotel where we had our reception—the rental of which was Sam Hallowell's wedding gift to me. My arms are looped around Wesley's neck and my head is turned. He is leaning in, his eyes closed, whispering something to me.

I have tried so, so hard to remember what my handsome husband, breathtaking in his tuxedo, was saying. I'd like to believe it was *You are the most beautiful thing I've ever seen* or *I can't wait to start our life together*. But that is the stuff of novels and movies, and in reality, I am pretty sure we were planning our escape from a roomful of well-wishers so that I could pee.

The reason I know this is because although I cannot remember the conversation that Wesley and I had when that photograph was taken, I do remember the one we had afterward. There was a line at the ladies' room off the main lobby, and Wesley gallantly volunteered to stand guard at the men's room so that no one would enter while I was inside. It took me a significant amount of time to maneuver my wedding gown and do my business, and when I finally made it out of the bathroom, a good ten minutes had passed. Wesley was still outside the door, my sentry, but now he was holding a valet claim ticket.

"What's that?" I asked. We didn't have a car then; we'd taken public transport to our own wedding.

Wesley shook his head, chuckling. "Some dude just walked up to me and asked me to bring his Mercedes around."

We laughed and gave the ticket to the bellhop desk. We laughed, because we were in love. Because when life is full of good things, it does not seem important if an old white guy sees a Black man in a fancy hotel and naturally assumes he must work there.

AFTER A MONTH OF WORKING at McDonald's, I begin to see the paradox between service and sanitary food preparation. Although all orders are supposed to be prepared in less than fifty seconds, most items on the menu take longer than that to cook. McNuggets and Filet-O-Fish fry for almost four minutes. Chicken Selects take six minutes, and weighing in longest in the fry vat are crispy chicken breasts. Ten-to-one meat takes thirty-nine seconds to cook; four-to-one meat takes seventy-nine seconds. The grilled chicken is actually steamed while it cooks. Apple pies bake for twelve minutes, cookies for two. And yet in spite of all this, we employees are supposed to have the customer walking out the door in ninety seconds—fifty for food prep, forty for a meaningful interaction.

The managers love me, because unlike most of the staff, I do not have to juggle class schedules with my shifts. After decades of working nights, I don't mind coming in at 3:45 A.M. to open grill, which takes a while to heat up before we unlock the doors at 5:00. Because of my flexibility, I am usually given my favorite job—cashier. I like talking to the customers. I consider it a personal challenge to make them smile before they walk away from the counter. And after literally having women throw things at my head in the thick of labor, being berated for mayo instead of mustard really doesn't faze me.

Most of our regulars come in the mornings. There are Marge and Walt, who wear identical yellow sweat suits and walk three miles from their house and then get matching hotcake meals with orange juice. There's Allegria, who's ninety-three and comes once a week in her fur coat, no matter how warm it is outside, and eats an Egg McMuffin, no meat, no cheese, no muffin. There's Consuela, who gets four large iced coffees for all the girls at her salon.

This morning, one of the homeless folks who pepper the streets of New Haven wanders in. Sometimes my manager will give them food, if it's about to be thrown out—like the fries that go unsold after five minutes. Sometimes they come in to warm up. Once, we had a man pee in the bathroom sink. Today, the man who enters has long, tangled hair, and a beard that reaches his belly. His stained T-shirt reads NAMASTAY IN BED, and there is dirt crusted underneath his fingernails.

"Hello," I say. "Welcome to McDonald's. Can I take your order?"

He stares at me, his eyes rheumy and blue. "I want a song."

"I beg your pardon?"

"A song." His voice escalates. "I want a song!"

My manager on duty, a tiny woman named Patsy, steps up to the counter. "Sir," she says, "you need to move along."

"*I want a fucking song!*"

Patsy flushes. "I'm calling the police."

"No, wait." I meet the man's eye and start crooning Bob Marley. I used to sing "Three Little Birds" to Edison as a lullaby every night; I'll probably remember the words till the day I die.

The man stops screaming and shuffles out the door. I paste a smile on my face so that I can greet the next customer. "Welcome to McDonald's," I say and find myself looking at Kennedy McQuarrie.

She is dressed in a shapeless charcoal suit, and she's holding on to a little girl with strawberry-blond curls erupting from her scalp in a crazy tumble. "I want the pancakes *with* the egg sandwich," the girl chatters.

"Well, that's not an option," Kennedy says firmly, and then she notices me. "Oh. Wow. Ruth. You're . . . working here."

Her words strip me naked. What did she expect me to do while she was trying to build a case? Dip into my endless savings?

"This is my daughter, Violet," Kennedy says. "Today is a sort of treat. We, uh, don't come to McDonald's very often."

"Yes we do, Mommy," Violet pipes up, and Kennedy's cheeks redden.

I realize she doesn't want me to think of her as the kind of mother who would feed her kids our fast food for breakfast, no more than I want her to think of me as someone who would work at this job if I had any other choice. I realize that we both desperately want to be people we really aren't.

It makes me a little braver.

"If I were you," I whisper to Violet, "I'd pick the pancakes."

She clasps her hands and smiles. "Then I want the pancakes."

"Anything else?"

"Just a small coffee for me," Kennedy replies. "I have yogurt at the office."

"Mm-hmm." I punch the screen. "That'll be five dollars and seven cents."

She unzips her wallet and counts out a few bills.

"So," I ask casually. "Any news?" I say this in the same tone I might ask about the weather.

"Not yet. But that's normal."

Normal. Kennedy takes her daughter's hand and steps back from the counter, in just as much of a hurry to get out of this moment as I am. I force a smile. "Don't forget the change," I say.

* * *

A WEEK INTO MY CAREER as a Dalton School student, I developed a stomachache. Although I didn't have a fever, my mama let me skip school, and she took me with her to the Hallowells'. Every time I thought about stepping through the doors of the school, I got a stabbing in my gut or felt like I was going to be sick or both.

With Ms. Mina's permission, my mother wrapped me in blankets and settled me in Mr. Hallowell's study with saltines and ginger ale and the television to babysit me. She gave me her lucky scarf to wear, which she said was almost as good as having her with me. She checked in on me every half hour, which is why I was surprised when Mr. Hallowell himself entered. He grunted a hello, crossed to his desk, and leafed through a stack of paperwork until he found what he was looking for—a red file folder. Then he turned to me. "You contagious?"

I shook my head. "No, sir." I mean, I didn't *think* I was, anyway.

"Your mother says you're sick to your stomach."

I nodded.

"And it came on suddenly after you started school this week . . ."

Did he think I was faking? Because I wasn't. Those pains were real.

"How *was* school?" he asked. "Do you like your teacher?"

"Yes, sir." Ms. Thomas was small and pretty and hopped from the desk of one third grader to another like a starling on a summer patio. She always smiled when she said my name. Unlike my school in Harlem last year—the school my sister was still attending—this school had large windows and sunlight that spilled into the hallways; the crayons we used for art weren't broken into nubs; the textbooks weren't scribbled in, and had all their pages. It was like the schools we saw on television, which I had believed to be fiction, until I set foot in one.

"Hmph." Sam Hallowell sat down next to me on the couch. "Does it feel like you've eaten a bad burrito? Comes and goes in waves?"

Yes.

"Mostly when you think about going to school?"

I looked right at him, wondering if he could read minds.

"I happen to know exactly what's ailing you, Ruth, because I caught that bug once too. It was just after I took over programming at the

network. I had a fancy office and everyone was falling all over each
other to try to make me happy, and you know what? I felt sick as a
dog." He glanced at me. "I was sure that any minute everyone was
going to look at me and realize I didn't belong there."

I thought of what it felt like to sit down in the beautiful wood-
paneled cafeteria and be the only student with a bag lunch. I remembered how Ms. Thomas had shown us pictures of American heroes, and
although everyone knew who George Washington and Elvis Presley
were, I was the only person in the class who recognized Rosa Parks and
that made me proud and embarrassed all at once.

"You are not an impostor," Sam Hallowell told me. "You are not
there because of luck, or because you happened to be in the right place
at the right moment, or because someone like me had connections.
You are there because you are *you*, and that is a remarkable accomplish-
ment in itself."

That conversation is in my thoughts as I now listen to the principal
at Edison's magnet high school tell me that my son, who will not even
swat a bug, punched his best friend in the nose during their lunch period today, the first day back after Thanksgiving vacation. "Although
we're cognizant of the fact that things at home have been . . . a challenge, Ms. Jefferson, obviously we don't tolerate this kind of behavior,"
the principal says.

"I can assure you it won't happen again." All of a sudden I'm back
at Dalton, feeling lesser than, like I should be grateful to be in this
principal's office.

"Believe me, I'm being lenient because I know there are extenuat-
ing circumstances. This should technically go on Edison's permanent
record, but I'm willing to waive that. Still, he'll be suspended for the
rest of the week. We have a zero tolerance policy here, and we can't let
our students go around worrying for their own safety."

"Yes, of course," I murmur, and I duck out of the principal's office,
humiliated. I am used to coming to this school wrapped in a virtual
cloud of triumph: to watch my son receive an award for his score on a
national French exam; to applaud him as he's crowned Scholar-Athlete
of the Year. But Edison is not crossing a stage with a wide smile right

now, to shake the principal's hand. He is sprawled on a bench just out-side the office door, looking for all the world like he doesn't give a damn. I want to box his ears.

He scowls when he sees me. "Why did you come here like *that*?"

I look down at my uniform. "Because I was in the middle of a shift when the principal's office called me to say my son was going to be expelled."

"Suspended . . ."

I round on him. "You do *not* get to speak right now. And you most definitely do not get to correct me." We step out of the school, into a day that bites like the start of winter. "You want to tell me why you hit Bryce?"

"I thought I don't get to speak."

"Don't you back-talk me. What were you *thinking*, Edison?"

Edison looks away from me. "You know someone named Tyla? You work with her."

I picture a thin girl with bad acne. "Skinny?"

"Yeah. I've never talked to her before in my life. Today she came up at lunch and said she knew you from McDonald's, and Bryce thought it was hilarious that my mother got a job there."

"You should have ignored him," I reply. "Bryce wouldn't know how to do a good honest day's work if you held a gun to his head."

"He started talking smack about you."

"I told you, he's not worth the energy of paying attention."

Edison clenches his jaw. "Bryce said, 'Why is yo mama like a Big Mac? Because she's full of fat and only worth a buck.'"

All the air rushes from my lungs. I start toward the front door of the school. "I'm going to give that principal a piece of my mind."

My son grabs my arm. "No! Jesus, I'm already the punch line for everyone's jokes. Don't make it worse!" He shakes his head. "I'm so sick of this. I hate this fucking school and its fucking scholarships and its fucking fakeness."

I don't even tell Edison to watch his mouth. I can't breathe.

All my life I have promised Edison that if you work hard, and do well, you will earn your place. I've said that we are not impostors; that what we strive for and get, we deserve. What I neglected to tell him was that at any moment, these achievements might still be yanked away.

It is amazing how you can look in a mirror your whole life and think you are seeing yourself clearly. And then one day, you peel off a filmy gray layer of hypocrisy, and you realize you've never truly seen yourself at all.

I am struggling to find the correct response here: to tell Edison that he was right in his actions, but that he could beat up every boy in that school and it would not make a difference in the long run. I am struggling to find a way to make him believe that in spite of this, we have to put one foot in front of the other every day and pray it will be better the next time the sun rises. That if our legacy is not entitlement, it must be hope.

Because if it's not, then we become the shiftless, the wandering, the conquered. We become what they think we are.

EDISON AND I TAKE THE bus home in silence. As we turn the corner of our block, I tell him he's grounded. "For how long?" he asks.

"A week," I say.

He scowls. "This isn't even going on my record."

"How many times I tell you that if you want to be taken seriously, you gotta be twice as good as everyone else?"

"Or maybe I could punch more white people," Edison says. "Principal took me pretty seriously for doing *that*."

My mouth tightens. "*Two* weeks," I say.

He storms away, taking the porch stairs in one leap, pushing through the front door, nearly knocking down a woman standing in front of it, holding a large cardboard box.

Kennedy.

I'm so angry about Edison's suspension that I've completely forgotten we have picked this afternoon to review the State's discovery. "Is this a bad time?" Kennedy asks delicately. "We can reschedule . . ."

I feel a flush rise from my collar to my cheeks. "No. This is fine—something . . . unexpected . . . came up. I'm sorry you had to hear that; my son is not usually so rude." I hold the door open so that she can enter my house. "It gets harder when you can't give them a swat on the behind anymore because they're bigger than you are."

She looks shocked, but covers it quickly with a polite smile.

As I take her coat to hang up, I glance at the couch and single arm-chair, the tiny kitchen, and try to see it through her eyes. "Would you like something to drink?"

"Water would be great."

I go to the kitchen to fill a glass—it's only steps away from her, separated by a counter—while Kennedy glances at the photographs on the mantel. Edison's latest school photo is there, as well as one of us on the Mall in Washington, D.C., and the picture of Wesley and me on our wedding day.

She begins to unpack the box of files she lugged inside as I sit down on the couch. Edison is in his bedroom, stewing. "I've had a look through the discovery," Kennedy begins, "but this is where I really need your help. It's the baby's chart. I can read legalese, but I'm not fluent in medical."

I open the file, my shoulders stiffening when I turn the photo-copied page of Marie's Post-it note. "It's all accurate—height, weight, Apgar scores, eyes and thighs—"

"What?"

"An antibiotic eye ointment and a vitamin K shot. It's standard for newborns."

Kennedy reaches across me and points to a number. "What's that mean?"

"The baby's blood sugar was low. He hadn't nursed. The mom had gestational diabetes, so that wasn't particularly surprising."

"Is that your handwriting?" she asks.

"No, I wasn't the delivery nurse. That was Lucille; I took over for her after her shift ended." I flip the page. "This is the newborn assessment—the form *I* filled out. Temperature of ninety-eight point one," I read, "nothing concerning about his hair whorls or fontanels;

Accu-Chek at fifty-two—his sugar was improving. His lungs were clear. No bruising or abnormal shaping of the skull. Length nineteen point five inches, head circumference thirteen point five inches." I shrug. "The exam was perfectly fine, except for a possible heart murmur. You can see where I noted it in the file and flagged the pediatric cardiology team."

"What did the cardiologist say?"

"He never got a chance to diagnose it. The baby died before that." I frown. "Where are the results of the heel stick?"

"What's that?"

"Routine testing."

"I'll subpoena it," Kennedy says absently. She starts tossing around papers and files until she finds one labeled with the seal of the medical examiner. "Ah, look at this . . . *Cause of death: hypoglycemia leading to hypoglycemic seizure leading to respiratory arrest and cardiac arrest,*" Kennedy says. "Cardiac arrest? As in: a congenital heart defect?"

She hands me the report. "Well, I was right, for what it's worth," I say. "The baby had a grade-one patent ductus."

"Is that life-threatening?"

"No. It usually closes up by itself the first year of life."

"Usually," she repeats. "But not *always.*"

I shake my head, confused. "We can't say the baby was sick if he wasn't."

"The defense doesn't have the burden of proof. We can say anything—that the baby was exposed to Ebola, that a distant cousin of his died of heart disease, that he was the first kid to be born with a chromosomal abnormality inconsistent with life—we just have to lay out a trail of bread crumbs for the jury and hope they're hungry enough to follow."

I sift through the medical file again until I find the photocopy of the Post-it note. "We could always show them this."

"That does not create doubt," Kennedy says flatly. "That, in fact, makes the jury think you might have a reason for being pissed off in the first place. Let it go, Ruth. What really matters here? The pain from just a little bruise to your ego? Or the guillotine hanging over your head?"

My hand tightens on the paper, and I feel the sting of a paper cut. "It was not a little bruise to my ego."

"Great. Then we're in agreement. You want to win this case? Help me find a medical issue that shows the baby might still have died, even if you'd taken every single measure possible to save it."

I almost tell her, then. I almost say that I tried to resuscitate that child. But then I would have to admit that I had lied to Kennedy in the first place, when here I stand, telling her it's wrong to lie about a cardiac anomaly. So instead, I stick my finger in my mouth and suck at the wound. In the kitchen, I find a box of Band-Aids and carry them back to the table, wrap one around my middle finger.

This is not a case about a heart murmur. She knows it, and I know it.

I look down at my kitchen table, and run my thumbnail against the grain of the wood. "You ever make your little girl peanut butter and jelly sandwiches?"

"What?" Kennedy glances up. "Yes. Sure."

"Edison, he was a picky eater when he was little. Sometimes he decided he didn't want the jelly, and I'd have to try to scrape it off. But you know, you can't ever really take the jelly off a peanut butter and jelly sandwich, once it's there. You can still taste it."

My lawyer is looking at me as if I've lost my mind.

"You told me this lawsuit isn't about race. But that's what started it. And it doesn't matter if you can convince the jury I'm the reincarnation of Florence Nightingale—you can't take away the fact that I am Black. The truth is, if I looked like you, this would not be happening to me."

Something shutters in her eyes. "First," Kennedy says evenly, "you might very well have been indicted no matter what race you were. Grieving parents and hospitals that are trying to keep their insurance premiums from going through the roof create a perfect recipe for finding a fall guy. Second, I am not disagreeing with you. There are definite racial overtones in this case. But in my professional opinion, bringing them up in court is more likely to hinder than to help you secure an acquittal, and I don't think that's a risk you should take just to make yourself feel better about a perceived slight."

"A perceived slight," I say. I turn the words over in my mouth, running my tongue across the sharp edges. "A *perceived* slight." I lift my chin and stare at Kennedy. "What do you think about being white?"

She shakes her head, her face blank. "I *don't* think about being white. I told you the first time we sat down—I don't see color."

"Not all of us have that privilege." I reach for the Band-Aids and shake them across all her charts and folders and files. "Flesh color," I read on the box. "Tell me, which one of these is flesh color? *My* flesh color?"

Two bright spots bloom on Kennedy's cheeks. "You can't blame me for that."

"Can't I?"

She straightens her spine. "I am not a racist, Ruth. And I understand that you're upset, but it's a little unfair of you to take it out on me, when I'm just trying to do my best—my professional best—to help you. For God's sake, if I'm walking down a street and a Black man is coming toward me and I realize I'm going the wrong way, I keep going the wrong direction instead of turning around so he won't automatically think I'm afraid of him."

"That's overcompensating, and that's just as bad," I say. "You say you don't see color . . . but that's *all* you see. You're so hyperaware of it, and of trying to look like you aren't prejudiced, you can't even understand that when you say *race doesn't matter* all I hear is you dismissing what *I've* felt, what *I've* lived, what it's like to be put down because of the color of my skin."

I don't know which one of us is more surprised by my outburst. Kennedy, for being confronted by a client she thought was grateful to bask in the glow of her professional advice, or I, for letting loose a beast that must have been hiding inside me all these years. It had been lurking, just waiting for something to shake my unshakable optimism, and free it.

Tight-lipped, Kennedy nods. "You're right. I don't know what it's like to be Black. But I do know what it's like to be in a courtroom. If you bring up race in court, you will lose. Juries like clarity. They like being able to say, *Because A, therefore B.* Sprinkle racism over that, and everything gets cloudy." She starts gathering up her files and reports, jamming them back in her briefcase. "I'm not trying to make it seem like your feelings don't matter to me, or that I don't believe racism is real. I'm just trying to get you acquitted."

Doubt is like frostbite, shivering at the edges of my mind.

"Maybe we both need to cool down," Kennedy says diplomatically. She gets to her feet and walks to the door. "I promise you, Ruth. We can win this case, without bringing any of that up."

After the door closes behind her, I sit, my hands folded in my lap. *How,* I think, *is that winning?*

I pick at the edge of the Band-Aid on my finger. Then I walk to the vase on the shelf near the television. I pull out the manila envelope and rummage through the checks until I find what I'm looking for.

Wallace Mercy's business card.

Turk

FRANCIS LIKES TO OPEN UP HIS HOME TO GUYS IN THE MOVEMENT EVERY other Sunday afternoon. Once the crews stopped roaming the streets looking for people to mess up, we hardly ever saw each other. You can reach a lot of people through the World Wide Web, but it's a cold, impersonal community. Francis recognizes that, which is why twice a month the street is packed with cars with license plates from as far away as New Jersey and New Hampshire, enjoying an afternoon of hospitality. I'll put on the football game for the guys, and the women congregate in the kitchen with Brit, organizing the potluck dishes and trading gossip like baseball cards. Francis takes it upon himself to entertain the older kids with colorful lectures. You can stand at a distance and almost see words blazing from his mouth, like he is a dragon, as the boys sit mesmerized at his feet.

It's been almost three months since we've had a Sunday session. We haven't seen these people since Davis's funeral. To be honest, I haven't really thought about it, since I'm still stumbling through the days like a zombie. But when Francis tells me to post an invitation on Lonewolf.org, I do it. You just don't say no to Francis.

And so, the house is full again. The tone, though, is a little different. Everyone wants to seek me out, ask how I'm doing. Brit is in our bedroom with a headache; she didn't even want to pretend to be social.

But Francis is still the happy host, pulling the caps off beers and complimenting the ladies on their haircuts or blue-eyed babies or the deliciousness of their brownies. He finds me sitting by myself near the garage, where I've gone to dump a bag of trash. "People seem to be having a good time," he says.

I nod. "People like free beer."

"It's only free if you're not me," Francis replies, and then he looks at me shrewdly. "Everything all right?" he asks, and by *everything* he means *Brit*. When I shrug, he purses his lips. "You know, when Brit's mama left, I didn't understand why I was still here. Thought about checking out, if you know what I mean. I was taking care of my six-month-old, and I still couldn't find the will to stick around. And then one day, I just *got* it: the reason we lose people we care about is so we're more grateful for the ones we still have. It's the only possible explanation. Otherwise, God's a sorry son of a bitch."

He claps me on the back and walks into the tiny fenced backyard. The young teens who've been dragged here by their parents are suddenly alert, awakened to his magnetism. He sits down on a stump and starts his version of Sunday School. "Who likes mysteries?" There is nodding, a general buzz of assent. "Good. Who can tell me who Israel is?"

"That's a pretty crappy mystery," someone mutters and is elbowed by the boy beside him.

Another boy calls out, "A country filled with Jews."

"Raise your hand," Francis says. "And I didn't ask *what* Israel is. I asked *who*."

A kid who's just getting fuzz over his upper lip waves and is pointed to. "Jacob. He started being called that after he fought the angel at Peniel."

"And we have a winner," Francis says. "Israel went on to have twelve sons—that's where the twelve tribes of Israel come from, you follow . . ."

I walk back into the kitchen, where a few women are talking. One of them is holding a baby who's fussing. "All's I know is she doesn't sleep through the night anymore and I'm so tired I actually walked out the front door in my pajamas yesterday headed to work before I realized what I was doing."

"I'm telling you," one girl says. "I used whiskey, rubbed on the gums."

"Can't start them too early," says an older woman, and everyone laughs.

Then they see me standing there, and the conversation drops like a stone from a cliff. "Turk," says the older woman. I don't know her name, but I recognize her face; she's been here before. "Didn't see you come in."

I don't respond. My eyes are glued to the baby, who is red-faced, waving her fists. She is crying so hard she can't catch her breath.

My arms are reaching out before I can stop myself. "Can I . . . ?"

The women glance at each other, and then the baby's mother places her into my arms. I can't get over how light the baby is, rigid arms and legs kicking as she shrieks. "Shh," I say, patting her. "Quiet, now."

I rub my hand on her back. I let her curl like a comma over my shoulder. Her cries become hiccups. "Look at you, the Baby Whisperer," her mother says, smiling.

This is how it could have been.

This is how it *should* have been.

Suddenly I realize that the ladies are not looking at the baby anymore. They are staring at something behind me. I turn around, the baby fast asleep, tiny bubbles of spit on the seam of her lips.

"Jesus," Brit says, an accusation. She turns and runs out of the kitchen. I hear the door to the bedroom slam behind her. "Excuse me," I say, trying to juggle the baby back to her mother as gently and as quickly as possible. Then I run to Brit.

She's lying on our bed, facing away from me. "I fucking hate them. I hate them for being in my house."

"Brit. They're just trying to be nice."

"That's what I hate the most," she says, her voice a blade. "I hate the way they look at me."

"That's not what—"

"All I wanted was a fucking drink of water from my own sink. Is that too much to ask?"

"I'll get you water . . ."

"That's not the point, Turk."

"What *is* the point?" I whisper.

Brit rolls over. Her eyes are swimming with tears. "Exactly," she says, and she starts to cry, just as hard as that baby was crying, but even after I gather her into my arms and hold her tight and rub her back she doesn't stop.

It feels just as foreign to be soothing Brit while she sobs as it was for me to cradle an infant. This is not the woman I married. I wonder if I buried that fierce spirit along with the body of my son.

We stay there, in the cocoon of the bedroom, long after the sun sets and the cars drive away and the house is empty again.

THE NEXT NIGHT WE ARE all sitting in the living room watching television. My laptop is open; I'm writing a post for Lonewolf.org about something that happened in Cincinnati. Brit brings me a beer and curls up against me, the first contact she's initiated since, well, I can't even remember. "What are you working on?" she asks, craning her neck so that she can read what's on my screen.

"White kid got body-slammed by two niggers at school," I say. "They broke his back, but they didn't get charged. You can bet if it were the other way around, the White kids would have been charged with assault."

Francis points the remote at the television and grunts. "That's because Cincinnati is in the ninety-ninth percentile of shit schools," he adds. "It's an all-black administration. What do we *really* want for our kids?"

"That's good," I say, typing in his words. "I'm gonna end with that."

Francis flips through the cable stations. "How come there's Black Entertainment TV but no White Entertainment TV?" he asks. "And people say there's no reverse racism." He turns off the television and stands up. "I'm headed to bed."

He kisses Brit on the forehead and leaves for the night, headed to his side of the duplex. I expect her to get up, too, but she makes no move to leave.

"Doesn't it kill you?" Brit asks. "The waiting?"

I glance up. "How do you mean?"

"It's like there's nothing *immediate* anymore. You don't know who's reading the stuff you post." She pivots to face me, sitting cross-legged. "Things used to be so much clearer. I learned my colors by looking at the shoelaces of the guys my dad was meeting up with. White Power and neo-Nazis had red or white laces. SHARPs were blue or green."

I smirk. "I have a hard time imagining your father meeting with SHARPs." Skinheads Against Racial Prejudice are the biggest race traitors you'll ever meet; they target those of us who are fighting the good fight by trying to get rid of lesser races. They think they're fucking Batman, every one of them.

"I didn't say it was a . . . friendly meeting," Brit replies. "But actually, sometimes he did. You did what you had to do—even if it seemed to go against all reason—because you were seeing the big picture." She glances up at me. "You know Uncle Richard?"

Not personally, but Brit did. He was Richard Butler, the head of Aryan Nations. He died when Brit was about seventeen.

"Uncle Richard was friends with Louis Farrakhan."

The leader of the Nation of Islam? This was news to me. "But . . . he's . . ."

"Black? Yeah. But he hates Jews and the federal government as much as we do. Daddy always says the enemy of my enemy is my friend." Brit shrugs. "It was kind of an unspoken understanding: after we worked together to bring down the system, then we'd fight each other."

We'd win, of that I have no doubt.

She looks at me carefully. "What do we *really* want for our kids?"

Brit says, repeating Francis's earlier comment. "I know what I want for *my* kid. I want him to be remembered."

"Baby, you know we won't forget him."

"Not us," Brit says, her words suddenly hard. *"Everyone."*

I look at her. I know what she's saying: that typing a blog may indeed crumble foundations, but it's far more dramatic—and faster—to blow the building up from the top down.

To some extent I'd been too late for the Skinhead Movement, which had its heyday ten years before I was born. I imagined a world where when people saw me coming, they ran away. I thought about how Francis and I had spent the past two years trying to convince crews that anonymity was more insidious—and terrifying—than overt threats. "Your father won't go along with this," I say.

Brit leans down and kisses me, softly, pulling away so I am left wanting more. God, I've missed this. I missed *her.*

"What my father doesn't know can't hurt him," she answers.

RAINE IS PUMPED TO GET my phone call. It's been two years since I've seen him; he didn't make it to my wedding, because his wife had just had their second baby. When I tell him I'm in Brattleboro for the day, he invites me to his house for lunch. He's moved, so I jot the address down on a napkin.

At first I'm sure I'm in the wrong place. It's a little ranch on a cul-de-sac, with a mailbox that is shaped like a cat. There's a bright red plastic slide on the front lawn and a ticky-tacky wooden snowman hanging near the front door. The welcome mat says HI! WE'RE THE TESCOS!

Then a slow grin spreads over my face. The smart bastard. He's taking hiding in plain sight to a whole new level. I mean, who would ever expect that the dad living next door who power-washes his porch and lets his kid ride a bike with training wheels up and down the driveway is actually a White Supremacist?

Raine opens the door before I even get a chance to knock. He's holding a chunky toddler in his arms, and poking out from between the towers of his legs is a shy little girl wearing a tutu and a princess crown. He grins, reaching out to embrace me. I can't help but notice he is wearing sparkling pink nail polish.

"Bro," I say, glancing at his fingers. "Nice fashion statement."

"You should see how good I am at tea parties. Come in! Man, it's good to see you."

I walk inside, and the little girl ducks behind Raine's legs. "Mira," he says, crouching down, "this is Turk, Daddy's friend."

She sticks her thumb into her mouth, like she's sizing me up.

"She's not great with strangers," Raine says. He juggles the baby in his arms. "This bruiser here is Isaac."

I follow him inside, past toys that are littered like confetti, and into the living room. Raine gets me a cold one, but he doesn't take a beer for himself. "I'm drinking alone?"

He shrugs. "Sal doesn't like when I drink in front of the kids. Doesn't think it sets a great example, and some crap like that."

"Where is Sally?" I ask.

"At work! She does radiology at the VA. I'm kind of in between jobs, so I'm home with the hobbits."

"Cool," I say, taking a long pull from the bottle.

Raine sets Isaac on the floor. He starts stumbling around like a very tiny drunk. Mira runs down the hallway into her bedroom, her feet pounding like a round of artillery. "So what's up with you, man?" Raine asks. "You good?"

I rest my elbows on my knees. "I could be better. It's kind of what brought me here."

"Trouble in paradise?"

I realize that Raine has no idea Brit and I had a baby. That we lost that baby. I start to tell him the whole story—from that nigger nurse to the moment Davis stopped breathing. "I'm calling on all the squads. From the Vermont NADS all the way down to the Maryland State Skinheads. I want a day of vengeance to honor my son."

When Raine doesn't respond, I lean forward. "I'm talking vandalism. Good old-fashioned fights. Firebombs. Anything short of a casualty, I figure. It's up to the individual squads and their leaders. But something visible that gets us noticed. And I know it goes against what we've been working toward by blending in, but maybe it's time for a little reminder of our power, you know? There's strength in numbers. If we make a statement that's big enough, they can't arrest us *all*." I look him in the eye. "We deserve this. *Davis* deserves this."

Just then Mira dances down the hallway and drops a crown on her father's head. He pulls it off, looking soberly at the cheap foil circle. "Baby, can you go draw me a picture? That's a good girl." He follows her with his eyes as she goes back to her room. "I'm guessing you didn't hear," Raine says to me.

"Hear what?"

"I'm out, man. I'm not with the Movement anymore."

I stare at him, shocked. Raine was the one who had gotten me into White Power in the first place. Once I had joined NADS, we were brothers for life. It wasn't like this was a job you could just walk away from. It was a calling.

Suddenly I remember the line of swastika tattoos Raine had up and down his arm. I look at his shoulders, his biceps. The swastikas have been repurposed into a sleeve of vines. You can't even tell the symbols were there in the first place.

"It happened a couple years ago. Sal and I had gone to a rally that summer, like you and me and the boys used to, and everything was great except there were guys waiting in line to screw a skinchick in her tent. It freaked Sal out, taking our baby to a place where that was happening. So I started going to the rallies by myself, leaving Sal with the baby. Then we got called into preschool because Mira tried to bury some Chinese kid in the sandbox, because she said she was playing kitty and that's what cats do with their shit. I acted like I was shocked, but as soon as we got out of the building I told Mira what a good girl she was. Then one day I was in the grocery store with Mira. She was, oh, maybe turning three. We were waiting to check out, with a full cart. People were staring at me, you know, because of my tats and all, and I was used to that. Anyway, standing behind us in line, was a black man. And Mira, sweet as could be, said, *Daddy, look at the nigger.*" Raine looks up. "I didn't think nothing of it. But then the woman in front of us in line said to me, *Shame on you.* And the checkout clerk said, *How dare you teach that to an innocent baby?* Before I knew it the whole store was yelling and Mira started to cry. So I grabbed her and left the whole cart of food behind and I ran out to our truck. That was the moment I started thinking maybe I wasn't doing the right thing. I mean, I thought it was my duty to raise my kids to be race warriors—but maybe I wasn't doing Mira any favors. Maybe all I was doing was setting her up for a life where everyone would hate her."

I stare at him. "What else are you going to tell me? You volunteer at the local temple? Your best friend's a gook?"

"Maybe the shit we've been saying all these years isn't legit. It's the ultimate bait and switch, man. They promised us we'd be part of something bigger than us. That we'd be proud of our heritage and our race. And maybe that's, like, ten percent of the whole deal. The rest is just hating everyone else for existing. Once I started thinking that, I couldn't stop. Maybe that's why I felt like shit all the time, like I wanted to fucking bust someone's face in constantly, just to remind myself that I could. That's okay for me. But it's not how I want my kid to grow up." He shrugs. "Once word got around that I wanted out, I knew it was a matter of time. One of my own guys jumped me in a parking lot after Sal and I went to a movie. He messed me up bad enough that I had to get stitches. But then, that was that."

I look at Raine, who used to be my best friend, and it's like the light shifts and I realize I'm looking at something completely different. A coward. A loser.

"It doesn't change anything," Raine says. "We're still brothers, right?"

"Sure," I say. "Always."

"Maybe you and Brit can come up here and go skiing this winter," he suggests.

"That would be awesome." I finish my beer and stand up, make an excuse about having to get back before dark. As I drive away, Raine is waving, and so is baby Isaac.

I know I'll never see them again.

* * *

TWO DAYS LATER I HAVE met with former squad leaders up and down the Eastern Seaboard. With the exception of Raine, they are all active posters on Lonewolf.org, and they all knew about Davis before I even started to relay the story. They all have histories with Francis—they heard him speak at a rally once; they knew a guy he killed; they were personally tapped by him to lead a crew.

Exhausted and hungry, I park on the street in front of our place. When I see the flicker of the television in the living room—even though it's nearly 2:00 A.M.—I suck in my breath. I'd been hoping to just slide into the house unnoticed, but now I'm going to have to come up with some fake excuse for Francis about why I've been running around behind his back.

To my surprise, though, it's not Francis who's got insomnia. Brit is sitting on the couch, wrapped in one of my sweatshirts, which reaches her thighs like a dress. I cross the room, lean down, and drop a kiss on the crown of her head. "Hey, baby," I say. "Can't sleep?"

She shakes her head. I glance at the television, where the Wicked Witch of the West is leaning close to Dorothy, making a threat. "Did you ever watch this?"

"Yeah. You want me to tell you how it ends?" I joke.

"No, I mean *really* watch it. It's like a whole fairy tale about White Power. The wizard who's pulling everyone's strings is a little Jew. The villain is a weird color and works with monkeys."

I kneel down in front of her, drawing her attention. "I did what I promised. I met with all the guys who used to run squads. But no one wants to take a risk. Your dad did too good a job drumming into them that our new approach is to infiltrate, I guess. They just don't want to run the risk of going to prison."

"Well, you and I could—"

"Brit, if something goes down, the first place the cops will look is anyone connected to the Movement. And we're already named in the media, thanks to the lawsuit." I hesitate. "You know I'd do anything for you. But you've only just started to come back to me. If I get sent away to do time, it would be like losing you all over again." I wrap my arms around her. "I'm sorry, baby. I thought I could make it work."

She kisses me. "I know. It was worth a try."

"Come to bed?"

Brit turns off the television, comes into the bedroom with me. Slowly I peel off the sweatshirt she's wearing; I let her tug my boots and jeans off. When we get under the covers, I press against her. But when I go to move between her legs, I'm soft, slipping out of her.

She looks at me in the dark, her eyes hooded, her arm crossed over her soft belly. "Is it me?" she asks, in a voice so small I have to reach for it.

"No," I swear. "You're beautiful. It's stupid shit in my head."

She rolls away. Even like that, I can feel her skin heat up, red with shame.

"I'm sorry," I say to her back.

Brit doesn't answer.

In the middle of the night I wake up and reach for her. I'm not thinking, which is why I do it. Maybe if I get out of my own way, I can find comfort. My hand snakes over the sheets, searching, but Brit is gone.

IN THE BEGINNING THERE WERE many of us, and we were all different. You could be Aryan Nations but not a Skinhead, depending on whether or not you bought into Christian Identity theology. White Supremacists were more academic, publishing treatises; Skinheads were more violent, preferring to teach a lesson with their fists. White Separatists were the guys buying land in North Dakota and trying to divide the country so that anyone nonwhite would be kicked over the perimeter they created. Neo-Nazis were a cross between Aryan Nations and the Aryan Brotherhood in prisons—if there was a violent street gang criminal element to the Movement, they were it. There were Odinists and Creationists and disciples of the World Church of the Creator. But in spite of the ideology that split us into factions, we'd all come together one day of the year to celebrate: April 20, the birthday of Adolf Hitler.

There were birthday festivals scattered around the country, kind of like the old KKK rallies that I went to as a teen. They were usually on someone's back forty, or on a piece of conservation land no one ever monitored, or in whatever passed for an alpine village. Directions were by word of mouth, turns marked off with tiny flags no bigger than those used by electric dog fences, except these weren't pink plastic but SS red.

I'd probably been to five Aryan festivals since I joined up with the White Power Movement, but this one was special. At this one, I was getting married.

Well, in spirit at least. Technically Brit and I would have to go to city hall next week and fill out the legal forms. But spiritually, it would happen tonight.

I was twenty-two years old, and this was the pinnacle of my life.

Brit didn't want me around while she was fussed over by the girls, so I wandered the festival. Overall, there were far fewer people here than at the rallies I'd gone to five years ago, mostly because the feds had started cracking down wherever we congregated. But even so, there were the usual groups of drunks, some brawling, some pissing behind the portable tents where vendors sold everything from corn dogs to thongs printed with the words SKINHEAD LOVE. There was a kid zone with coloring books and a bouncy castle that had a big-ass SS flag draped in the back, like in the Sportpalast where Hitler used to give his speeches. At the end of the row of food and merchandise vendors were the tattoo artists, who were in high demand during festivals like this.

I cut in line, which I knew would piss off the guy I cut. We had the necessary scuffle, and I gave him a bloody nose, and then he shut up and let me take his place. When I sat down in front of the tattoo artist, he looked at me. "What's it going to be?"

Francis and I had been working for six months now to convince squads to stop flaunting sun-wheel tattoos and shaved heads and suspenders and to start looking like ordinary Joes. Part of that meant wearing long sleeves or getting acid treatments to cover up the ink on our faces. But today was a special day. Today, I wanted everyone to know what I stood for.

When I left that tent, there were eight Gothic letters, one inked on each of my finger knuckles. On the right hand, when I made a fist, it read H-A-T-E. On the left, the side closest to my heart, was L-O-V-E.

At sunset, it was time. In the distance was the throaty roar of motorcycles, and everyone who was still at the festival formed two lines. I waited, my hands clasped in front of me, the skin still red and swollen from the new tats.

Then suddenly, the crowd parted, and I could see Brit, backlit in the oranges and yellows of the end of day. She wore a white lace dress that made her look like a cupcake, and her Doc Martens. I started smiling. I smiled so hard that I thought my jaw would crack.

When she was close enough to touch, I tucked her arm into mine. If the world had ended at that moment, I would have been okay with it. We started to walk down the makeshift aisle. As we passed, arms flew up, everyone Sieg Heiling. At the end of the line stood Francis. He smiled at us, his eyes bright and sharp. He had presided over dozens of Aryan weddings, but this one was different. "Ladybug," he said, husky. "Aren't you something?" Then he turned to me. "You fuck with her and I will kill you."

"Yes, sir," I managed.

"Brittany," Francis began, "do you promise to obey Turk and continue the heritage of the White race?"

"I do," she vowed.

"And Turk, will you honor this woman in war as your Aryan bride?"

"I will," I said.

We turned toward each other. I looked her in the eye, unwavering, as we recited the Fourteen Words, the mantra David Lane created when he was running the Order: *We must secure the existence of our people and a future for White children.*

I kissed Brit, while behind us, someone lit a wooden swastika to brand this moment. I swear I felt a shift in me that day. Like I really had handed over half my heart to this woman, and she had given me hers, and the only way we would both continue to survive was with this patchwork.

I was dimly aware of Francis speaking, of people clapping. But I was pulled toward Brit, like we were the last two people on earth.

We might as well have been.

Kennedy

"MY CLIENT HATES ME," I TELL MICAH, AS WE ARE STANDING IN THE kitchen washing dishes.

"I'm sure she doesn't hate you."

I glance at him. "She thinks I'm a racist."

"She has a point," Micah says mildly, and I turn to him, my eyebrows shooting up to my hairline. "You're white and she's not, and you both happen to live in a world where white people have all the power."

"I'm not saying that her life hasn't been harder than mine," I argue. "I'm not one of those people who thinks that just because we elected a black president we're magically postracial. I work with minority clients every day who've been screwed by the healthcare system and the criminal justice system and the educational system. I mean, prisons are run as a business. *Someone's* profiting from keeping a steady stream of people going to jail."

We had hosted some of Micah's colleagues for dinner. I'd had high hopes of serving a gourmet meal but wound up making a taco bar and offering a store-bought bakery pie that I passed off as being homemade after I broke off the edges of the crust a little to make it slightly less perfect. Throughout the evening, my mind wandered. Granted, when conversation drifted toward rates of retinal nerve fiber layer loss in contralateral eyes of glaucoma patients with unilateral progression, I couldn't be blamed. But I already was obsessing over my earlier argument with Ruth. If I was in the right, how come I couldn't stop rehashing what I'd said?

"But you just don't bring up race in a criminal trial," I say. "It's like one of those unspoken rules, you know, like *Don't use your brights in oncoming traffic* . . . or *Don't be the asshole who brings a full cart to the twelve items or less lane.* Even the cases based on stand-your-ground laws steer clear of it, and ninety-nine percent of the time it's a white guy in Florida who got scared by a black kid and pulled a trigger. I get that Ruth feels singled out by her employer. But none of that has to do with a murder charge."

Micah passes me a platter to dry. "Don't take this the wrong way, babe," he says, "but sometimes when you're trying to explain something and you think you're dropping a hint, you're actually more like a Mack truck."

I turn to him, waving my dish towel. "What if one of your patients had cancer, and you were trying to treat it, but she also kept telling you she had poison ivy. Wouldn't you tell her it was more important to focus on getting rid of the cancer, and *then* you'd take care of the rash?"

Micah considers this. "Well, I'm not an oncologist. But sometimes, when you've got an itch, you keep scratching it and you don't even realize that you're doing it."

I am totally lost. "What?"

"It was *your* metaphor."

I sigh. "My client hates me," I say again.

Just then the phone rings. It is nearly 10:30, the time for calls about heart attacks and accidents. I grab the receiver with a damp hand. "Hello?"

"Is this Kennedy McQuarrie?" booms a deep voice, one I know but cannot place.

"It is."

"Excellent! Ms. McQuarrie, this is Reverend Wallace Mercy."

The Wallace Mercy?

I don't even realize I've said that aloud until he chuckles. "Rumors of my superstardom have been greatly exaggerated," he paraphrases. "I am calling about a friend we have in common—Ruth Jefferson."

Immediately, I go into lockdown mode. "Reverend Mercy, I'm not at liberty to discuss a client."

"I assure you, you can. Ruth has asked me to serve as an adviser, of sorts . . ."

I clench my teeth. "My client hasn't signed anything stating that."

"The release, yes, of course. I emailed one to her an hour ago. It will be on your desk tomorrow morning."

What. The. Hell. Why would Ruth go and sign something like that without consulting me? Why wouldn't she even mention that she'd been talking to someone like Wallace Mercy?

But I already know the answer: because I told Ruth her case had nothing to do with racial discrimination, that's why. And Wallace Mercy is about nothing *but* racial discrimination.

"Listen to me," I say, my heart pounding so hard that I can hear its pulse in every word. "Getting Ruth Jefferson acquitted is *my* job, not *yours*. You want to boost your ratings? Don't think you're going to do it on my back."

I end the call, punching the button with such vehemence that the handset goes spinning out of my hand and skitters across the kitchen floor. Micah turns off the faucet. "Damn cordless phones," he says. "It was so much more satisfying back when you could slam them down, right?" He approaches me, his hands in his pockets. "You want to tell me what that was all about?"

"That was Wallace Mercy on the phone. Ruth Jefferson wants him to *advise* her."

Micah whistles long and low. "You're right," he says. "She hates you."

* * *

RUTH OPENS THE DOOR IN her nightgown and bathrobe. "Please," I say. "I only need five minutes of your time."

"Isn't it a little late?"

I don't know if she's talking about the fact that it's almost 11:00 P.M. or the fact that we parted on such a divisive note early this afternoon. I choose to assume the former. "I knew if I called you'd recognize my number and ignore it."

She considers this. "Probably."

I pull my sweater more tightly around me. After Wallace Mercy's call, I got in the car and started driving. I didn't even grab a coat first. All I could think was that I needed to intercept Ruth before she mailed back that release form.

I take a deep breath. "It's not that I don't care about how you were treated—I do. It's that I know having Wallace Mercy involved is going to cost you in the short run, if not the long run."

Ruth watches me shiver again. "Come in," she says, after a moment.

The couch is already made up with pillows and sheets and a blanket, so I sit at the kitchen table as her son pokes his head out of the bedroom. "Mama? What's going on?"

"I'm fine, Edison. Go to bed."

He looks dubious, but he backs up and closes the door.

"Ruth," I beg, "don't sign that release."

She takes a seat at the table, too. "He promised me that he wouldn't interfere with whatever you're doing in court—"

"You'll sabotage yourself," I say bluntly. "Think about it—angry mobs in the street, your face on TV every night, legal pundits weighing in on the case on morning shows—you don't want them taking control of the narrative of this case before *we* have a chance to." I gesture to the closed door of Edison's bedroom. "What about your son? Are you ready to have him dragged into the public eye? Because that's what happens when you become a symbol. The world knows everything about you, and your past, and your family, and crucifies you. Your name will be just as familiar as Trayvon Martin's. You're never going to get your life back."

She meets my gaze. "Neither did he."

The truth of that statement separates us like a canyon. I look down into that abyss and see all the reasons why Ruth shouldn't do this; she looks down and no doubt sees all the reasons why she *should*.

"Ruth, I know you have no reason to trust me, especially given the way white people have treated you recently. But if Wallace Mercy grandstands, you won't be safe. The last thing you want is for your case to be tried in the media. Please, let's do this my way. Give it a chance." I hesitate. "I'm begging you."

She folds her arms. "What if I tell you I want the jury to know what happened to me? To hear my side of the story?"

I nod, striking a bargain. "Then we put you on the stand," I promise.

THE MOST INTERESTING THING ABOUT Jack DeNardi is that he has a rubber band ball on his desk the size of a newborn's head. Other than that he is exactly what you would expect to find working in a dingy cubicle in the Mercy–West Haven Hospital office: paunch, gray skin, comb-over. He's a paper pusher, and the only reason I'm here is that I'm fishing. I want to see if there's anything they'd say about Ruth that might help her—or that is going to hurt her.

"Twenty years," Jack DeNardi says. "That's how long she worked here."

"How many times in those twenty years was Ruth promoted?" I ask.

"Let's see." He pores through the files. "Once."

"Once in twenty years?" I say, incredulous. "Doesn't that seem low to you?"

Jack shrugs. "I'm really not at liberty to discuss that."

"Why is that?" I press. "You're part of a hospital. Isn't your job to help people?"

"Patients," he clarifies. "Not employees."

I snort. Institutions are allowed to scrutinize their personnel and find and label every flaw—but no one ever turns the magnifying glass back on them.

He scrolls through some more paperwork. "The term used in her most recent performance review was *prickly*."

I'm not going to disagree with that.

"Clearly Ruth Jefferson is qualified. But from what I can gather in her file, she was passed over for promotions because she was seen by her superiors as a little . . . uppity."

I frown. "Ruth's superior, Marie Malone . . . how long has she been working here?"

He enters a few keystrokes into his computer. "Roughly ten years."

"So someone who worked here for ten years was giving *Ruth* orders—dubious ones at that—and maybe Ruth questioned them from time to time? Does that sound like she's being uppity . . . or just assertive?"

He turns to me. "I couldn't say."

I stand up. "Thanks for your time, Mr. DeNardi." I gather my coat and my briefcase, and just before I cross the threshold I turn. "Uppity . . . or assertive. Is it possible the adjective changes depending on the color of the employee?"

"I resent that implication, Ms. McQuarrie." Jack DeNardi presses his lips together. "Mercy–West Haven does not discriminate based on race, creed, religion, or sexual orientation."

"Oh, okay. I see," I say. "Then it was just dumb luck that Ruth Jefferson was the employee you chose to throw to the wolves."

As I walk out of the hospital, I consider that none of this conversation can or will be used in court. I'm not even sure what made me turn back at the last minute and toss that final question to the HR employee.

Except, perhaps, that Ruth is rubbing off on me.

THAT WEEKEND, A COLD RAIN pelts the windows. Violet and I sit at the coffee table, coloring. Violet is scribbling across the page, without any regard for the predrawn outline of a raccoon in her coloring book.

"Grandma likes to color inside the lines," my daughter informs me. "She says it's the right way."

"There is no right way or wrong way," I say automatically. I point to her explosion of reds and yellows. "Look how pretty yours is."

Who came up with that rule anyway? Why are there even lines?

When Micah and I went on our honeymoon to Australia, we spent three nights camping in the red center of the country, where the ground was cracked like a parched throat and the night sky looked like a bowl of diamonds that had been upended. We met an Aboriginal man, who showed us the Emu in the Sky, the constellation near the Southern Cross that is not a dot-to-dot puzzle, like our constellations, but the spaces in between the dots—nebulas swirling against the Milky Way to form the long neck and dangling legs of the great bird. I couldn't find it, at first. And then, once I did, it was all I could see.

When my cellphone starts to ring and I recognize Ruth's number, I immediately pick up. "Is everything all right?" I ask.

"Fine." Ruth's voice sounds stiff. "I was wondering if maybe you had any free time this afternoon."

I glance at Micah, who's come into the living room. *Ruth*, I mouth.

He scoops up Violet, tickling her, letting me know that I have all the time I need. "Of course," I say. "Was there something in the discovery you wanted to talk about?"

"Not exactly. I need to go shopping for a birthday gift for my mama. And I thought you might like to come along."

I recognize an olive branch when I see it. "I'd like that," I say.

As I drive to Ruth's, I think about all the reasons this is a colossal mistake. When I was starting out as public defender, I spent my salary, which didn't even cover my groceries for the week, on my clients when I could see they needed a clean set of clothes or a hot meal. It took me a while to realize that helping my clients couldn't extend to my bank account. Ruth seems too proud to drag me to a mall and hint that she could really use a new pair of shoes, however. I think maybe she just wants to clear the air between us.

But as we drive to the mall, all we discuss is the weather—when the rain is going to stop, if it might turn to sleet. Then we talk about where we will be spending the upcoming holidays. At Ruth's suggestion, I park near T.J.Maxx. "So," I say. "Are you looking for something in particular?"

She shakes her head. "I'll know it when I see it. There are items that just scream my mama's name, usually ones covered in sequins." Ruth smiles. "The way she dresses for church, you'd think she was headed to a black-tie wedding. I always figured it was because she wears a uniform all week long, maybe this was her way of cutting loose."

"Did you grow up here in Connecticut?" I ask, as we get out of the car.

"No. Harlem. I used to take the bus into Manhattan every day with my mama to work, and then get dropped off at Dalton."

"You and your sister went to Dalton?" I ask.

"I did. Adisa wasn't quite as . . . scholarly minded. It was Wesley who made me settle in Connecticut."

"How did you two meet?"

"At a hospital," Ruth says. "I was a nursing student, on an L and D ward, and there was a woman having a baby whose husband was in the service. She had tried and tried to contact him. She was delivering twins a month early, and she was scared, and convinced she was gonna have those babies alone. Suddenly when she was in the middle of pushing, a guy comes flying in, wearing camo. He takes one look at her and drops like a stone. Since I was just a student, I was stuck taking care of the fainter."

"So wait," I say. "Wesley was married to someone else when you met?"

"That's what I assumed. When he came to, he started hitting on me, turning up the charm. I thought he was the biggest jackass I'd ever met, flirting while his wife was delivering his twins, and I told him so. Turned out they weren't his babies. His best friend was the father, but was out training and couldn't get furlough, so Wesley promised to take his place and help the guy's wife till he got there." Ruth laughs. "That's about when I started thinking maybe he wasn't the biggest jackass after all. We had some good years, Wesley and me."

"When did he pass away?"

"When Edison was seven."

I can't imagine losing Micah; I can't imagine raising Violet by my-self. What Ruth has done with her life, I realize, is braver than any-thing I've ever done. "I'm sorry."

"Me too," Ruth sighs. "But you know, you go on, right? Because what other choice have you got?" She turns to me. "Mama taught me that, as a matter of fact. Maybe I'll find it embroidered on a pillow."

"In glitter," I say, and we walk through the store doors.

Ruth tells me about Sam Hallowell, whose name rings a faint bell, and how her mother has been working as a domestic in that household for almost fifty years. She talks about Christina, who gave her her first illicit sip of brandy when she was twelve, from her father's liquor cabi-net, and who paid her way through trigonometry, buying the answers to tests off an exchange student from Beijing. She tells me, too, how Christina tried to give her money. "She sounds awful," I admit.

Ruth considers this. "She's not. It's just what she knows. She never learned any other way of being."

We move through the aisles, trading stories. She confesses that she wanted to be an anthropologist, until she studied Lucy the *Australo-pithecus*: *How many women from Ethiopia do* you *know named Lucy?* I tell her how my water broke in the middle of a trial, and the dick of a judge wouldn't give me a continuance. She tells me about Adisa, who con-vinced her when she was five that the reason Ruth was so pale by com-parison was because she was turning into a ghost, that she'd been born black as a berry but was fading away little by little. I tell her about the client I hid in my basement for three weeks, because she was so sure her husband was going to kill her. She tells me about a man who, in the middle of labor, told his girlfriend she needed to wax. I confess that I haven't seen my father, who is in an institution for Alzheimer's, in over a year, because the last time I was so sad I couldn't shake the visit for months. Ruth admits that walking through Adisa's neighborhood scares her.

I am starving, so I grab a box of caramel corn from a display and open it as we talk, only to find Ruth staring at me. "What are you doing?" she asks.

"Eating?" I say, my mouth full of popcorn. "Take some. It's my treat."

"But you haven't paid for it yet."

I look at her like she's crazy. "I'm *going* to, obviously, when we leave. What's the big deal?"

"I mean—"

But before she can answer, we are interrupted by an employee. "Can I help you find something?" she asks, looking directly at Ruth.

"Just browsing," Ruth says.

The woman smiles, but she doesn't leave. She trails us at a distance, like a child's toy being dragged on a string. Ruth either doesn't notice or doesn't choose to notice. I suggest gloves or a nice winter scarf, but Ruth says her mother has one lucky scarf she's owned forever, and she'd never trade up. Ruth keeps up a steady patter of conversation until we find a section of bargain basement DVDs. "This might be fun. I could do up a whole bunch of her favorite shows, and package them with microwave popcorn and call it movie night." She begins sifting through the barrels of DVDs: *Saved by the Bell. Full House. Buffy the Vampire Slayer*.

"*Dawson's Creek*," I say. "Man, does that take me back. I was absolutely going to grow up and marry Pacey."

"Pacey? What kind of name is that?"

"Didn't you ever watch it?"

Ruth shakes her head. "I've got about ten years on you. And if there was ever a white-girl show, this was it."

I reach deep into the barrel and pull out a season of *The Cosby Show*. I think about showing it to Ruth, but then hide it underneath a box of *The X-Files*, because what if she thinks that the only reason I'm picking it is the color of their skin? But Ruth plucks it out of my hand. "Did you watch this when it was on TV?"

"Of course. Didn't everyone?" I say.

"I guess that was the point. If you make the most functional family on TV a black one, maybe white folks won't be quite as terrified."

"Don't know that I'd use the words *Cosby* and *functional* in the same sentence these days," I muse, as the T.J.Maxx employee walks up to us again.

"Everything all right?"

"*Yeah,*" I say, getting annoyed. "We'll let you know if we need help."

Ruth decides on *ER*, because her mother has a crush on George Clooney, along with mittens that have real rabbit fur sewed along the edges. I pick up a pair of pajamas for Violet, and a pack of undershirts for Micah. When we walk up to the cash register, the manager follows us. I pay first, handing over my credit card to the cashier, and then wait for Ruth to finish her transaction.

"Do you have any ID?" the cashier asks. Ruth pulls out her license and Social Security card. The cashier looks at her, then at the picture on the license, and rings up the items.

As we are leaving the store, a security guard stops us. "Ma'am," he says to Ruth, "can I see your receipt?"

I start to rummage in my bag so that he can check mine, too, but he waves me away. "You're fine," he says dismissively, and he turns his attention back to Ruth, matching the contents of the bag with what's been rung up.

That's when I realize that Ruth didn't want me to come here with her because she needed help picking out a present for her mother.

Ruth wanted me to come here so that I could understand what it was like to be her.

The manager hovering, in case of shoplifting.

The wariness of the cashier.

The fact that out of a dozen people leaving T.J.Maxx at the same time, Ruth was the only one whose bag was checked.

I can feel my cheeks redden—embarrassed on Ruth's behalf, embarrassed because I didn't realize what was going on even as it was happening. When the security guard gives Ruth back the bag, we leave the store, running through the driving rain to my car.

Inside, we sit, out of breath and soaked. The rain is a sheet between us and the world. "I get it," I say.

Ruth looks at me. "You haven't even *begun* to get it," she replies, not unkindly.

"But you didn't *say* anything," I point out. "Do you just get used to it?"

"I don't imagine you ever get used to it. But you figure out how to let it go."

I hear her words about Christina, echoing in my mind: *She never learned any other way of being.*

Our eyes meet. "True confession? The worst grade I got in college was for a course on black history. I was the only white girl in the seminar. I did fine on exams, but half of the grade was participation, and I never opened my mouth that semester, not once. I figured if I did, I'd say the wrong thing, or something stupid that made me sound prejudiced. But then I worried that all those other kids thought I didn't give a damn about the subject because I never contributed to the discussion."

Ruth is quiet for a moment. "True confession? The reason we don't talk about race is because we do not speak a common language."

We sit for a few moments, listening to the rain. "True confession? I never really liked *The Cosby Show*."

"True confession?" Ruth grins. "Neither did I."

THROUGHOUT DECEMBER, I DOUBLE DOWN on my efforts to keep my nose to the grindstone. I sort through discovery, I write pretrial motions, and I catch up on the other thirty cases vying with Ruth's for a moment of my attention. After lunch, I am supposed to depose a twenty-three-year-old who was beaten up by her boyfriend when he found out she was sleeping with his brother. However, the witness gets into a fender-bender on the way so we have to reschedule, leaving me with two hours free. I look down at the mountains of paperwork surrounding my desk and make a snap decision. I poke my head over the edge of my cubicle, toward where Howard is sitting. "If anyone asks," I tell him, "say I had to go out to buy tampons."

"Wait. Really?"

"No. But then they'll be embarrassed, and it serves them right for checking up on me."

It's unseasonably warm—almost fifty degrees. I know that when the weather is good my mother usually picks Violet up from school and walks her to the playground. They have a snack—apples and nuts—and then Violet plays on the jungle gym before heading home. Sure enough, Violet is hanging upside down from the monkey bars, her skirt tickling her chin, when she sees me. "Mommy!" she cries, and with a grace and athleticism that must have come from Micah's genes, she flips herself to the ground and races toward me.

As I lift her into my arms, my mother turns around on the bench. "Did you get fired?" she asks.

I raise a brow. "Is that honestly the first thing that pops into your mind?"

"Well, the last time you made an impromptu visit in the middle of the day I think it was because Micah's father was dying."

"Mommy," Violet announces, "I made you a Christmas present at school and it's a necklace and also birds can eat it." She squirms in my embrace, so I set her down, and immediately she runs back to the play structure.

My mother pats the spot on the bench beside her. She is bundled up in spite of the temperature, has her e-reader on her lap, and beside her is a little Tupperware bento box with apple slices and mixed nuts. "So," she says, "if you still have a job, to what do we owe this very excellent surprise?"

"A car accident—not mine." I pop a handful of nuts into my mouth. "What are you reading?"

"Why, sugar, I'd never read while my grandbaby is on a jungle gym. My eyes never leave her."

I roll my eyes. "What are you reading?"

"I don't remember the name. Something about a duchess with cancer and the vampire who offers to make her immortal. Apparently it's a genre called sick lit," my mother says. "It's for book club."

"Who chose it?"

"Not me. I don't pick the books. I pick the wine."

"The last book I read was *Everyone Poops*," I say, "so I guess I can't really pass judgment."

I lean back, tilting my face to the late afternoon sun. My mother pats her lap, and I stretch out on the bench, lying down. She plays with my hair, the way she used to when I was Violet's age. "You know the hardest thing about being a mom?" I say idly. "That you never get time to be a kid anymore."

"You never get time, period," my mother replies. "And before you know it, your little girl is off saving the world."

"Right now she's just enjoying stuffing her face," I say, holding out my hand for more nuts. I slip one between my lips and almost immediately spit it out. "Ugh, God, I hate Brazil nuts."

"Is that what those are?" my mother says. "They taste like feet. They're the poor bastard stepchildren of the mixed nuts tin, the ones nobody likes."

Suddenly I remember being about Violet's age, and going to my grandmother's home for Thanksgiving dinner. It was packed with my aunts and uncles and cousins. I loved the sweet potato pie she made, and the doilies on her furniture, which were all different, like snowflakes. But I did my absolute best to avoid Uncle Leon, my grandfather's brother, who was the relative that was too loud, too drunk, and who always seemed to kiss you on the lips when he was aiming for your cheek. My grandmother used to put a big bowl of nuts out as an appetizer, and Uncle Leon would man the nutcracker, shelling them and passing them to the kids: walnuts and hazelnuts and pecans, cashews and almonds and Brazil nuts. Except he never called them Brazil nuts. He'd hold up a wrinkled, long brown shell. *Nigger toes for sale*, he'd say. *Who wants a nigger toe?*

"Do you remember Uncle Leon?" I ask abruptly, sitting up. "What he used to call them?"

My mother sighs. "Yes. Uncle Leon was a bit of a character."

I hadn't even known what the N-word meant, back then. I'd laughed, like everyone else. "How come no one ever said something to him? How come you didn't shut him up?"

She looks at me, exasperated. "It wasn't like Leon was ever gonna change."

"Not if he had an audience," I point out. I nod toward the sandbox, where Violet is shoulder to shoulder with a little black girl, chipping away at the packed sand with a stick. "What if she repeated what Leon used to say, because she doesn't know better? How do you think that would go over?"

"Back then, North Carolina wasn't like it is here," my mother says.

"Maybe that wouldn't have been the case if people like you had stopped making excuses."

I feel bad as soon as the words leave my mouth, because I know I'm berating my mother when I really want to beat up on myself. Legally I still know that the soundest course for Ruth is to avoid any discussion of race, but morally, I'm having a hard time reconciling that. What if the reason I have been so quick to dismiss the racial elements of Ruth's case is not because our legal system can't bear that load, but because I was born into a family where black jokes were as much of the holiday tradition as my grandmother's bone china and sausage stuffing? My own mother, for God's sake, grew up with someone like Ruth's mom in the house—cooking, cleaning, walking her to school, taking her to playgrounds like this one.

My mother is quiet for so long that I know I've offended her. "In 1954, when I was nine years old, a court ruled that five black children could come to my school. I remember one boy in my class who said they had horns, hidden in their fuzzy hair. And my teacher, who warned us that they might try to steal our lunch money." She turns to me. "The night before they came to school, my daddy held a meeting. Uncle Leon was there. People talked about how white children would be bullied, and how there'd be classroom control issues, because those kids didn't know how to behave. Uncle Leon was so mad his face was red and sweaty. He said he didn't want his daughter to be a guinea pig. They were planning to picket outside the school the next day, even though they knew there would be police there, making sure the kids could get inside. My daddy swore he would never sell Judge Haw-thorne another car again."

She starts collecting the nuts and the apples, packing them up. "Beattie, our maid, she was there that night too. Serving lemonade and cakes she'd made that afternoon. In the middle of the meeting I got bored, and went into the kitchen, and found her crying. I'd never seen

Beattie cry before. She said that her little boy was one of those five who'd be bused in." My mother shakes her head. "I didn't even know she had a little boy. Beattie had been with my family since before I could walk or talk, and I didn't ever consider she might belong with someone other than us."

"What happened?" I ask.

"Those children came to school. The police walked them inside. Other kids called them horrible names. One boy got spit on. I remember him walking by me, the saliva running down into his white collar, and I wondered if he was Beattie's son." She shrugs. "Eventually there were more of them. They kept to themselves, eating together at lunch and playing together at recess. And we kept to ourselves. I can't say it was much of a desegregation, really."

My mother nods toward Violet and her little friend, sprinkling grass over their mud pies. "This has been going on so much longer than either of us, Kennedy. From where you stepped in, in your life, it looks like we've got miles to go. But me?" She smiles in the direction of the girls. "I look at that, and I guess I'm amazed at how far we've come."

AFTER CHRISTMAS AND NEW YEAR'S, I find myself doing the work of two public defenders, literally, because Ed is vacationing with his family in Cozumel. I'm in court representing one of Ed's clients, who violated a restraining order, so I decide to check the docket to see which judge has been assigned to Ruth's case. One typical pastime for lawyers is storing away the details of the personal lives of judges—who they marry, if they're wealthy, if they go to church every weekend or just on high-water-mark holidays, if they're dumber than a bag of hammers, if they like musical theater, if they go out drinking with attorneys when they are off the clock. We store away these facts and rumors like squirrels put away nuts for winter, so that when we see who is assigned to our case, we can pull out the minutiae and figure out if we have a fighting chance of winning.

When I see who it is, my heart sinks.

Judge Thunder lives up to his name. He's a hanging judge, and he prejudges cases, and if you get convicted, you're going away for a long, long time. I know this not from hearsay, however, but from personal experience.

Before I was a public defender, when I was clerking for a federal judge, one of my colleagues became tangled up in an ethical issue involving a conflict of interest from his previous job at a law firm. I was part of the team that represented him, and after years of building the case, we went to trial in front of Judge Thunder. He hated any kind of media circus, and the fact that a federal judge's clerk was caught in an ethical violation had turned our trial into just that. Even though we had an airtight case, Thunder wanted to set a precedent for other attorneys, and my colleague was convicted and sentenced to six years. If that wasn't shocking enough, the judge turned to all of us who had been on the defense team. "You should be ashamed of yourselves. Mr. Dennehy has fooled you all," Judge Thunder scolded. "But he hasn't fooled this court." For me, it was the last straw. I had been burning the candle at both ends, working for about a week without sleep. I was sick as a dog, on cold medication and heavy doses of prednisone, exhausted and demoralized after losing the case—so perhaps I was not as gracious or lucid as I could have been in that moment.

I might have told Judge Thunder he could suck my dick.

What ensued was a chambers conference where I begged to not be disbarred and assured the judge that I did not have, in fact, any male genitalia and had actually said, *Such magic!* because I was so impressed by his ruling.

I've had two cases in front of Judge Thunder since then. I've lost both.

I resolve not to tell Ruth about my history with the judge. Maybe the third time is a charm.

I button my coat, getting ready to leave the courthouse, giving myself a silent pep talk the whole way. I'm not going to let a tiny setback like this affect the whole case for me, not when we have jury selection next month.

As I walk out of the building, I hear the swell of gospel music.

On the New Haven Green is a sea of black people. Their arms are linked. Their voices harmonize and fill the sky: *We shall overcome.* They carry posters with Ruth's name and likeness on them.

Front and center is Wallace Mercy, singing his heart out. And beside him, her elbow tucked in his, is Ruth's sister, Adisa.

Ruth

I'M WORKING THE CASH REGISTER, GETTING TOWARD THE END OF MY shift, when my arches ache and my back hurts. Although I took as many extra shifts as I could, it was a bleak and meager Christmas, and Edison spent most of it sullen and moody. He's been back at school for a week, but there's been a seismic shift in him—he barely talks to me, grunting out responses to my questions, riding the knife edge of rudeness until I call him on it; he's stopped doing his homework at the kitchen table and instead vanishes into his room and blares Drake and Kendrick Lamar; his phone buzzes constantly with texts, and when I ask him who needs him so desperately he says it's nobody I know. I have not received any more calls from the principal, or emails from his teachers telling me he's slacking on his work, but that doesn't mean I'm not anticipating them.

And then what will I do? How am I supposed to encourage my son to be better than most people expect him to be? How can I say, with a straight face, *you can be anything you want in this world*—when I struggled and studied and excelled and still wound up on trial for something I did not do? Every time Edison and I get into it these days, I can see that challenge in his eyes: *I dare you. I dare you to say you still believe that lie.*

School has let out; I know this because of the influx of teens who explode into the building like a holiday, filling the space with bright ribbons of laughter and teasing. Inevitably they know someone working table and call out, begging for free McNuggets or a sundae. Usually they don't bother me; I prefer to be busy rather than slow. But today, a girl comes up to me, her blond ponytail swinging, holding her phone while her friends crowd around to read an incoming text with her. "Welcome to McDonald's," I say. "Can I help you?"

There is a line of people behind her, but she looks at her friend. "What should I tell him?"

"That you can't talk because you're meeting up with someone," one of the girls suggests.

Another girl shakes her head. "No, don't write anything. Keep him waiting."

Like the customers behind her in line, I am starting to get annoyed. "Excuse me," I try again, pasting a smile on my face. "Are you ready to order?"

She glances up. She has blush on her cheeks that has glitter in it; it makes her look awfully young, which I'm sure is not what she's going for. "Do you have onion rings?"

"No, that's Burger King. Our menu is up there." I point overhead. "If you're not ready, maybe you can step aside?"

She looks at her two friends, and her eyebrows shoot up to her hairline as if I've said something offensive. "Don't worry, mama, I was jus' aksin' . . . "

I freeze. This girl isn't Black. She's about as far from Black as possible. So why is she talking to me like that?

Her friend cuts in front of her and orders a large fries; her other friend has a Diet Coke and a snack wrap. The girl orders a Happy Meal, and as I angrily stuff the items into the box, the irony is not lost on me.

Three customers later, I'm still watching her out of the corner of my eye as she eats her cheeseburger.

I turn to the runner who's working at the register with me. "I'll be right back."

I walk into the dining area where the girl is still holding court with her friends. ". . . so I said, right to her face, *Who lit the fuse on your tampon?*—"

"Excuse me," I interrupt. "I did not appreciate the way you spoke to me at the counter."

A hot blush burns in her cheeks. "Wow, okay. I'm sorry," she says, but her lips twitch.

My boss suddenly is standing beside me. Jeff is a former middle manager at a ball bearing plant who got cut when the economy tanked, and he runs the restaurant like we are giving out state secrets and not French fries. "Ruth? Is there a problem?"

There are *so* many problems. From the fact that I am not this girl's *mama* to the fact that she will not remember this conversation an hour from now. But if I choose this particular moment to stand up for myself, I will pay a price. "No, sir," I tell Jeff, and in silence, I walk back to my register.

MY DAY ONLY GETS WORSE when I leave work and see six missed phone calls from Kennedy. I immediately ring her back. "I thought you agreed that working with Wallace Mercy was a bad idea," she hammers, without even saying hello.

"What? I did. I *do*."

"So you had no idea that he was leading a march in your honor today in front of the courthouse?"

I stop walking, letting the foot traffic funnel around me. "You gotta be kidding. Kennedy, I did *not* talk to Wallace."

"Your sister was shoulder to shoulder with him."

Well, mystery solved. "Adisa tends to do whatever she wants."

"Can't you control her?"

"I've been trying for forty-four years but it hasn't worked yet."

"Try harder," Kennedy tells me.

Which is how I wind up taking the bus to my sister's apartment, instead of going right home. When Donté lets me in, Adisa is sitting on the couch playing Candy Crush on her phone, even though it is nearly dinnertime. "Well, look what the cat drug in," she says. "Where you been?"

"It's been crazy since New Year's. Between work, and going over things for trial, I haven't had a free minute."

"I came by the other day, did Edison tell you?"

I kick her feet off the couch so there's room for me to sit. "Did you come over to tell me your new best friend is Wallace Mercy?"

Adisa's eyes light up. "You see me on the news today? It was just my elbow and up to here on my neck, but you can tell it's me by the coat. I wore the one with the leopard collar—"

"I want you to stop," I say. "I don't need Wallace Mercy."

"Your white lawyer tell you that?"

"Adisa," I sigh. "I never wanted to be someone's poster child."

"You didn't even give Reverend Mercy a chance. You know how many of our people have had experiences like yours? How many times they been told no because of their skin color? This is bigger than just your story, and if some good can come out of what happened to you, why not let it?" Adisa sits up. "All he wants is a chance to sit down with us, Ruth. On national television."

Alarm bells ring in my head. "*Us*," I repeat.

Adisa's gaze slides away. "Well," she admits, "I indicated that I might be able to change your mind."

"So this isn't even about helping me move forward. It's about *you* getting recognition. Jesus, Adisa. This is a new low, even for you."

"What's *that* supposed to mean?" She gets to her feet and stares down at me, her hands balanced on her hips. "You really think I'd use my baby sister like that?"

I challenge her. "You really gonna stand here drenched to the bone and tell me it's not raining?"

Before she can answer there is a loud crash as a door falls back on its hinges and slams into the wall. Tabari swaggers out from one of the bedrooms with a friend. "You rob a trucker fuh that hat, yo?" He laughs. They are amped up, loud, their pants riding so low I don't know why they even bother to wear them. All I can think is that I'd never let Edison out of the house like that, like he was looking to intimidate.

Then Tabari's friend turns around and I realize it's my son.

"Edison?"

"Ain't it nice," Adisa says, smiling. "The cousins hanging?"

"What are you doing here?" Edison says, in a tone that lets me know this is not a pleasant surprise.

"Don't you have homework to do?"

"Did it."

"College applications?"

He looks at me, his eyes hooded. "They ain't due for another week."

Ain't?

"What's the problem?" he asks. "You're always telling me how important *family* is." He says that word as if it is a swear.

"Where exactly are you and Tabari going?"

Tabari looks up. "The movies, Auntie," he says.

"The movies." *Like hell*, I think. "What film are you seeing?"

He and Edison exchange a look and start laughing. "We gonna pick when we get there," Tabari says.

Adisa steps forward, arms crossed. "You got a problem with that, Ruth?"

"Yes. Yes I do," I explode. "Because I think it's a lot more likely that your son is going to take Edison down by the basketball court to smoke weed than to see the next Oscar nominee."

My sister's jaw drops. "You judging my family," she hisses, "when *you* on trial for murder?"

I grab Edison's arm. "You're coming with me," I announce, and then I turn to Adisa. "Have fun doing your interview with Wallace Mercy. Just make sure you tell him, and the adoring public, that you and your sister are no longer on speaking terms."

With that, I drag my son out of her home. I rip the hat off his head when we get downstairs and tell him to pull up his pants. We are halfway to the bus station before he says a word. "I'm sorry," Edison begins.

"You better be," I answer, rounding on him. "You lost your damn mind? I didn't raise you to be like this."

"Tabari's not as bad as his friends."

I start walking, and I don't look back. "Tabari is not my son," I say.

WHEN I WAS PREGNANT WITH Edison, all I knew was that I didn't want the experience of giving birth to be anything like Adisa's—who claimed to not even realize she was pregnant for six months when she had her first baby, and who practically had her second on the subway. Me, I wanted the best care I could get, the finest doctors. Since Wesley was on a tour of duty, I enlisted Mama as my birthing coach. When it was time, we took a taxi to Mercy–West Haven because Mama couldn't drive and I was in no state to. I had planned for a natural birth, because as a labor and delivery nurse I'd written this moment in my head a thousand times, but just like any well-laid plan, that wasn't in the cards for me. As I was being wheeled into the OR for a C-section, Mama was singing Baptist hymns, and when I came to after the procedure, she was holding my son.

"Ruth," she said to me, her eyes so full of pride they were a color I'd never seen before. "Ruth, look at what God made for you."

She held the baby out to me, and I suddenly realized that although I'd planned my first birth down to the minute, I hadn't organized a single second of what might come afterward. I had no idea how to be a mother. My son was stiff in my arms, and then he opened his mouth and started wailing, like this world was an affront to him.

Panicked, I looked up at my mama. I was a straight-A student; I was an overachiever. I had never imagined that this—the most natural of all relationships—would make me feel so incompetent. I jiggled the baby in my arms, but that only made him cry louder. His feet kicked like he was traveling on an imaginary bicycle; his arms flailed, each tiny finger flexed and rigid. His screams grew tighter and tighter, an uneven seam of anger punctuated by the tiny knots of his hiccups. His cheeks were red with effort, as he tried to tell me something I was not equipped to understand.

"Mama?" I begged. "What do I do?"

I held out my arms to her, hoping she would take him and calm him down. But she just shook her head. "You tell him who you are to him," she instructed, and she took a step back, as if to remind me I was in this by myself.

So I bent my face close to his. I pressed his spine up under my heart, where it had been for so many months. "Your name is Edison Wesley Jefferson," I whispered. "I am your mama, and I'm going to give you the best life I can."

Edison blinked. He stared up at me through his dark eyes, as if I were a shadow he had to distinguish from the rest of this new, strange world. His cries hitched twice, a train headed off its track, and then crashed into silence.

I could tell you the exact minute my son relaxed into his new surroundings. I know this detail because it was the moment I did the same.

"See," Mama said, from somewhere behind me, somewhere outside the circle of just us two. "I told you so."

KENNEDY AND I MEET EVERY two weeks, even when there's no new information. Sometimes she'll text me, or stop by McDonald's to say hello. At one of these visits she invites me and Edison over for dinner.

Before going to Kennedy's home, I change three times. Finally Edison knocks on the bathroom door. "We going to your lawyer's," he asks, "or to meet the queen?"

He's right. I don't know why I'm nervous. Except that this feels like crossing a line. It's one thing to have her here to review information about my case, but this invitation didn't have any work attached to it. This invitation was more like . . . a social call.

Edison is dressed in a button-down shirt and khaki pants and has been told on penalty of death that he will behave like the gentleman I know him to be, or I will whup him when he gets home. When we ring the doorbell, the husband—Micah, that's his name—answers, with a girl tucked under his arm like a rag doll. "You must be Ruth," he says, taking the bouquet I offer and shaking my hand warmly, then shaking Edison's. He pivots, then turns the other way. "My daughter, Violet, is around here somewhere . . . I just saw her . . . I'm sure she'll want to say hello." As he twists, the little girl whips around, her hair flying, her giggles falling over my feet like bubbles.

She slips out of her dad's arm, and I kneel down. Violet McQuarrie looks like a tiny version of her mama, albeit dressed in a Princess Tiana costume. I hold out a Mason jar that is filled with miniature white lights, and flip the switch so that it illuminates. "This is for you," I tell her. "It's a fairy jar."

Her eyes widen. "Wow," Violet breathes, and she takes it and runs off.

I get to my feet. "It also doubles as an excellent night-light," I tell Micah, as Kennedy comes out of the kitchen, wearing jeans and a sweater and an apron.

"You made it!" she says, smiling. She has spaghetti sauce on her chin.

"Yes," I answer. "I must have driven past your place a hundred times. I just didn't know, you know, that you lived here."

And still wouldn't, had I not been indicted for murder. I know she's thinking it, too, but Micah saves the moment. "Drink? Can I get you something, Ruth? We have wine, beer, gin and tonic . . ."

"Wine would be nice."

We sit down in the living room. There is already a cheese plate on the coffee table. "Look at that," Edison murmurs to me. "A basketful of crackers."

I shoot him a look that could make a bird fall from the sky.

"It's so nice of you to invite us into your home," I say politely.

"Well, don't thank me yet," Kennedy replies. "Dinner with a four-year-old is not exactly a gourmet dining experience." She smiles at Violet, who is coloring on the other side of the coffee table. "Needless to say we don't entertain much these days."

"I remember when Edison was that age. I am pretty sure we ate a variation of macaroni and cheese every night for a full year."

Micah crosses his legs. "Edison, my wife tells me you're quite the student."

Yes. Because I neglected to mention to Kennedy that of late, he's been suspended.

"Thank you, sir," Edison replies. "I've been applying to colleges."

"Oh yeah? That's great. What do you want to study?"

"History, maybe. Or politics."

Micah nods, interested. "Are you a big fan of Obama?"

Why do white people always assume that?

"I was kind of young when he was running," Edison says. "But I went around with my mom campaigning for Hillary, when she was running against him. I guess because of my dad I'm sensitive to military issues, and her position on the Iraq War made more sense at the time; she was vocally in favor of invasion and Obama was opposed from the start."

I puff up with pride. "Well," Micah says, impressed. "I look forward to seeing your name on a ticket one day."

Violet, clearly bored by this conversation, steps over my legs to hold out a crayon to Edison. "Wanna color?" she asks.

"Um, yeah, okay," Edison replies. He sinks down to his knees, shoulder to shoulder with Kennedy's girl, so that he can reach the coloring book. He starts making Cinderella's dress green.

"No," Violet interrupts, a tiny despot. "That's supposed to be *blue*." She points to Cinderella's dress in the coloring book, half hidden beneath Edison's broad palm.

"Violet," Kennedy says, "we let our guests make their own choices, remember?"

"That's okay, Mrs. McQuarrie. I wouldn't want to mess with Cinderella," Edison answers.

The little girl proudly hands him the right color crayon, a blue one. Edison bends his head and starts to scribble again.

"Next week you start jury selection?" I ask. "Should I be worried about that?"

"No, of course not. It's just—"

"Edison?" Violet asks. "Is that a chain?"

He touches the necklace he's been wearing lately, ever since he started hanging with his cousin. "Yeah, I guess so."

"So that means you're a slave," she states matter-of-factly.

"Violet!" Both Micah and Kennedy shout her name simultaneously.

"Oh my God, Edison. Ruth. I'm so sorry," Kennedy blusters. "I don't know where she would have heard that—"

"In school," Violet announces. "Josiah told Taisha that people who look like her used to wear chains and their history was that they were slaves."

"We'll discuss this later," Micah says. "Okay, Vi? It's not something to talk about now."

"It's okay," I say, even though I can feel the unease in the room, as if someone has taken away all the oxygen. "Do you know what a slave is?"

Violet shakes her head.

"It's when someone owns someone else."

I watch the little girl turn this over in her head. "Like a pet?"

Kennedy puts her hand on my arm. "You don't have to do this," she says quietly.

"Don't you think I already *had* to, once?" I glance at her daughter again. "Kind of like a pet, but also different. A long time ago, people who looked like you and your mama and daddy found a place in the world where people looked like me, and like Edison, and like Taisha. And we were doing things so fine there—building homes, and cooking food, making something out of nothing—that they wanted it in their country too. So they brought over the people who looked like me, without asking our permission. We didn't have a choice. So a slave— that's just someone who doesn't have a choice in what they do, or what's done to them."

Violet sets down her crayon. Her face is twisted in thought.

"We weren't the first slaves," I tell her. "There are stories in a book I like, called the Bible. The Egyptians made Jewish people slaves who would build cities for them. They were able to make the Jewish people slaves because the Egyptians were the ones with the power."

Then, like any other four-year-old, Violet bounces back to her spot beside my son. "Let's color Rapunzel instead," she announces—but then she hesitates. "I mean," she corrects, "do *you* want to color Rapunzel?"

"Okay," Edison says.

I may be the only person who notices, but while I've been explaining, he has taken off that chain from his neck and slipped it into his pocket.

"Thank you," Micah says, sincere. "That was a really perfect Black history lesson."

"Slavery isn't Black history," I point out. "It's *everyone's* history."

A timer goes off, and Kennedy stands up. When she goes into the kitchen, I murmur something about wanting to help her and follow her. Immediately, she turns, her cheeks burning. "I am so, so sorry for that, Ruth."

"Don't be. She's a baby. She doesn't know any better yet."

"Well, you did a much better job explaining than I ever would have."

I watch her reach into the oven for a lasagne. "When Edison came home from school and asked if we were slaves, he was about the same age as Violet. And the last thing I wanted was to have that talk and leave him feeling like a victim."

"Violet told me last week she wished she could be just like Taisha, because she gets to wear beads in her hair."

"What did you say?"

Kennedy hesitates. "I don't know. I probably bungled it. I said something about how everyone's different and that's what makes the world great. I swear, when she asks me things about race I turn into a freaking Coke commercial."

I laugh. "In your defense, you probably don't talk about it quite as much as I do. Practice makes perfect."

"But you know what? When I was her age, I had a Taisha in my class too—except her name was Lesley. And God, I wanted to be her. I used to dream that I'd wake up Black. No joke."

I raise my brows in mock horror. "And give up your winning lottery ticket? No way."

She looks at me, and we both laugh, and in that instant we are merely two women, standing over a lasagne, telling the truth. In that instant, with our flaws and confessions trailing like a slip from a dress, we have more in common than we have differences.

I smile, and Kennedy smiles, and for that moment, at least, we really, really see each other. It's a start.

Suddenly Edison comes into the kitchen holding out my cellphone. "What's the matter?" I tease. "Don't tell me you were fired because you made Ariel a brunette?"

"Mama, it's Ms. Mina," he says. "I think you better take it."

ONE CHRISTMAS, WHEN I WAS ten, I got a Black Barbie. Her name was Christie, and she was just like the dolls Christina had, except for the skin color, and except for the fact that Christina had a whole shoe box full of Barbie clothes and my mama couldn't afford those. Instead, she made Christie a wardrobe out of old socks and dish towels. She glued me a dream house out of shoe boxes. I was over the moon. This was even better than Christina's collection, I told Mama, because I was the only person in the world who had it. My sister, Rachel, who was twelve, made fun of me. "Call them what you want," she told me. "But they're just knockoffs."

Rachel's friends were mostly the same age as her, but they acted like they were sixteen. I didn't hang out with them very often, because they went to school in Harlem and I commuted to Dalton. But on weekends, if they came over, they made fun of me because I had wavy hair, instead of kinks like theirs, and because my skin was light. "You think you all that," they'd say, and then they'd giggle into each other's shoulders as if this were the punch line to a secret joke. When my mother made Rachel babysit me on weekends, and we would take the bus to a shopping center, I sat in the front while they all sat in the back.

They called me Afrosaxon, instead of by my name. They sang along to music I didn't know. When I told Rachel that I didn't like her friends making fun of me, she told me to stop being so sensitive. "They just crackin' on you," she said. "Maybe if you let it slide a little, they'd like you more."

One day, I ran into her friends when I was on my way home from school. This time, though, Rachel wasn't with them. "Ooh, look what we got here," said the tallest one, Fantasee. She yanked at my French braid, which was how the girls in my school were wearing their hair those days. "You think you so fancy," she said, and the three of them surrounded me. "What? Can't you talk for yourself? You need your sister to do it for you?"

"Stop," I said. "Leave me alone. Please."

"I think someone needs to remember where she from." They grabbed at my backpack, unzipping it, throwing my schoolwork into the puddles on the ground, shoving me into the mud. Fantasee grabbed my Christie doll and dismembered her. Suddenly, like an avenging angel, Rachel arrived. She pulled Fantasee away and smacked her across the face. She tripped one of the other girls and pummeled the third. When they were all flattened, she stood over them with her fist. They crawled away, crabs in the gutter, and then scrambled to their feet and ran. I crouched down next to my broken Christie, and Rachel knelt beside me. "You okay?"

"Yeah," I said. "But you . . . you hurt your friends."

"I got other friends," Rachel answered. "You're my only sister." She tugged me to my feet. "C'mon, let's get you clean."

We walked home in silence. Mama took one look at my hair and my ripped tights and hustled me into a bath. She put ice on Rachel's knuckles.

Mama glued Christie back together, but her arm kept popping out and there was a permanent dent in the back of her head. Later that night, Rachel crawled into my bed. She'd done that when we were little, during thunderstorms. She handed me a chair that was made out of an empty cigarette pack, a yogurt cup, and some newspaper. Trash, that she had glued and taped together. "I thought Christie could use this," she said.

I nodded, turning it over in my hands. Probably it would break apart when Christie first sat in it, but that wasn't the point. I lifted up the covers and Rachel fitted herself to me, her front to my back. We rode out the night like that, like we were Siamese twins, sharing a heart that beat between us.

MY MOTHER SUFFERED HER FIRST stroke while she was vacuuming. Ms. Mina heard the crash of her body falling down, and found her lying on the edge of the Persian rug with her face pressed up against the tassel, as if she was inspecting it. She suffers her second stroke in the ambulance en route to the hospital. She is dead on arrival when we get there. I find Ms. Mina waiting for us, sobbing and overwrought. Edison stays with her, while I go to see Mama.

Some kind nurse has left the body for me. I go into the small curtained cubicle and sit down beside her. I take her hand; it's still warm. "Why didn't I call you last night?" I murmur. "Why didn't I go visit you this past weekend?"

I sit on the edge of the bed, then tuck myself under her arm for a moment, lying with my ear against her still chest. This is the last chance I will have to be her baby.

It is a strange thing, being suddenly motherless. It's like losing a rudder that was keeping me on course, one that I never paid much mind to before now. Who will teach me how to parent, how to deal with the unkindness of strangers, how to be humble?

You already did, I realize.

In silence, I cross to the sink. I fill a basin with warm, soapy water, and I place it beside my mama. I pull down the sheet that was left on her, after emergency intervention failed. I have not seen my mama naked in ages, but it is like looking in a mirror that distorts by years. This is what my breasts will look like, my belly. These are the stretch marks by which she remembered me. This is the curve of a spine that has worked hard to make her useful. These are the laugh lines that fan from her eyes.

I begin to wash her, the way I would wash a newborn. I run the cloth up the length of her arms and down her legs. I wipe between her toes. I sit her up, leaning her against the strength of my chest. She weighs next to nothing. As the water drips down her back, I rest my head on her shoulder, a one-sided embrace. She brought me into this world. I will help her leave it.

When I am finished, I cradle her in my arms, setting her back gently against the pillow. I pull the sheet up and tuck it beneath her chin. "I love you, Mama," I whisper.

The curtain is yanked open, and Adisa stands there. In counterpoint to my quiet grief, she is wailing, sobbing loudly. She throws herself on Mama, clutching fistfuls of the sheet.

Like any fire, I know she'll burn out. So I wait until her cries become hiccups. When she turns and sees me standing there, I truly think it's the first time she realizes that I'm even in the room.

I don't know if she holds out her arms to me or I hold out my arms to her, but we hold on for dear life. We talk over each other—*Did Mina call you? Had she been feeling poorly? When was the last time you spoke to her?* Shock and anguish run in loop, from me to her and back again.

Adisa hugs me tight. My hand tangles in her braids. "I told Wallace Mercy to find himself a new interview subject," she whispers.

I draw away just long enough to meet her eye.

Adisa shrugs, as if I've asked a question. "You're my only sister," she says.

MAMA'S FUNERAL IS AN AFFAIR with a capital *A*, which is exactly how she'd want it. Her longtime church in Harlem is packed with parishioners who have known her for years. I sit in the front row beside Adisa, staring at the giant wooden cross hanging on the chancel wall, between two massive panes of stained glass, with a fountain beneath. On the altar is Mama's casket—we got the fanciest one money could buy, which is what Ms. Mina insisted on, and she's the one who is paying for the funeral. Edison stands near Pastor Harold, looking shell-shocked, wearing a black suit that is too short at his wrists and ankles, and his basketball sneakers. He is wearing reflective sunglasses, although we are inside. At first I thought that was disrespectful, but then I realized why. As a nurse, I see death visit all the time, but this is his first experience; he was too little to remember his daddy being sent home in a flag-draped coffin.

A long snake of folks shuffles down the aisle, a macabre dance to look in Mama's open casket. She is wearing her favorite purple dress with sequins at the shoulders, and the black patent pumps that made her feet hurt, and the diamond studs that Ms. Mina and Mr. Sam gave her one year for Christmas that she never wore because she was so afraid one would fall out and she would lose it. I wanted to bury her in her lucky scarf, but in spite of turning her apartment upside down, I could not find it to bring to the undertaker. "She looks like she's at peace," I hear, over and over. Or "She looks just like herself, don't she?" Neither one of these is true. She looks like an illustration in a book, two-dimensional, when she ought to be leaping off the page.

When everyone has had a chance to file by, Pastor Harold starts the service. "Ladies and gentlemen, brothers and sisters . . . this is not a sad day," he says. He smiles gently at my niece Tyana, who's sobbing into little Zhanice's tiny Bantu knots. "This is a happy day, for we are here to celebrate our beloved friend and mother and grandmother, Louanne Brooks, who is finally at peace and walking beside the Lord. Let us begin with prayer."

I bow my head, but sneak a glance around the church, which groans at the seams with well-wishers. They all look like us, except for Ms. Mina and Christina, and in the back, Kennedy McQuarrie and an older woman.

It surprises me to see her here, but then, of course she knows about Mama. I was at her house when I heard.

Still, it feels like a blurred line, like wine and cheese at her home was. Like I am trying to put her in a box and she keeps escaping the confines.

"Our friend Louanne was born in 1940," the pastor says, "to Jermaine and Maddie Brooks, the youngest of four. She had two daughters, and made the best of her life after their daddy left, raising them to be good, strong women. She devoted her life to serving others, creating a happy home for the family that employed her for over fifty years. She won more ribbons at our church fair for her pies and cakes than anyone else in this congregation, and I do believe that at least ten pounds around my middle can be credited to Lou's sweets. She loved gospel music and *The View* and baking and Jesus, and is survived by her daughters and her six beloved grandchildren."

The choir sings Mama's favorite hymns: "Take My Hand, Precious Lord," and "I'll Fly Away." Then the pastor returns to the podium. He lifts his eyes to the congregation. "God is good!" he calls.

"All the time!" everyone responds.

"And He has called His angel home to glory!"

After a round of *Amen*s, he invites those so moved to stand and witness the impact Mama made on their lives. I watch some of her friends get up, moving slowly, as if they know they might be next. *She helped me through breast cancer,* one says. *She taught me how to sew a hem. She never lost at bingo.* It is illuminating—I knew Mama in one way, but to them, she was something different—a teacher, a confidante, a partner in crime. As their stories shape who Mama used to be, people are crying, rocking, calling out their praise.

Adisa squeezes my hand, and takes to the podium. "My mama," she says, "was strict." The crowd laughs at this truth. "She was strict about manners, and homework, and dating, and how much bare skin we could show when we went out in public. There was a ratio, right, Ruth? It changed depending on the season, but it cramped my style year-round." Adisa smiles faintly, turning in to herself. "I remember how once, she put out a place setting at the dinner table for my attitude, and she told me, *Girl, when you leave the table,* that *can stay behind.*"

Oh yes she did, I hear behind me.

"The thing is, I was a wild child. Maybe I still am. And Mama rode us on things that other parents never seemed to care about. At the time, it seemed so unfair. I asked her what difference it would make in God's grand scheme if I wore a red pleather miniskirt, and she said something I will never forget. *Rachel*, she told me, *I got precious little time for you to belong to me. I'm gonna make sure it isn't any shorter than it has to be.* I was too young, and too much of a rabble-rouser, to understand what she meant. But now I do. See, what I didn't realize back then was the flip side of that coin: I had precious little time for her to be my mama."

Teary, she steps down, and I stand up. To be honest, I didn't know Adisa could be such a good speaker, but then again, she has always been the brave one. Me, I recede into the background. I had not wanted to talk at the funeral, but Adisa said people would be expecting it, and so I did. *Tell a story*, she suggested. So I take the podium, clearing my throat, and grip the edge of the wood with overwhelming panic. "Thank you," I say, and the microphone squeals. I step back. "Thank you for coming out to say goodbye to Mama. She would have loved knowing you all cared, and if you hadn't come you know she'd be up in Heaven throwing shade about your manners." I glance out—that was supposed to be a joke, but no one is really laughing.

Swallowing, I forge on. "Mama always put herself last. You all know that she'd feed anyone and everyone—God forbid you ever left our home hungry. Like Pastor Harold, I bet all of you have had her blue-ribbon pies and cakes. Once, she was baking a Black Forest cake for a church contest, and I insisted on helping. I was of the age where I was no help at all, of course. At some point, I dropped the measuring spoon into the batter and was too embarrassed to tell her, so it got baked into the cake. When the judge at the contest cut into the cake, and found the spoon, Mama knew exactly what had happened. But instead of getting mad at me, she told the judge it was a special trick she used to make the cake moist. You probably remember how the next year, several of the cakes entered in the contest had metal measuring spoons baked inside them—well, now you know why." There is a titter of laughter, and I let out a breath I had not even realized I'd been holding. "I heard people say Mama was proud of her ribbons, of her baking, but you know, that isn't true. She worked hard at that. She worked hard at everything. Pride, she would tell us, is a sin. And in fact the only thing I ever saw her take pride in was me and my sister."

As I say the words, I remember the look on her face when I told her about the indictment. *Ruth*, she had said, when I came home from jail and she wanted to see me face-to-face, to make sure I was all right, *how could this happen to* you? I knew what she meant. I was her golden child. I had escaped the cycle. I had achieved. I had busted through the ceiling she spent her life butting her head against. "She was so proud of me," I repeat, but the words are viscous, balloons that pop when they hit the air, that leave a faint stench of disappointment.

It's all right, baby, I hear, from the crowd. And: *Mm-hmm, you okay*.

My mother never said as much, but *was* she still proud of me? Was it enough that I was her daughter? Or was the fact that I was on trial for a murder I didn't commit like one of those stains she worked so hard to get out?

There is more to my speech, but it is gone. The words on my little index card might as well be written in hieroglyphs. I stare at them, but nothing makes sense anymore. I can't imagine a world where I might go to prison for years. I can't imagine a world where my mother isn't.

Then I remember something she told me once, the night I went to Christina's slumber party. *When you're ready for us, we'll be waiting on you.* At that moment, I feel another presence I haven't felt before. Or maybe one I never noticed. It's solid as a wall, and warm to the skin. It's a community of people who know my name, even when I don't always remember theirs. It's a congregation that never stopped praying for me, even when I flew from the nest. It's friends I did not know I had, who have memories of me that I've pushed so far to the back of my mind, I've forgotten.

I hear the flow of the fountain behind me, and I think about water, how it might rise above its station as mist, flirt at being a cloud, and return as rain. Would you call that falling? Or coming home?

I don't know how long I stand there, weeping. Adisa comes to me, her shawl open like the great black wings of a heron. She wraps me in the feathers of unconditional love. She bears me away.

* * *

AFTER THE CHOIR SINGS "SOON and Very Soon," as the casket is carried from the church and we file out behind it; after the graveside ceremony, where the pastor speaks yet again, we reconvene at my mother's apartment—the small space where I grew up. The church ladies have done their duty; there are giant bowls of potato salad and coleslaw and platters of fried chicken set out on pretty pink tablecloths. There are silk flowers on almost every horizontal space, and someone has thought to bring folding chairs, although there isn't nearly enough room for everyone to sit.

I take refuge in the kitchen. I look over the stacked plates of brownies and lemon squares, and then walk to a tiny bookshelf above the sink. There's a small black and white composition book there, and I open it, nearly brought to my knees by the spiky hills and valleys of Mama's handwriting. *Sweet potato pie*, I read. *Coconut dreams. Chocolate Cake to Break a Man.* I smile at that last recipe—it was what I had cooked for Wesley, before he proposed, to which Mama only said, *I told you so.*

"Ruth," I hear, and I turn around to find Kennedy and the other white woman she brought with her looking awkward and out of place in my mama's kitchen.

I reach into the abyss and find my manners. "Thank you for coming. It means a lot."

Kennedy takes a step forward. "I'd like you to meet my mother. Ava."

The older woman holds out her hand in that southern way, like a limp fish, pressing just the tips of her fingers to the tips of mine. "My condolences. It was a lovely service."

I nod. Really, what is there to say?

"How are you holding up?" Kennedy asks.

"I keep thinking Mama's going to tell me to go tell Pastor Harold to use a coaster on her good coffee table." I don't have the words to tell her what it really feels like, seeing her with her own mother, knowing I don't have that option. What it's like being the balloon, when someone lets go of the string.

Kennedy glances down at the open book in my hands. "What's that?"

"A recipe book. It's only half finished. Mama kept telling me she was going to write down all her best ones for me, but she was always too busy cooking for someone else." I realize how bitter I sound. "She wasted her *life*, slaving away for someone else. Polishing silver and cooking three meals a day and scrubbing toilets so her skin was always raw. Taking care of someone else's baby."

My voice breaks on that last bit. Falls off the cliff.

Kennedy's mother, Ava, reaches into her purse. "I asked to come here today, with Kennedy," she says. "I didn't know your mom, but I knew someone like her. Someone I cared for very much."

She holds out an old photo, the kind with scalloped edges. It is a picture of a Black woman wearing a maid's uniform, holding a little girl in her arms. The girl has hair as light as snow, and her hand is pressed against her caregiver's cheek in shocking contrast. There's more than just duty between them. There's pride. There's love. "I didn't know your mother. But, Ruth—she didn't waste her life."

Tears fill my eyes. I hand the photo back to Ava, and Kennedy pulls me into an embrace. Unlike the stiff hugs I remember from white women like Ms. Mina or my high school principal, this one does not feel forced, smug, inauthentic.

She lets go of me, so that we are eye to eye. "I'm sorry for your loss," Kennedy says, and something crackles between us: a promise, a hope that when we go to trial, those same words will not cross her lips.

Kennedy

On my sixth wedding anniversary, Micah gives me the stomach flu.

It started last week with Violet, like most transmittable viruses that enter our household. Then Micah began throwing up. I told myself I did not have time to get sick, and thought I was safe until I bolted upright in the middle of the night, bathed in sweat, and made a beeline for the bathroom.

I wake up with my cheek pressed against the tile floor, and Micah standing over me. "Don't look at me like that," I say. "All smug because you've already been through this."

"It gets better," Micah promises.

I moan. "Wonderful."

"I was going to make you breakfast in bed, but instead I opted for ginger ale."

"You're a prince." I push myself upright. The room spins.

"Whoa. Steady, girl." Micah crouches beside me, helping me to my feet. Then he sweeps me into his arms and carries me into the bedroom.

"In any other circumstance," I say, "this would be very romantic."

Micah laughs. "Rain check."

"I'm trying really hard not to vomit on you."

"I can't tell you how much I appreciate that," he says gravely, and he crosses his arms. "Would you like to have a fight now about how you're not going into the office? Or do you want to finish your ginger ale first?"

"You're using my tactics against me. That's the kind of either-or I offer Violet—"

"See, and *you* think I never listen."

"I'm going to work," I say, and I try to get on my feet, but I black out. When I blink a moment later, Micah's face is inches from mine. "I'm not going to work," I whisper.

"Good answer. I already called Ava. She's going to come over and play nurse."

I groan. "Can't you just kill me instead? I don't think I can handle my mother. She thinks a shot of bourbon cures everything."

"I'll lock the liquor cabinet. You need anything else?"

"My briefcase?" I beg.

Micah knows better than to say no to that. As he goes downstairs to retrieve it, I prop myself up on pillows. I have too much to do to *not* be working, but my body doesn't seem to be cooperating.

I drift off in the few minutes it takes Micah to come back into the bedroom. He's trying to gently put the briefcase on the floor so he doesn't disturb me, but I reach for it, overestimating my strength. The contents of the leather folio spill all over the bed and onto the floor, and Micah crouches to pick them up. "Huh," he says, holding up a piece of paper. "What are you doing with a lab report?"

It's wrinkled, having slipped between files to get wedged at the bottom of my bag. I have to squint, and then a run of graphs comes into focus. It's the newborn screening results that I subpoenaed from the Mercy–West Haven Hospital, the ones that had been missing from Davis Bauer's file. They came in this week, and given my lack of understanding of chemistry, I barely glanced at the charts, figuring I'd show them to Ruth sometime after her mother's funeral. "It's just some routine test," I say.

"Apparently not," Micah replies. "There's abnormality in the blood work."

I grab it out of his hand. "How do you know that?"

"Because," Micah says, pointing to the cover letter I didn't bother to read, "it says here there's *abnormality in the blood work.*"

I scour the letter, addressed to Dr. Marlise Atkins. "Could it be fatal?"

"I have no idea."

"You're a doctor."

"I study eyes, not enzymes."

I look up at him. "What did you get me for our anniversary?"

"I was going to take you out to dinner," Micah admits.

"Well," I suggest, "take me to see a neonatologist instead."

WHEN WE SAY, IN AMERICA, that you have a right to be tried by a jury of your peers, we're not exactly telling the truth. The pool of jurors is not as random as you'd think, thanks to careful scrutiny by the defense and the prosecution to eliminate both ends of the bell curve—the people most likely to vote against our clients' best interests. We weed out the folks who believe that people are guilty until proven innocent, or who tell us they see dead people, or who hold grudges against the legal system because they were once arrested. But we also prune on a case-by-case basis. If my client is a draft dodger, I try to limit jurors who have proudly served. If my client is a drug addict, I don't want a juror who lost a family member to an overdose. Everyone has prejudices. It's my job to make sure that they work in favor of the person I'm representing.

So although I would never play the race card once the trial starts—as I've spent months explaining to Ruth—I'm damn well going to stack the odds before it begins.

Which is why, before we begin voir dire to choose jurors, I march into my boss's office and tell him I was wrong. "I'm feeling a little overwhelmed after all," I say to Harry. "I was thinking I might need a co-chair."

He takes a lollipop out of a jar he keeps on his desk. "Ed's got a shaken-baby trial starting this week—"

"I wasn't talking about Ed. I was thinking of Howard."

"Howard." He looks at me, baffled. "The kid who still brings his meals in a lunchbox?"

It's true that Howard is fresh out of law school and that so far, in the few months he's been at the office, has only done misdemeanors—domestics and a few disorderlies. I offer my smoothest grin. "Yeah. You know, he'll just be an extra pair of hands for me. A runner. And in the meantime, it would be good for him to get trial experience."

Harry unwraps the lollipop and sticks it in his mouth. "Whatever," he says, his teeth gripped on the stem.

With his blessing, or the closest I'm going to get to one, I head back to my cubicle and poke my head over the divider that separates me from Howard. "Guess what," I tell him. "You're going to second-chair the Jefferson case. Voir dire's this week."

He glances up. "Wait. What? Really?"

It's a big deal for a rookie who is still doing scut work in the office. "We're leaving," I announce, and I grab my coat, knowing he will follow.

I do need an extra pair of hands.

I also need them to be black.

HOWARD SCRAMBLES AT MY SIDE as we walk through the halls of the courthouse. "You don't speak to the judge unless I've told you to," I instruct. "Don't show any emotions, no matter what theatrical display Odette Lawton puts on—prosecutors do that to make themselves feel like they're Gregory Peck in *Mockingbird*."

"Who?"

"God. Never mind." I glance at him. "How old are you, anyway?"

"Twenty-four."

"I have sweaters older than you," I mutter. "I'll give you the discovery to read over tonight. This afternoon I'm going to need you to do some fieldwork."

"Fieldwork?"

"Yeah, you have a car, right?"

He nods.

"And then, once we actually get the jurors inside, you're going to be my human video camera. You're going to record every tic and twitch and comment that each potential juror makes in response to my questions, so that we can go over it and figure out which candidates are going to fuck us over. It's not about who's *on* the jury . . . it's about who's *not* on it. Do you have any questions?"

Howard hesitates. "Is it true that you once offered Judge Thunder a blow job?"

I stop walking and face him, my hands on my hips. "You don't even know how to clean out the coffee machine yet, but you know *that*?"

Howard pushes his glasses up his nose. "I plead the Fifth."

"Well, whatever you heard, it was taken out of context and it was prednisone-induced. Now shut up and look older than twelve, for God's sake." I push open the door to Judge Thunder's chambers to find him sitting behind his desk, with the prosecutor already in the room. "Your Honor. Hello."

He glances at Howard. "Who's this?"

"My co-counsel," I reply.

Odette folds her arms. "As of when?"

"About a half hour ago."

We all stare at Howard, waiting for him to introduce himself. He looks at me, his lips pressed firmly together. *You don't speak to the judge unless I've told you to.* "Speak," I mutter.

He holds out a hand. "Howard Moore. It's an honor, Your . . . um . . . Honor."

I roll my eyes.

Judge Thunder produces a huge stack of completed questionnaires, which are sent out to people who are called for jury duty. They are full of practical information, like where the recipient lives and where he or she works. But they also include pointed questions: *Do you have any problems with the presumption of innocence? If a defendant doesn't testify, do you assume he is hiding something? Do you understand that the*

Constitution gives the defendant the right to not say anything? If the State proves this case beyond reasonable doubt, would you have any moral qualms about convicting the defendant?

He splits the pile in half. "Ms. Lawton, you take this bunch for four hours; and Ms. McQuarrie, you take these. We'll reconvene at one P.M., switch piles, and then voir dire begins in two days."

As I drive Howard back to our office, I explain what we are looking for. "A solid defense juror is an older woman. They have the most empathy, the most experience, and they're less judgmental, and they're really hard on young punks like Turk Bauer. And beware of Millennials."

"Why?" Howard asks, surprised. "Aren't young people less likely to be racist?"

"You mean like Turk?" I point out. "The Millennials are the *me* generation. They usually think everything revolves around them, and make decisions based on what's going on in their lives and how it will affect their lives. In other words, they're minefields of egocentrism."

"Got it."

"Ideally we want a juror who has a high social status, because those people tend to influence other jurors when it comes to deliberations."

"So we're looking for a unicorn," Howard says. "A supersensitive, racially conscious, straight white male."

"He could be gay," I reply, serious. "Gay, Jewish, female—anything that can help them identify with discrimination in any form is going to be a bonus for Ruth."

"But we don't know any of these candidates. How do we become psychic overnight?"

"We don't become psychic. We become detectives," I say. "You're going to take half the surveys and drive to the addresses that are listed on them. You want to find out whatever you can. Are they religious? Are they rich? Poor? Do they have political campaign signs on the lawn? Do they live above where they work? Do they have a flagpole in the front yard?"

"What does *that* have to do with anything?"

"More often than not that's someone who's extremely conservative," I explain.

"Where are you going to be?" he asks.

"Doing the same thing."

I watch Howard leave, plugging the first address into his phone GPS. Then I wander the halls of the office asking other public defenders if they've had any of these folks on their panels—a lot of the jurors get recycled. Ed is about to head out the door to court, but he glances at the sheaf of papers. "I remember this guy," he says, pulling one survey free. "He was part of my jury on Monday—grand larceny case. He raised his hand during my opening statement and asked if I had a business card."

"Are you kidding me?"

"Sadly," Ed says, "no. Good luck, kiddo."

Ten minutes later, I've plugged an address into my GPS and find myself driving through Newhallville. I lock the doors for safety's sake. Presidential Gardens, the apartment building between Shelton and Dixwell Avenues, is a lower-income pocket of the city, with a quarter of the residents living below the poverty line, and the streets that bracket the residences are rife with drug traffic. Nevaeh Jones lives in this building, somewhere. I watch a little boy run out the door of one building, not wearing a coat, and start jogging when the cold hits him. He wipes his nose on his sleeve in midstride.

Will a woman from this area see Ruth and think she's being railroaded? Or will she see the socioeconomic difference between them and be resentful?

It's a hard call. In Ruth's unique case, the best juror may not be one with the same color skin.

I put a question mark at the top of the survey—this is one I'll have to consider further. Driving slowly out of the neighborhood, I wait until I see children playing outside and then pull over to the curb and call Howard's cell. "So?" I ask when he picks up. "How's it going?"

"Um," he says. "I'm sort of stuck."

"Where?"

"East Shore."

"What's the problem?"

"It's a gated community. There's a low fence and I could look over it, but I'd have to get out of the car," Howard says.

"Then get out of the car."

"I can't. See, back when I was in college, I kind of made a rule for myself—don't get out of the car unless there's a happy, living black person in sight." He exhales. "I've been waiting for forty-five minutes, but the only people in this part of New Haven are white."

That's not necessarily a bad thing for Ruth. "Can't you just go peek over the wall? Make sure she doesn't have a Trump sign on her lawn?"

"Kennedy—there are neighborhood watch signs all over the place. What do you think is going to happen if they see a black man trying to peek over a wall?"

"Oh," I say, embarrassed. "I get it." I look out the window to where three kids are jumping into piles of leaves; I think of the little black boy I saw streaking away from Presidential Gardens. Ed told me last week that he defended a twelve-year-old involved in a gang shooting with two seventeen-year-olds, and that the prosecution was gunning to have all three tried as adults. "Give me an hour and then meet me at 560 Theodore Street in East End. And, Howard? When you arrive, it's safe to get out of the car," I say. "I live there."

I LIGHTLY DROP THE BAG of Chinese food onto the desk of my home office. "I have goodies," I say, taking out the lo mein and laying claim to it.

"So do I," Howard says, and he points to a stack of papers he's printed out.

It's 10:00 P.M., and we've set up camp at my home. I left Howard there all afternoon to do online research while Odette and I swapped stacks of surveys. For hours, I've battled traffic, sussed out more jurors by neighborhood, and scanned the plaintiff and defendant lists at the courthouse to see if any of the potential jurors have been criminally prosecuted or have relatives that were criminally prosecuted.

"I found three guys who were charged with domestics, a woman whose mother got convicted of arson, and a lovely little old lady whose grandson's meth lab was busted last year," Howard announces.

The screen reflects, glowing green around Howard's face as he scans the page. "Okay," he says, opening a plastic container of soup and drinking from the side without a spoon. "God, I'm starving. So here's the thing: you can get some good dirt on Facebook, but it depends on privacy settings."

"Did you try LinkedIn?"

"Yeah," he says. "It's a gold mine."

He beckons me to the floor, where he's spread out the surveys and has paper-clipped printouts to each one. "This guy? We love him," Howard says. "He's a social justice educator at Yale. And even better—his mother is a nurse." I hold up my hand, he high-fives. "This is my second favorite."

He passes me the survey. Candace White. She's forty-eight years old, African American, a librarian, mother of three. She looks like someone who could be friends with Ruth, not just rule in favor of the defense.

Her favorite TV show is *Wallace Mercy*.

I may not want Reverend Mercy messed up in Ruth's case, but the people who watch him are definitely going to have sympathy for my client.

Howard is still listing his finds. "I've got three ACLU memberships. And this girl ran a whole tribute to Eric Garner on her blog. A series called *I Can't Breathe Either*."

"Nice."

"On the other end of the spectrum," Howard says, "this lovely gentleman is the deacon of his church and also supports Rand Paul and advocates the repeal of all civil rights laws."

I take the survey from his hand and put a red *X* through the name at the top.

"Two people who posted about reducing funding for welfare," Howard says. "I'm not sure what you want to do about that."

"Put them in the middle pile," I reply.

"This girl updated her status three hours ago: *Jesus Christ some chink just sideswiped my car.*"

I place her survey on top of the Rand Paul advocate's, as well as someone whose profile pic on Twitter is Glenn Beck. There are two candidates Howard has nixed because they liked Facebook pages for Skullhead and Day of the Sword. "Is that some *Game of Thrones* thing?" I ask, baffled.

"They're white power bands," Howard says, and I am pretty sure he blushes. "I found a group called Vaginal Jesus too. But none of our potential jurors listen to them."

"Thank God for small mercies. What's the big pile in the middle?"

"Indeterminate," Howard explains. "I have a few pictures of people making gun gang signs, a handful of stoners, one idiot who took a video of himself shooting up heroin, and thirty selfies of people who are rocked-off-their-gourd drunk."

"Doesn't it just warm the cockles of your heart to know that we entrust the legal system to these folks?"

I'm joking, but Howard looks at me soberly. "To tell you the truth, today's been a little shocking. I mean, I had no idea how people live their lives, and what they do when they think no one's looking—" He glances at a photo of a woman brandishing a red Solo cup. "Or even when they *are.*"

I spear a Peking ravioli with my chopstick. "When you start to see the seedy underbelly of America," I say, "it makes you want to live in Canada."

"Oh, and there's this," Howard says, pointing to the computer screen. "Do with it what you will." He reaches across me for a Peking ravioli.

I frown at the Twitter handle: @*WhiteMight.* "Which juror is it?"

"It's not a juror," he says. "And I'm pretty sure Miles Standup is a fake name." He clicks twice on the profile picture: a newborn infant.

"Why have I seen that photo before . . . ?"

"Because it's the same picture of Davis Bauer that people were holding up outside the courthouse before the arraignment. I checked the news footage. I think that's Turk Bauer's account."

"The Internet is a beautiful thing." I look at Howard with pride. "Well done."

He looks at me, hopeful, over the white lip of the paper carton. "So we're finished for the night?"

"Oh, Howard." I laugh. "We've only just begun."

ODETTE AND I MEET THE next morning at a diner to cross-check the survey numbers of the potential jurors that we each want to decline. In the rare occasion when our numbers match (the twenty-five-year-old who just got out of a psychiatric hospital; the man who was arrested last week) we agree to let them go.

I don't know Odette very well. She is tough, no-nonsense. At legal conferences, when everyone else is getting drunk and doing karaoke, she is the one sitting in the corner drinking club soda with lime and filing away memories she can use to exploit us later. I've always thought of her as an uptight piece of work. But now I'm wondering: when she goes shopping, is she, like Ruth, asked to show her receipts before exiting the store? Does she mutely hand them over? Or does she ever snap and say she is the one who puts shoplifters on trial?

So, in an attempt to offer an olive branch, I smile at her. "It's going to be quite a trial, huh?"

She stuffs her folder of surveys into her briefcase. "They're all big trials."

"But *this* one . . . I mean . . ." I stumble, trying to find the words.

Odette meets my gaze. Her eyes are like chips of flint. "My interest in this case is the same as your interest in this case. I am prosecuting it because everyone else in my office is overworked and maxed out, and it landed on my desk. And I do not care if your client is black, white, or polka-dotted. Murder is remarkably monochromatic." With that she stands up. "I'll see you tomorrow," Odette says, and she walks away.

"Nice chatting with you too," I mutter.

At that moment, Howard blusters in. His glasses are askew and his shirt is untucked in the back and he looks like he's already had about ten cups of coffee. "I was doing some background research," he begins, sitting down in the chair Odette just vacated.

"When? In the shower?" I know exactly when we stopped working last night, which leaves little room for free time.

"So, there was a study done by SUNY Stony Brook in 1991 and 1992 by Nayda Terkildsen, about how white voters assess black politicians who are running for office, and how prejudice affects that, and how that changes for people who actively try *not* to act prejudiced—"

"First," I say, "we are not using a defense based on race, we are using one based on science. Second, Ruth is not running for office."

"Yeah, but there are crossover implications in the study that I think could tell us a lot about the potential jurors," Howard says. "Just hear me out, okay? So Terkildsen took a random sample of about three hundred and fifty white people from the jury pool in Jefferson County, Kentucky. She made up three sets of packets about a fake candidate for governor that had the same biography, the same résumé and political platform. The only difference was that in some of the head shots, the candidate was a white man. In others, it was Photoshopped to be a light-skinned black man or a dark-skinned black man. The voters were asked to identify if they were racially biased, and if they tended to be aware of that racial bias."

I motion with my hands to hurry him up.

"The white politician got the most positive responses," Howard says.

"Big surprise."

"Yeah, but that's not the interesting part. As prejudice increased, the rating of the light-skinned black man dropped quicker than the rating of the dark-skinned black man. But when prejudiced voters were divided into those who were aware of their racism and those who generally weren't, things changed. The people who didn't care if they looked prejudiced were harder on the dark-skinned black man than on the light-skinned black man. The voters who were worried about what people would think of them if they were racist, however, rated the dark-skinned black way higher than the light-skinned black. You get it, right? If a white person is trying extra hard to *not* look racist, they're going to overcompensate for their prejudice by suppressing their real feelings about the darker-skinned person."

I stare at him. "Why are you telling me this?"

"Because Ruth *is* black. Light-skinned, but still black. And you can't necessarily trust the white people in that jury pool if they tell you they aren't prejudiced. They may be a lot more implicitly racist than they show on the outside, and that makes them wild cards for the jury."

I look down at the table. Odette is wrong. Murder is not monochromatic. We know that from the school-to-prison pipeline. There are so, so many reasons the cycle is hard to break—and one of them is that white jurors come into a trial with bias. They are far more likely to make concessions for a defendant who looks like them than for one who doesn't.

"All right," I say to Howard. "What's your plan?"

WHEN I CRAWL INTO BED that night, Micah is already asleep. But then he reaches out and wraps his arm around me. "No," I say. "I am too tired to do anything right now."

"Even thank me?" he says.

I turn to face him. "Why?"

"Because," he says. "I found you a neonatologist."

Immediately I sit up. "And?"

"And we're going to see him this weekend. He's a guy I knew from med school."

"What did you tell him?"

"That my crazy lawyer wife is going all Lysistrata on me until I can get her an expert in the field."

I laugh, then frame Micah's face with my hands and kiss him, long and slow. "Go figure," I say. "I've gotten my second wind."

In one quick move he grabs me and rolls, so that I am pinned beneath him. His smile gleams in the light of the moon. "If you'll do that for a neonatologist," he murmurs, "what would you give me if I found you something *really* impressive, like a parasitologist? Or a leprolo-gist?"

"You spoil me," I say, and I pull him down to me.

I MEET RUTH AT THE back entrance of the courthouse, just in case Wal-lace Mercy has decided that jury selection is worth his time and energy. She is wearing a plum suit that I went with her to buy at T.J.Maxx last week, and a crisp white shirt. Her hair is pulled back and knotted at the nape of her neck. She looks every inch the professional, and I would have assumed she is at court because she is an attorney if not for the fact that her knees are shaking so uncontrollably they are knocking together.

I take her arm. "Relax. Honestly, this isn't worth getting nervous over."

She looks at me. "It's just suddenly . . . very real."

I introduce her to Howard, and as they shake hands I see some-thing almost imperceptible pass between them—an acknowledgment that it is surprising for both of them to be in this courthouse, for dif-ferent reasons. Howard and I flank Ruth as we walk into the court-room and take our seats at the defense table.

For all that Judge Thunder is an asshole to us attorneys, juries eat him up. He looks the part, with wavy silver hair and grave lines of ex-perience bracketing his mouth, forming parentheses around whatever wisdom he has yet to speak. When our hundred potential jurors are jammed into the courtroom, he gives preliminary instructions.

"Remember," I whisper to Howard, leaning behind Ruth's back. "Your job is to take notes. So many notes that your hand cramps. If one of those jurors flinches at a certain word, I need to know the word. If they fall asleep, I want to know when."

He nods as I scan the faces of the potential jurors. I recognize some, from their Facebook photos. But even those I don't recall have expressions I am used to seeing: there are the faces of those I secretly call Boy Scouts, who are delighted to be performing this duty to their

country. There are the Morgan Stanleys—businessmen who keep
checking their watches because their time is clearly more important
than spending the day in a jury box. There are the Repeat Offenders,
who have been through this process before and wonder why the hell
they've been called again.

"Ladies and gentlemen, I'm Judge Thunder, and I'd like to welcome you to my courtroom."

Oh, good grief.

"In this case, the State is represented by our prosecutor Odette
Lawton. Her job is to prove this case by reason of evidence, beyond a
reasonable doubt. The defendant is represented by Kennedy McQuarrie." As he begins to list the charges that Ruth was indicted for—
murder and involuntary manslaughter—her knee starts trembling so
hard I reach under the table and press it flat.

"I will explain to you later what those charges mean," Judge Thunder says. "But at this moment, is there any member of the panel who
knows the parties in this case?"

One juror raises his hand.

"Can you approach the bench?" the judge asks.

Odette and I move closer for the conference as a noise machine is
turned on so that the rest of the jury cannot hear what this guy says.
He points to Odette. "She locked up my brother on a drug charge, and
she's a lying bitch."

Needless to say, he's excused.

After a few more blanket queries, the judge smiles at the group.
"All right, folks. I'm going to excuse you, and the bailiff will take you
to the jury lounge. We'll be calling you in one at a time so that the
counselors can ask some individual follow-ups. Please don't talk about
your experiences with your fellow jurors. As I told you, the State has
the burden of proof. We haven't started to take evidence yet, so I urge
you to keep an open mind and to be honest with your answers in front
of the court. We want to make sure you are comfortable sitting as a
juror in this case, just as the parties involved have the right to feel that
their process can be judged by someone fair and impartial."

If only the judge were the same, I think.

Voir dire is a cocktail party without any booze. You want to schmooze your jurors, you want them to like you. You want to act interested in their careers, even if that career is quality control at a Vaseline plant. As each individual juror is paraded before you, you rate him or her. A perfect juror is a 5. A bad juror is a 1.

Howard will list the reasons that a juror isn't acceptable, so we can keep them straight. Ultimately we'll wind up taking 3s and 4s and 5s, because we have only seven peremptory strikes we can use to kick a juror out of the pool without having to give a reason. And we don't want to use those all up at once, because what if there's a *bigger* problem juror yet to come?

The first man to take the stand is Derrick Welsh. He's fifty-eight and has bad teeth and is wearing an untucked plaid shirt. Odette greets him with a smile. "Mr. Welsh, how are you doing today?"

"All right I guess. A little hungry."

She smiles. "Me too. Tell me, have we ever worked on any cases together?"

"No," he says.

"What do you do for a living, Mr. Welsh?"

"I run a hardware store."

She asks him about his children and their ages. Howard taps me on the shoulder. He's been frantically sifting through the surveys. "This is the one whose brother is a cop," he whispers.

"I read *The Wall Street Journal*," Welsh is saying, when I turn back. "And Harlan Coben."

"Have you heard about this case?"

"A little bit. On the news," he admits. "I know the nurse was accused of killing a baby."

Beside me, Ruth flinches.

"Do you have any opinion about whether the defendant is guilty of that offense?" Odette asks.

"As far as I know, in our country everyone's innocent till they're proven guilty."

"How do you see your role as a juror?"

He shrugs. "I guess listen to evidence . . . and do what the judge says."

"Thank you, Your Honor," Odette says, and she sits down.

I rise from my seat. "Hi there, Mr. Welsh," I say. "You have a relative in law enforcement, don't you?"

"My brother is a police officer."

"Does he work in this community?"

"For fifteen years," the juror replies.

"Does he ever tell you about his job? What kinds of people he deals with?"

"Sometimes . . ."

"Has your store ever been vandalized?"

"We were robbed once."

"Do you think the increase in crime is due to an influx of minorities in the community?

He considers this. "I think it has more to do with the economy. People lose jobs, they get desperate."

"Who do you think has the right to dictate medical treatment— the family of the patient or the medical professional?" I ask.

"It's a case-by-case thing . . ."

"Have you or someone in your family had a bad outcome at a hospital?"

Welsh's mouth tightens. "My mother died on the operating table during a routine endoscopy."

"Did you blame the doctor?"

He hesitates. "We settled."

And a flag is on the field. "Thank you," I say, and as I sit down I look at Howard and shake my head.

The second potential juror is a black man in his late sixties. Odette asks him how far he went in school, if he is married, who he lives with, what his hobbies are. Most of these questions are on the survey, but sometimes you want to ask them again, to look the person in the eye when he tells you he does Civil War reenactments, for example, to see if he's just into history or if he's a gun nut. "I understand you're a security guard at a mall," she says. "Do you consider yourself a member of law enforcement?"

"I guess in a small sense," he replies.

"Mr. Jordan, you know we're looking for an impartial jury," Odette says. "It surely has not escaped your notice that you and the defendant are both people of color. Might that impact your ability to make a fair decision?"

He blinks. After a moment, he replies to Odette, "Is there anything about *your* color that makes *you* unfair?"

I think Mr. Jordan might be my favorite person in the world right now. I stand up as Odette finishes her questioning. "Do you think black people are more likely to commit crimes than white people?" I ask.

I already know the answer, so that's not why I'm asking.

I want to see how he reacts to me, a white woman, posing a question like that.

"I believe," he says slowly, "that black people are more likely to wind up in jail than white folks."

"Thank you, sir," I say, and I turn toward Howard, nodding imperceptibly, as if to say: *That is a* ten.

There are several witnesses who fall somewhere in between horrific and perfect, and then juror number 12 takes the stand. Lila Fairclough is the perfect age for a juror, blond and spry. She teaches in the inner city in a racially integrated classroom. She's very polite and professional with Odette, but she smiles at me the minute I stand up. "My daughter's going to be in the school district where you work," I tell her. "It's why we moved there."

"She'll love it," the woman says.

"Now, here I am, Ms. Fairclough, a white woman representing a black woman, who's facing one of the most serious accusations that can be brought against a person. I have some concerns, and I'd like to talk about them, because it's just as critical for you to feel comfortable on this jury as it is for me to feel comfortable representing my client. You know, we all talk about prejudice being a bad thing, but it's a reality. For example, there are certain kinds of cases I could never be impaneled on. I mean, I love animals. If I see someone being cruel to them I can't be objective—I'm just so angry that my anger supersedes any rational thought. If that was the case, I'd have a hard time believing anything the defense told me."

"I totally get your point, but I don't have a biased bone in my body," Ms. Fairclough assures me.

"If you got on the bus and there were two seats available—one next to an African American man and one next to an elderly white woman, where would you sit?"

"In the first available seat." She shakes her head. "I know what you're getting at, Ms. McQuarrie. But honestly, I don't have a problem with black people."

That's when Howard drops his pen.

I hear it like a gunshot. I spin around, meet his eye, and start to fake an Oscar-worthy coughing fit. This was our prearranged signal. I choke as if I am hacking out a lung, and drink from the glass of water on the defense table, and then rasp at the judge, "My colleague will finish up here, Your Honor."

When Howard stands up, he starts swallowing convulsively. I'm sure that the judge is going to think the entire defense team has the plague, when I see the reaction on Lila Fairclough's face.

She freezes the minute Howard steps in front of her.

It's infinitesimal, the time between that and how fast she stretches her lips into a smile. But that doesn't mean I haven't witnessed it. "I'm so sorry, Ms. Fairclough," he says. "Just a couple more questions.

"What's the percentage of black children in your classroom?"

"Well, I have a class of thirty, and eight of my children are African American this year."

"Do you find that the African American children have to be disciplined more frequently than the white children?"

She starts twisting her ring on her finger. "I treat all my students equally."

"Let's step outside of your classroom for a moment. Do you think in general that African American children have to be disciplined more frequently than white kids?"

"Well, I haven't read studies on it." Twist, twist. "But I can tell you I'm not part of the problem."

Which, of course, means that she thinks there *is* a problem.

WHEN WE FINISH THE INDIVIDUAL questioning, and the first set of fourteen jurors are led back to the holding room, Howard and I huddle together and sort through who, if anyone, we want to strike for cause. "Are we ready to discuss excusals?" Judge Thunder asks.

"I'd like to excuse juror number ten," Odette says, "the one who indicated that a black person can't get a fair job, let alone a fair trial."

"No objection," I answer. "I'd like to excuse juror number eight, whose daughter was raped by a black man."

"No objection," Odette says.

We excuse a man whose wife is dying, and a mother with a sick baby, and a man who supports his family of six and whose boss has told him he cannot miss a week of work without risking his job.

"I'd like to excuse juror number twelve," I say.

"No way," Odette says.

Judge Thunder frowns at me. "You haven't developed a challenge for cause, Counselor."

"She's racist?" I explain, but it sounds ridiculous even to me. The woman teaches black students and swore she wasn't prejudiced. I might know she has implicit bias based on her reaction to Howard and her nervous tic of twisting her ring, but if I explain our little experiment to Odette or the judge, I'll be in trouble.

I know if I call her in for further questioning, it won't do any good. Which means that I either have to accept her as a juror or must use one of my peremptory strikes.

Odette has exercised one strike against a nurse, and another against a community organizer who admitted that he can find injustice anywhere. I've dismissed a woman who lost an infant, a man who sued a hospital for malpractice, and one of the guys who—thanks to Howard and Facebook—I know went to a white power music festival.

Howard leans across Ruth so he can whisper in my ear. "Use it," he says. "She's going to be trouble, even if she doesn't look it."

"Counselor," the judge demands, "are we all invited to your little gossip session?"

"I'm sorry, Your Honor—a moment to consult with my co-counsel?" I turn back to Howard. "I can't. I mean, I have another eighty-six jurors to get through here, and only four more strikes. Satan could be part of the next pool, for all we know." I meet his gaze. "You were right. She's biased. But she doesn't *think* she is, and she doesn't want to be *seen* that way. So maybe, just maybe, it'll swing in our favor."

Howard looks at me for a long second. I can tell he wants to speak his mind, but he just nods. "You're the boss," he says.

"We accept juror number twelve," I tell the judge.

"I'd like to strike juror number two," Odette continues.

That is my black security guard, my perfect ten. Odette knows this, which is why she is willing to use a peremptory strike against him. But I am up like a shot before she even finishes her sentence. "Your Honor, sidebar?" We approach the bench. "Judge," I say, "this is a blatant violation of *Batson*."

James Batson was an African American man who was tried for burglary in Kentucky by an all-white jury. During the voir dire phase of the trial, when the jurors were being selected, the prosecutor used peremptory strikes against six potential jurors—four of whom were black. The defense tried to discharge the jury on the grounds that Batson was not being tried by a representative sample of the community, but the judge denied it, and Batson wound up being convicted. In 1986, the Supreme Court ruled in Batson's favor, stating that a prosecutor's use of peremptory strikes in a criminal case could not be based solely on race.

Since then, any time a black person gets bounced from a jury, any defense attorney worth his or her salt will cry *Batson*.

"Your Honor," I continue, "the Sixth Amendment guarantees the right of a defendant to be tried by a jury of his or her peers."

"Thank you, Ms. McQuarrie, I know very well what the Sixth Amendment says."

"I didn't mean to imply otherwise. New Haven is a very diverse county, and the jury needs to reflect that diversity, and right now this gentleman is the only black juror in this pool of fourteen."

"You have *got* to be kidding," Odette says. "You're saying *I'm* racist?"

"No, I'm saying that it's a lot easier for you to stack a jury in the State's favor without being called on it *because* of your race."

The judge turns to Odette. "What's your reason for exercising your peremptory strike, Counselor?"

"I found him argumentative," she says.

"This is the first group of jurors," Judge Thunder warns me. "Don't get your knickers in a twist."

Maybe it's the fact that he is so blatantly favoring the prosecution right now. Maybe it is that I want to show Ruth I am going to bat for her. Maybe it's just because he used the word *knickers* and it made me remember my steroid rant against him. For whatever reason, or maybe all of them, I straighten my spine and take this opportunity to unbalance Odette before we even get started. "I want a hearing on this," I demand. "I want Odette to produce her notes. We had other argumentative people on this panel, and I want to know if she documented that characteristic for the other jurors."

Rolling her eyes, Odette climbs into the witness box. I have to admit, there's enough public defender pride in me to love seeing a prosecutor in there, effectively caged. She glares at me as I approach. "You indicated that juror number two was argumentative. Did you listen to the responses of juror number seven?"

"Of course I did."

"How did you find his demeanor?" I ask.

"I found him friendly."

I look down at Howard's excellent notes. "Even when you asked him about African Americans and crime and he came out of his seat and said you were implying he was a racist? Is that not argumentative?"

Odette shrugs. "His tone was different than juror number two's."

"Coincidentally, so was his skin color," I say. "Tell me, did you make any notes about juror number eleven being argumentative?"

She glances down at her chart. "We were moving quickly. I didn't write down everything I was thinking, because it wasn't important."

"Because it wasn't important," I clarify, "or because that juror was white?" I turn to the judge. "Thank you, Your Honor."

Judge Thunder turns to the prosecutor. "I'm not going to allow the peremptory challenge. You're not getting me into a *Batson* situation this early in the game, Ms. Lawton. Juror number two remains on the panel."

I slide into my seat beside Ruth, pretty damn pumped. Howard is blinking at me like I'm a goddess. It's not every day you get to school a prosecutor. Suddenly Ruth passes a note to me. I unfold it, read the two simple words: *Thank you.*

WHEN THE JUDGE DISMISSES US for the day, I tell Howard to go home and get some sleep. Ruth and I leave the courthouse together; I peek outside first to make sure that the coast is clear of media. It is—but I know that will change as soon as we start the trial.

When we reach the parking lot, however, neither one of us seems to be in a great hurry to leave. Ruth keeps her head ducked, and I know her well enough by now to know that something's on her mind. "You want to go grab a glass of wine? Or do you have to get back to Edison?"

She shakes her head. "He's out more than I am these days."

"You don't sound thrilled about that."

"Right now I'm not exactly his role model," Ruth says.

We walk around the corner to a bar that I've been to many times before, celebrating victory or drowning defeat. It's full of lawyers I know, so I squirrel us into a booth way in the back. We both order pinot noir, and when the glasses arrive, I toast. "Here's to an acquittal."

I notice that Ruth doesn't lift her glass.

"Ruth," I say gently, "I know this was the first time you've been in court. But trust me—today went really, really well."

She swirls the wine in her glass. "My mama used to tell a story about how, once, she was pushing me in a stroller in our neighborhood in Harlem, and two black ladies passed her. One of them said to the other, *She walkin' around like that her baby. That ain't her baby. I hate when nannies do that.* I was light-skinned, compared to Mama. She laughed it off, because she knew the truth—I was hers, through and through. But the thing is, growing up, it wasn't the white kids who made me feel worst about myself. It was the black kids." Ruth looks up at me. "That prosecutor made it all come flooding back today. Like, she was out to *get* me."

"I don't know if it's all that personal for Odette. She just likes to win."

It strikes me that this is a conversation I have never had with someone who is African American. Usually I am so conscious of not being seen as prejudiced that I would be paralyzed by the fear of saying something that would be offensive. I've had African American clients before, but in those cases I was very clearly setting myself up to be the one with all the answers. Ruth has seen that mask slip.

With Ruth, I know I can ask a stupid white girl question, and that she will answer me without judging my ignorance. Likewise, if I step on her toes, she'll tell me so. I think about the time she explained to me the difference between weaves and extensions; or how she asked me about sunburn, and how long it takes for blistered skin to start peeling. It's the difference between dancing along the eggshell crust of acquaintance and diving into the messy center of a relationship. It's not always perfect; it's not always pleasant—but because it is rooted in respect, it is unshakable.

"You surprised me today," Ruth admits.

I laugh. "Because I'm actually good at what I do?"

"No. Because half the questions you asked were based on race." She meets my gaze. "After all this time telling me that doesn't happen in a courtroom."

"It doesn't," I say bluntly. "Come Monday, when the trial starts, everything changes."

"You'll still let me speak?" Ruth confirms. "Because I need to say my piece."

"I promise." I set my wineglass down. "Ruth, you know, just because we pretend racism has nothing to do with a case doesn't mean we aren't aware of it."

"Then why pretend?"

"Because it's what lawyers do. I lie for a living. If I thought it was going to get you acquitted, I could tell the jury that Davis Bauer was a werewolf. And if they believe it, shame on them."

Ruth's eyes meet mine. "It's a distraction. It's a clown waving in your face, so you don't notice the sleight of hand going on behind him."

It's strange to hear my work described that way, but it's not entirely untrue. "Then I guess all we can do is drink to forget." I lift my glass.

Ruth finally takes a sip of her wine. "There isn't enough pinot noir in the world."

I run my thumb around the edge of my cocktail napkin. "Do you think there will ever be a time when racism doesn't exist?"

"No, because that means white people would have to buy into being equal. Who'd *choose* to dismantle the system that makes them special?"

Heat floods my neck. Is she talking about me? Is she suggesting that the reason I won't buck the system is because I, personally, have something to lose?

"But then," Ruth muses, "maybe I'm wrong."

I lift my glass, clink it against hers. "To baby steps," I toast.

AFTER ONE MORE DAY OF jury selection, we have our twelve plus two alternates. I spend the weekend holed up in my home office preparing for Monday's opening arguments of the trial, taking off only Sunday afternoon to meet the neonatologist. Micah met Ivan Kelly-Garcia in his freshman orgo class, when—during the midterm—Ivan rushed in with only a half hour left during the exam, dressed like a giant hot dog, grabbed an exam booklet, and aced the test. The previous night was Halloween, and he'd passed out drunk in a sorority house, and woke up to realize he was about to forgo his entire future as a doctor. Ivan not only went on to become Micah's study partner in orgo but also to go to Harvard Med and become one of the best neonatologists in the tristate area.

He's thrilled to hear from Micah after so many years, and he's even outwardly thrilled to host his insane lawyer wife and one very crabby four-year-old who should not have been awakened from her car seat nap. Ivan lives in Westport, Connecticut, in a sedate colonial, with his wife—a woman who managed to make homemade guacamole and salsa for us *after* her fifteen-mile morning marathon training run. They don't have any kids yet, but they do have a giant Bernese mountain dog, which is currently either babysitting Violet or licking her to death.

"Look at us, bro," Ivan says. "Married. Employed. *Sober*. Remember that time we dropped acid and I decided to climb a tree but forgot I'm scared of heights?"

I look at Micah. "*You* dropped acid?"

"You probably didn't tell her about Sweden, either," Ivan muses.

"Sweden?" I look between the two men.

"Cone of silence," Ivan says. "Bro code."

The thought of Micah—who prefers his boxer shorts *ironed*—as a bro makes me stifle a laugh.

"My wife's trying her first murder case," Micah segues smoothly, "so I apologize in advance if she asks you ten thousand questions."

Under my breath I whisper, "I'm totally getting that whole story from you later." Then I smile at Ivan. "I was hoping you could explain newborn screening."

"Well, basically, it was a game changer for infant mortality. Thanks to something called tandem mass spectrometry, which is done at the state lab, we can identify a handful of congenital diseases that can be treated or managed. I'm sure your daughter had it done, and you probably were never the wiser."

"What kinds of diseases?" I ask.

"Oh, a whole science nerd dictionary: biotinidase deficiency— that's when the body can't reuse and recycle enough free biotin. Congenital adrenal hyperplasia and congenital hypothyroidism, which are hormone deficiencies. Galactosemia, which prevents an infant from processing a certain sugar that's in milk, breast milk, and formula. Hemoglobinopathies, which are problems with red blood cells. Amino acid disorders, which cause amino acids to build up in the blood or the urine; and fatty acid oxidation disorders, which keep bodies from turning fat into energy; and organic aciduria disorders, which are sort of a hybrid between the two. You've probably heard of some of them, like sickle cell, which affects a lot of African Americans. Or PKU," Ivan says. "Babies who have that one can't break down certain types of amino acids, and they build up in the blood or the urine. If you don't know your kid has the disease, it leads to cognitive impairment and seizures. But if it's flagged right after birth, it can be managed with a special diet and prognosis is excellent."

I hand him the lab results. "The lab says there was an abnormality in this patient's newborn screening."

He flips through the first few pages. "Bingo—this kid has MCADD. You can tell by the spikes on the mass spectrometry graph here at C-six and C-eight—that's the acylcarnitine profile." Ivan looks up at us. "Oh, okay, yeah. English. Well, the acronym is short for medium-chain acyl-coenzyme A dehydrogenase deficiency. It's an autosomal recessive disorder of fatty acid oxidation. Your body needs energy to do stuff— move, function, digest, even breathe. We get our fuel from food, and store it in our tissues as fatty acids until we need it. At that point, we oxidize those fatty acids to create energy for bodily functions. But a baby with a fatty acid oxidation disorder can't do that, because he's missing a key enzyme—in this case, MCADD. That means once his energy stores are depleted, he's in trouble."

"Meaning . . . ?"

He hands me back the packet. "His blood sugar will tank, and he'll be tired, sluggish."

Those words trigger a flag in my mind. Davis Bauer's low blood sugar was blamed on his mother's gestational diabetes. But what if that wasn't the case? "Could it cause death?"

"If it's not diagnosed early. A lot of these kids are asymptomatic until something acts like a trigger—an infection, or an immunization, or fasting. Then, you get a rapid decline that looks an awful lot like sudden infant death syndrome—basically the baby goes into arrest."

"Could a baby who arrests still be saved, if he has MCADD?"

"It really depends on the situation. Maybe. Maybe not."

Maybe, I think, is an excellent word for a jury.

Ivan looks at me. "I'm guessing, if there's a lawsuit involved, that the patient didn't make it?"

I shake my head. "He died when he was three days old."

"What day was the kid born?"

"Thursday. The heel stick was done on a Friday."

"What time was it sent off to the state lab?" Ivan asks.

"I don't know," I admit. "Does that make a difference?"

"Yeah." He leans back in his chair, eyeing Violet, who is now trying to ride the dog. "The lab in Connecticut is closed on Saturday and Sunday. If the screening sample was sent out from the hospital after, say, midday on Friday, it didn't reach the lab till after the weekend." Ivan looks at me. "Which means if this kid had been born on a Monday instead, he would have had a fighting chance."

stage two

Pushing

She wanted to get at the hate of them all, to pry at it and work at it until she found a little chink, and then pull out a pebble or a stone or a brick and then a part of the wall, and, once started, the whole edifice might roar down and be done away with.

—RAY BRADBURY, *The Illustrated Man*

Ruth

WE ALL DO IT, YOU KNOW. DISTRACT OURSELVES FROM NOTICING HOW time's passing. We throw ourselves into our jobs. We focus on keeping the blight off our tomato plants. We fill up our gas tanks and top off our Metro cards and do the grocery shopping so that the weeks look the same on the surface. And then one day, you turn around, and your baby is a man. One day, you look in the mirror, and see gray hair. One day, you realize there is less of your life left than what you've already lived. And you think, *How did this happen so fast? It was only yesterday when I was having my first legal drink, when I was diapering him, when I was young.*

When this realization hits, you start doing the math. *How much time do I have left? How much can I fit into that small space?*

Some of us let this realization guide us, I guess. We book trips to Tibet, we learn how to sculpt, we skydive. We try to pretend it's not almost over.

But some of us just fill up our gas tanks and top off our Metro cards and do the grocery shopping, because if you only see the path that's right ahead of you, you don't obsess over when the cliff might drop off.

Some of us never learn.

And some of us learn earlier than others.

ON THE MORNING OF THE trial, I knock softly on Edison's door. "You almost ready?" I ask, and when he doesn't answer, I turn the knob and step inside. Edison is buried under a pile of quilts, his arm flung over his eyes. "Edison," I say more loudly. "Come on! We can't be late!"

He's not asleep, I can tell by the depth of his breathing. "I'm not going," he mutters.

Kennedy had requested that Edison miss school and attend the trial. I didn't tell her that these days, going to school has been less of a priority for him, as evidenced by the number of times I've been called about him skipping class. I've pleaded, I've argued, but getting him to listen to me has become a Herculean task. My scholar, my serious, sweet boy, is now a rebel—holed up in his room listening to music so loud it makes the walls shake or texting friends I did not know he had; coming home past curfew smelling of hard liquor and weed. I have fought, I have cried, and now, I am not sure what else to do. The whole train of our lives is in the process of derailing; this is only one of the cars skidding off the tracks.

"We talked about this," I tell him.

"No we didn't." He squints at me. "You talked *at* me."

"Kennedy says that someone who's seen as maternal is harder to picture as a murderer. She says that the picture you present to the jury is sometimes more important than the evidence."

"Kennedy says. Kennedy says. You talk like she's Jesus—"

"She is," I interrupt. "At least, she is right now. All my prayers are going to her, because she is the only thing that stands between me and a conviction, Edison, which is why I'm asking—no, *begging* you to do this one thing for me."

"I got stuff to do."

I arch a brow. "Like what? Skip school?"

Edison rolls away from me. "Why don't you just leave?"

"In about a week," I snap, "your wish might just come true."

The truth has teeth. I hold my hand over my mouth, like I could will back the words. Edison fights to blink back tears. "I didn't mean that," he mumbles.

"I know."

"I don't want to go to the trial because I don't think I can listen to what they say about you," he confesses.

I put my hands on either side of his face. "Edison, you know me. They *don't*. No matter what you hear in that courtroom, no matter what lies they try to tell—you remember that everything I have ever done has been for you." I cup his cheek, follow the track of a tear with the pad of my thumb. "You're going to make something of yourself. People are going to know your name."

I can hear the echo of my mama telling me the same thing. *Be careful what you wish for*, I think. After today, people *will* know my name. But not for the reasons she had hoped.

"What happens to *you* matters," I tell Edison. "What happens to me doesn't."

His hand comes up, encircling my wrist. "It matters to *me*."

Oh, there *you are*, I think as I look into Edison's eyes. This is the boy I know. The boy I hooked my star on.

"It seems," I say lightly, "that I am in need of a date to my own trial."

Edison lets go of my wrist. He holds out his arm, crooked at the elbow, old-fashioned and courtly, even though he is still wearing his pajamas, even though I have a scarf wrapped around my hair, even though this is not a ball we are attending, but more of a gauntlet to run. "It would be my pleasure," he says.

LAST NIGHT, KENNEDY HAD SHOWED up at my house unexpected. Her husband and daughter were with her; she had come straight from some town about two hours away and was bursting to share her news with me: MCADD had shown up in Davis Bauer's newborn screening.

I stared at the results she showed me, the same ones a doctor friend of her husband's had explained to her. "But that's . . . that's . . ."

"Lucky," she finished. "For you, anyway. I don't know if these results were missing from the file accidentally, or if someone tanked them purposely because they knew it would make you less culpable. But what's important is that we have the information now, and we're going to ride it to an acquittal."

MCADD is a much more dangerous medical condition than a grade one patent ductus, the heart ailment Kennedy had planned to raise. It is not a lie, anymore, to say that the Bauer baby had had a life-threatening disorder.

She wouldn't be lying in court. Just me.

I had tried a half dozen times to come clean to Kennedy, especially as our relationship shifted from a professional track into a personal one. But as it turned out, that just made it worse. At first I couldn't tell her that I had intervened and touched Davis Bauer when he was seizing because I didn't know if I could trust her, or how the truth would reflect on my case. But now, I couldn't tell her because I was ashamed to have ever lied in the first place.

I burst into tears.

"Those better be tears of happiness," she said. "Or gratitude for my remarkable legal talent."

"That poor baby," I managed. "It's so . . . arbitrary."

But I wasn't crying for Davis Bauer, and I wasn't crying because of my own dishonesty. I was crying because Kennedy had been right all along—it really didn't matter if the nurse attending to Davis Bauer was Black or white or purple. It didn't matter if I tried to resuscitate that baby or not. None of it would have made a difference.

She put her hand on my arm. "Ruth," Kennedy reminded me. "Bad things happen to good people every day."

MY CELLPHONE RINGS JUST AS the bus pulls up to our stop downtown. Edison and I step off as Adisa's voice fills my ear. "Girl, you not gonna believe this. Where you at?"

I look at a sign. "College Street."

"Well, walk toward the green."

I get my bearings, turning with Edison in tow. The courthouse stands a block away from the public park, and Kennedy has given me express directions *not* to approach from this direction, because I will be bombarded by press.

But surely it can't hurt to see what's going on from a distance.

I hear them before I see them, their strong voices braided together in harmony and climbing to the sky like Jack's beanstalk, aimed for Heaven. It is a sea of faces, so many shades of brown, singing "Oh, Freedom." In the front, on a small makeshift dais with a network logo backdrop behind him, is Wallace Mercy. Police form a human barrier, their arms outstretched, as if they are trying to cast a spell to prevent violence. Meanwhile, Elm Street itself is lined with news vans, their dishes craned to the sun, while reporters clutch their microphones with their backs to the green and cameramen film a stream of footage.

"My God," I breathe.

"I didn't have anything to do with it, but that's for you," Adisa says proudly. "You should march right up those front steps with your head held high."

"I can't." Kennedy and I have a prearranged meeting spot.

"Okay," Adisa says, but I can hear the disappointment in her voice.

"I'll see you in there," I tell her. "And, Adisa? Thanks for coming."

She tsks. "Where else would I be?" she says, and then the line goes dead.

EDISON AND I WANDER PAST oblivious Yale students, wearing backpacks like tortoise shells; past the Gothic buildings of the residential colleges that are safely walled off behind black gates; past the Poetry Lady—the homeless woman who will recite a few lines for a donation. When we reach the parish house on Wall Street, we slip behind the building unnoticed, into an empty lot.

"Now what?" Edison asks. He is wearing the suit he wore to Mama's funeral. On any other day, he might be a boy going to a college interview.

"Now we wait," I tell him. Kennedy has a plan to sneak me into the back entrance, where I won't attract media attention. She's asked me to trust her.

Fool that I am, I do.

Turk

LAST NIGHT, WHEN I COULDN'T FALL ASLEEP, I WATCHED SOME CABLE show that was on at 3:00 A.M. about how Indians used to live. They showed a reenactment, a dude in a loincloth, setting fire to a pile of leaves on the long line of a tree that had been split lengthwise. Then, after it burned, he scraped it out with what looked like a clamshell, repeating the process until the canoe was hollowed out. That's what I feel like, today. Like someone has rubbed me raw from the inside, until I'm empty.

It's kind of surprising, because I've been waiting so long for today. I thought for sure I'd have the energy of Superman. I was going to war for my son, and nothing was going to stop me.

But, strangely, I have a sense that I've reached the combat zone and found it deserted.

I'm tired. I'm twenty-five years old and I have lived enough for ten men.

Brit comes out of the bathroom. "All yours," she says. She is wearing a bra and her panty hose, which the prosecutor told her to wear, so that she looks conservative.

"And you," she suggested, "should wear a hat."

Fuck that.

As far as I'm concerned, this is the memorial my son deserves: if I cannot have him back, I will make sure the people responsible for it are punished, and that others like them are left trembling with fear.

I run the hot water and hold my hands under the faucet. Then I lather up with shaving cream. I rub this all over my scalp and start to use my straightedge to scrape my head smooth.

Maybe it's the fact that I could not sleep; or I suppose the crater that's taken up residence inside me is making me shaky—for whatever reason, I nick myself just above the left ear. It stings like a mother as the soap runs into the cut.

I press a washcloth against my head, but scalp wounds take a little while to clot. After a minute I just let go, watch the streak of blood run down my neck, under my collar.

It looks like a red flag, coming from my swastika tattoo. I'm mesmerized by the combination: the white soap, the pale skin, the vivid stain.

FIRST WE DRIVE IN THE opposite direction of the courthouse. There's frost on the front windshield of the pickup and it's sunny, the kind of day that looks perfect until you realize how cold it is when you step outside. We are dressed up—me in the suit jacket that Francis and I share, and Brit in a black dress that used to hug her body and that now hangs on it.

We're the only car in the lot. After I park, I get out and come around to Brit's side. This is not because I'm such a gentleman but because she won't get out. I kneel down beside her, put my hand on her knee. "It's okay," I say. "We can lean on each other."

She juts out her chin, like I've seen her do when she thinks someone is about to dismiss her as weak or ineffective. Then she unfolds herself from the truck. She is wearing flat shoes, the way Odette Lawton told her to, but her coat is short and only reaches to the hip, and I can tell the wind whips through the fabric of her dress fast. I try to stand between her and the gusts, as if I could change up the weather for her.

When we get there, the sun is just hitting the headstone in a way that makes it sparkle. It's white. Blinding white. Brit bends down and traces the letters of Davis's name. The day of his birth, the hopscotch leap to his death. And just one word under that: LOVE.

Brit had wanted it to say LOVED. Those were the directions she gave me for the granite carver. But at the last minute I changed it. I was never going to stop, so why make it past tense?

I told Brit the carver had been the one to screw up. I didn't admit it had been my idea all along.

I like the idea that the word on my son's grave matches the tattoo on the knuckles of my left hand. It's like I carry him with me.

We stand at the grave until Brit gets too cold. There is a peach fuzz of lawn, seeded after the funeral, already brown. A second death.

THE FIRST THINGS I SEE at the courthouse are the niggers.

It's like the whole park in the middle of New Haven is covered with them. They're waving flags and singing hymns.

It's that asshole from television, Wallace Something. The one who thinks he's a reverend and probably got ordained online for five bucks. He's giving some kind of nigger history lesson, talking about Bacon's Rebellion. "In response, my brothers and sisters," he says, "Whites and blacks were separated. If they united, it was believed they could do too much damage together. And by 1705, indentured servants who were Christian—and White—were given land, guns, food, money. Those who were not were enslaved. Our land and livestock was taken. Our arms were taken. If we lifted a hand to a White man, our very lives could be taken." He raises his arms. "History is told by Americans of Anglo descent."

Damn straight. I look at the size of the crowd listening to him. I think of the Alamo, where a handful of Texans held off an army of spics for twelve days.

I mean, they lost, but still.

Suddenly, out of the sea of black, I see a White fist raised. A symbol.

The crowd shifts as the man walks toward me. A big dude, with a bald head and a long red beard. He stops in front of me and Brit and holds out his hand. "Carl Thorheldson," he says, introducing himself. "But you know me as Odin45."

It is the handle of a frequent poster on Lonewolf.org.

His companion shakes my hand, too. "Erich Duval. WhiteDevil."

They are joined by a woman with twins, little silver-haired toddlers each balanced on a hip. Then a dude in camo. Three girls with heavy black eyeliner. A tall man in combat boots with a toothpick clenched between his teeth. A young guy with thick-framed hipster glasses and a laptop in his arms.

A steady stream closes ranks around me—people I know by a shared interest in Lonewolf.org. They are tailors and accountants and teachers, they are Minutemen patrolling the borders in Arizona and militia in the hills of New Hampshire. They are neo-Nazis who never decredited. They have been anonymous, hiding behind the screens of usernames, until now.

For my son, they're willing to be outed once again.

Kennedy

On the morning of the trial, I oversleep. I shoot out of bed like a cannonball, throwing water on my face and yanking my hair into a bun at the nape and stuffing myself into my panty hose and my best navy trial suit. Literally three minutes of grooming, and I'm in the kitchen, where Micah is standing at the stove. "Why didn't you wake me up?" I demand.

He smiles and gives me a quick kiss. "I love you too, moon of my life," he says. "Go sit down next to Violet."

Our daughter is at the table, looking at me. "Mommy? You're wearing two different shoes."

"Oh, God," I mutter, pivoting to go back to the bedroom, but Micah grabs my shoulder and steers me to a seat.

"You're going to eat this while it's hot. You need energy to take down a skinhead and his wife. Otherwise, you're going to run out of steam, and I know from personal experience that the only option for food in that courthouse is something brown they are trying to pass off as coffee and a vending machine of granola bars from the Jurassic period." He puts down a plate—two fried eggs, toast with jam, even hash browns. I am so hungry that I've already finished the eggs before he can set down the last of my breakfast—a steaming latte in his old Harvard Med School mug. "Look," he jokes, "I even served you your coffee in the White Privilege cup."

I burst out laughing. "Then I'll take it with me in the car for luck. Or guilt. Or something."

I kiss Violet on the crown of her head and grab my matching shoe from the bedroom closet, along with my phone, charger, computer, and briefcase. Micah's waiting for me at the door with the mug of coffee. "In all seriousness? I'm proud of you."

I let myself have this one moment. "Thanks."

"Go forth and be Marcia Clark."

I wince. "She's a prosecutor. Can I be Gloria Allred?"

Micah shrugs. "Just knock 'em dead."

I am already walking toward the driveway. "Pretty sure that's the last thing you're supposed to say to someone who's about to try her first murder case," I reply, and I slip into the driver's seat without spilling a drop of my coffee.

I mean, that's got to be a sign, right?

I DRIVE AROUND THE FRONT of the courthouse just to see what's happening, even though I've arranged to meet Ruth somewhere I know she won't be accosted. A circus, that's really the only way to describe it. On one end of the green, Wallace Freaking Mercy is broadcasting live, preaching to a crowd through a megaphone. "In 1691 the word *white* was used in court for the first time. Back then, this nation went by the one-drop rule," I hear him say. "You needed only one drop of blood to be considered black in this country . . ."

On the other end of the green is a cluster of white people. At first I think they are watching Wallace's shenanigans, and then I see one hoisting the picture of the dead baby.

They begin to march through the group that is listening to Wallace. There are curses, shoving, a punch thrown. The police immediately join the fray, pushing the blacks and the whites apart.

It makes me think of a magic trick I did last year to impress Violet. I poured water into a pie pan and dusted the top with pepper. Then I told her the pepper was afraid of Ivory soap, and sure enough, when I dipped the bar of soap into the bowl, the pepper flew to the edges.

To Violet, it was magic. Of course I knew better—what caused the pepper to run from the soap was surface tension.

Which, really, is kind of what's going on here.

I drive around to the parish house on Wall Street. Immediately, I see Edison, standing lookout—but no Ruth. I get out of my car, feeling my heart sink. "Is she . . . ?"

He points across the lot, to where Ruth is standing on the sidewalk, looking at the foot traffic across the street. So far, nobody has noticed her, but it's a risk. I go to drag her back, touching her arm, but she shakes me away. "I would like a moment," she says formally.

I back off.

Students and professors pass, their collars turned up against the wind. A bicycle whizzes by, and then the dinosaur bulk of a bus sighs at the curb, belching out a few passengers before moving away again. "I keep having these . . . thoughts," Ruth says. "You know, all weekend long. How many more times will I get to take the bus? Or cook breakfast? Is this the last time I'll write out a check for my electricity bill? Would I have paid more attention last April when the daffodils first came up, if I'd known I wasn't going to see them again?"

She takes a step toward a line of adolescent trees planted in a neat row. Her hands wrap around one narrow trunk as if she's throttling it, and she turns her face to the bare branches overhead.

"Look at that sky," Ruth says. "It's the kind of blue you find in tubes of oil paint. Like color, boiled down to its essence." Then she turns to me. "How long does it take to forget this?"

I put my arm around her shoulders. She's shaking, and I know it has nothing to do with the temperature. "If I have anything to say about it," I tell her, "you'll never find out."

Ruth

WHEN EDISON WAS LITTLE, I ALWAYS KNEW WHEN HE WAS GETTING UP to no good. I could sense it, even if I couldn't see it. *I've got eyes in the back of my head,* I would tell him, when he was amazed that even if I turned away, I knew he was trying to steal a snack before dinner.

Maybe that is why, even though I am facing forward like Kennedy told me to, I can feel the stares of everyone sitting behind me in the gallery.

They feel like pinpricks, arrows, tiny bug bites. It takes all my concentration to not slap at the back of my neck, swat them away.

Who am I kidding? It takes all my concentration not to stand up and run down the aisle and out of this courtroom.

Kennedy and Howard are bent together, deep in a strategy session; they don't have time to talk me down from the ledge. The judge has made it clear that he won't tolerate disruption from the gallery, and that he has a zero tolerance policy—first strike, you're out. Certainly that is keeping the white supremacists in check. But they are not the only ones whose eyes are boring into me.

There are a whole host of Black people, many faces I recognize from my mother's funeral, who have come to lift me up on their prayers. Directly behind me are Edison and Adisa. They are holding hands on the armrest between their seats. I can feel the strength of that bond, like a force field. I listen to their breathing.

All of a sudden I'm back in the hospital, doing what I did best, my hand on the shoulder of a woman in labor and my eyes on the screen that monitors her vitals. "Inhale," I'd order. "Exhale. Deep breath in . . . deep breath out." And sure enough, the tension would leach out of her. Without that strain, progress could be made.

It's time to take my own advice.

I draw in all the air I can, nostrils flaring, breathing so deeply I envision the vacuum I create, the walls bending inward. My lungs swell in my chest, full to bursting. For a second I hold time still.

And then, I let go.

ODETTE LAWTON DOES NOT MAKE eye contact with me. She is completely focused on the jury. She is one of them. Even the distance she puts between herself and the defense table is a way of reminding the people who will decide my fate that she and I have *nothing* in common. No matter what they see when they look at our skin.

"Ladies and gentlemen of the jury," she says, "the case you are about to hear is horrible and tragic. Turk and Brittany Bauer were, like many of us, excited to become parents. In fact the best day of their lives was October first, 2015. On that day, their son Davis was born." She rests her hand on the rail of the jury box. "Unlike all parents, however, the Bauers have some personal preferences that led them to feel uncomfortable with an African American nurse caring for their child. You may not like what they believe, you may not agree with them, but you cannot deny their just due as patients in the hospital to make decisions about the medical care of their baby. Exercising that privilege, Turk Bauer requested that only certain nurses attend to his infant. The defendant was not one of them—and, ladies and gentlemen, that was a slight she could not stomach."

If I weren't so terrified, I would laugh. That's it? That's the way

Odette glossed over the racism that led to that damn Post-it note on the file? It's almost impressive, the way she so neatly flipped it so that before the jury got a glance at the ugliness, they were looking at something else entirely: patients' rights. I glance at Kennedy, and she shrugs the tiniest bit. *I told you so.*

"On Saturday morning, little Davis Bauer was taken to the nursery for his circumcision. The defendant was alone in that room when the baby went into distress. So what did she do?" Odette hesitates. "Nothing. This nurse with over twenty years of experience, this woman who had taken an oath to administer care as best she could, *just stood there.*" Turning, she points to me. "The defendant stood there, and she watched that baby struggle to breathe, and she let that baby die."

Now I can feel the jury picking me over, jackals at carrion. Some of them seem curious, some stare with revulsion. It makes me want to crawl under the defense table. Take a shower. But then I feel Kennedy squeeze my hand where it rests on my lap, and I lift my chin. *Do not let them see you sweat,* she'd said.

"Ruth Jefferson's behavior was wanton, reckless, and intentional. Ruth Jefferson is a murderer."

Hearing the word leveled at me, even though I have been expecting it, still takes me by surprise. I try to build a levee against the shock of it, by picturing in quick succession all the babies I have held in my arms, the first touch they've had for comfort in this world.

"The evidence will show that the defendant stood there doing nothing while that infant fought for his life. When other medical professionals came in and prodded her into action, she used more force than was necessary and violated all the professional standards of care. She was so violent to this little baby boy that you will see the bruising in his autopsy photos."

She faces the jury once more. "We have all had our feelings hurt, ladies and gentlemen," Odette says. "But even if you don't feel that a choice was made correctly—even if you find it a moral affront—you don't retaliate. You don't cause harm to an innocent, to get back at the person who's wronged you. And yet this is exactly what the defendant did. Had she acted in accordance with her training as a medical professional, instead of being motivated by rage and retaliation, Davis Bauer would be alive today. But with Ruth Jefferson on the job?" She looks me square in the eye. "That baby didn't stand a chance."

Beside me, Kennedy rises smoothly. She walks toward the jury, her heels clicking on the tile floor. "The prosecutor," she says, "will have you believe this case is black and white. But not in the way that you think. I'm representing Ruth Jefferson. She is a graduate of SUNY Plattsburgh who went on to get a nursing degree at Yale. She has practiced as a labor and delivery nurse for over twenty years in the state of Connecticut. She was married to Wesley Jefferson, who died overseas serving in our military. By herself, she raised a son, Edison, an honor student who is applying to college. Ruth Jefferson is not a monster, ladies and gentlemen. She is a good mother, she was a good wife, and she is an exemplary nurse."

She crosses back to the defense table and puts her hand on my shoulder. "The evidence is going to show that one day, a baby died during Ruth's shift. Not just any baby, though. The infant was the child of Turk Bauer, a man who hated her because of her skin color. And what happened? When the baby died, he went to the police and blamed Ruth. In spite of the fact that the pediatrician—who you will hear from—commended Ruth for the way she fought to save that infant during his respiratory arrest. In spite of the fact that Ruth's boss—who you will hear from—told Ruth not to touch this child, when the hospital had no right to tell her to abandon her duty as a nurse."

Kennedy walks toward the jury again. "Here is what the evidence will show: Ruth was confronted with an impossible situation. Should she follow the orders of her supervisor, and the misguided wishes of the baby's parents? Or should she do whatever she possibly could to save his life?

"Ms. Lawton said that this case was tragic, and she is right. But again, not for the reason you think. Because nothing Ruth Jefferson did or didn't do would have made a difference for little Davis Bauer. What the Bauers—and the hospital—did not know at the time is that the baby had a life-threatening condition that had gone unidentified. And it wouldn't have mattered if it were Ruth in the room with him, or

Florence Nightingale. There is simply no way Davis Bauer would have survived."

She spreads her hands, a concession. "The prosecutor would have you believe that the reason we are here today is negligence. But it was not Ruth who was inattentive—it was the hospital and the state lab, which failed to promptly flag a severe medical condition in the infant that, if diagnosed sooner, might have saved his life. The prosecutor would have you believe that the reason we are here today is rage and retaliation. That's true. But it's not Ruth who was consumed by anger. It was Turk and Brittany Bauer, who, lost in grief and pain, wanted to find a scapegoat. If they could not have their son, alive and healthy, they wanted someone else to suffer. And so, they targeted Ruth Jefferson." She looks at the jury. "There has already been one innocent victim. I urge you to prevent there being a second."

I HAVEN'T SEEN CORINNE IN months. She looks older, and there are circles under her eyes. I wonder if she is with the same boyfriend, if she's been ill, what crisis has overtaken her life lately. I remember how when we got salads down in the cafeteria and ate them in the break room, she would give me her tomatoes and I would pass over my olives.

If the past few months have taught me anything, it's that friendship is a smoke screen. The people you think are solid turn out to be mirrors and light; and then you look down and realize there are others you took for granted, those who are your foundation. A year ago, I would have told you that Corinne and I were close, but that turned out to be proximity instead of connection. We were default acquaintances, buying each other Christmas gifts and going out for tapas on Thursday nights not because we had so much in common, but because we worked so hard and so long that it was easier to continue our shorthand conversation than to branch out and teach someone else the language.

Odette asks Corinne to give her name, her address. Then she asks, "Are you employed?"

From the witness stand, Corinne makes eye contact with me, and then her gaze slides away. "Yes. At Mercy–West Haven Hospital."

"Do you know the defendant in this matter?"

"Yes," Corinne admits. "I do."

But she doesn't, not really. She never did.

To be fair, I guess, I didn't really know who I was, either.

"How long have you known her?" Odette asks.

"Seven years. We worked together as nurses on the L and D ward."

"I see," the prosecutor says. "Were you both working on October first, 2015?"

"Yes. We started our shift at seven A.M."

"Did you care for Davis Bauer that morning?"

"Yes," Corinne says. "But I took over for Ruth."

"Why?"

"Our supervisor, Marie Malone, asked me to."

Odette makes a big to-do about entering a certified copy of the medical record into evidence. "I'd like to refer you to exhibit twenty-four, in front of you. Can you tell the jury what it is?"

"A medical records folder," Corinne explains. "Davis Bauer was the patient."

"Is there a note in the front of the file?"

"Yes," Corinne says, and she reads it aloud. *"No African American personnel to care for this patient."*

Each word, it's a bullet.

"As a result of this, the patient was reassigned from the defendant to you, correct?"

"Yes."

"Did you observe Ruth's reaction to that note?" Odette asks.

"I did. She was angry and upset. She told me that Marie had taken her off the case because she's Black, and I said that didn't sound like Marie. You know, like, there must have been more going on. She didn't want to hear it. She said, 'That baby means nothing to me.' And then she stormed off."

Stormed off? I went down the staircase, instead of taking the elevator. It is remarkable how events and truths can be reshaped, like wax that's sat too long in the sun. There is no such thing as a fact. There is only how you saw the fact, in a given moment. How you reported the fact. How your brain processed that fact. There is no extrication of the storyteller from the story.

"Was Davis Bauer a healthy baby?" the prosecutor continues.

"It seemed that way," Corinne admits. "I mean, he wasn't nursing a lot, but that wasn't particularly significant. Lots of babies are logy at first."

"Were you at work on Friday, October second?"

"Yes," Corinne says.

"Was Ruth?"

"No. She wasn't supposed to come in at all, but I'm pretty sure we were shorthanded and she got pulled in to do a double—seven p.m., running straight into Saturday."

"So you were Davis's nurse all day Friday?"

"Yes."

"Did you perform any routine procedures on the infant?"

Corinne nods. "At around two-thirty I did the heel stick. It's a standard blood test—it wasn't done because the baby was sick or anything. All newborns get it, and it goes off to the state lab for analysis."

"Did you have any concerns about your patient that day?"

"He was still having trouble latching on for breast feeding, but again, that's not extraordinary for a first-time mom and a newborn." She smiles at the jury. "Blind leading the blind, and all that."

"Did you have any conversation with the defendant about Davis Bauer when she came on shift?"

"No. In fact she seemed to ignore him completely."

It is like an out-of-body experience—sitting right here, in plain sight, and hearing these people discuss me as if I am not present.

"When did you next see Ruth?"

"Well, she was still on duty when I came back on shift at seven a.m. She'd pulled an all-nighter, and was scheduled to leave at eleven a.m."

"What happened that morning?" Odette asks.

"The baby was being circumcised. Usually the parents don't like to see that happen in front of them, so we take the infant to the nursery.

We give them a little bit of sweeties—basically sugar water—to calm them down a little, and the pediatrician does the procedure. When I wheeled in the bassinet, Ruth was waiting in the nursery. It had been a crazy morning, and she was taking a breather."

"Did the circumcision go as planned?"

"Yes, no complications. The protocol is to monitor the baby for ninety minutes to make sure there's no bleeding, or any other sort of issue."

"Is that what you did?"

"No," Corinne admits. "I was called for an emergency C-section for one of my other patients. Our charge nurse, Marie, accompanied me to the OR, which is her job. That meant Ruth was the only nurse left on the floor. So I grabbed her and asked her to watch over Davis." She hesitates. "You have to understand, we're a tiny hospital. We have a skeletal staff. And when a medical emergency happens, decisions are made quickly."

Beside me, Howard scribbles a note.

"A stat C-section takes twenty minutes, tops. I assumed I'd be back in that nursery before the infant even woke up."

"Did you have any concern about leaving Davis in Ruth's care?"

"No," she says firmly. "Ruth's the best nurse I've ever met."

"How long were you gone?" Odette asks.

"Too long," Corinne says softly. "By the time I got back, the baby was dead."

The prosecutor turns to Kennedy. "Your witness."

Kennedy smiles at Corinne as she walks toward the witness stand. "You say you worked with Ruth for seven years. Would you consider yourself friends?"

Corinne's eyes dart to me. "Yes."

"Have you ever doubted her commitment to her career?"

"No. She has pretty much been a role model for me."

"Were you in the nursery for any of the time that a medical intervention was taking place with Davis Bauer?"

"No," Corinne says. "I was with my other patient."

"So you didn't see Ruth take action."

"No."

"And," Kennedy adds, "you didn't see Ruth *not* take action."

"No."

She holds up the piece of paper Howard has passed to her. "You stated, and I quote, *When a medical emergency happens, decisions are made quickly.* Do you remember saying that?"

"Yes . . ."

"Your stat C-section was a medical emergency, right?"

"Yes."

"Wouldn't you also say that a newborn suffering a respiratory seizure qualifies as a medical emergency?"

"Um, yes, of course."

"Were you aware that there was a note in the file that said Ruth was not to care for this baby?"

"Objection!" Odette says. "That's not what the note said."

"Sustained," the judge pronounces. "Ms. McQuarrie, rephrase."

"Were you aware that there was a note in the file that said no African American personnel could care for the baby?"

"Yes."

"How many Black nurses work in your department?"

"Just Ruth."

"Were you aware when you grabbed Ruth to fill in for you that the baby's parents had expressed the desire to prohibit her from caring for their newborn?"

Corinne shifts on the wooden seat. "I didn't think anything was going to happen. The baby was fine when I left."

"The whole reason for monitoring a baby for ninety minutes after a circumcision is because with neonates, things can change on a dime, isn't that right?"

"Yes."

"And the fact is, Corinne, you left that baby with a nurse who was forbidden from ministering to him, correct?"

"I had no other choice," Corinne says, defensive.

"But you *did* leave that infant in Ruth's care?"

"Yes."

"And you *did* know that she wasn't supposed to touch that baby?"

"Yes."

"So you screwed up, essentially, two times over?"

"Well—"

"Funny," Kennedy interrupts. "No one accused *you* of killing that baby."

LAST NIGHT, I DREAMED ABOUT Mama's funeral. The pews were full, and it wasn't winter, but summer. In spite of the air-conditioning and people waving fans and programs, we were all slick with sweat. The church wasn't a church but a warehouse that looked like it had been repurposed after a fire. The cross behind the altar was made of two charred beams fitted together like a puzzle.

I was trying to cry, but I didn't have any tears left. All the moisture in my body had become perspiration. I tried to fan myself, but I didn't have a program.

Then the person sitting beside me handed me one. "Take mine," she said.

I looked over to say thank you, and realized Mama was in the chair next to me.

Speechless, I staggered to my feet.

I peered into the coffin, to see who—instead—was inside.

It was full of dead babies.

MARIE WAS HIRED TEN YEARS after I was. Back then she was an L & D nurse, just like me. We suffered through double shifts and complained about the lousy benefits and survived the remodeling of the hospital. When the charge nurse retired, Marie and I both threw our names into the ring. When HR went with Marie, she came to me, devastated. She said that she was hoping I'd get the job, just so she didn't have to apologize for being the one who was chosen. But really, I was okay with it. I had Edison to watch after, in the first place. And being charge nurse meant a lot more administrative work and less hands-on with patients.

As I watched Marie settle into her new role, I thanked my lucky stars that it had worked out the way it had.

"The baby's father, Turk Bauer, had asked to speak to a supervisor," Marie says, replying to the prosecutor. "He had a concern about the care of his infant."

"What were the contents of that conversation?"

She looks into her lap. "He did not want any Black people touching his baby. He told me that at the same time he revealed a tattoo of a Confederate flag on his forearm."

There is actually a gasp from someone in the jury.

"Had you ever experienced a request like this from a parent?"

Marie hesitates. "We get patient requests all the time. Some women prefer female doctors to deliver their babies, or they don't like being treated by a med student. We do our best to make our patients comfortable, whatever it takes."

"In this case, what did you do?"

"I wrote a note and stuck it in the file."

Odette asks her to examine the exhibit with the medical file, to read the note out loud. "Did you speak to your staff about this patient request?"

"I did. I explained to Ruth that there had been a request to have her step down, due to the father's philosophical beliefs."

"What was her reaction?"

"She took it as a personal affront," Marie says evenly. "I didn't mean it that way. I told her it was just a formality. But she walked out and slammed the door of my office."

"When did you see the defendant again?" Odette asks.

"Saturday morning. I was in the ER with another patient, who had suffered a complication during delivery. As nurse supervisor, I'm required to make that transfer with the attending nurse, who happened to be Corinne. Corinne had left Ruth watching over her other patient—Davis Bauer—postcircumcision. So as soon as I possibly could, I ran back to the nursery."

"Tell us what you saw, Marie."

"Ruth was standing over the bassinet," she says. "I asked her what she was doing, and she said, *Nothing*."

The room closes in on me, and the muscles of my neck and arms tighten. I feel myself frozen again, mesmerized by the blue marble of the baby's cheek, the stillness of his small body. I hear her instructions:

Ambu bag.

Call the code.

I am swimming, I am in over my head, I am wooden.

Start compressions.

Hammering with two fingers on the delicate spring of rib cage, attaching the leads with my other hand. The nursery too cramped for all the people suddenly inside. The needle inserted subcutaneous into the scalp, the blue barrage of swear words as it slips out before striking a vein. A vial rolling off the table. Atropine, squirted into the lungs, coating the plastic tube. The pediatrician, flying into the nursery. The sigh of the Ambu bag being tossed in the trash.

Time? 10:04.

"Ruth?" Kennedy whispers. "Are you all right?"

I cannot get my lips to move. I am in over my head. I am wooden. I am drowning.

"The patient developed wide complex bradycardia," Marie says.

Tombstones.

"We were unable to oxygenate him. Finally, the pediatrician called the time of death. We didn't realize that the parents were in the nursery. There was just so much going on . . . and . . ." She falters. "The father—Mr. Bauer—he ran to the trash can and took the Ambu bag out. He tried to put it on the tube that was still sticking out of the baby's throat. He begged us to show him what to do." She wipes a tear away. "I don't mean to . . . I'm . . . I'm sorry."

I manage to jerk my head a few degrees and see that there are several women in the jury box who are doing the same thing. But me, there are no tears left in me.

I am drowning in everyone *else's* tears.

Odette walks toward Marie and hands her a box of tissues. The soft sound of sobs surrounds me, like cotton batting on all sides. "What happened next?" the prosecutor asks.

Marie dabs at her eyes. "I wrapped Davis Bauer in a blanket. I put his hat back on. And I gave him to his mother and father."

I am wooden.

I close my eyes. And I sink, I sink.

IT TAKES ME A FEW minutes to focus on Kennedy, who has already started the cross-examination of Marie when I clear my head. "Did any patient ever complain to you about Ruth's expertise as a nurse, prior to Turk Bauer?"

"No."

"Did Ruth provide substandard care?"

"No."

"When you wrote that note in the infant's chart, you knew there would only be two nurses working at any given time, and that there might be a possibility the patient might be left without supervision at some point during his hospital stay?"

"That's not true. The other nurse on duty would have covered."

"And what if that nurse was busy? What if," Kennedy says, "she got called away on an emergency C-section, for example, and the only nurse remaining on the floor was in fact African American?"

Marie's mouth opens and closes, but no sound emerges.

"I'm sorry, Ms. Malone—I didn't quite get that."

"Davis Bauer was not left unsupervised at any point," she insists. "Ruth was there."

"But you—her supervisor—you had prohibited her from ministering to this particular patient, isn't that right?"

"No, I—"

"Your note barred her from actively treating this particular patient—"

"In *general*," Marie explains. "Obviously not in the case of *emergency*."

Kennedy's eyes flash. "Was that written in the patient's chart?"

"No, but—"

"Was that written on your Post-it note?"

"No."

"Did you advise Ruth that in certain circumstances her Nightingale pledge as a nurse should supersede what you'd ordered?"

"No," Marie murmurs.

Kennedy folds her arms. "Then how," she asks, "was Ruth supposed to know?"

WHEN COURT BREAKS FOR LUNCH, Kennedy offers to get us a bite to eat, so that Edison and I don't have to run a gauntlet of press. I tell her I'm not hungry. "I know it doesn't feel like it," she tells me. "But this was a good start."

I give her a look that tells her exactly what I'm thinking: there is no way that jury isn't going to be thinking of Turk Bauer trying to resuscitate his own son.

After Kennedy leaves us, Edison sits down beside me. He loosens his tie. "You all right?" I ask him, squeezing his hand.

"I can't believe you're the one asking me that."

A lady walks by us and sits beside Edison on the bench outside the courtroom. She is deeply involved in a text conversation on her phone. She laughs and frowns and tsks, a human opera of one. Then finally she looks up as if she's just realized where she is.

She sees Edison beside her, and shifts just the tiniest bit, to put a hair of space between them. Then she smiles, as if this will make everything all right.

"You know," I say, "I'm sort of hungry."

Edison grins. "I'm *always* hungry."

We rise in tandem and sneak out the back of the courthouse. I don't even care at this point if I run into the entirety of the media, or Wallace Mercy himself. I wander down the street with my arm tucked into Edison's until we find a pizza place.

We order slices and sit down, waiting to be called. In the booth, Edison hunches over his Coca-Cola, sucking hard on the straw until he reaches the bottom of the glass and slurps. I, too, am lost in my thoughts and my memories.

I guess I didn't realize that a trial is not just a sanctioned character assassination. It is a mind game, so that the defendant's armor is chipped away one scale at a time, until you can't help but wonder if maybe what the prosecution is saying is true.

What if I *had* done it on purpose?

What if I'd hesitated not because of Marie's Post-it note but because, deep down, I *wanted* to?

I am distracted by Edison's voice. Blinking, I come back to center. "Did they call our name?"

He shakes his head. "Not yet. Mama, can I . . . can I ask you something?"

"Always."

He mulls for a moment, as if he is sifting through words. "Was it . . . was it really like that?"

There is a bell at the front counter. Our food is ready.

I make no move to retrieve it. Instead I meet my son's gaze. "It was worse," I say.

THE ANESTHESIOLOGIST WHO IS CALLED that afternoon as a witness for the State is someone I do not know very well. Isaac Hager doesn't work on my floor unless a code is called. Then, he arrives with the rest of the team. When he came to minister to Davis Bauer I did not even know his name.

"Prior to responding to the code," Odette asks, "had you ever met this patient?"

"No," Dr. Hager says.

"Had you ever met his parents?"

"No."

"Can you tell us what you did when you reached the nursery?"

"I intubated the patient," Dr. Hager replies. "And when my colleagues couldn't get an IV in, I tried to help."

"Did you make any comments to Ruth during this process?" Odette asks.

"Yes. She was doing compressions, and I instructed her at several times to stop so that we could see if the patient was responding. At one point, when I felt she was a little aggressive with her chest compressions, I told her so."

"Can you describe what she was doing?"

"Chest compressions on an infant involve pressing the sternum down a half inch, about two hundred times a minute. The complexes on the monitor were too high; I thought Ruth was pushing down too hard."

"Can you explain what that means to a layperson?"

Dr. Hager looks at the jury. "Chest compressions are the way we manually make a heart beat, if it's not doing it by itself. The point is to physically push the cardiac output . . . but then let up on your thrust long enough to let blood fill the heart. It's not unlike plunging a toilet. You have to push down, but if you keep doing that and don't pull up, creating suction, the bowl won't fill with water. Likewise, if you do compressions too fast or too hard, you're pumping, pumping, pumping, but there's no blood circulating in the body."

"Do you remember what you said to Ruth, exactly?"

He clears his throat. "I told her to lighten up."

"Is it unusual for an anesthesiologist to suggest a modification to the person who is doing compressions?"

"Not at all," Dr. Hager says. "It's a system of checks and balances. We're all watching each other during a code. I might just as well have been watching to see if both sides of the chest were rising, and if they weren't, I would have told Marie Malone to bag harder."

"How long was Ruth overly aggressive?"

"Objection!" Kennedy says. "She's putting words in the witness's mouth."

"I'll rephrase. How long was the defendant aggressive with her chest compressions?"

"It was only slightly aggressive, and for less than a minute."

"In your expert medical opinion, Doctor," Odette asks, "could the defendant's actions have caused harm to the patient?"

"The act of saving a life can look pretty violent, Ms. Lawton. We slice open skin, we crack ribs, we shock with extreme voltage." Then he turns to me. "We do what we have to do, and when we are lucky, it works."

"Nothing further," the prosecutor says.

Kennedy approaches Dr. Hager. "Emotions were running very high in that nursery, weren't they?"

"Yes."

"Those compressions that Ruth was doing—were they adversely affecting the infant's life?"

"On the contrary. They were keeping him alive while we attempted medical intervention."

"Were they contributory to the infant's death?"

"No."

Kennedy leans on the railing of the jury box. "Is it fair to say that in that nursery, everyone was trying to save that baby's life?"

"Absolutely."

"Even Ruth?"

Dr. Hager looks right at me. "Yes," he says.

THERE IS A RECESS AFTER the anesthesiologist's testimony. The judge leaves, and the jury is removed from their box. Kennedy spirits me away to a conference room, where I am supposed to stay, so that I remain safely sequestered from the media.

I want to talk to Edison. I want a hug from Adisa. But instead I sit at a small table in a room with hissing fluorescent lights, trying to untangle this chess game in my head.

"You ever wonder?" I ask. "What you'd do, if you weren't a lawyer?"

Kennedy glances at me. "Is this your way of telling me I'm doing a shitty job?"

"No, I'm just thinking. About . . . starting over."

She unwraps a piece of gum and passes me the rest of the packet. "Don't laugh, but I wanted to be a pastry chef once."

"Really?"

"I went to culinary school for three weeks. I was eventually conquered by phyllo. I just don't have the patience for it."

A smile dances over my face. "Go figure."

"What about you?" Kennedy asks.

I look up at her. "I don't know," I admit. "I've wanted to be a nurse since I was five. I feel like I'm too old to start over, and even if I had to, I wouldn't know where else to go."

"That's the problem with having a *calling*," Kennedy says. "It doesn't just pay the rent."

A calling. Is that why I unwrapped Davis Bauer's blanket when he wasn't breathing? "Kennedy," I begin, "there's something—"

But she interrupts. "You could go back to school. Get a medical degree or become a PA," she suggests. "Or work as a private caregiver."

Neither of us says the truth that squeezes into the small room with us: *convicted felon* doesn't look good on a résumé.

When she sees my face, her eyes soften. "It's going to work out, Ruth. There's a grand plan."

"What if?" I say softly. "What if the grand plan doesn't come to pass?"

She sets her jaw. "Then I will do whatever I can to get your sentence minimized."

"I'd have to go to prison?"

"Right now the State's leveled several charges against you. At any time if they decide they don't have the evidence to support them, they might drop a greater charge in favor of conviction on a lesser one. So if they can't prove murder, but they think they have negligent homicide locked up, Odette may play it safe." She meets my gaze. "Murder has a minimum sentence of twenty-five years. But negligent homicide? Less than a year. And to be honest, they're going to have a very hard time proving intent. Odette's going to have to tiptoe through her questioning of Turk Bauer or the jury's going to hate him."

"You mean as much as I do?"

Kennedy's eyes sharpen. "Ruth," she warns, "I never want to hear you say those words out loud again. Do you understand?"

In an instant, I realize Kennedy is not the only one thinking six moves ahead. So is Odette. She *wants* the jury to hate Turk Bauer. She wants them outraged, offended, morally disgusted.

And that's exactly how she will prove motive.

I'VE ALWAYS ADMIRED DR. ATKINS, the pediatrician, but after hearing her list her credentials and rattle off her CV, I'm even more impressed. She is one of those rare individuals who has more awards and honors than you'd ever expect, because she's humble enough to not mention it herself. She is also the first witness to take the stand who looks directly at me and smiles before turning her attention to the prosecutor.

"Ruth had already done the newborn exam," Dr. Atkins says. "She was concerned about a potential heart murmur."

"Was that a significant concern?" Odette asks.

"No. A lot of babies are born with an open patent ductus. A teensy little hole in the heart. It usually closes up by itself, the first year of life. However, to be safe, I scheduled a pediatric cardiology consult prior to patient discharge."

I know, from Kennedy, that Odette will be assuming the medical issue Kennedy referenced in her opening statement is this heart murmur. That she's downplaying it, already, for the jury.

"Dr. Atkins, were you working on Saturday, October third—the day of Davis Bauer's death?"

"Yes. I came in to do the patient's circumcision at nine A.M."

"Can you explain that procedure?"

"Of course, it's a very simple operation during which the foreskin of a male infant's penis is removed. I was running a little late because I had another patient with an emergency."

"Was anyone else present?"

"Yes, two nurses. Corinne and Ruth. I asked Ruth if the patient was ready, and she said she was no longer his nurse. Corinne confirmed that the infant was ready for the procedure, and I performed it without incident."

"Did Ruth say anything to you about the circumcision?"

Dr. Atkins pauses. "She said maybe I should sterilize the baby."

Behind me, in the gallery, someone whispers: *Bitch*.

"How did you respond?"

"I didn't. I had work to do."

"How did the procedure go?"

The pediatrician shrugs. "He was crying afterward, like all infants do. We swaddled him tight, and he drifted off." She looks up. "When I left, he was sleeping . . . well . . . like a baby."

"Your witness," Odette says.

"Doctor, you've worked at the hospital for eight years?" Kennedy begins.

"Yes." She laughs a little. "Wow. Time flies."

"During that time, have you worked with Ruth before?"

"Frequently, and joyously," Dr. Atkins says. "She is a terrific nurse who goes above and beyond for her patients."

"When Ruth made the comment about sterilizing the infant, how did you perceive her statement?"

"As a joke," Dr. Atkins says. "I knew she was kidding. Ruth isn't the type to be malicious about patients."

"After Davis Bauer's circumcision, were you still working in the hospital?"

"Yes, on a different floor, in the pediatric clinic."

"Were you made aware of an emergency in the nursery?"

"Yes. Marie had called the code. When I arrived, Ruth was compressing the chest."

"Did Ruth do everything according to the highest standards of care?"

"As far as I could see, yes."

"Did she indicate any animus or bias against this child?" Kennedy asks.

"No."

"I'd like to jump back a bit," Kennedy says. "Did you order any blood work to be done on Davis Bauer after his birth?"

"Yes, the newborn screening that's done by the state of Connecticut."

"Where does the blood work go?"

"The state lab in Rocky Hill tests it. We don't do it in-house."

"How is it transported to the state lab?"

"By courier," Dr. Atkins says.

"When was Davis Bauer's blood taken for the screening?"

"At two-thirty P.M., on Friday, October second."

"Did you ever receive the results of the newborn screening test from the Connecticut state lab?"

Dr. Atkins frowns, considering this. "Actually, I don't remember seeing them. But of course by then it was a moot point."

"What is the purpose of the test?"

She lists a series of rare diseases. Some are caused by genetic mutation. Some are issues with not having enough of an enzyme or protein in the body. Others result from not being able to break down enzymes or proteins. "Most of you have never heard of these conditions," Dr. Atkins says, "because most babies don't have them. But the ones that do—well, some of the disorders are treatable if caught early. If we make accommodations through diet or medicine or hormone therapy, we can often prevent significant growth delays and cognitive impairment by starting immediate treatment."

"Are any of these conditions fatal?"

"Some, if they're left untreated."

"You did not have the benefit of the results of this test when Davis Bauer had a seizure, did you?" Kennedy asks.

"No. The state lab is closed on weekends. We usually don't get Friday's results back until Tuesday."

"What you're saying," Kennedy mulls, "is that it takes almost twice as long to get the test results back if the baby has the misfortune to be born at the end of the workweek."

"That's true, unfortunately."

I can see the jury perking up, writing down notes, listening intently. Behind me, Edison shifts. Maybe Kennedy is right. Maybe all they need is science.

"Are you aware of a disorder called MCADD?" Kennedy asks.

"Yes. It's a fatty acid oxidation disorder. Basically, an infant who has it will have trouble breaking down fats, and that means the blood sugar drops to dangerously low levels. It can be managed with early detection—a careful diet, frequent feedings."

"Let's say it isn't detected. What happens?"

"Well, infants who have MCADD have a significant risk of death during the first clinical episode of hypoglycemia—when that blood sugar goes south."

"What would that look like?"

"They'd be sleepy, logy. Irritable. They wouldn't nurse well."

"Let's say, hypothetically, a baby with undiagnosed, untreated MCADD was about to be circumcised. Is there anything about that procedure that might have exacerbated the disease?"

The pediatrician nods. "Normally there would be fasting after six A.M., because of the upcoming surgery. For a baby with MCADD, that would lead to low blood sugar—a potential episode of hypoglycemia. Instead, ten percent dextrose would have been given to the baby prior and afterward."

"You drew blood from Davis Bauer during the code, didn't you?"

"Yes."

"Can you tell the jury the results of his blood sugar at that time?" Kennedy asks.

"Twenty."

"At what level is a newborn considered hypoglycemic?"

"Forty."

"So Davis Bauer's blood sugar was dangerously low?"

"Yes."

"Would it have been enough to cause a child with untreated, undiagnosed MCADD to go into respiratory failure?"

"I can't say for sure. But it's possible."

Kennedy lifts a file. "I'd like to enter this as exhibit forty-two," she says. "It's the newborn screening result of Davis Bauer, which was sub-poenaed by the defense."

Odette stands like a shot. "Your Honor, what is this stunt? Defense hasn't shared this with the prosecution—"

"That's because I received these results just days ago. They were *conveniently* missing from the discovery, however, for *months*," Kennedy replies. "Which I could claim as obstruction of justice . . ."

"Approach." The judge calls both lawyers to the bench. A machine is turned on so that I cannot hear what they're saying, and neither can the jury. When they finish, though, it's after much hand waving and a dark flush on Kennedy's face. But the record is handed to the clerk to be entered as evidence.

"Dr. Atkins, can you tell us what you're looking at?" Kennedy asks.

"It's a newborn screening test result," the pediatrician says, sifting through the pages. Then she stops. "Oh, my God."

"Is there any particular finding of interest in the results, Dr. Atkins? The results that didn't get processed because the state lab was closed all weekend? The results you didn't receive until *after* the death of Davis Bauer?"

The pediatrician looks up. "Yes. Davis Bauer screened positive for MCADD."

KENNEDY IS HIGH ON HERSELF when court is dismissed that first day. She's talking fast, like she's had four big cups of coffee, and she seems to feel like we won our case, even though the prosecution has only just begun and we haven't started the defense. She tells me I should drink a big glass of wine to celebrate a phenomenal day of testimony, but honestly, all I want to do is go home and crawl into bed.

My head is aching with images of Davis Bauer, and with the look on Dr. Atkins's face when she realized what the test results said. True, Kennedy had shared them with me two nights ago, but this was even more devastating. To see someone else from the hospital—someone I liked and trusted—silently thinking, *If only* . . . It recentered me a little.

Yes, this is a trial against me.

Yes, I was blamed for something I shouldn't have been blamed for.

But at the end of the day, there's still a dead baby. There's still a mama who doesn't get to watch him grow up. I could be acquitted; I could become a shining light for Wallace Mercy's message; I could sue in civil court for damages and get a payout that makes my nerves about Edison's college bills disappear—and still, I would know that nobody had really *won* this case.

Because you can't erase the colossal, tragic loss of a life at its very beginning.

That's what's running through my mind as I wait for the hallways to clear, so that Edison and I can go home without attracting attention. He is waiting for me on a bench outside the conference room. "Where's your aunt?"

He shrugs. "She said she wanted to get home before the snow really started."

I glance out the window, where flakes are falling. I've been turned inward so much, I hadn't even noticed an oncoming storm. "Let me just use the restroom," I tell Edison, and I walk down the empty hall.

I go into the stall and do my business, flush, and come out to wash my hands. Standing at the sink is Odette Lawton. She glances at me in the mirror, puts the cap on her lipstick. "Your lawyer had a good first day," she concedes.

I don't know what to say, so I just let the hot water run over my wrists.

"But if I were you, I wouldn't get too complacent. You may be able to convince Kennedy McQuarrie you're Clara Barton, but I know what you were thinking after that racist put you in your place. And they were *not* healing thoughts."

It is too much. Something bubbles up inside me, a geyser, a realization. I shut the faucet, dry my hands, and face her. "You know, I have spent my life doing everything right. I have studied hard and smiled pretty and played by the rules to get where I am. And I know you have too. So it is *really* hard for me to understand why an intelligent, professional African American woman would go out of her way to put down another intelligent, professional African American woman."

There is a flicker in Odette's eyes, like a breath on a flame. Just as quickly, it's gone, replaced by a steel stare. "This has nothing to do with race. I'm just doing my job."

I throw my paper towel into the trash, put my hand on the door handle. "Aren't you lucky?" I say. "No one told you you couldn't."

THAT NIGHT I AM SITTING at the kitchen table, just lost in my thoughts, when Edison brings me a cup of tea. "What's this for, baby?" I say, smiling.

"I thought you could use it," he tells me. "You look tired."

"I am," I confess. "I am so damn tired."

We both know I'm not talking about the first two days of testimony, either.

Edison sits down beside me, and I squeeze his hand. "It's exhausting, isn't it? Trying so hard to prove that you're better than they expect you to be?"

He nods, and I know he understands what I'm saying. "Court's different than I thought it would be, from what I've seen on TV."

"Longer," I say, at the same time he says, "Boring."

We both laugh.

"I was talking a little to that Howard dude, during one of the recesses," Edison says. "It's pretty cool, his job. And Kennedy's. You know, the whole idea that everyone has the right to a good attorney, even if they can't pay for it." He looks at me, a question wreathed around his features. "You think I'd be a good lawyer, Mama?"

"Well, you're smarter than me, and Lord knows you know how to argue," I tease. "But, Edison, you'll be a star at whatever you choose to do."

"It's funny," he says. "I'd want to do what they do—work for people who can't afford legal representation. But it's kind of like my whole life has prepared me for the other side, instead—the prosecution."

"How do you mean?"

He shrugs. "The State's got the burden of proof," Edison says. "Kind of like we do, every day."

* * *

THE SNOW FALLS HARD AND fast that night, so that the plows can't keep up, and the world becomes completely white. I wear my winter boots with the same skirt I've worn all week—I've been changing up the blouse—and stuff my dress shoes into a Stop & Shop bag. The radio is full of school closings, and the bus Edison and I have been taking breaks down, so we have to hurry to a different line and transfer twice. As a result, we reach the courthouse five minutes late. I've texted Kennedy, and know we don't have time to sneak in through the back. Instead, she meets me on the steps of the courthouse, where immediately microphones are shoved at me and people call me a killer. Edison's arm comes around me and I duck against his chest, letting him form a barrier.

"If we're lucky Judge Thunder had trouble digging his car out today," she mutters.

"It was the public transport sys—"

"I don't care. You don't give the court any extra reasons to dislike you."

We race into the courtroom, where Odette is sitting smugly at the prosecution table, looking like she arrived at 6:00 A.M. For all I know, she sleeps here. Judge Thunder enters, bent at the waist, and we all rise. "I was rear-ended by a cretin on the way to work, and as a result, my back is officially out," he says. "My apologies for the delay."

"Are you all right, Your Honor?" Kennedy says. "Do you need to call a doctor?"

"As much as I appreciate your display of sympathy, Ms. McQuarrie, I imagine you'd prefer I was incapacitated somewhere in a hospital. Preferably without painkillers available. Ms. Lawton, call your witness before I forgo this judicial bravery and take a Vicodin."

The first witness for the prosecution today is the detective who interviewed me after my arrest. "Detective MacDougall," Odette begins, after walking him through his name and address, "where are you employed?"

"In the town of East End, Connecticut."

"How did you become involved in the case we're examining today?"

He leans back. He seems to spill over the chair, to fill the entire witness stand. "I got a call from Mr. Bauer, and I told him to come down to the station so I could take his complaint. He was pretty distraught at the time. He believed that the nurse who had been taking care of his son had intentionally withheld emergency care, which led to the baby's death. I interviewed the medical personnel involved in the case, and had several meetings with the medical examiner . . . and with you, ma'am."

"Did you interview the defendant?"

"Yes. After securing an arrest warrant, we went to Ms. Jefferson's house and knocked on the door—loudly—but she didn't come."

At that, I nearly rise out of my chair. Howard and Kennedy each put a hand on my shoulder, holding me down. It was 3:00 A.M. They did not knock, they pounded until the doorjamb was busted. They held me at gunpoint.

I lean toward Kennedy, my nostrils flaring. "This is a lie. He is *lying* on the stand," I whisper.

"Ssh," she says.

"What happened next?" asks the prosecutor.

"No one answered the door."

Kennedy's hand clamps tighter on my shoulder.

"We were concerned that she might be fleeing through the back door. So I advised my team to use the battering ram to gain entrance to the home."

"Did you in fact gain entrance and arrest Ms. Jefferson?"

"Yes," the detective says, "but first we were confronted with a large Black subject—"

"*No,*" I say under my breath, and Howard kicks me under the table.

"—whom we later determined to be Ms. Jefferson's son. We were also concerned about officer safety, so we conducted a cursory search of the bedroom, while we handcuffed Ms. Jefferson."

They tossed aside my furniture. They broke my dishes. They pulled my clothes off hangers. They tackled my son.

"I advised her of her rights," Detective MacDougall continues, "and read her the charges."

"How did she react?"

He grimaces. "She was uncooperative."

"What happened next?"

"We brought her to the East End station. She was fingerprinted and photographed and put in a holding cell. Then my colleague, Detective Leong, and I brought her into a conference room and again advised her she had the right to have her lawyer there, to not say anything, and that if she wanted to stop answering questions at any time she was free to do so. We told her that her responses could and would be used in court. And then I asked her if she understood all that. She initialed every paragraph, saying that she did."

"Did the defendant request an attorney?"

"Not at that time. She was very willing to explain her version of events. She maintained that she did not touch the infant until he started to code. She also admitted that she and Mr. Bauer did not—how did she put it?—*see eye to eye.*"

"Then what happened?"

"Well, we wanted to let her know that we were looking out for her. If it was an accident, we said, just tell us, and then the judge would go easy on her and we could straighten out the mess and she could get on with raising her boy. But she clammed up and said she didn't want to talk anymore." He shrugs. "I guess it *wasn't* an accident."

"Objection," Kennedy says.

Judge Thunder winces, trying to pivot toward the court reporter. "Sustained. Strike the witness's last comment from the record."

But it hangs in the space between us, like the glow of a neon sign after the plug has been pulled.

I feel negative pressure on my shoulder and realize Kennedy has released me. She stands in front of the detective. "You had a warrant?"

"Yes."

"Did you call Ruth to tell her you'd be coming? Ask her to come voluntarily to the station?"

"That's not what we do with murder warrants," MacDougall says.

"What time was your warrant issued?" ——

"Five P.M. or so."

"And what time did you actually get to Ruth's house?"

"About three A.M."

Kennedy looks at the jury as if to say, *Can you believe this?* "Any particular reason for the delay?"

"It was fully intentional. One of the tenets of law enforcement is to go when someone is least expecting you. That disarms the suspect and moves the process along."

"When you knocked on Ruth's door, then, and she didn't immediately welcome you with a coffee cake and a big hug, is it possible that was because she was fast asleep at three in the morning?"

"I can't speak to the defendant's sleep habits."

"The cursory search you did . . . in fact didn't you actually empty the drawers and cabinets and knock over furniture and otherwise destroy Ms. Jefferson's home when she was handcuffed and unable to access any weapon?"

"You never know when a weapon might be within someone's reach, ma'am."

"Isn't it also true that you pushed her son to the ground and pulled his arms behind his back to subdue him?"

"That's standard procedure for officer safety. We didn't know that was Ms. Jefferson's son. We saw a large, angry Black youth who was visibly upset."

"Really?" Kennedy says. "Was he wearing a hoodie too?"

JUDGE THUNDER STRIKES THAT COMMENT from the record, and when Kennedy sits down, she looks just as surprised by her outburst as I am. "Sorry," she murmurs. "That just slipped out." The judge, though, is furious. He calls counsel up for a sidebar. There is a noise machine again that prevents me from hearing what he says, but from the color of his face, and the full-throttle anger as he laces into my lawyer, I know he didn't ask her up there to praise her.

"That," Kennedy tells me, a little white around the gills when she returns, "is why you don't bring up race in a courtroom."

Judge Thunder decides that his back spasm merits adjournment for the rest of the day.

Because of the snow, it takes us longer to get home. When Edison and I turn the corner on our block, we are damp and exhausted. A man is trying to dig out his car using only his gloved hands. Two neighborhood boys are in the thick of a snowball fight; one missile smacks against Edison's back.

There is a car sitting in front of our house. It's a black sedan with a driver, which isn't something you see very often around here, at least not once you get off the Yale campus. As I approach, the rear door opens and a woman stands up. She is wearing a ski parka and furry boots and is buried under a layer of wool—a hat, a scarf. It takes me a moment to realize that this is Christina.

"What are you doing here?" I ask, truly surprised. In all the years I've been in East End, Christina has not come to visit. In all the years, I haven't invited her.

It's not that I'm ashamed of my home. I love where I live, *how* I live. It's that I did not think I could handle the excessive way she'd exclaim about how cute the space was, how cozy, how *me*.

"I've been in court for the last two days," she admits, and I'm shocked. I've scanned that gallery. I haven't noticed her there, and Christina is very hard to overlook.

She unzips her coat, revealing a ratty flannel shirt and baggy jeans, as far away from her couture sheaths as possible. "I wore camouflage," she says, smiling shyly. She looks over my shoulder, to Edison. "Edison! My God, I haven't seen you since you were shorter than your mother . . ."

He jerks his chin, an awkward hello.

"Edison, why don't you go inside?" I suggest, and when he does, I meet Christina's gaze. "I don't understand. If the press found out that you were here—"

"Then I'd tell them to go screw themselves," she says firmly. "The hell with Congress. I told Larry I was coming, and that it wasn't negotiable. If anyone from the press asks, I'm just going to tell them the truth: that you and I go way back."

"Christina," I ask again, "what are you doing *here*?"

She could have texted. She could have called. She could have simply sat in the courtroom to lend moral support. But instead, she has been waiting in front of my door for God knows how long.

"I'm your *friend*," she says quietly. "Believe it or not, Ruth, this is what friends do." She looks up at me, and I realize she has tears in her eyes. "What they said happened to you—the police breaking in. The handcuffs. The way they attacked Edison. I never imagined . . ." She falters, then gathers up the weeds of her thoughts and offers me the saddest, truest bouquet. "I didn't know."

"Why *would* you?" I reply—not angry, not hurt, just stating a fact. "You'll never have to."

Christina wipes at her eyes, smearing her mascara. "I don't know if I ever told you this story," she says. "It's about your mother. It was a long time ago, when I was in college. I was driving back home from Vassar for Thanksgiving break, and there was a hitchhiker on the side of the road on the Taconic Parkway. He was a Black man, and he had a bum leg. He was literally walking on crutches. So I pulled over and asked if he needed a ride. I took him all the way to Penn Station, so that he could get on a train to visit his family in D.C." She folds her coat more tightly around her. "When I got home, and Lou came into my room to help me unpack, I told her what I'd done. I thought she'd be proud of me, being a Good Samaritan and all. Instead, she got so angry, Ruth! I swear, I'd never seen her like that. She grabbed my arms and shook me; she couldn't even speak at first. *Don't you ever, ever do that again*, she told me, and I was so shocked I promised I wouldn't." Christina looks at me. "Today I sat in that courtroom and I listened to that detective talk about how he busted in your door in the middle of the night and pushed you down and held back Edison and I kept hearing Lou's voice in my head, after I told her about the Black hitchhiker. I knew your mama reacted that way to me because she was scared. But all these years, I thought she was trying to keep me safe. Now, I know she was trying to keep *him* safe."

I realize that for years, I've made the assumption that Christina looks at me as someone from her past to be tolerated, an unfortunate to be helped. As children I felt like we were equals. But as we got older, as we became more aware of what was different about us, instead of what was similar, I felt a wedge drive between us. I secretly criticized her for making judgments about me and my life without asking me questions directly. She was the diva and I was the supporting player in her story. But I conveniently forgot to point out to myself that *I* was the one who'd cast her in that role. I'd blamed Christina for building that invisible wall without admitting I'd added a few bricks of my own.

"I left the money under your welcome mat," I blurt out.

"I know," Christina says. "I should have superglued it to your palm."

There's a foot of space, and a world of contrast, between Christina and me. Yet I, too, know how hard it is to peel back the veneer of your life, and to peek at the real. It's like waking up in a room and getting out of bed and realizing the furniture has been completely rearranged. You will eventually find your way out, but it's going to be slow going, and you're bound to get some bruises along the way.

I reach out and squeeze Christina's hand. "Why don't you come inside?" I say.

THE NEXT DAY IS FRIGID and clear. The memory of yesterday's snowstorm has been scraped off the highways and the temperature keeps some of the crowd away from the front steps of the courthouse. Even Judge Thunder seems settled, made complacent by either whatever drugs he got for his sore back or the fact that we are nearing the end of the prosecution's witnesses. Today, the first person called is the state medical examiner, Dr. Bill Binnie, who studied under the famous Henry Lee. He is younger than I would have imagined, with delicate hands that flutter during his responses, like trained birds sitting in his lap; and he has movie-star looks, so the ladies in the jury are hanging on his responses, even when they are simply the boring litany of all the accomplishments on his CV. "When did you first hear about Davis Bauer, Doctor?" the prosecutor asks.

"My office received a phone message from Corinne McAvoy, a nurse at Mercy–West Haven Hospital."

"Did you respond?"

"Yes. After retrieving the infant's body, we did an autopsy."

"Can you tell the court what that entails?"

"Sure," he says, turning to the jury. "I perform both an external and an internal examination. During the external exam, I look over the body for bruises and to see if there are any marks. I take measurements of the body, and the circumference of the head, and photograph the body. I take blood and bile samples. Then, to perform the internal examination, I make a Y incision in the chest, pull back the skin, and examine the lungs and the heart and the liver as well as other organs, checking for rupture, for gross abnormalities. We weigh and measure the organs. We take tissue samples. And then we send the samples to toxicology and await the results, in order to make a reasonable and factual conclusion about the cause of death."

"What were your findings of note during the autopsy?" Odette asks.

"The liver was slightly enlarged. There was slight cardiomegaly and a minimal grade one patent ductus, but other congenital defects were absent—there were no valvular or plumbing abnormalities."

"What does that mean?"

"The organ was a little large, and there was a small hole in the heart. However, the vessels weren't hooked up wrong," he says. "There were no septal defects."

"Were any of these findings something that suggested the cause of death?"

"Not really," the medical examiner says. "There was good reason for them. According to the patient's medical records, the mother had gestational diabetes during the pregnancy."

"What's that?"

"A condition that leads to high blood sugar for a mother during pregnancy. Unfortunately, that high blood sugar in mothers also has an effect on their infants."

"How so?"

"Infants who are born to mothers with diabetes are often bigger than other babies. Their livers, hearts, and adrenal glands may be enlarged. These infants are also often hypoglycemic after birth because of increased insulin levels in the blood. Again, based on the medical records I studied, the patient's postnatal lab work indicated low blood sugar, as did the femoral stick done during the code. All of the findings of the autopsy, as well as the low blood sugar, would be consistent with an infant born to a diabetic mother."

"What about the hole in the baby's heart? That sounds serious . . ."

"It sounds worse than it is. In most cases, the patent ductus closes up by itself," Dr. Binnie says, and he glances at the jury. The woman who is a teacher, juror number 12, actually starts fanning herself.

"Were you able to determine how the baby died, then?"

"Actually," the medical examiner says. "That's more complicated than most people think. We medical geeks make a distinction between the way a person died and the actual change in the body that causes the termination of life. For example, let's say there is a gunshot and someone dies. The cause of death is the gunshot wound. But the mechanism of death—the actual physical event that ended his life—would be exsanguination—loss of blood."

He turns his attention from Odette to the jury. "And then, there's manner of death—how it came about. Was the gunshot wound an accident? A suicide? Was it a deliberate assault? That becomes important—well—when we're sitting in a courtroom like this."

The prosecutor enters another exhibit. "What you're about to see," Odette warns the jury, "may be extremely disturbing."

She sets up on an easel a photograph of the body of Davis Bauer.

I feel my breath catch in my throat. Those tiny fingers, the bow of the legs. The acorn of his penis, still bloodied from the circumcision. If not for the bruises, the blue tint to his skin, he might be asleep.

I had taken this body from the morgue. I had held him in my own arms. I had rocked him toward Heaven.

"Doctor," Odette begins, "could you tell us—" But before she can finish, there is a crash in the gallery. We all spin around to see Brittany Bauer standing, her eyes wild. Her husband stands in front of her, holding her shoulders. I can't tell if he's trying to keep her subdued or keep her upright.

"Let me go," she shrieks. "That's my *son!*"

Judge Thunder raps his gavel. "I'll have order," he demands, and not unkindly, "Ma'am, please sit back down . . ."

But Brittany points a shaking finger directly at me. It might as well be a Taser for the current that runs through my bones. "You fucking killed my baby." She stumbles into the aisle, approaching me, while I stand caught in the spell of her hate. "I'll make you pay for this, if it's the last thing I do."

Kennedy calls out to the judge as he smacks his gavel again and calls the bailiff. Brittany Bauer's father tries to calm her down, too, but to no avail. There is a shudder of shock and gossip as she is escorted from the courtroom. Her husband is frozen, caught between comforting her and staying for the testimony. After a moment he turns and runs out the double doors.

When the judge calls order, we all face forward again, riveted by that giant poster of the dead infant. One of the jurors bursts into tears and it takes two others to calm her, and then, Judge Thunder calls a recess.

Beside me, Kennedy exhales. "Oh, shit," she says.

FIFTEEN MINUTES LATER, EVERYONE BUT Brittany and Turk Bauer has returned to the courtroom. And yet their absence is almost even more visible, as if the negative space is a constant reminder of why we had to break in the first place. Odette leads the medical examiner through a series of photographs of the baby's body, from every angle possible. She has him explain the different test results, what was standard, what was deviant from the norm. Finally, she asks, "Were you able to determine the cause of death for Davis Bauer?"

Dr. Binnie nods. "For Davis Bauer, the cause of death was hypoglycemia, leading to hypoglycemic seizure, leading to respiratory and then cardiac arrest. In other words, low blood sugar made the infant seize, stop breathing, and that in turn stopped his heart. The method of death was asphyxiation. And the manner was undetermined."

"Undetermined? Does that mean the defendant's actions had nothing to do with the baby's death?" Odette asks.

"On the contrary. It just means that it was not patently clear whether this was a violent or a natural death."

"How did you go about researching that?"

"I read the medical records, of course, as well as a police report that provided information."

"Such as?"

"Mr. Bauer told the police that Ruth Jefferson was aggressively beating on his son's chest. The bruising we found on the sternum could support that allegation."

"Was there anything else in the police report that led you to fill out the report the way you did?"

"According to multiple accounts, there was an indication that the defendant did not take any resuscitative efforts until other personnel came into the room."

"Why was that important to the autopsy results?"

"It goes to the manner of death," Dr. Binnie says. "I don't know how long that infant was in respiratory distress. If the respiratory failure had been alleviated sooner, it's possible that the cardiac arrest would never have occurred." He looks at the jury. "Had the defendant acted, it's possible that none of us would be sitting here."

"Your witness," Odette says.

Kennedy rises. "Doctor, was there anything in the police report that indicated there was foul play or intentional trauma to this infant?"

"I already mentioned the bruising to the sternum . . ."

"Yes, you did. But isn't it possible that the bruising might also be consistent with vigorous, medically necessary CPR?"

"It is," he concedes.

"Is it possible that there might be other scenarios—other than foul play—that might have led to the death of this baby?"

"It's possible."

Kennedy asks him to review the neonatal screening results she entered into evidence earlier. "Doctor, would you mind taking a look at exhibit forty-two?"

He takes the file and thumbs through it.

"Can you tell the jury what you're looking at?"

He glances up. "Davis Bauer's newborn screening results."

"Did you have access to this information while you were performing your autopsy?"

"I did not."

"You work at the state lab where these tests were performed, don't you?"

"Yes."

"Can you explain the highlighted section on page one?"

"It's a test for a fatty acid oxidation disorder called MCADD. The results were abnormal."

"Meaning what?"

"The state would return these results to the hospital nursery, and the doctor would have been immediately notified."

"Do infants with MCADD show symptoms from birth?"

"No," the medical examiner says. "No. That's one of the reasons the state of Connecticut screens for it."

"Dr. Binnie," Kennedy says, "you were aware of the fact that the infant's mother had gestational diabetes, and that the baby had low blood sugar, correct?"

"Yes."

"You stated earlier that the diabetes was what caused the hypoglycemia in the newborn, didn't you?"

"Yes, that was my conclusion at the time of the autopsy."

"Isn't it also possible that hypoglycemia might be caused by MCADD?"

He nods. "Yes."

"Isn't it possible that a newborn's listlessness and lethargy and poor appetite might be caused by MCADD?" Kennedy asks.

"Yes," he admits.

"And an enlarged heart—is it potentially a side effect not only of maternal gestational diabetes . . . but also of this particular metabolic disorder?"

"Yes."

"Dr. Binnie, did you learn from the hospital records that Davis Bauer had MCADD?"

"No."

"Had these results come in in a timely manner, would you have used them to determine the cause of death and manner of death in your autopsy results?"

"Of course," he says.

"What happens to an infant who has the disorder yet has gone undiagnosed?"

"They are often clinically asymptomatic until something happens to cause metabolic decompensation."

"Like what?"

"An illness. An infection." He clears his throat. "Fasting."

"Fasting?" Kennedy repeats. "Like the kind of fasting done prior to a baby's circumcision?"

"Yes."

"What happens to a baby who is undiagnosed with MCADD, and who suffers one of these acute episodes?"

"You might see seizures, vomiting, lethargy, hypoglycemia . . . coma," the doctor says. "In about twenty percent of cases, the infant can die."

Kennedy walks toward the jury box and turns so that her back is facing them, so that she is watching the witness with them. "Doctor, if Davis Bauer had MCADD, and if no one at the hospital knew it, and if the medical protocol was to have him fast three hours prior to his circumcision like any other infant *without* the disorder, *and* if an acute metabolic episode occurred in his little body—isn't there a chance Davis Bauer would be dead even if Ruth Jefferson had performed every conceivable medical intervention?"

The medical examiner looks at me, his gray eyes soft with an apology. "Yes," he admits.

Oh my God. Oh my God. The energy in court has changed. The gal-

lery is so quiet I can hear the rustle of clothing, the murmur of possibility. Turk and Brittany Bauer are still gone, and in their absence,
hope blooms.

Howard, beside me, breathes a single word. "Day-umm."

"Nothing further, Your Honor," Kennedy says, and she walks back
to the defense table, winking at me. *I told you so.*

MY CONFIDENCE IS SHORT-LIVED. "I'd like to redirect," Odette says, and
she gets up before Dr. Binnie can be dismissed. "Doctor, let's say that
this abnormal result had come into the nursery in a timely fashion.
What would have happened?"

"There are some abnormal results that require a letter to be sent to
the parents in due course—suggesting genetic counseling," the medical examiner says. "But this one—it's a red flag, one any neonatologist
would consider emergent. The baby would be monitored closely and
tested to confirm the diagnosis. Sometimes we send the family to a
metabolic treatment center."

"Isn't it true, Doctor, that many children with MCADD are not
formally diagnosed for weeks? Or months?"

"Yes," he says. "It depends on how quickly we can get the parents
in for a confirmation."

"A *confirmation*," she repeats. "Then an abnormal result on the
newborn screening is not a final diagnosis."

"No."

"Did Davis Bauer ever come in for more testing?"

"No," Dr. Binnie says. "He didn't have the chance."

"So you cannot say, beyond a reasonable medical doubt, that Davis
Bauer had MCADD."

He hesitates. "No."

"And you cannot say, beyond a reasonable medical doubt, that
Davis Bauer died of a metabolic disorder."

"Not entirely."

"And in fact, the defendant and her legal team might be grasping
at straws to try to throw some shade in another direction, any direction

that doesn't point to Ruth Jefferson intentionally harming an innocent newborn first by withholding treatment and then by reacting so forcefully she left bruises on his tiny body?"

"Objection!" Kennedy roars.

"I'll withdraw," Odette says, but the damage is done. Because the last words that jury has heard may as well be bullets, shooting my optimism out of the sky.

THAT NIGHT EDISON IS SILENT on the way home. He tells me he has a headache, and almost as soon as we have walked in the door and I'm starting supper, he comes back through the living room with his coat on and tells me he is going out to clear his head. I don't stop him. How can I? How can I say anything that will erase whatever he's been through, sitting behind me every day so far like a shadow, listening to someone try to make me into someone he never believed I could be?

I eat by myself, but really, I just pick at the food. I cover the rest with tinfoil and sit at the kitchen table waiting for Edison. I tell myself I will eat when he returns.

But an hour passes. Two. When it is after midnight and he does not come back and will not answer my texts, I put my head down on the pillow of my arms.

I find myself thinking about the Kangaroo Suite, at the hospital. It's a room with an unofficial name that has a mural of the marsupial on the inside. It's where we put the mothers who have lost their babies.

I have always hated that term—*lost*—to be honest. Those mothers, they know just where their infants are. They would in fact do anything, *give* anything, even their own lives, to get them back.

In the Kangaroo Suite, we let the parents spend time with an infant who has died for as long as they'd like. I'm sure Turk and Brittany Bauer were put in there with Davis. It's a corner room, next to the charge nurse's office, intentionally set aside from other labor and delivery rooms, as if grief is a communicable disease.

This isolation means that the parents don't have to walk past all the other rooms with healthy babies and mothers in them. They don't have to hear the cries of newborns coming into the world, when their own child has left it.

In the Kangaroo Suite, we put the birthing mothers who knew, thanks to ultrasounds, that their babies would be born in a way that was incompatible with life. Or the mothers who had to terminate late, because of some gross anomaly. Or the ones who delivered normally, and who—to their great shock—lived both the greatest moment of their lives and the worst within hours of each other.

If I was a nurse who was assigned to a patient whose baby died, I'd do handprints of the baby in plaster. Or hair samples. I had professional photographers I could call, who knew how to take a picture of the deceased and touch it up so that it looked beautiful and vibrant and alive. I'd put together a memory box, so that when the parents left the hospital, it was not empty-handed.

The last patient I had who had used the Kangaroo Suite was a woman named Jiao. Her husband was getting a master's degree at Yale and she was an architect. For her entire pregnancy, she had too much amniotic fluid, and would come in weekly to have an amniocentesis to check the baby, and to siphon off fluid. One night I took four liters of fluid off her, to give you a sense. And obviously that's not normal; that's not healthy. I asked her doctor what she thought it was—was the baby missing an esophagus possibly? A baby in utero normally ingests amniotic fluid, yet clearly if that much was accumulating, the baby wasn't swallowing it. But the ultrasounds were normal, and no one could convince Jiao that this was a problem. She was certain the baby was going to be fine.

One day she came in and the baby had hydrops—fluid collection under his skin. She stayed with us for a week, and then her doctor tried to induce, but the baby couldn't tolerate it. Jiao had a C-section. The baby had pulmonary hypoplasia—the lungs just didn't function. He died in her arms quickly after birth, puffy, swollen, as if he were jointed of marshmallows.

Jiao was put in the Kangaroo Suite, and like many mothers who had to come to terms with the fact that their babies had not survived, she was robotic, numb. But unlike other mothers, she did not cry, and she refused to see the baby. It was as if she had this image in her mind for a perfect little boy, and she could not reconcile anything less than that. Her husband tried to get her to hold the baby; her mother tried to get her to hold the baby; her doctor tried to get her to hold the baby. Finally, when she was on her eighth hour of catatonia, I wrapped the baby in warm blankets and put a tiny hat on his head. I carried him back into Jiao's room. "Jiao," I said, "would you like to help me give him a bath?"

Jiao didn't respond. I looked at her husband, her poor husband, who nodded, encouraging.

I filled a basin with warm water and took a stack of wipes. Gently, at the foot of Jiao's bed, I unwrapped her baby. I dipped a cloth in warm water and ran it over her baby's sausage legs, his blue arms. I wiped his swollen face, his stiff fingers.

Then I handed Jiao a damp cloth. I pressed it into her palm.

I don't know if the water shocked her into awareness, or if it was the baby. But with my hand guiding her she washed every fold and curve of her baby. She wrapped him in the blanket. She held him to her breast. Finally, with a sob that sounded like she was tearing a piece of herself away, she offered the body of her child back to me.

I managed to hold it together while I carried her infant out of the Kangaroo Suite. And then, as she collapsed in her husband's arms, I lost it. I just lost it. I sobbed over that baby the whole way to the morgue, and when I got there, I couldn't let him go any easier than his mother had.

Now, the key turns in the lock, and Edison slips inside. His eyes are adjusting to the darkness; he is creeping because he expects me to be asleep. Instead, in a clear voice, I say his name from my spot at the kitchen table.

"Why aren't you asleep?" he asks.

"Why weren't you home?"

I can see him clearly, a shadow among shadows. "I was alone. I was out walking."

"For six hours?" I blurt.

"Yes. For six hours," Edison challenges. "Why don't you just put a GPS chip on me, if you don't trust me?"

"I do trust you," I say carefully. "It's the rest of the world I'm not so sure about."

I stand so that we are only inches apart. All mothers worry, but Black mothers, we have to worry a little bit more. "Even walking can be dangerous. Just *being* can be dangerous, if you are in the wrong place at the wrong time."

"I'm not stupid," Edison says.

"I know that better than anyone. That's the problem. You are smart enough to make excuses for people who aren't. You give the benefit of the doubt when other people don't. That is what makes you *you*, and that is what makes you remarkable. But you need to start being more careful. Because I may not be here much longer to . . ." My sentence snaps, unravels. "I may have to leave you."

I see his Adam's apple jerk down, and then back, and I know what he has been thinking about all this time. I imagine him walking the streets of New Haven, trying to outdistance himself from the fact that this trial is coming to an end. And that when it does, everything will be different.

"Mama," he says, his voice small. "What am I supposed to do?"

For a moment, I try to decide how to sum up a life's worth of lessons in my response. Then I look at him, my eyes shining. "Thrive," I say.

Edison wrenches away from me. A moment later, the door to his bedroom slams shut. Music whitewashes all the other sounds I try in vain to discern.

I think I know now why it is called the Kangaroo Suite. It's because even when you no longer have a child, you carry him forever.

It's the same when a parent is ripped away from the child, but the suite is the size of the world. At Mama's funeral, I put a handful of cold dirt from her grave in the pocket of my good wool coat. Some days I wear that coat inside the house, just because. I sift through the soil, hold it tight in my fist.

I wonder what Edison will keep of me.

Turk

I PUT MY HANDS ON BOTH SIDES OF BRIT'S FACE AND TOUCH MY FORE-head to hers. "Breathe," I tell her. "Think of Vienna."

Neither of us has ever been to Vienna, but Brit found an old picture in an antique shop once that she hung on the wall of our bedroom. It shows the fancy city hall building, the plaza in front of it filled with pedestrians and mothers towing children by the hand—all of them white. We always thought that we could save up for a vacation there, one day. When Brit was putting together a birthing plan, Vienna was one of the words I was supposed to use to help her focus.

It doesn't escape me that I'm whispering the same word I used to calm her when she was delivering Davis—but now I'm repeating it to help her stop seeing the image of our dead son.

Suddenly the door to the conference room opens and the prosecutor walks in. "That was a nice touch. The jury loves a mother who's acting so distraught that she can't control herself. But the threat in open court? Not the wisest move."

Brit bristles. She pushes away from me and gets up in the lawyer's face. "I am not acting," she says, her voice dangerously soft. "And you don't get to tell me what's a good idea and what's not, bitch."

I grasp her arm. "Baby, why don't you go wash up? I'll take care of this."

Brit doesn't even blink. Just keeps herself like a wall in front of Odette Lawton, like an alpha dog standing over another mutt until it has the good sense to cower. Then, abruptly, she walks away and slams the door behind her.

I know it is already a big deal that Brit and I are allowed in the courtroom, even though we are going to testify. There was a hearing about it and everything, before the trial began. That goddamned public defender thought she could keep us away by asking for all witnesses to be sequestered, but the judge said we deserved to be there because we were Davis's parents. I'm sure the prosecutor doesn't want to give him any good reason to rethink his decision.

"Mr. Bauer," the lawyer says, "you and I need to talk."

I fold my arms. "Why don't you just do what you're supposed to do? Win this case?"

"It's a little hard when your wife is acting like an intimidating thug and not a grieving mother." She stares at me. "I can't call her as a witness."

"What?" I say. "But we did all that practicing—"

"Yes, but I don't trust Brittany," she says flatly. "Your wife is a wild card. And you do not put a wild card in the witness box."

"The jury needs to hear from Davis's mother."

"Not if I can't be certain she won't start screaming racist slurs at the defendant." She eyes me coolly. "You and your wife may detest me and everyone who looks like me, Mr. Bauer. And frankly I don't care. But I am the best chance—the *only* chance—you have to get justice for your son. So not only will I tell you what is a good idea and a bad idea, I will also be calling all the shots. And that means your wife is not testifying."

"The judge and the jury will think something's off if she isn't a witness."

"The judge and the jury will think she's distraught. And you will be a solid witness in your own right."

Does this mean that I loved Davis less? Because my grief isn't enough to keep me from censoring myself, like Brit?

"Yesterday you heard the defense introduce the theory that your son had an undiagnosed metabolic disease?"

It was when the pediatrician was on the stand. There was a lot of medical jargon I did not understand, but I got the gist of it. "Yeah, yeah. I get it," I say. "It was a Hail Mary pass."

"Not quite. While you were gone, the medical examiner verified the results. Davis screened positive for MCADD. I did my best to get the jury to discount his testimony, but the bottom line is the defense planted a seed that's already taken root: that your baby was tested for a potentially fatal disorder and the results arrived too late. And if none of that had happened, he might still be alive."

I feel my knees giving out, and I sit heavily on the tabletop. My baby boy was actually sick, and we didn't know? How could a hospital overlook that?

It's so . . . random. So pointless.

The prosecutor touches my arm, and I can't help it, I flinch. "Don't do it. Don't get lost in your own head. I'm telling you this so you can't be surprised during a cross-examination. But all Kennedy McQuarrie has done is find a *possible* diagnosis. It was never confirmed. Davis wasn't treated. She could have just as well said that your son would develop heart disease as an adult, because that's what his genetic pre-disposition is. That doesn't mean it would ever happen."

I think of my grandfather, dropping dead of a heart attack.

"I am telling you this because when we go back in there," Odette says, "I'm going to call you to the stand. And you're going to answer just the way we rehearsed in my office. All you need to remember is that there is no room for *maybe* in this trial. There is no *this might have happened*. It already *did* happen. Your son is dead."

I nod. There is a body. And someone has to pay.

Do you swear to tell the truth?

My hand flexes on the leather Bible. I don't read it a lot anymore.

But swearing on it makes me remember Big Ike, from back when I was in jail. And Twinkie.

I think about him a lot, to be honest. I imagine he's out now. Maybe eating the Chef Boyardee he craved. What would happen if I ran into him on the street? At a Starbucks? Would we do the man hug thing? Or would we pretend we didn't know each other? He knew what I was, on the outside, just like I knew what he was. But in jail, things were different, and what I'd been taught to believe didn't hold true. If we crossed paths now, would he still be Twinkie to me? Or would he just be another nigger?

Brit is finally back in the courtroom, anchored beside Francis. When she returned from the bathroom, her face still damp from wiping it with a towelette and her nose and cheeks pink, I said that I'd told the prosecutor no one tells my wife how to grieve. And that I couldn't bear the thought of Brit having another breakdown, so I told Odette Lawton there was no way she was putting my wife on the stand. I told Brit that I loved her, and it hurt me too much to see her hurting.

She bought it.

Do you swear to tell the truth?

"Mr. Bauer," the prosecutor asks, "was this your first child with your wife, Brittany?"

Sweat breaks out on my back. I can feel jurors staring at the swastika tattoo on my head. Even the ones who are pretending not to look are sneaking glances. I curl my hands around the base of the chair. The wood feels good. Solid. A weapon. "Yes. We were very excited."

"Did you know it was going to be a boy?"

"No," I reply. "We wanted it to be a surprise."

"Were there any complications during the pregnancy?"

"My wife had gestational diabetes. The doctor told us that wasn't a big deal, as long as she watched her diet. And she did. She wanted a healthy kid as much as me."

"How about the delivery, Mr. Bauer? Was it a normal birth?"

"Everything went smoothly," I say, "but then again, I wasn't doing the heavy lifting, exactly." The ladies on the jury smile, just like the prosecutor said they would, if I made myself seem like any other father.

"And where did you and your wife have the baby?"

"Mercy–West Haven Hospital."

"Did you get to hold your son, Davis, after he was born, Mr. Bauer?"

"Yeah," I say. When we rehearsed this in the prosecutor's office, as if we were actors learning lines, she told me how effective it would be if I teared up. I said I couldn't cry on demand, for fuck's sake, but now, thinking back on the moment Davis was born, I'm getting choked up. It's crazy, isn't it, that you can love a girl so much you can actually create another human being? It's like rubbing two sticks together and getting fire—all of a sudden there's something alive and intense there that did not exist a minute before. I can remember Davis's feet kicking against me. His head in the palm of my hand. Those stormy, unfocused eyes, puzzling me out. "I've never felt that way in my life," I confess. I'm off script, and I don't care. "I thought it was a lie, when people said they fell in love with a baby at first sight. But it's the truth. It was like I could see my whole future right there in his face."

"Did you know any of the hospital staff prior to going to that particular hospital?"

"No. Brit's OB worked there, so it was sort of a done deal."

"Did you have a good experience at this hospital, Mr. Bauer?"

"No," I say firmly. "I did not."

"Was it like that from the moment your wife was admitted?"

"No. That was fine. So was the labor and delivery."

The prosecutor walks toward the jury box. "So when did things change?"

"When another nurse took over after the first one went off shift. And she was black."

The prosecutor clears her throat. "Why was this an issue, Mr. Bauer?"

Unconsciously, I reach up and rub the tattoo on my scalp. "Because I believe in the superiority of the White race."

Some of the jurors stare harder at me, curious. Some shake their heads. Others look into their laps.

"So you're a White Supremacist," the prosecutor says. "You believe that black people, people like me, should be subordinate."

384 small great things

"I'm not anti-black," I tell her. "I'm pro-White."

"You understand that many people in the world—in fact, many people here—might find your beliefs offensive."

"But hospitals have to treat all patients," I say, "even the ones whose ideas they might not like. If a school shooter gets injured when the cops try to take him out and he's brought to the ER, the doctors do surgery to save his life, even if he's killed a dozen other people. I know the way my wife and I live is not the way others choose to live. But the great thing about this country is that we all have a right to believe whatever we want."

"What did you do when you found out there was a black nurse caring for your newborn son?"

"I made a request. I asked that she not touch my baby."

"Is the African American nurse you are referring to here today?"

"Yes." I point to Ruth Jefferson. I think maybe she shrinks back in her chair.

I want to think that, anyway.

"Who did you ask?" the prosecutor says.

"The head of the nurses," I reply. "Marie Malone."

"As a result of that conversation, what happened?"

"I don't know, but she got reassigned."

"At some point, did the defendant interact with your son again?"

I nod. "Davis was being circumcised. It was supposed to be no big deal. They were going to take him to the nursery and bring him back as soon as it was done. But the next thing I know, all hell breaks loose. People were screaming, calling for help, crash carts were being pushed down the hall, everyone was running toward the nursery. My kid was in there, and I just . . . I guess Brit and I *knew*. We got to the nursery and there was a crowd of people huddled around my son, and that woman, she had her hands on my baby again." I swallow. "She was hurting him. She was jackhammering on his chest so hard she was practically breaking him in half."

"Objection!" the other lawyer says.

The judge purses his lips. "I'll allow it."

"How did you react, Mr. Bauer?"

"I didn't say anything. Brit and I, we were both shocked. I mean, they told us this procedure was *nothing*. We were supposed to go *home* that afternoon. It was like my brain couldn't process what was right before my eyes."

"Then what happened?"

The jury, I realize, is on the edge of their seats. Every face is turned toward me. "The doctors and the nurses, they were moving so fast I couldn't tell whose hands were whose. Then the pediatrician came in—Dr. Atkins. She worked for a little bit on my son, and then she . . . then she said there was nothing else to do." The words become three-dimensional, a movie I can't turn away from. The pediatrician looking at the clock. The way the others all stepped back, their hands in the air, like someone was pointing a gun at them. My son, too still.

A sob belches out of me. I hold tight to the chair. If I let go, my fists will take over. I will find someone to punish. I look up, and for just one second, I let them all see how empty I am inside. "She said my son was dead."

Odette Lawton walks toward me with a box of Kleenex. She puts it on the railing between us, but I don't make a move to take a tissue. I am glad, right now, that Brit doesn't have to go through this. I don't want her to have to relive that moment.

"What did you do next?"

"I couldn't let them stop." The words feel like glass on my tongue. "If they weren't going to save him, I was. So I went to the trash and I pulled out the bag they were using to help Davis breathe. I tried to figure out how to attach it again. I wasn't going to quit on my own kid."

I hear a sound, a high-pitched keen, one that I recognize from the weeks that Brit did not get out of bed, but shook our home with the force of her grieving. She is hunched over in her seat in the gallery, a human question mark, as if her whole body is asking why this happened to us.

"Mr. Bauer," the prosecutor says gently, drawing my attention back. "Some people here would call you a White Supremacist, and would say that you were the one who started this ball rolling by requesting that an African American nurse be removed from the care of your child. They might even blame you for your own misfortune. How would you respond?"

I take a deep breath. "All I was trying to do was give my baby the best chance in life he could possibly have. Does that make me a White Supremacist?" I ask. "Or does that just make me a father?"

DURING THE RECESS, ODETTE COACHES me in the conference room. "*Her* job is to do whatever she can to make the jury hate you. A little bit of that is okay, because it shows the jury the nurse's motive. But just a little. *Your* job is to do whatever you can to make them see what they have in common with you, not what sets you apart. This is supposed to be a case about how much you loved your son. Don't screw it up by focusing on who you hate."

She leaves Brit and me alone for a few minutes, before we are called back to the courtroom. "Her," Brit says, as soon as the door closes behind her. "I hate *her*."

I turn to my wife. "Do you think she's right? Do you think we brought this down on ourselves?"

I have been thinking about what Odette Lawton said: if I hadn't spoken out against the black nurse, would this have ended differently? Would she have tried to save Davis the minute she realized he wasn't breathing? Would she have treated him like any other critical patient, instead of wanting to hurt me like I'd hurt her?

My son would be five months old now. Would he be sitting up on his own? Would he smile when he saw me?

I believe in God. I believe in a God who recognizes the work we are doing for Him on this earth. But then why would He punish His warriors?

Brit stands up, a look of disgust rippling her features. "When did you become such a pussy?" she asks, and she turns away from me.

* * *

In the last few weeks of Brit's pregnancy, our neighbors—a pair of beaners from Guatemala who'd probably jumped a barbed-wire fence to get into this country—got a new puppy. It was one of those little fluffy things that looks like an evil cotton ball with teeth, and never stopped barking. Frida, that was the dog's name, and it used to come into our yard and shit on our lawn, and when it wasn't doing that, it was yipping. Every time Brit lay down to take a nap, that stupid mop head would start up again and wake her. She'd get pissed, and then *I'd* get pissed, and I'd stomp over and bang on the door and tell them if they didn't muzzle their goddamned animal I would get rid of it.

Then one day, I came home from a drywall job to find the beaner digging a hole under an azalea bush, and his hysterical wife holding a shoe box in her arms. When I came into the house, Brit was sitting on the couch. "Guess their dog died," she announced.

"So I see."

She reached behind her and held up a bottle of antifreeze. "Tastes sweet, you know. Daddy told me to keep it away from our puppy, when I was little."

I stared at her for a second. "You poisoned Frida?"

Brit met my gaze with so much nerve that for a second, I could only see Francis in her. "I couldn't get any sleep," she said. "It was either our baby, or that fucking dog."

Kennedy McQuarrie probably drinks pumpkin spice lattes. I bet she voted for Obama and donates after watching those commercials about sad dogs and believes the world would be a bright shiny place if we all could *just get along.*

She's exactly the kind of bleeding-heart liberal I can't stand.

I keep this front and center in my head as she walks toward me. "You heard Dr. Atkins testify that your son had a condition called MCADD, didn't you?"

"Well," I say. "I heard her say that he screened positive for it."

The prosecutor's coached me on that one.

"Do you understand, Mr. Bauer, that a baby with undiagnosed MCADD whose blood sugar drops might go into respiratory failure?"

"Yes."

"And do you understand that a baby who goes into respiratory failure might go into cardiac failure?"

"Yes."

"And that same baby might die?"

I nod. "Yeah."

"Do you also understand, Mr. Bauer, that in none of those events would it make a difference whether or not a nurse attempted every medical intervention possible to save that baby's life? That the baby could still possibly die?"

"Possibly," I repeat.

"Do you realize that in that scenario, if your son was that baby, Mother Teresa herself could not have saved him?"

I fold my arms. "But that *wasn't* my son."

She cocks her head. "You heard the medical testimony from Dr. Atkins, which was corroborated by Dr. Binnie. Your baby did indeed have MCADD, Mr. Bauer, isn't that true?"

"I don't know." I jerk my head toward Ruth Jefferson. "She killed him before he could get tested for sure."

"You really, truly believe that?" she asks. "In the face of scientific evidence?"

"I do," I grit out.

Her eyes spark. "You do," she repeats, "or you *have* to?"

"What?"

"You believe in God, Mr. Bauer, don't you?"

"Yes."

"And you believe things happen for a reason?"

"Yes."

"Mr. Bauer, do you use the Twitter handle @WhiteMight?"

"Yeah," I say, but I have no idea what that has to do with her questions. They feel like a blast of wind that comes from a different direction every time.

She enters a computer printout into evidence. "Is this a post from your Twitter account, made last July?" I nod. "Can you read it out loud?"

"'We all get what's coming to us,'" I say.

"Then I guess your son got what was coming to him, right?"

My hands clench on the railing of the witness stand. "What did you say?" My voice is low, hot.

"I said your son must have gotten what he deserved," she repeats.

"My son was innocent. An Aryan warrior."

She ignores my response. "Come to think of it, I guess you got what you deserved, too . . ."

"Shut your mouth."

"That's why you're accusing an innocent woman of a death that was completely and utterly arbitrary, isn't it? Because if you believe instead what's *really* true—namely that your son carried a genetic disease—"

I stand up, fuming. "Shut up—"

The prosecutor is yelling, and this bitch lawyer is yelling over her. "You can't accept the fact that your son's death was absolutely senseless and nothing more than bad luck. You have to blame Ruth Jefferson, because if you don't, then *you're* the one to blame, because you and your wife somehow created an *Aryan* child with a flaw in his DNA. Isn't that right, Mr. Bauer?"

Out of the corner of my eye, I see Odette Lawton walk toward the judge. But I'm already out of my seat, leaning over the rail of the witness box. The monster that has been sleeping inside me is suddenly awake and breathing fire. "You bitch," I say, going for Kennedy McQuarrie's throat. I am already halfway over the railing when some blockhead fake cop bailiff tackles me. "You're a fucking race traitor!"

Distantly, I hear the judge banging a gavel, calling for the witness to be removed. I feel myself being dragged out of the courtroom, my shoes scuffing on the floor. I hear Brit calling my name, and Francis's rally cry, and the thunderous applause of the Lonewolf.org posters.

I don't remember much after that. Except that I blinked, and suddenly I was no longer in the courtroom. I was in a cell somewhere with cement-block walls and a cot and a toilet.

It feels like forever, but it is only a half hour before Odette Lawton shows up. I almost laugh when the deputy opens the cell door, and she is standing there. My savior is a black woman. Go figure.

"That," she says, "was beyond foolish. There have been numerous times I've wanted to kill a defense attorney, but I've never actually *tried*."

"I didn't even touch her," I say with a scowl.

"The jury *does not care*. I have to tell you, Mr. Bauer, that your outburst in there undid any advantage the State might have had in this case. There's nothing else I can do."

"What do you mean?"

She looks at me. "The prosecution rests."

But I won't. Ever.

Kennedy

IF I COULD TURN CARTWHEELS INTO JUDGE THUNDER'S OFFICE, I WOULD.

I leave Howard sitting with Ruth in a conference room. There is an excellent chance I can get this entire case tossed out. I've filed my motion for judgment of acquittal, and I can tell, as soon as I get into the judge's office, that Odette already knows she's sunk. "Judge," I begin, "we know this baby died, which is tragic, but there's been absolutely no evidence of any willful, wanton, or reckless conduct by Ruth Jefferson. The allegation of murder made by the State isn't supported, and as a matter of law, it must be dismissed."

The judge turns to Odette. "Counselor? Where's the evidence of premeditation? Of malice?"

Odette dances around a response. "I'd consider a public comment about sterilizing a baby a strong indicator."

"Your Honor, that was the bitter response of a woman who'd been subject to discrimination," I argue. "It became uncomfortably relevant in light of later events. But it still doesn't point to a plan for murder."

"I must agree with Ms. McQuarrie," Judge Thunder says. "Spiteful, yes; murderous, not by the letter of the law. If attorneys were held accountable for the vindictive comments you make about judges after a case doesn't go your way, you'd all be charged with murder. Count One is dismissed, and, Ms. McQuarrie, your motion on judgment of acquittal for murder is granted."

As I walk down the hallway toward the conference room to tell my client the excellent news, I check behind me to make sure the coast is clear, and then skip a little in my heels. I mean, it's not every day the tide of a murder trial turns in your direction; and it's certainly not every day that happens with your *first* murder trial. I let myself imagine how Harry will call me into his office, and in his gruff way, tell me I surprised him. I picture him letting me have my own share of the big cases from now on, and promoting Howard to cover my current duties.

Beaming, I let myself into the conference room. Howard and Ruth turn to me, hopeful. "He threw out the murder charge," I say, grinning.

"Yaaaas!" Howard pumps his fist in the air.

Ruth is more cautious. "I know this is good news . . . but how good?"

"*Excellent,*" I say. "Negligent homicide is a whole different animal, legally. The worst-case scenario—a conviction—carries almost no jail time, and honestly, our medical evidence was so strong that I'd be shocked if the jury doesn't acquit—"

Ruth throws her arms around my neck. "Thank you."

"Just think," I say. "By this weekend, this could all be over. I'll go into court tomorrow and say the defense rests and if the jury comes back with a verdict as quickly as I think they will—"

"Wait," Ruth interrupts. "What?"

I step back. "We've created reasonable doubt. That's all we have to do to win."

"But I haven't testified," Ruth says.

"I don't think you should get on the stand. Right now, things are going *really* well for us. If the last thing the jury has in their heads is that whack job Turk Bauer trying to come after me, you already have all their support."

She stands very, very straight. "You promised."

"I promised I would do my best to get you acquitted, and I have."

Ruth shakes her head. "You *promised* I could say my piece."

"But the beauty of this is you don't *have* to," I point out. "The jury hands back the verdict, and then you go get your job back. You get to pretend this never happened."

Ruth's voice is soft, but steel. "You think I can pretend this never happened?" she asks. "I see this every day, everywhere I go. You think I'm going to just walk in and get my job back? You think I'm not always going to be that black nurse who caused trouble?"

"Ruth," I say, incredulous. "I'm ninety-nine percent sure this jury is going to find you not guilty. What more could you possibly want?"

She tilts her head. "You still have to ask?"

I know what she is talking about.

Namely, everything I *refused* to talk about, in court: what it is like to know that you are a target, because of the color of your skin. What it means to work hard, to be an impeccable employee, and have none of that make a difference in the face of prejudice.

True, I had said she could have a moment to tell the jury her side of the story. But what's the point, if we've already given them a peg on which to hang their exoneration?

"Think of Edison," I say.

"I *am* thinking of my son!" Ruth replies, heated. "I'm thinking of what he'll make of a mother who didn't speak for herself." She narrows her eyes. "I know how the law works, Kennedy. I know the State has the burden of proof. I also know that you have to put me on the stand if I ask you to. So I suppose the question is: Are you going to do your job? Or are you going to be just one more white person who lied to me?"

I turn to Howard, who is watching our volley like we're the Women's Singles Final at the U.S. Open. "Howard," I say evenly, "would you step out for a moment so I can speak to our client alone?"

He jerks his chin and slips outside. I turn on Ruth. "What the *hell*? Now is *not* the time to stand on principle. You have to trust me on this. If you get on the stand and start talking about race, you'll erase the lead we currently have in the jury's favor. You'll be talking about issues that will alienate them and make them uncomfortable. Plus, the fact that you're upset and angry will come through loud and clear and negate any sympathy they have for you right now. I've already said everything the jury needs to hear."

"Except the truth," Ruth says.

"What are you talking about?"

"I tried to resuscitate that baby. I told you I didn't touch him at first. I told everyone that. But I did."

I feel sick to my stomach. "Why didn't you tell me this before?"

"At first I lied because I thought I was going to lose my job. Then I lied because I didn't know if I could trust you. And then, every time I tried to tell you the truth, I was so embarrassed that I'd hidden it for this long it got harder and harder." She takes a deep breath. "This is what I should have told you, the first day we met: I wasn't supposed to touch the baby; it was in the medical file. But when he went blue, I unwrapped him. I moved him around. I tapped his feet and turned him on his side, all the things you do when you're trying to get a baby responsive again. Then I heard footsteps and I wrapped him up tight again. I didn't want anyone seeing me do what I wasn't supposed to be doing."

"Why rewrite history, Ruth?" I ask, after a moment. "The jury could hear that and think you tried your hardest. But they could also think you screwed up, and did something that made him die."

"I want them to know that I did my job," she says. "You keep telling me this doesn't have anything to do with the color of my skin—that it's about my competence. Well, in addition to everything else, I want them to know that I *am* a good nurse. I tried to save that baby."

"You have this idea that if you get on the stand, you'll be able to tell your story and be in control—and that's not how it works. Odette is going to shred you. She'll do everything she can to point out that this means you're a liar."

Ruth looks at me. "I'd rather they think I'm a liar than a murderer."

"If you get up there and give a different version than the one we've already presented," I explain carefully, "you lose your credibility. I lose *my* credibility. I know what's best for you. There's a reason we're called *counsel*—you're supposed to listen to me."

"I'm tired of following orders. Last time I followed orders, I got into this mess." Ruth folds her arms. "You are putting me on that stand tomorrow," she says flatly. "Or I'm going to tell the judge that you won't let me testify."

And just like that, I know I'm going to lose this case.

ONE NIGHT, WHEN RUTH AND I were preparing for the trial, we'd been working in my kitchen and Violet had been high on life, running in circles around the house in her underwear and pretending to be a unicorn. Her shrieks punctuated our discussions, and then suddenly the sound wasn't joy but pain. A moment later, Violet started sobbing, and we both ran to the living room, where Violet was lying on the floor bleeding profusely from the temple.

I felt my knees wobble, but before I could even reach for my daughter, Ruth had her cradled in her arms, and had pressed the bottom of her shirt up to the wound. "Hey now," she soothed. "What happened?"

"I slipped," Vi hiccuped, as her blood soaked Ruth's shirt.

"And I see you've got a little cut here," Ruth said calmly. "One I'm gonna take care of." She started ordering me around my own house, efficiently getting me to fetch a damp washcloth, antibiotic ointment, and a butterfly bandage from a first aid kit. She never let go of Violet, and she never stopped talking to her. Even when she suggested that we drive to Yale–New Haven to see if maybe a stitch was in order, Ruth was steely, measured, while I continued to freak out, wondering if Violet would have a scar, if I would be flagged by CPS for not watching my kid more closely or letting her run in socks on a slippery wooden floor. When Violet needed two stitches, it wasn't me she clung to but Ruth, who promised her that if we sang really loud, she wouldn't feel anything. And so the three of us belted "Let It Go" at the top of our lungs, and Violet never cried. Later that night, when she had a clean bandage on her forehead and was asleep in her bed, I thanked Ruth.

You're good at what you do, I told her.

I know, she said.

That's all she wants. To let people know she was treated unfairly because of her race, and for her reputation as a caregiver to remain intact, even if it means it will be tarnished by a guilty verdict.

"Drinking alone," Micah says, when he comes home from the hospital and finds me in the dark, in the kitchen, with a bottle of Syrah. "That's the first sign, you know."

I lift up my glass, and take a long swallow. "Of what?"

"Adulthood, probably," he admits. "Hard day at the office?"

"It started out great. Legendary, even. And then went to hell very quickly."

Micah sits down next to me and loosens his tie. "Do you want to talk about it? Or should I get my own bottle?"

I push the Syrah toward him. "I thought I had an acquittal in the bag," I sigh. "And then Ruth went and decided to ruin it all."

While he pours himself a glass of wine, I tell him everything. From the way Turk Bauer spouted his rhetoric of hate to the look in his eyes when he came after me; from the rush of adrenaline I got when my motion for judgment of acquittal was granted to Ruth's admission about resuscitating the baby to the dizzy realization that I had to put Ruth on the stand if she demanded it. Even if it was going to tank my chances of winning my first murder case.

"What am I supposed to do tomorrow?" I ask. "No matter what I ask Ruth on the stand, she's going to be incriminating herself. And that doesn't even begin to consider what the prosecutor's going to do to her on cross." I shudder, thinking about Odette, who doesn't even know that this boon is about to be granted. "I can't believe I was so close," I say softly. "I can't believe she's going to ruin it."

Micah clears his throat. "Radical thought number one: maybe you need to take yourself out of this equation."

I've drunk enough that he's a little fuzzy at the edges, so maybe I've just misheard. "I beg your pardon?"

"*You* weren't close. *Ruth* was."

I snort. "That's semantics. We both win, or we both lose."

"But she has more at stake than you do," Micah says gently. "Her reputation. Her career. Her life. This is the first trial that really matters to you, Kennedy. But it's the only one that matters to Ruth."

I scrub a hand through my hair. "What's radical thought number two?"

"What if the best thing for Ruth *isn't* winning this case?" Micah replies. "What if the reason this is so important to her isn't because of *what* she's going to say . . . but rather the fact that she is finally being given the chance to say it?"

Is it worth being able to say what you need to say, if it means you land in prison? If it nets you a conviction? That goes against everything I've ever been taught, everything I've ever believed.

But I'm not the one on trial.

I press my fingers against my temples. Micah's words circle in my mind.

He takes his glass and empties it into mine. "You need it more than I do," he says, and he kisses me on the forehead. "Don't stay up too late."

ON FRIDAY MORNING, AS I am hurrying to meet Ruth in the parking lot, I pass the memorial on the green near City Hall. It commemorates Sengbe Pieh, who was one of the slaves involved in the *Amistad* mutiny. In 1839 a ship carried a group of Africans taken from their home to be slaves in the Caribbean. The Africans revolted, killed the captain and cook, and forced other sailors on board to head back toward Africa. The sailors, though, tricked the Africans, and headed north— where the ship was boarded by U.S. authorities. The Africans were imprisoned in a warehouse in New Haven, pending trial.

The Africans revolted because a mulatto cook had heard that the white crew planned to kill the blacks and eat the meat themselves. The whites on board believed the Africans were cannibals.

Neither side was right.

When I reach the parking lot, Ruth won't even make eye contact with me. She starts walking quickly toward the courthouse, Edison by her side, until I grab her by the arm. "Are you still determined to do this?"

"Did you think if I slept on it I'd change my mind?" she asks.

"I had *hoped*," I admit. "I'm begging you, Ruth."

"Mama?" Edison looks at her face, and then mine, confused.

I raise my brows as if to say, *Think of what you're doing to him.*

She slips her arm through her son's elbow. "Let's go," she replies, and she starts walking again.

The crowds have swelled in front of the courthouse; now that the media have reported that the prosecution's side of the case is finished, the taste for blood is getting stronger. I see Wallace Mercy and his crew from the corner of my eye, maintaining their vigil. Maybe I should have sicced Wallace on Ruth; maybe he could have convinced her to duck her head and let justice be served in her favor. But then again, knowing Wallace, he would not turn down an opportunity to speak his mind. He'd probably have offered to coach Ruth in whatever it is she feels the need to say.

Howard is pacing in front of the courtroom. "So," he says nervously. "Are we resting? Or . . ."

"Yes," I say bluntly. "Or."

"Just in case you wanted to know, the Bauers are back. They're in the gallery."

"Thanks, Howard," I say with sarcasm. "Now I feel even better."

I speak to Ruth just once more, moments before we are asked to rise at the judge's arrival. "I will give you just one piece of advice," I whisper. "Be as cool and calm as possible. The minute you raise your voice, the prosecution is going to be all over you. And the way you answer me should be exactly the same way you respond when Odette's cross-examining you."

She looks at me. It's quick, how our eyes meet, but it's enough for me to see the flicker in them, the fear. I open my mouth, sensing the weakness, intending to reel her back in, but then I remember what Micah said. "Good luck," I say.

I rise, and call Ruth Jefferson to the stand.

She looks smaller in the box, somehow. Her hair is pulled back in a low bun, as usual. Have I noticed before how severe that looks? Her hands are folded in her lap tightly. I know it's because she's trying to keep herself from shaking, but the jury doesn't. To them, it just looks like she's excessively formal, prim. She repeats the oath quietly, without betraying any emotion. I know it's because she feels like she is on display. But shyness can be mistaken for haughtiness, and that could be a fatal flaw.

"Ruth," I begin, "how old are you?"

"Forty-four," she says.

"Where were you born?"

"Harlem, in New York City."

"Did you go to school there?"

"Only for a couple of years. Then I transferred to Dalton on a scholarship."

"Did you complete college?" I ask.

"Yes, I went to SUNY Plattsburgh as an undergrad, and then got my nursing degree at Yale."

"Can you tell us how long that program was?"

"Three years."

"When you graduate as a nurse, do you take an oath?"

She nods. "It's called the Florence Nightingale pledge," Ruth says.

I enter a piece of paper into evidence and present it to her. "Is this the pledge?"

"Yes."

"Will you read it aloud?"

"'Before God and those assembled here, I solemnly pledge to adhere to the code of ethics of the nursing profession; to cooperate faithfully with the other members of the nursing team and to carry out faithfully and to the best of my ability the instructions of the physician or the nurse'"—she falters here—"'who may be assigned to supervise my work.'" Ruth takes a deep breath, forging ahead. "'I will not do anything evil or malicious and I will not knowingly give any harmful drug or assist in malpractice. I will not reveal any confidential information that may come to my knowledge in the course of my work. And I pledge myself to do all in my power to raise the standards and prestige of practical nursing. May my life be devoted to service and to the high ideals of the nursing profession.'" She looks up at me.

"Is that oath fundamental to you as a nurse?"

"We take it very seriously," Ruth confirms. "It's like the equivalent of the Hippocratic oath for doctors."

"How long have you been employed at Mercy–West Haven Hospital?"

"Just over twenty years," Ruth says. "My whole career."

"What are your responsibilities?"

"I am a neonatal nurse. I help deliver babies, I am in the OR during C-sections, I care for the mothers and then postdelivery, for the newborns."

"How many hours a week did you work?"

"Forty-plus," she replies. "We often were asked to pull some overtime."

"Ruth, are you married?"

"I'm a widow," she says. "My husband was a soldier who died in Afghanistan. It happened about ten years ago."

"Do you have any children?"

"Yes, my son, Edison. He's seventeen." Her eyes shine, and she searches Edison out in the gallery.

"Do you recall coming to work the morning of October first, 2015?"

"Yes," Ruth says. "I came in at seven A.M. for a twelve-hour shift."

"Were you assigned to watch Davis Bauer?"

"Yes. His mother had delivered early that morning. I was assigned to do typical postpartum care of Brittany Bauer, and a nurse's newborn exam."

She describes the exam, and says she conducted it in the hospital room.

"So Brittany Bauer was present?"

"Yes," Ruth says. "So was her husband."

"Was there any significant finding during this exam?"

"I noted a heart murmur in the file. It wasn't something I felt that we needed to be alarmed about—it's a very common condition for newborns. But it was definitely something for the pediatrician to check out the next time she came back, which was why I wrote it down."

"Did you know Mr. and Mrs. Bauer prior to the birth of their son?"

"No," Ruth replies. "I met them when I came into the room. I congratulated them on their beautiful baby boy, and explained I was there to do a routine check."

"How long were you in the room with them?"

"Ten to fifteen minutes."

"Did you have any verbal exchange with the parents at that time?"

"I mentioned the murmur, and that it wasn't any reason for concern. And I told them his sugar levels had improved since birth. Then after I cleaned the baby up, I suggested we try to have him nurse."

"What response did you get?"

"Mr. Bauer told me to get away from his wife. Then he said he wanted to speak to my supervisor."

"How did that make you feel, Ruth?"

"I was shocked," she admits. "I didn't know what I'd done to upset them."

"What happened next?"

"My boss, Marie Malone, put a note in the baby's file, stating that no African American staff should come in contact with the infant. I questioned her about it, and she said it was done at the request of the parents, and that I would be reassigned."

"When did you next see the baby?"

"Saturday morning. I was in the nursery when Corinne—the baby's new nurse—brought him in for a circ."

"What were your responsibilities that morning?"

She frowns. "I had two—no, three patients. It had been a crazy night; I'd worked a shift I wasn't supposed to work because another nurse was out sick. I had gone into the nursery to grab clean linens, and to scarf down a PowerBar, because I hadn't eaten at all during my shift."

"What happened after the baby was circumcised?"

"I wasn't in the room, but I assumed it all went normally. Then Corinne grabbed me and asked me to watch over him because another one of her patients had to be rushed to the OR, and protocol required that a postcirc baby be monitored."

"Did you agree?"

"I didn't really have a choice. There was literally no one else to do it. I knew Corinne or Marie, my charge nurse, would be back quickly to take over."

"When you first saw the baby, how did he look?"

"Beautiful," Ruth says. "He was swaddled and fast asleep. But a few moments later I looked down and saw that his skin was ashen. He was making grunting noises. I could see he was having trouble breathing."

I walk toward the witness box, and set my hand on the rail. "What did you do in that instant, Ruth?"

She takes a deep breath. "I unwrapped the swaddling. I started touching the baby, tapping his feet, trying to get him to respond."

The jury looks puzzled. Odette sits back in her chair, arms crossed, a smile breaking over her face.

"Why did you do that? When you'd been told by your supervisor to *not* touch that baby?"

"I had to," Ruth confesses. I can see it, the way she breaks free, like a butterfly from a chrysalis. Her voice is lighter, the lines bracketing her mouth soften. "It's what any good nurse would do in that situation."

"Then what?"

"The next step would have been to call a code, to get a whole team in to resuscitate. But I heard footsteps. I knew someone was coming and I didn't know what to do. I thought I'd get in trouble if someone saw me interacting with the baby, when I had been told not to. So I wrapped him up again, and stepped back, and Marie walked into the nursery." Ruth looks down at her lap. "She asked me what I was doing."

"What did you say, Ruth?"

When she glances up, her eyes are wide with shame. "I said I was doing nothing."

"You lied?"

"Yes."

"More than once, apparently—when you were later questioned by the police, you stated that you did not engage in any resuscitative efforts for that baby. Why?"

"I was afraid I was going to lose my job." She turns to the jury, pleading her case. "Every fiber of my being told me I had to help that infant . . . but I also knew I'd be reprimanded if I went against my supervisor's orders. And if I lost my job, who would take care of my son?"

"So you basically faced either assisting in malpractice, or violating your supervisor's order?"

She nods. "It was a lose-lose situation."

"What happened next?"

"The code team was called in. My job was to do compressions. I did my best, we all did, but in the end it wasn't enough." She looks up. "When the time of death was called, and when Mr. Bauer took the Ambu bag out of the trash and tried to continue efforts himself, I could barely hold it together." Like an arrow searching for its mark, her eyes hone in on Turk Bauer, in the gallery. "I thought: *What did I miss? Could I have done anything different?*" She hesitates. "And then I thought: *Would I have been allowed to?*"

"Two weeks later you received a letter," I say. "Can you tell us about it?"

"It was from the Board of Health. Suspending my license to practice as a nurse."

"What went through your mind when you received it?"

"I realized that I was being held responsible for the death of Davis Bauer. I knew I'd be suspended from my job, and that's what happened."

"Have you been employed since?"

"I went on public assistance, briefly," Ruth says. "Then I got a job at McDonald's."

"Ruth, how has your life changed in the aftermath of this incident?"

She takes a deep breath. "I don't have any savings anymore. We live from week to week. I'm worried about my son's future. I can't use my car because I can't afford to register it."

I turn my back, but Ruth isn't finished speaking.

"It's funny," she says softly. "You think you're a respected member of a community—the hospital where you work, the town where you live. I had a wonderful job. I had colleagues who were friends. I lived in a home I was proud of. But it was just an optical illusion. I was never a member of any of those communities. I was tolerated, but not welcomed. I was, and will always be, different from them." She looks up. "And because of the color of my skin, I will be the one who's blamed."

Oh God, I think. *Oh God, oh God, shut up, Ruth. Don't go here.* "Nothing further," I say, trying to cut our losses.

Because Ruth is no longer a witness. She's a time bomb.

WHEN I SIT BACK DOWN at the defense table, Howard is gaping. He pushes me a piece of paper: *WHAT IS GOING ON???*

I write back on the bottom: *That was an example of what you NEVER want a witness to do.*

Odette strides toward the witness stand. "You were instructed not to touch that baby?"

"Yes," Ruth says.

"And until today you said that you had not touched that baby until you were expressly told to by your charge nurse?"

"Yes."

"Yet now you testified on your direct examination that you in fact *did* touch that baby while he was in distress?"

Ruth nods. "That's true."

"So which is it?" Odette presses. "Did you or didn't you touch Davis Bauer when he initially stopped breathing?"

"I did."

"So let me get this straight. You lied to your supervisor?"

"Yes."

"And you lied to your colleague Corinne?"

"Yes."

"You lied to the risk management team at Mercy–West Haven, didn't you?"

She nods. "Yes."

"You lied to the police?"

"Yes, I did."

"Even though you realize they have a duty and a moral obligation to try to find out what happened to that dead infant?"

"I know but—"

"You were thinking of saving your job," Odette corrects, "because deep down you knew you were doing something shady. Isn't that right?"

"Well—"

"If you lied to *all* these people," Odette says, "why on earth should this jury believe anything you say right now?"

Ruth turns to the men and women crammed into the jury box. "Because I'm telling them the truth."

"Right," Odette says. "But that's not your only secret confession, is it?"

Where is she going with this?

"At the moment that the baby died—when the pediatrician called the time of death—deep down, you didn't really give a damn, right, Ruth?"

"Of course I did!" She sits up in her chair. "We were working so hard, just like we would for any patient—"

"Ah, but this wasn't just any patient. This was the baby of a white supremacist. The baby of a man who had dismissed your years of experience and nursing expertise—"

"You're wrong."

"—a man who called into question your ability to do your job simply because of the color of your skin. You resented Turk Bauer, and you resented his baby, didn't you?"

Odette is a foot away from Ruth now, yelling into her face. Ruth closes her eyes with every blast, as if she's facing a hurricane. "No," she whispers. "I never thought that."

"Yet you heard your colleague Corinne say you were angry after you were told you could no longer care for Davis Bauer, correct?"

"Yes."

"You worked twenty years at Mercy–West Haven?"

"Yes."

"You testified that you were an experienced, competent nurse and that you loved your job, is that fair to say?"

"It is," Ruth admits.

"Yet the hospital had no problem taking the wishes of the patient into consideration over respect for their own employee, and dismissing you from the professional role you'd maintained all those years?"

"Apparently."

"That must have made you furious, right?"

"I was upset," she concedes.

Hold it together, Ruth, I think.

"Upset? You said, and I quote, *That baby means nothing to me.*"

"It was something that came out in the heat of the moment—"

Odette's eyes gleam. "The heat of the moment! Is that also what happened when you told Dr. Atkins to sterilize the baby during his circumcision?"

"It was a joke," Ruth says. "I shouldn't have said it. That was a mistake."

"What *else* was a mistake?" Odette asks. "The fact that you stopped ministering to that baby while he fought to breathe, simply because you were afraid of how it might affect *you?*"

"I had been told to do nothing."

"So you made the conscious choice to stand over that poor tiny infant who was turning blue, while you thought, *What if I lose my job?*"

"No—"

"Or maybe you were thinking: *This baby doesn't deserve my help. His parents don't want me touching him because I'm black, and they're gonna get their wish.*"

"That's not true—"

"I see. You were thinking: *I hate his racist parents?*"

"No!" Ruth holds her hands to her head, trying to drown out Odette's voice.

"Oh, so maybe it was: *I hate this* baby *because I hate his racist parents?*"

"No," Ruth explodes, so loud that it feels like the walls of the courtroom are shaking. "I was thinking that baby was better off dead than raised by *him*."

She points directly at Turk Bauer, as a curtain of silence falls over the jury and the gallery and, yes, me. Ruth holds her hand over her mouth. *Too fucking late*, I think.

"O-objection!" Howard sputters. "Move to strike!"

At the same exact moment, Edison runs out of the courtroom.

I GRAB RUTH'S WRIST AS soon as we are dismissed and drag her to the conference room. Howard is smart enough to know to stay away. Once the door is closed, I turn on her. "Congratulations. You did *exactly* what you weren't supposed to do, Ruth."

She walks to the window, her back to me.

"Have you made your point? Are you happy you got up on the stand to testify? All the jury is going to see now is an angry black woman. One who was so pissed off and vengeful that I wouldn't be surprised if the judge regrets dismissing the count of murder. You just gave those fourteen jurors every reason to believe you were mad enough to let that baby die before your eyes."

Slowly, Ruth turns around. She is haloed by the afternoon sunlight, otherworldly. "I didn't *get* angry. I *am* angry. I have been angry for years. I just didn't let it show. What you don't understand is that three hundred and sixty-five days a year, I have to think about not looking or sounding *too black*, so I play a role. I put on a game face, like a layer of plaster. It's exhausting. It's so goddamned exhausting. But I do it, because I don't have bail money. I do it because I have a son. I do it because if I don't, I could lose my job. My house. Myself. So instead, I work and smile and nod and pay my bills and stay silent and pretend to be satisfied, because that is what you people want—no—*need* me to be. And the great, sad shame is that for too many years of my sorry life, I have bought into that farce. I thought if I did all those things, I could be one of you."

She walks toward me. "Look at you," Ruth sneers. "You're so proud of being a public defender and working with people of color who need help. But did you ever think our misfortune is directly related to your good fortune? Maybe the house your parents bought was on the market because the sellers didn't want *my* mama in the neighborhood. Maybe the good grades that eventually led you to law school were possible because your mama didn't have to work eighteen hours a day, and was there to read to you at night, or make sure you did your homework. How often do you remind yourself how lucky you are that you own your house, because you were able to build up equity through generations in a way families of color can't? How often do you open your mouth at work and think how awesome it is that no one's thinking you're speaking for everyone with the same skin color you have? How hard is it for you to find a greeting card for your baby's birthday with a picture of a child that has the same color skin as her? How many times have you seen a painting of Jesus that looks like you?" She stops, breathing heavily, her cheeks flushed. "Prejudice goes both ways, you know. There are people who suffer from it, and there are people who profit from it. Who died and made you Robin Hood? Who said I ever needed saving? Here you are on your high horse, telling me I screwed up this case that you worked so hard on; patting yourself on the back for being an advocate for a poor, struggling black woman like me . . . but you're part of the reason I was down on the ground to begin with."

We are inches apart. I can feel the heat of her skin; I can see myself reflected in her pupils as she starts to speak again. "You told me you could represent me, Kennedy. You can't represent me. You don't *know* me. You never even tried." Her eyes lock on mine. "You're fired," Ruth says, and she walks out of the room.

* * *

FOR A FEW MINUTES, I stand alone in the conference room, fighting an army of emotions. So this is why it's called a *trial*. I have never felt so furious, ashamed, humiliated. In all the years I've practiced law, I have had clients who hated me, but no one ever sacked me.

This is how Ruth feels.

Okay, I get it: she has been wronged by a lot of white people. But that doesn't mean she can so effortlessly lump me with them, judge one individual by the rest.

This is how Ruth feels.

How dare she accuse me of not being able to represent her, just because I'm not black? How dare she say I didn't try to get to know her? How dare she put words in my mouth? How dare she tell me what I'm thinking?

This is how Ruth feels.

Groaning, I throw myself toward the door. The judge is expecting us in chambers.

Howard is framed in the doorway as soon as it opens. Jesus Christ, I'd forgotten about him. "She fired you?" he says and then sheepishly adds, "I was kind of eavesdropping."

I start striding down the hall. "She can't fire me. The judge will never let her do that this late in the trial." The legal claim Ruth will make is ineffective assistance of counsel, but if anyone was ineffective here, it was the client. She tanked her own acquittal.

"So what happens now?"

I stop walking and turn to him. "Your guess is as good as mine," I say.

TOWARD THE END OF A CASE, a defense attorney will raise a motion for judgment of acquittal. But this time, when I step before Judge Thunder with Odette, he looks at me like I have some nerve to even be raising this issue. "There's no proof that Davis Bauer's death resulted from Ruth's actions. Or inactions," I add feebly, because at this point, even *I'm* not sure what to believe.

"Your Honor," Odette says. "It's clear that this is a last-ditch effort of desperation for the defense, given what we all just heard during that testimony. In fact I would humbly ask the court to reverse the decision on your previous motion to throw out the charge of murder. Clearly, Ruth Jefferson just gave proof of malice."

My blood freezes. I knew Odette would come out swinging, but I hadn't anticipated *this*. "Your Honor, the ruling has to stand. You already dismissed the murder charge. Double jeopardy applies; Ruth can't be charged twice with the same crime."

"In this one instance," Judge Thunder says grudgingly, "Ms. McQuarrie is correct. You've already had your bite at the apple, Ms. Lawton, and I already rejected the murder charge. I will, however, reserve my right to rule on the defense's renewed motion for judgment of acquittal." He looks at us each in turn. "Closing arguments start Monday morning, Counselors. Let's try not to make this any more of a shit show than it's already been, all right?"

I tell Howard to take the rest of the day off, and I drive home. My head feels cluttered, my mind too tight in my skull, as if I'm fighting a cold. When I get to my house, it smells of vanilla. I step into the kitchen to find my mother wearing a Wonder Woman apron while Violet kneels on one of the kitchen stools, her hand in a bowl of cookie dough. "Mommy!" she cries, raising sticky fists. "We're making you a surprise so pretend you can't see."

There's something about her phrase that sticks in my throat. *Pretend you can't see.*

Out of the mouths of babes.

My mother takes one look at me and frowns over Violet's head. "You okay?" she mouths silently.

In response, I sit down next to Violet and take a scoop of the cookie dough with my fingers and start eating.

My daughter is a lefty, in spite of the fact that Micah and I are not. We even have an ultrasound picture of her sucking her left thumb in utero. "What if it's that simple?" I murmur.

"What if *what's* that simple?"

I look at my mom. "Do you think the world is biased toward righties?"

"Um, I can't say I've ever thought about it."

"That's because," I point out, "*you're* a righty. But think about it. Can openers, scissors, even desks at college that fold out from the side—they're all meant for right-handed people."

Violet lifts up the hand that is holding her spoon, frowning at it. "Baby girl," my mother says, "why don't you go wash up so you can taste the first batch that comes out of the oven?"

She slithers off the stool, her hands held up like Micah's before he enters an operating room.

"Do you want to give the child nightmares?" my mother scolds. "Honestly, Kennedy! Where is this even coming from? Does this have to do with your case?"

"I've read that lefties die young because they're more accident prone. When you were growing up, didn't nuns slap the kids who wrote with their left hands?"

My mother puts a hand on her hip. "One man's curse is another's boon, you know. Lefties are supposed to be more creative. Weren't Michelangelo and da Vinci and Bach all left-handed? And back in medieval times you were lucky to be a lefty, because the majority of men fought with a sword in their right hand and a shield in their left, which meant you could pull off a sneak attack"—she reaches toward me with a spatula, poking me on the right side of my chest—"like this."

I laugh. "Why do you even know that?"

"I read romance novels, sugar," she says. "Don't worry about Violet. If she really wants to, you know, she can always teach herself to be ambidextrous. Your father, *he* was just as good with his right hand as with his left one—writing, hammering, even getting to second base." She grins. "And I am *not* talking about batting practice."

"*Ew,*" I say. "Stop." But meanwhile, my brain is spinning: What if the puzzle of the world was a shape you didn't fit into? And the only way to survive was to mutilate yourself, carve away your corners, sand yourself down, modify yourself to fit?

How come we haven't been able to change the puzzle instead?

"Mom?" I ask. "Can you stay with Vi for a few more hours?"

* * *

I REMEMBER READING A NOVEL once that said the native Alaskans who came in contact with white missionaries thought, at first, they were ghosts. And why shouldn't they have thought that? Like ghosts, white people move effortlessly through boundaries and borders. Like ghosts, we can be anywhere we want to be.

I decide it's time to feel the walls around me.

The first thing I do is leave my car in the driveway and walk a mile to a bus stop. Chilled to the bone, I duck into a CVS to warm up. I stop in front of a display I've never paused at before and take down a purple box. Dark and Lovely Healthy-Gloss relaxer. I look at the pretty woman in the picture. *For medium hair textures,* I read. *Straight, sleek, and shiny hair.* I scan the instructions, the multiple-step process needed to get hair that looks like mine after I blow it dry.

Next I reach for a bottle, Luster's Pink oil moisturizer hair lotion. A black tub of Ampro Pro Styl. A satin bonnet that claims to minimize frizz and breakage at night.

These products are foreign to me. I have no idea what they do, why they're necessary for black people, or how to use them. But I bet Ruth could name five shampoos white people use, just off the top of her head, thanks to ubiquitous television commercials.

I walk downtown, where for a little while I sit on a bench for another bus and watch two homeless people soliciting strangers on the street. They target mostly well-dressed white people in business suits, or college students plugged into their headphones, and maybe one in six or seven reaches into his or her pocket for change. Of the two homeless people, one routinely gets a donation more often than the other. She's elderly, and white. The other one—a young black man—is given a wider berth.

The Hill neighborhood of New Haven is among the most notorious in the city. I've had dozens of clients from there—mostly involved in selling drugs near the Church Street South low-income housing. That's also where Adisa, Ruth's sister, lives.

I wander the streets. There are kids running, chasing each other. Girls huddled together, speaking a flurry of Spanish. Men stand on street corners, arms folded, silent sentries. I am the only white face in the vicinity. It is already starting to get dark out when I duck into a bodega. The cashier at the counter stares at me as I walk through the aisles. I can feel her gaze like lightning between my shoulder blades. "Can I help you?" she asks finally, and I shake my head and walk out.

It's unsettling, not seeing someone who looks like me. People I pass don't make eye contact. I am the stranger in their midst, the sore thumb, the one that is not like the others. And yet, at the very same instant, I have become invisible.

When I get to Church Street South, I walk around the buildings. Some of the apartments, I know, have been condemned for mold, for structural damage. It is like a ghost town: curtains pulled tight, residents holed up inside. Beneath a stairwell, I see two young men, passing cash. An old lady tries to haul her oxygen tank up the stairs above them. "Excuse me," I call out. "Can I give you a hand?"

All three of them stare at me, frozen. The men glance up, and one puts a hand on the waistband of his jeans, from which I think I see the hilt of a gun protruding. My legs are jelly. Before I can back away, the old woman says, "*No hablo inglés,*" and climbs the steps double time.

I had wanted to live like Ruth did, just for an afternoon, but not if it meant I'd be in danger. Yet danger, it's relative. I have a husband with a good job and a house that's paid off, and I don't have to worry that something I say or do is going to threaten my ability to put food on the table or pay my bills. For me, danger looks different: it's whatever can separate me from Violet, from Micah. But no matter what face you put on your own personal bogeyman, it gives you nightmares. It has the power to terrify, and to make you do things you wouldn't normally think you'd do, all in an effort to stay safe.

For me, that means running through a night that's tunneling tighter around me, until I can be sure I'm not being followed. Several blocks away, I slow down at an intersection. By now, my pulse isn't racing, the sweat has cooled beneath my arms. A man about my age approaches, pushing the same pedestrian walk button, waiting. His dark skin is pocked on the cheeks, a road map of his life. His hands hold a thick book, but I cannot make out the title.

I decide to try one more time. I nod down toward the book. "Is it good? I'm looking for something to read."

He glances at me, and lets his gaze slide away. He doesn't respond.

I feel my cheeks burning as the walk signal illuminates. We cross the street side by side in silence, and then he turns away, ducking down a street.

I wonder if he was really intending to go down that street, or if he just wanted to put distance between us. My feet hurt, my whole body is shaking with the cold, and I'm feeling utterly defeated. I realize it was a short-lived experiment, but at least I tried to understand what Ruth was saying. I tried.

I.

As I trudge up to the hospital where Micah works, I think about that pronoun. I consider the hundreds of years that a black man could have gotten into trouble for talking to a white woman. In some places in this country, it's still the case, and the repercussions are vigilante justice. For me, the dire consequence of that stoplight conversation was feeling snubbed. For him, it was something else entirely. It was two centuries of history.

Micah's office is on the third floor. It's remarkable how, the minute I walk through the doors of that hospital, I am in my element again. I know the healthcare system; I know how I will be treated; I know the rituals and the responses. I can stride past the information desk without anyone questioning where I'm going or why I am there. I can wave to the staff in Micah's department and let myself into his office.

Today is a surgery day for him. I sit in his desk chair, my coat unbuttoned, my shoes off. I stare at the model of the human eye on his desk, a three-dimensional puzzle, as my thoughts speed like a cyclone. Every time I close my eyes, I see the old woman at Church Street South, shrinking away from my offer of help. I hear Ruth's voice, telling me I am fired.

Maybe I deserve to be.

Maybe I'm wrong.

I've spent months so focused on getting an acquittal for Ruth, but if I'm really going to be honest, the acquittal was for *me*. For my first murder trial.

I've spent months telling Ruth that a criminal lawsuit is no place to bring up race. If you do, you can't win. But if you don't, there are still costs—because you are perpetuating a flawed system, instead of trying to change it.

That's what Ruth has been trying to say, but I haven't listened. She's brave enough to risk losing her job, her livelihood, her *freedom* to tell the truth, and I'm the liar. I'd told her race isn't welcome in the courtroom, when deep down I know it's already there. It always *has* been. And just because I close my eyes doesn't mean it's gone away.

Witnesses swear on Bibles in court to tell the truth, the whole truth, and nothing but the truth. But lies of omission are just as damning as any other falsehood. And to finish out Ruth Jefferson's case without stating, overtly, that what happened to her happened because of the color of her skin might be an even bigger loss than a conviction.

Maybe if there were lawyers more courageous than I am, we wouldn't be so scared to talk about race in places where it matters the most.

Maybe if there were lawyers more courageous than I am, there would not be another Ruth somewhere down the line, being indicted as the result of another racially motivated incident that no one wants to admit is a racially motivated incident.

Maybe if there were lawyers more courageous than I am, fixing the system would be as important as acquitting the client.

Maybe I should be more courageous.

Ruth accused me of wanting to save her, and perhaps that was a fair assessment. But she doesn't need saving. She doesn't need my advice, because really, who am I to give it, when I haven't lived her life? She just needs a chance to speak. To be heard.

I am really not sure how much time passes before Micah enters.

He is wearing scrubs, which I've always thought were sexy, and Crocs, which totally *aren't*. His face lights up when he sees me. "This is a nice surprise."

"I was in the neighborhood," I tell him. "Can you give me a ride home?"

"Where's your car?"

I shake my head. "Long story."

He gathers up some files and checks a stack of messages, then reaches for his coat. "Everything all right? You were a million miles away when I walked in."

I lift the eye model and turn it over in my hands. "I feel like I've been standing underneath an open window, just as a baby gets tossed out. I grab the baby, right, because who wouldn't? But then another baby gets tossed out, so I pass the baby to someone else, and I make the catch. This keeps happening. And before you know it there are a whole bunch of people who are getting really good at passing along babies, just like I'm good at catching them, but no one ever asks who the fuck is throwing the babies out the window in the first place."

"Um." Micah tilts his head. "What baby are we talking about?"

"It's not a baby, it's a metaphor," I say, irritated. "I've been doing my job, but who cares, if the system keeps on creating situations where my job is necessary? Shouldn't we focus on the big picture, instead of just catching whatever falls out the window at any given moment?"

Micah's staring at me like I've lost my mind. Behind his shoulder a poster hangs on the wall: the anatomy of the human eye. There is the optic nerve, the aqueous humor, the conjunctiva. The ciliary body, the retina, the choroid. "For a living," I murmur, "you make people see."

"Well," he says. "Yeah."

I look directly at him. "That's what I need to do too."

Ruth

EDISON ISN'T AT HOME, AND MY CAR IS GONE.

I wait for him, text him, call him, pray, but there is no response. I imagine him walking the streets, hearing my voice ring out in his ears. He is wondering if he has it in him, too, the capacity for rage. If nature or nurture matters more; if he is doubly damned.

Yes, I hated that racist father for belittling me. Yes, I hated the hospital for sticking by his side. I don't know if that bled over into my ability to care for a patient. I can't tell you that for a moment, it didn't cross my mind. That I didn't look down at that innocent baby and think of the monster he would grow up to be.

Does that make me the villain here? Or does that just make me human?

And Kennedy. What I said wasn't in my mind, it was in my heart. I do not regret a syllable. Every time I think about what it felt like to be the one who walked out of that room—who had that *privilege*, for once—I feel dizzy, like I'm flying.

When I hear steps outside, I fly to the door and open it, but it is not my son—just my sister. Adisa stands with her arms crossed. "Figured you'd be home," she says, pushing her way into my living room. "After that, I didn't imagine you'd be sticking around the courthouse."

She makes herself comfortable, draping her coat over a kitchen chair, sitting down on the couch, putting her feet up on the coffee table.

"Have you seen Edison? Is he with Tabari?" I ask.

She shakes her head. "Tabari's home babysitting."

"I'm worried, A."

"About Edison?"

"Among other things."

Adisa pats the couch beside her. I sit down, and she reaches for my hand and squeezes it. "Edison's a smart boy. He'll wind up on his feet."

I swallow. "Will you ... watch him for me? Make sure that he doesn't just, you know, give up?"

"If you making out your will, I always liked those black leather boots of yours." She shakes her head. "Ruth, relax."

"I can't relax. I can't sit here and think that my son is going to throw away his whole future and it's my fault."

She looks me in the eye. "Then you're just gonna have to make sure you're here to monitor him."

But we both know that's not in my hands. Before I know it, I am bent at the waist, punched in the gut by a truth so raw and so frightening that I can't breathe: I have lost control of my future. And it's my own damn fault.

I didn't play by the rules. I did what Kennedy told me not to. And now I'm paying the price for using my voice.

Adisa's arm goes around me, pressing my face against her shoulder. It isn't until she does that that I realize I'm sobbing. "I'm scared," I gasp.

"I know. But you always got me," Adisa vows. "I will bake you a cake with a file in it."

That makes me hiccup on a laugh. "No you won't."

"You're right," she says, reconsidering. "I can't bake for shit." Suddenly she pushes off the couch and reaches into the pocket of her coat. "I thought you should have this."

I know by the smell—a hint of perfume, with the sharp scent of laundry soap—what she is giving me. Adisa tosses the coil of my mother's lucky scarf into my lap, where it unfurls like a rose. "*You* took this? I looked everywhere for it."

"Yeah, because I figured you'd either take it for yourself or bury Mama in it, and she didn't need luck anymore, but God knows I do." Adisa shrugs. "And so do you."

She sits down next to me again. This week her fingernails are bright yellow. Mine are chewed down to the flesh. She takes the scarf and wraps it around my neck, tucking in the ends the way I used to for Edison, her hands coming to rest on my shoulders. "There," she says, like I am ready to be sent into the storm.

AFTER MIDNIGHT, EDISON RETURNS. HE is wild-eyed and fidgety, his clothes damp with sweat. "Where have you been?" I demand.

"Running." But who runs carrying a knapsack?

"We have to talk . . ."

"I have nothing to say to you," he tells me, and he slams the door to his bedroom.

I know he must be disgusted by what he saw in me today: my anger, my admission that I am a liar. I walk up to the door, press my palms to the particleboard, ball my hand into a fist to knock, to force this conversation, but I can't. There is nothing left in me.

I don't make up my bed; instead I fall asleep fitfully on the couch. I dream about Mama's funeral, again. This time, she is sitting beside me in the church, and we are the only people present. There is a coffin on the altar. *It's a shame, isn't it?* Mama says.

I look at her, and then I look at the coffin. I cannot see over the lip. So I get to my feet heavily, only to realize that they are rooted to the church floor. Vines have grown up around the ankles, and through the wooden boards on the ground. I try to move, but I am bound.

Straining in my shoes, I manage to peer over the edge of the open coffin so that I can see the deceased.

From the neck down, it's a skeleton, flesh melted from the bones.

From the neck up, it has my face.

I wake up, my heart hammering, only to realize that the pounding is coming from somewhere else. *Déjà vu*, I think, as I swivel toward the door, shaking from the force of the knocks. I leap up and reach the knob, and the moment I do, the door flies back on its hinges, nearly throwing me down in the process. But the police that flood my home push me out of the way. They dump out drawers, they knock over chairs. "Edison Jefferson?" one of them yells, and my son steps out, sleepy and tousled.

He is immediately grabbed, handcuffed, dragged toward the door. "You're under arrest for a Class C felony hate crime," the officer says.

What?

"Edison," I cry. "Wait! This is a mistake!"

Another cop comes out of Edison's bedroom carrying his knapsack, unzipped, in one hand, and a can of red spray paint in the other. "Bingo," he says.

Edison turns toward me as best he can. "I'm sorry, Mama, I *had* to," he says, and then he is yanked out the door.

"You have the right to remain silent . . ." I hear, and just as quickly as the police entered, they are gone.

The stillness paralyzes me, presses in on my temples, my throat. I am suffocating, I am being crushed. I manage to scrabble my hands over the coffee table to find my cellphone, which is charging. Yanking it out of the wall, I dial, even though it is the middle of the night. "I need your help."

Kennedy's voice is sure and strong, as if she's been expecting me. "What's wrong?" she asks.

Kennedy

IT'S JUST AFTER 2:00 A.M. WHEN MY CELLPHONE RINGS, AND I SEE RUTH'S name flash. Immediately I'm awake. Micah sits up, alert the way doctors always are, and I shake my head at him. *I've got this.*

Fifteen minutes later, I pull up to the East End police department.

I walk up to the desk sergeant as if I have every right to be there. "You brought in a kid named Edison Jefferson?" I ask. "What's the charge?"

"Who are you?"

"The family lawyer."

Who was fired hours ago, I think silently. The officer narrows his eyes. "Kid didn't say anything about a lawyer."

"He's seventeen," I point out. "He's probably too terrified to remember his own name. Look, let's not make this any harder than it has to be, okay?"

"We got him on security cameras at the hospital, spray-painting the walls."

Edison? Vandalizing? "You sure you have the right kid? He's an honor student. College-bound."

"Security guards ID'd him. And we tagged him driving a car with out-of-date plates registered to Ruth Jefferson. To his front door."

Oh. Crap.

"He was painting swastikas, and wrote *'Die Nigger.'*"

"What?" I say, stunned.

That means it's not just vandalism. It's a hate crime. But it doesn't make any sense. I open my purse, look at how much cash I have. "Okay, listen. Can you get him a special arraignment? I'll pay for the magistrate to come, so he can get out of here tonight."

I am taken back to the holding cell, where Edison is sitting on the floor, his back to the wall, his knees hunched up to his chin. Tears lattice his cheeks. The minute he sees me he stands up and walks toward the bars. "What were you *thinking*?" I demand.

He wipes his nose on his sleeve. "I wanted to help my mama."

"What about getting your ass thrown in jail helps your mother right now?"

"I wanted to get Turk Bauer in trouble. If it wasn't for him, none of this ever would have happened. And after today, everyone was blaming her, and they should have been blaming him . . ." He looks up at me, his eyes red. "She's the victim here. How come nobody sees that?"

"I will help you," I tell him. "But what you and I talk about is privileged information, which means you shouldn't tell your mother anything about it." What I'm thinking, though, is that Ruth will find out soon enough. Probably when she reads the front page of the damn paper. It's just too good: SON OF KILLER NURSE ARRESTED FOR HATE CRIME. "And for the love of God, don't say a word in front of the magistrate."

Fifteen minutes later, the magistrate comes to the holding cell. Special arraignments are like magic tricks; all sorts of rules can be bent when you are willing to pay extra. There's an officer acting as prosecutor, and me, and Edison, and the judge-for-hire. Edison's charge is read, and his Miranda rights. "What's going on here?" the magistrate asks.

I jump in. "Your Honor, this is a very unique circumstance, an isolated incident. Edison is a varsity athlete and an honor student who's never been in trouble before; his mother is on trial right now for negligent homicide, and he's frustrated. Emotions are running very high right now, and this was a hugely misguided attempt to support his mother."

The magistrate looks at Edison. "Is that true, young man?"

Edison looks at me, unsure if he should answer. I nod. "Yes, sir," he says quietly.

"Edison Jefferson," the magistrate says, "you have been charged with a racially motived hate crime. This is a felony, and you'll be arraigned in court on Monday. You will not have to answer any questions, and you have the right to an attorney. If you can't afford an attorney, one will be appointed to you. I see that you have Ms. McQuarrie here on your behalf, and the case will be referred to the public defender's office formally in superior court. You cannot leave the state of Connecticut, and I have the obligation to advise you that if you are arrested for any other offense while this case is pending, you can be held at the state prison." He stares down Edison. "Stay out of trouble, boy."

The whole thing takes an hour. We are both wide awake when we get into my car so that I can drive Edison home. The glow of the rearview mirror brackets my eyes as I steal glances at him in the passenger seat. He's holding one of Violet's toys—a little fairy with pink wings. It is impossibly tiny in his large hands. "What the fuck, Edison?" I say quietly. "People like Turk Bauer are horrible. Why are you stooping to that level?"

"Why are *you*?" he asks, turning toward me. "You're pretending that what they do doesn't even matter. I sat through that whole trial; it barely even came up."

"What barely came up?"

"Racism," he says.

I suck in my breath. "It may never have been explicitly discussed during the trial, but Turk Bauer was on full display—a museum-quality exhibit."

He looks at me, one eyebrow cocked. "You really think Turk Bauer is the only person in that courtroom who's a racist?"

We pull into a spot in front of Ruth's home. The light is on inside, buttery and warm. She throws open the front door and comes out onto the steps, pulling her cardigan more tightly around her body. "Thank the Lord," she murmurs, and she folds Edison into her embrace. "What happened?"

Edison glances at me. "She told me not to tell you."

Ruth snorts. "Yeah, she's good at that."

"I spray-painted a swastika on the hospital. And . . . some other stuff."

She holds him at arm's length, waiting.

"I wrote 'Die Nigger,'" Edison murmurs.

Ruth slaps him across the face. He reels back, holding his cheek. "You fool, why would you do that?"

"I thought Turk Bauer would get blamed. I wanted people to stop saying awful things about you."

Ruth closes her eyes for a moment, like she is fighting for control. "What happens now?"

"He'll be arraigned in court on Monday. The press will probably be there," I say.

"What am I going to do?" she asks.

"You," I tell her, "are going to do nothing. I'll handle this."

I see her fighting, struggling to accept this gift. "Okay," Ruth says.

I notice that this whole time, she keeps contact with her son. Even after swatting him, her hand is on his arm, his shoulder, his back. When I drive away, they are still standing together on the porch, tangled in each other's regret.

BY THE TIME I GET home, it is four in the morning. It seems stupid to crawl into bed, and anyway, I'm wired. I decide to clean up a little, and then to have a pancake breakfast waiting when Violet and Micah wake.

It's inevitable that over the course of a trial, my home office becomes more and more cluttered. But Ruth's case, it's a done deal. So I tiptoe into the extra bedroom I use and begin to pack up the discovery into its boxes. I stack files and folders and notes I made on the evidence. I try to find Ground Zero.

I accidentally bump a pile on the desk and knock it onto the floor. Picking up the pages, I scan the deposition from Brittany Bauer, which of course never came into play, and the photocopied results from the state laboratory that flagged Davis Bauer's metabolic disorder. It's a long, aggregate list of disorders. Most read *normal*, except of course the line for MCADD.

I glance over the rest of the list, which I never really focused on before, because I'd grabbed the brass ring and run with it. Davis Bauer seemed to be a normal infant in all other regards, his testing standard.

Then I turn the page over, and realize there's print on the back, too.

There, in a sea of ordinary, is the word *abnormal* again. This one is much farther down the list of aggregated results—less important maybe, less threatening? I cross-reference the result with the lab tests that were included in the subpoena, a mess of lists of proteins I can't pronounce, and scraggly graphs of spectrometry I do not know how to read.

I pause at a page that looks like a runny tie-dye. *Electrophoresis*, I read. *Hemoglobinopathy*. And at the bottom of the page, the results: *HbAS/heterozygous*.

I sit down at my computer and plug the result into Google. If this is something else that was medically wrong with Davis Bauer, I can introduce it, even now. I can call for a new trial, because of new evidence.

I can start over with a fresh jury.

Generally benign carrier state, I read, my hopes falling. So much for another potential cause of natural death.

Family to be tested/counseled.

The hemoglobins are listed in the order of hemoglobin present (F>A>S). FA = normal. FAS = carrier, sickle-cell trait. FSA = sickle beta-plus thalassemia.

Then I remember something Ivan said.

I sink to the floor, reaching for the stack of deposition transcripts, and begin to read.

Then, although it is only 4:30 A.M., I grab my phone and scroll through the history of incoming calls until I find the one I am looking for. "This is Kennedy McQuarrie," I say, when Wallace Mercy picks up, his voice thick with dreams. "And I need you."

ON MONDAY MORNING, THE STEPS are crowded with cameras and reporters, many now from out of state, who have picked up the story of the black kid who wrote a racial slur against his own kind, the son of a nurse on trial just down the hall for killing a white supremacist's baby. Although I have prepared a song and dance for Howard in case my stay isn't granted, Judge Thunder shocks me once again by agreeing to delay closing arguments until 10:00 A.M. so I can act as Edison's attorney before I pick up again as Ruth's—even if only to be formally fired.

The cameras follow us down the hallway, even though I tuck Ruth under one arm and instruct Howard to shield Edison. The entire arraignment takes less than five minutes. Edison is released on personal recognizance and a pretrial conference date is set. Then we dodge the press the whole way back.

I have never been so delighted to return to Judge Thunder's courtroom, in which no cameras or press are allowed.

We step inside and walk to the defense table, Edison slipping quietly into the row behind. But no sooner have we reached our spot than Ruth looks at me, frowning. "What are you doing?"

I blink. "What?"

"Just because you're representing Edison doesn't mean anything has changed," she replies.

Before I can respond, the judge takes the bench. He looks from me—clearly in the middle of a charged conversation with my client—to Odette, across the room. "Are the parties ready to proceed?" he asks.

"Your Honor?" Ruth says. "I would like to get rid of my lawyer."

I am pretty sure Judge Thunder thought nothing else in this trial could surprise him, until this moment. "Ms. Jefferson? Why on earth would you want to discharge your lawyer when the defense has rested? All that's left is a closing argument."

Ruth's jaw works. "It's personal, Your Honor."

"I would strongly recommend otherwise, Ms. Jefferson. She knows the case, and contrary to all expectation, she has been very prepared. She has your best interests in mind. It is my job to run this trial, and to make sure it's no longer delayed. We have a jury sitting in the box that has heard all the evidence; we don't have time for you to go find another attorney, and you are not equipped to represent yourself." He faces me. "Unbelievably, I am granting you another half-hour recess, Ms. McQuarrie, so you and your client can make nice."

I deputize Howard to stay with Edison so that the press can't get near him. Getting to our usual conference room will require running past the press, too, so instead I take Ruth out a back entrance and into the ladies' room. "Sorry," I say to a woman following us, and I lock the door behind us. Ruth leans against the bank of sinks and folds her arms.

"I know you think nothing's changed, and maybe it hasn't for you. But for me, it *has*," I say. "I hear you, loud and clear. I may not deserve it, but I'm begging you to give me one last chance."

"Why should I?" Ruth asks, a challenge.

"Because I told you once I don't see color . . . and now, it's *all* I see."

She starts for the door. "I don't need your pity."

"You're right." I nod. "You need equity."

Ruth stops walking, still facing away from me. "You mean equality," she corrects.

"No, I mean equity. Equality is treating everyone the same. But equity is taking differences into account, so everyone has a chance to succeed." I look at her. "The first one *sounds* fair. The second one *is* fair. It's equal to give a printed test to two kids. But if one's blind and one's sighted, that's not true. You ought to give one a Braille test and one a printed test, which both cover the same material. All this time, I've been giving the jury a print test, because I didn't realize that they're blind. That *I* was blind. Please, Ruth. I think you'll like hearing what I have to say."

Slowly, Ruth turns around. "One last chance," she agrees.

* * *

WHEN I STAND UP, I'M not alone.

Yes, there is a courtroom waiting for my closing argument, but I'm surrounded by the stories that have blazed through the media but have mostly been ignored in courts of law. The stories of Tamir Rice, of Michael Brown, of Trayvon Martin. Of Eric Garner and Walter Scott and Freddie Gray. Of Sandra Bland and John Crawford III. Of the female African American soldiers who wanted to wear their hair natural and the children in the Seattle school district who were told by the Supreme Court that cherry-picking students to maintain racial diversity was unconstitutional. Of minorities in the South, who've been left without federal protection while those states put laws into effect that limit their voting rights. Of the millions of African Americans who have been victims of housing discrimination and job discrimination. Of the homeless black boy on Chapel Street whose cup is never going to be as full as that of a white homeless woman.

I turn toward the jury. "What if, ladies and gentlemen, today I told you that anyone here who was born on a Monday, Tuesday, or Wednesday was free to leave right now? Also, they'd be given the most central parking spots in the city, and the biggest houses. They would get job interviews before others who were born later in the week, and they'd be taken first at the doctor's office, no matter how many patients were waiting in line. If you were born from Thursday to Sunday, you might try to catch up—but because you were straggling behind, the press would always point to how inefficient you are. And if you complained, you'd be dismissed for playing the birth-day card." I shrug. "Seems silly, right? But what if on top of these arbitrary systems that inhibited your chances for success, everyone kept telling you that things were actually pretty equal?"

I walk toward them, continuing. "I told you when we started this case that it was about Ruth Jefferson being presented with an impossible choice: to do her job as a nurse, or to defy her supervisor's orders. I told you that evidence would show Davis Bauer had underlying health conditions that led to his death. And that is true, ladies and gentlemen. But this case, it's about a lot more than I let on to you.

"Out of all the people who interacted with Davis Bauer at Mercy–

West Haven Hospital during his short life, only one of them is sitting in this courtroom at the defense table: Ruth Jefferson. Only one person is being charged with a crime: Ruth Jefferson. I spent an entire trial skirting a very important question: *Why?*

"Ruth is black," I say flatly. "That rubbed Turk Bauer, a white supremacist, the wrong way. He can't stand black people, or Asian people, or gay people, or anyone else who isn't like him. And as a result, he set into motion a chain of events that would lead to Ruth becoming a scapegoat for the tragic death of his son. But we are not supposed to talk about race in the criminal justice system. We're supposed to pretend it is merely the icing on the cake of whatever charge has been brought to the table—not the substance of it. We are supposed to be the legal guardians of a postracial society. But you know, the word *ignorance* has an even more important word at its heart: *ignore*. And I don't think it's right to ignore the truth any longer."

I look right at juror number 12, the teacher. "Finish this sentence," I say. "*I am . . . ?*" I pause at the blank. "Maybe you'd answer: *shy*. Or *blond. Friendly. Nervous, intelligent, Irish*. But the majority of you wouldn't say *white*. Why not? Because it's a given. It's identity that is taken for granted. Those of us who were lucky enough to be born white are oblivious to that good fortune. Now, we're all blissfully unmindful of lots of things. Probably, you did not give thanks for showering this morning, or for having a roof over your head last night. For eating breakfast and having clean underwear. That's because all those invisible privileges are easy to take in stride.

"Sure, it's so much easier to see the headwinds of racism, the ways that people of color are discriminated against. We see it now when a black man is accidentally shot by the police and a girl with brown skin is bullied by classmates for wearing a hijab. It's a little harder to see—and to own up to—the tailwinds of racism, the ways that those of us who aren't people of color have benefited just because we're white. We can go to a movie and be pretty certain that most of the main characters will look like us. We can be late for a meeting and not have it blamed on our race. I can go into Judge Thunder's chambers and raise an objection and not be told I'm playing the race card." I pause. "The vast majority of us do not come home from work and say, *Hooray! I didn't get stopped and frisked today!* The vast majority of us did not get into college and think, *I got into the school of my choice because the educational system really works in my favor.* We don't think these things, because we don't have to."

By now, the jury is getting uneasy. They shift and shuffle, and from the corner of my eye I see Judge Thunder regarding me narrowly, even though a closing argument is mine alone to give, and theoretically, if I wanted to read *Great Expectations* out loud, I could.

"I know you're thinking: *I'm not racist.* Why, we even had an example of what we think *real* racism looks like, in the form of Turk Bauer. I doubt there are many of you on the jury who, like Turk, believe that your children are Aryan warriors or that black people are so inferior they should not even be able to touch a white baby. But even if we took every white supremacist on the planet and shipped them off to Mars, there would still be racism. That's because racism isn't just about hate. We all have biases, even if we don't think we do. It's because racism is also about who has power . . . and who has access to it.

"When I started working on this case, ladies and gentlemen, I didn't see myself as a racist. Now I realize I am. Not because I hate people of different races but because—intentionally or unintentionally—I've gotten a boost from the color of my skin, just like Ruth Jefferson suffered a setback because of hers."

Odette is sitting with her head bowed at the prosecution table. I can't tell if she is delighted that I am building my own coffin out of words or if she is simply stunned that I have the balls to antagonize the jury at this late stage of the game. "There is a difference between active and passive racism. It's kind of like when you get on the moving walkway at the airport. If you walk down it, you're going to get to the other end faster than if you just stand still. But you're ultimately going to wind up in the same spot. Active racism is having a swastika tattoo on your head. Active racism is telling a nurse supervisor that an African American nurse can't touch your baby. It's snickering at a black joke. But passive racism? It's noticing there's only one person of color in your office and not asking your boss why. It's reading your kid's fourth-grade curriculum and seeing that the only black history covered is slavery, and not questioning why. It's defending a woman in court whose indictment directly resulted from her race . . . and glossing over that fact, like it hardly matters.

"I bet you feel uncomfortable right now. You know, so do I. It's hard to talk about this stuff without offending people, or feeling offended. It's why lawyers like me aren't supposed to say these things to juries like you. But deep down, if you've asked yourself what this trial is *really* about, you know it's more than just whether Ruth had anything to do with the death of one of her patients. In fact, it has very little to do with Ruth. It's about systems that have been in place for about four hundred years, systems meant to make sure that people like Turk can make a heinous request as a patient, and have it granted. Systems meant to make sure that people like Ruth are kept in their place."

I turn to the jury, beseeching. "If you don't want to think about this, you don't have to, and you can still acquit Ruth. I've given you enough medical evidence to show that there's plenty of doubt about what led to that baby's death. You heard the medical examiner himself say that had the newborn screening results come back in a more timely fashion, Davis Bauer might be alive today. Yes, you also heard Ruth get angry on the stand—that's because when you wait forty-four years to be given a chance to speak, things don't always come out the way you want them to. Ruth Jefferson just wanted the chance to *do her job*. To take care of that infant like she was trained to do."

I turn, finally, toward Ruth. She breathes in, and I feel it in my own chest. "What if people who were born on Monday, Tuesday, or Wednesday were never the subjects of extensive credit checks when they applied for loans? What if they could shop without fear of security tailing them?" I pause. "What if their newborn screening test results came back to the pediatrician in a timely manner, allowing medical intervention that could prevent their deaths? Suddenly," I say, "that type of arbitrary discrimination doesn't seem quite so silly, does it?"

Ruth

AFTER ALL THAT.

After months of telling me that race doesn't belong in a court of law, Kennedy McQuarrie took the elephant in the room and paraded it in front of the judge. She squeezed it into the jury box, so that those men and women couldn't help but feel the pinch.

I stare at the jury, all lost in thought and utterly silent. Kennedy comes to sit down beside me, and for a moment, I just look at her. My throat works while I try to put into words everything I am feeling. What Kennedy said to all those strangers, it's been the narrative of my life, the outline inside of which I have lived. But I could have screamed it from the rooftops, and it wouldn't have done any good. For the jurors to hear it, *really* hear it, it had to be said by one of their own.

She turns to me before I can speak. "Thank you," she says, as if I'm the one who's done her the favor.

Come to think of it, maybe I have.

The judge clears his throat, and we both look up to find him glaring. Odette Lawton has risen and is standing in the spot Kennedy just vacated. I stroke my mother's lucky scarf, looped around my neck, as she begins to speak. "You know, I admire Ms. McQuarrie and her rousing cry for social justice. But that's not what we're here for today. We are here because the defendant, Ruth Jefferson, abandoned the ethical code of her profession as a labor and delivery nurse and did not adequately respond to an infant's medical crisis."

The prosecutor approaches the jury. "What Ms. McQuarrie said . . . it's true. People have prejudices, and sometimes they make decisions that don't make sense to us. When I was in high school, I worked at McDonald's."

This surprises me; I try to imagine Odette timing fries, but I can't.

"I was the only Black kid working there. There were times I'd be at the register and I would see a customer walk in, look at me, and then go into another cashier's line to place their order. How did that make me feel?" She shrugs. "Not so great. But did I spit in their food? No. Did I drop the burger on the floor and then tuck it into the bun? No. I did my job. I did what I was supposed to do.

"Now let's look at Ruth Jefferson, shall we? She had a customer choose another line, so to speak, but did *she* continue to do what she was supposed to do? No. She did not take the directive to not care for Davis Bauer in stride as a simple patient request—she blew it up into a racial incident. She did not honor her Nightingale pledge to assist her patients—*no matter what*. She acted with complete disregard to the infant's welfare because she was angry, and she took her anger out on that poor child.

"It's true, ladies and gentlemen, that Marie Malone's directive to excuse Ruth as a caretaker for Davis Bauer was a racist decision, but it is not Marie on trial here for her actions. It is Ruth, for not adhering to the vow she made as a nurse. It's true, too, that many of you were made uncomfortable by Mr. Bauer and his beliefs, because they are extreme. In this country, he is allowed to express those views, even when they make others feel uneasy. But if you are going to say you are unnerved by how Turk Bauer is filled with hate, you must admit that Ruth, too, is filled with hate. You heard it, when she told you it was better for that baby to die than to grow up like his father. Perhaps that was the only moment she was candid with us. At least Turk Bauer is honest about his beliefs—as unpalatable as they may seem. Because Ruth, we know, is a liar. By her own admission, she *did* intervene and touch the infant in the nursery, in spite of telling her supervisor and Risk Management and the police that she did not. Ruth Jefferson started to save this baby—and what made her stop? Fear for her job. She put her own interests in front of the patient's . . . which is exactly what a medical professional should never do."

The prosecutor pauses. "Ruth Jefferson and her attorney can throw up a dog and pony show about tardy lab results, or the state of race relations in this country, or anything else," she says. "But it doesn't change the facts of this case. And it's never going to bring that baby back to life."

ONCE THE JUDGE HAS GIVEN instructions to the jury, they are led from the courtroom. Judge Thunder leaves, too. Howard jumps up. "I've never seen anything like that!"

"Yeah, and you probably never will again," Kennedy mutters.

"I mean, it was like watching Tom Cruise—*You can't handle the truth!* Like . . ."

"Like shooting myself in the foot," Kennedy finished. "On purpose."

I put my hand on her arm. "I know what you said back there cost you," I say.

Kennedy stares at me soberly. "Ruth, it's most likely going to cost *you* more."

She has explained to me that because the murder charge was thrown out before I testified, the jury has only the negligent homicide charge to decide. Although our medical evidence definitely creates reasonable doubt, an outburst of anger is like a poker burned into a juror's mind. Even if they're not deciding on a premeditated murder charge now, they might still feel like I didn't care for that baby as well as I possibly could. And whether that was even possible, under the circumstances, I don't know anymore.

I think about the night I spent in jail. I imagine spinning it out to many nights. Weeks. Months. I think about Liza Lott and how the conversation I have with her now would be very different than the one I had back then. I would start by saying that I'm not naïve anymore. I have been forged in a crucible, like steel. And the miracle about steel is that you can hammer it so thin it's stretched to its limit, but that doesn't mean it will break. "It was still worth hearing," I tell Kennedy.

She smiles a little. "It was worth saying."

Suddenly Odette Lawton is standing in front of us. I panic slightly. Kennedy also said that there was one other alternative the prosecutor might choose—to throw out *all* charges and start over with a grand jury, using my testimony to show malice in the heat of the moment, and with a new charge of second-degree murder.

"I'm getting the case against Edison Jefferson dismissed," Odette says briskly. "I thought you'd want to know."

My jaw drops. Of everything I thought she might say, *that* was not it.

She faces me and for the first time in this trial, meets my gaze. Except for our bathroom run-in, she has not made direct eye contact with me the entire time I was sitting at the defense table, glancing just past me or over my head. Kennedy says that's standard; it's the way prosecutors remind defendants they're not human.

It works.

"I have a fifteen-year-old daughter," Odette says, a fact and an explanation. Then she turns to Kennedy. "Nice closing, Counselor," she says, and she walks away.

"Now what?" I ask.

Kennedy takes a deep breath. "Now," she says, "we wait."

BUT FIRST, WE HAVE THE press to deal with. Howard and Kennedy formulate a plan to get me out of the courthouse with no media contact. "If we aren't able to avoid them completely," she explains, "the correct answer is *no comment*. We are waiting for the jury's decision. Period."

I nod at her.

"I don't think you get it, Ruth. They're going to be out for blood;

they are going to pick at you and goad you into exploding so that they can get it on tape. For the next five minutes, until you leave this building, you are blind, deaf, dumb. You understand?"

"Yes," I tell her.

My heart is a drum as we push through the double doors of the courtroom. Immediately there are flashes of lights, and microphones thrust in my face. Howard runs interference, shoving them away, as Kennedy barrels us through this circus: acrobat reporters, trying to reach over the heads of others to get a statement; clowns doing their act—the Bauers in a heated interview with one conservative news station—and me, trying to navigate my tightrope without falling.

Approaching us from the opposite direction is Wallace Mercy. He and his supporters form a human blockade, elbows locked, which means we will have to engage. Wallace and a woman stand in the middle; as I watch, they step forward to lead the rest. The woman wears a pink wool suit. Her close-cropped hair is dyed a hot red. She stands straight as an arrow, her arm tightly tucked through Wallace's.

I look to Kennedy, a silent question: *What do we do?*

But my question is answered for me. Wallace and the woman do not come toward us. Instead, they veer to the far side of the hallway, where Turk Bauer is still in conversation with a reporter, his wife and his father-in-law standing by his side.

"Brittany," the woman says, her eyes filling with tears. "Oh, Lord. Look at how beautiful you are."

She reaches toward Brittany Bauer as the cameras roll. But we are not in Judge Thunder's court, and she can say or do anything she pleases. So I see the woman's hand coming toward her as if in slow motion, and I know even before it happens that Brittany Bauer will push her away. "Get the hell away from me."

Wallace Mercy steps forward. "I think this is someone you want to meet, Ms. Bauer."

"She doesn't need to, Wallace," the woman murmurs. "We met twenty-six years ago, when I gave birth to her. Brit, honey, you remember me, don't you?"

Brittany Bauer's face blooms with color—shame, or anger, or both.

"*Liar*. You disgusting liar!" She lunges for the older woman, who goes down too easily.

People scramble to pull Brittany away, to lift the woman to safety. I hear shouts: *Help her!* And *Are you getting this on tape?*

Then I hear someone cry, "Stop!" The voice is deep and powerful and commanding, and just like that, Brit falls back.

She turns around, feral, glaring at her father. "You're just going to let that nigger say those things about me? About *us*?"

But her father is no longer looking at his daughter. He is ashen, staring at the woman who now stands with Wallace Mercy's contingent, Wallace's handkerchief pressed to her bleeding lip. "Hello, Adele," he says.

"I did *not* see this coming," I whisper, glancing at Kennedy.

And that's how I realize she *did*.

Turk

THE CAMERAS ARE ROLLING WHEN ALL HELL BREAKS LOOSE. ONE MINUTE, Brit and Francis are standing next to me, listening to me tell some right-wing radio personality that we have only just begun to fight, and then it becomes a literal declaration. A black woman marches up to Brit and touches her arm. Naturally, Brit recoils, and then the woman lobs a blatant lie: that Brittany Bauer, the princess of the White Power Movement, is actually half black.

I look to Francis, the way I have, well, for years. He taught me everything I know about hate; I would go to war beside him; in fact I *have*. I step back, waiting for Francis to let loose with his famous rhetoric, to cut this bitch down to size as an opportunist who wants her fifteen minutes of fame—except he doesn't.

He says the name of Brittany's mother.

I do not know much about Adele, because Brit doesn't, either. Just her name, and the fact that she cheated on Francis with a black dude and he was so furious that he gave her an ultimatum: leave him the baby and disappear from their lives forever, or die in your sleep. Wisely, she chose the former, and that was all Brit needed to know about her.

But I look at Brit's long dark hair.

We see what we're told to see.

She glances up, looking at Francis, too. "Daddy?"

Suddenly I can't breathe. I don't know who my wife is. I don't know who *I* am. For years I would have easily said I'd knife someone black before I'd sit down for coffee with them, and all this time, I've been living with one.

I made a *baby* with one.

Which means my own son, he was part-black, too.

There's a buzzing in my ears that feels like I'm free-falling, dropped from the airplane without a parachute. The ground, it's rushing up at me.

Brittany stands up, turning in a circle, her face pinched so tight it breaks my heart. "Baby," Francis offers, and she makes a low sound, deep in her throat.

"No," she says. "No."

Then she runs.

SHE IS SMALL, AND SHE is fast. Brit can move in and out of shadows, and why shouldn't she be able to? I mean, she learned, like me, from the best.

Francis tries to get the Lonewolf.org members who've been at court in solidarity to help us search for Brit, but there is a wall between us now. Some have already disappeared. I have no doubt that they will discontinue their user accounts, unless Francis can do enough damage control to stop them.

I am not sure that I even care.

I just want to find my wife.

We drive everywhere, looking for her. Our network, invisible but wide, is no longer available. We are alone in this, completely isolated.

Be careful what you wish for, I guess.

As I drive, searching the far corners of this city, I turn and look at Francis. "You feel like telling me the truth?"

"It was a long time ago," he says quietly. "Before I joined the

Movement. I met Adele at a diner. She served me pie. She put her name and phone number on the bill. I called." He shrugs. "Three months later, she was pregnant."

I feel my stomach turn as I think about sleeping with one of them. But then, I had done that, hadn't I?

"God help me, Turk, I loved her. Didn't matter if we were out dancing halfway into the night, or sitting at home watching television—I got to the point where I just didn't feel whole if she wasn't with me. And then we had Brit, and I started to get scared. It felt perfect, you know? And perfect means that something's bound to go wrong."

He rubs his forehead. "She went to church on Sundays, same church she'd gone to as a kid. A black church, with all that singing and hallelujah shit—I couldn't take it. I went fishing instead and told her that was my holy place. But the choir director, he started taking an interest in Adele. Told her she had the voice of an angel. They started spending a lot of time together, practicing all hours of the day or night." He shakes his head. "I don't know, maybe I went a little crazy. I accused her of cheating on me. Maybe she did, maybe she didn't. I messed her up some, which was wrong, I know. But I couldn't help it, she was tearing me apart, and I had to do something with all that hurt. You know what that's like, right?"

I nod.

"She ran to this other guy for comfort, and he took her in. Jesus, Turk, I drove her right to him. Next thing I know she says she's leaving me. I tell her that if she goes, it's empty-handed. I'm not letting her take my daughter away from me. I say that if she tries, it'll be the last thing she ever does." He looks at me, bleak. "I never saw her again."

"And you never told Brit?"

He shakes his head. "What was I going to say? I threatened to kill her mother? No. I started taking Brit to bars, leaving her in her car seat asleep while I went in to get drunk. That's where I met Tom Metzger."

I find it hard to imagine the leader of the White Alliance Army slugging a beer, but stranger things have happened.

"He was with some of his guys. He saw me get into my car, and refused to let me drive home when he saw Brit in the back. He drove us to my place and said I needed to get my act together for my kid. I was sloppy drunk by then; I told him how Adele had left me for a nigger. I guess I never mentioned that she was one too. Anyway, Tom gave me something to read. A pamphlet." Francis purses his lips. "That was the start. It was so much easier to hate them, than to hate myself."

My high beams cut across a train track, a place where Francis's squad used to hold court, back when they were active. "And now," Francis says, "I'm going to lose her too. She knows how to cover her tracks, how to disappear. I *taught* her."

He is riding a ragged edge of pain and shock, and frankly I don't have time for Francis's breakdown. I have more important things to do, like find my wife.

And I have one more idea.

WE HAVE TO BREAK INTO the graveyard; it's after dark now and the gates are locked. I scale the fence and hack at the lock with a sledgehammer from the back of my rig so that Francis can get inside, too. We let our eyes adjust, because we know Brit might run at the glimpse of a flashlight.

At first, I can't see her at all; it's that dark, and she is wearing a navy dress. But then I hear movement as I draw closer to Davis's grave. For a moment, the clouds covering the moon part, and the headstone gleams. There is a glint of metal, too.

"Don't come any closer," Brit says.

I hold up my palms, a white flag. Very slowly, I take another step. She slashes out once. It's a penknife, one she carries in her purse. I remember the day she bought it, at a White Power rally. She had held up various models, brandishing onyx, mother-of-pearl. She'd pressed a bedazzled one against my throat in a mock charge. *Which is more* me? she had teased.

"Hey, baby," I say gently. "It's time to come home."

"I can't. I'm a mess," she mutters.

"That's okay." I crouch down, moving the way I would if I were approaching a wild dog. I reach for her hand, but my palm slips out of hers.

I look down and see mine is bloody.

"Jesus Christ!" I cry, just as Francis shines his iPhone flashlight down on Brit from behind me, and lets out a cry. She is sitting with her back against Davis's grave. Her eyes are wide and wild, glassy. Her left arm has been sliced deeply seven or eight times. "I can't find it," she says. "I keep trying to get it out."

"Get what out, sweetheart?" I say, reaching for the blade again.

But she curls it away from me. "Her blood." As I watch, she picks up the knife and slashes her wrist.

The knife falls out of Brit's hand, and as her eyes roll back in her head, I lift her in my arms and start running to my truck.

IT'S A WHILE BEFORE BRIT is stable again, and that's a generous term. We are at Yale–New Haven, a different hospital than the one where she delivered Davis. Her lacerations have been stitched, her wrist has been wrapped; the blood has been washed from her body. She has been admitted to the psych ward, and I have to say, I'm grateful. I can't unravel the knots in her mind.

I can barely unravel the knots in mine.

I tell Francis to go home, get some rest. Me, I'll stay overnight in the visitors' lounge, just to make sure if Brit wakes up and needs me, she will know someone is here for her. But right now, she is unconscious, knocked out with sedatives.

A hospital after midnight is ghostly. Lights are low, and sounds are eerie—the squeak of a nurse's shoes, the moan of a patient, the beep and exhale of a blood pressure machine. I buy a knit cap from the gift store, one that has been knit for chemo patients, but I don't care. It covers my tattoo and right now I want to blend in.

I sit in the cafeteria, nursing a cup of coffee, and combing through the tangle of my thoughts. There's only so many things you can hate. There are only so many people you can beat up, so many nights you can get drunk, so many times you can blame other people for your own bullshit. It's a drug, and like any drug, it stops working. And then what?

My head actually aches from holding three incompatible truths in it: *1. Black people are inferior. 2. Brit is half black. 3. I love Brit with all my heart.*

Shouldn't numbers one and two make number three impossible? Or is she the exception to the rule? Was Adele one, too?

I think of me and Twinkie dreaming of the food we craved behind bars.

How many exceptions do there have to be before you start to realize that maybe the truths you've been told aren't actually true?

When I finish my coffee, I wander the halls of the hospital. I read a discarded newspaper in the lobby. I watch the flashing ambulance lights through the glass doors of the ER.

I stumble upon the preemie NICU by accident. Believe me, I don't want to be anywhere near a birthing pavilion; those scars are still tender for me, even if this is a different hospital. But I stand at the window beside another man. "She's mine," he says, pointing to a painfully small infant in a pink blanket. "Her name is Cora."

I panic a little; what creep hangs out in front of a nursery if he's not related to one of the babies? So I point to a kid in a blue blanket. There's a bit of a glare through his incubator, but even from here I can see the brown of his skin. "Davis," I lie.

My son was as white as I am, at least on the outside. He did not look like this newborn. But even if he had, now I realize I would have loved him. The truth is, if that baby were Davis, it wouldn't matter that his skin is darker than mine.

It would just matter that he is alive.

I bury my shaking hands in my coat, thinking of Francis, and of Brit. Maybe however much you've loved someone, that's how much you can hate. It's like a pocket turned inside out.

It stands to reason that the opposite should be true, too.

Kennedy

IN THE TIME THAT IT TAKES FOR THE JURY TO RETURN A VERDICT, I SIT through forty more arraignments, thirty-eight of which are black men. Micah performs six surgeries. Violet goes to a birthday party. I read an article on the front page of the paper, about a march at Yale by students of color, who want—among other things—to rechristen a residential college currently named for John C. Calhoun, a U.S. vice president who supported slavery and secession.

For two days, Ruth and I sit at the courthouse, and wait. Edison goes back to school, knuckling down with renewed enthusiasm—it's amazing what a little brush with the law can do for a kid who's flirting with delinquency. Ruth also has—with my blessing, and with me at her side—appeared on Wallace Mercy's television show, via remote camera. He championed her bravery, and handed her a check to cover some of the money she had lost from being out of work for months—donations from people as close as East End and as far as Johannesburg. Afterward, we read notes that were enclosed with some of the contributions:

I THINK ABOUT YOU AND YOUR BOY.

I DON'T HAVE MUCH, BUT I WANT YOU TO
KNOW YOU'RE NOT ALONE.

THANK YOU FOR BEING BRAVE ENOUGH TO
STAND UP, WHEN I DIDN'T.

We've heard about Brittany Bauer, who is suffering from what the prosecution calls stress and Ruth calls just plain crazy. No one has seen hide nor hair of Turk Bauer or Francis Mitchum.

"How did you know?" Ruth had asked me, immediately after the debacle that occurred when Wallace brought Adele Adams to the courthouse to "accidentally" cross paths with Francis and his daughter.

"I had a hunch," I told her. "I was looking through the neonatal screening, and I saw something none of us noticed before, because we were so focused on the MCADD: sickle-cell anemia. I remembered what the neonatologist said, about how that particular disease hits the African American community harder than others. And I also remembered Brit saying during her deposition that she never knew her mother."

"That's quite a long shot," Ruth had said.

"Yeah, that's why I did a little digging. One in twelve African Americans carry the sickle-cell trait. One in ten thousand white people carry it. Suddenly, it looked less like a wild card. So I called Wallace. The rest, that's on him. He found out the name of the mother from Brit's birth certificate, and tracked her down."

Ruth had looked at me. "But it had nothing to do with your case, really."

"Nope," I'd admitted. "That one, it was a gift from me to you. I figured there wasn't anything that could put a finer point on the hypocrisy of it all."

Now, as we come to the close of the second day with no word from the jury, we're all going a little stir-crazy. "What are you doing?" I ask Howard, who has been keeping the vigil with us. He's been typing furiously into his phone. "Hot date?"

"I've been looking up the sentencing difference for possession of crack versus cocaine," he says. "Up until 2010, a person convicted of possession with intent to distribute fifty grams or more of crack got a minimum of ten years in prison. To get the same sentence for cocaine, you had to distribute five *thousand* grams. Even now, the sentencing disparity ratio's eighteen to one."

I shake my head. "Why do you need to know this?"

"I'm thinking about appeal," he says brightly. "That's clearly a precedent for prejudice in sentencing, since eighty-four percent of people convicted for crack offenses are black, and black drug offenders are twenty percent more likely to be imprisoned than white drug offenders."

"Howard," I say, rubbing my temples. "Turn off your damn phone."

"This is bad, right?" Ruth says. She rubs her arms, although the radiator is belching and it's broiling in the room. "If they were going to acquit, it would have been quick, I bet."

"No news is good news," I lie.

AT THE END OF THE day, the judge calls the jury back into the courtroom. "Have you arrived at a verdict?"

The forewoman stands. "No, Your Honor. We're split."

I know the judge is going to give them an Allen charge, a glorified legal pep talk. He turns to the jury, imperial, to imbue them with resolve. "You know, the State has spent a great deal of money to put this trial on, and nobody knows the facts more than you all do. Talk to each other. Allow yourself to hear another's point of view. I encourage you to arrive at a verdict, so that we do not have to go through this all over again."

The jury is dismissed, and I look at Ruth. "You probably have to get back home."

She looks at her watch. "I have a little time," she admits.

So we walk downtown, shoulder to shoulder, huddled against the cold to grab a cup of coffee. We slip out of the biting wind into the buzzy chatter of a local shop. "After I realized I couldn't cut it as a pastry chef I used to dream about opening a coffee place," I muse. "I wanted to call it Grounds for Dismissal."

We are the next to order; I ask Ruth how she takes her coffee. "Black," she says, and suddenly we are both laughing so hard that the barista looks at us as if we are crazy, as if we are speaking a language she can't understand.

Which, I guess, is not all that far from the truth.

THE NEXT MORNING, JUDGE THUNDER summons Odette and me to chambers. "I got a note from the foreman. We have a hung jury. Eleven to one." He shakes his head. "I'm very sorry, ladies."

After he dismisses us, I find Howard pacing outside chambers. "Well?"

"Mistrial. They're deadlocked, eleven to one."

"Who's the holdout?" Howard asks, but it's a rhetorical question; he knows I don't have that information.

Suddenly, though, we both stop walking and face each other. "Juror number twelve," we say simultaneously.

"Ten bucks?" Howard asks.

"You're on," I tell him.

"I knew we should have used a peremptory strike on her."

"You haven't won that bet yet," I point out. But deep down, I imagine he's right. The teacher who couldn't admit to having any implicit racism would have been mightily offended by my closing argument.

Ruth is waiting for me in the conference room. She looks up, hopeful. "They can't reach a verdict," I say.

"So now what?"

"That depends," I explain. "The case can be tried again, later, with a new jury. Or else Odette just gives up and doesn't pursue this any further."

"Do you think she—?"

"I learned a long time ago not to pretend I can think like a prosecutor," I admit. "We're just going to have to see."

In the courtroom, the jury files in, looking exhausted. "Madam Foreman," the judge says. "I understand that the jury has been unable to reach a verdict. Is that correct?"

The foreman stands. "Yes, Your Honor."

"Do you feel that further time would enable you to resolve this case finally between the State and Ms. Jefferson?"

"Unfortunately, Your Honor, some of us just cannot see eye to eye."

"Thank you for your service," Judge Thunder says. "I am dismissing this jury."

The men and women exit. In the gallery, there are hushed whispers, as people try to understand what this means. I try to figure out in my head the odds that Odette will go back to a grand jury for that involuntary manslaughter charge.

"There is still one final thing that needs to be done in this trial," Judge Thunder continues. "I am prepared to rule on the defense's renewed motion for judgment of acquittal."

Howard looks at me over Ruth's head. *What?*

Holy shit. Judge Thunder is going to use the escape hatch I gave him as a matter of routine. I hold my breath.

"I have researched the law, and have reviewed the evidence in this case very carefully. There is no credible proof that the death of this child was causally related to any action or inaction of the defendant's." He faces Ruth. "I am very sorry you had to go through what you did at your workplace, ma'am." He smacks his gavel. "I grant the defense's motion."

In this humbling moment I learn that not only can I not think like a prosecutor, I am woefully off-base about the mental machinations of a judge. I turn, a dazed laugh bubbling up inside me. Ruth's brow is furrowed. "I don't understand."

He hasn't declared a mistrial. He's granted a bona fide acquittal.

"Ruth," I say, grinning. "You are free to go."

Ruth

FREEDOM IS THE FRAGILE NECK OF A DAFFODIL, AFTER THE LONGEST OF winters. It's the sound of your voice, without anyone drowning you out. It's having the grace to say yes, and more important, the right to say no. At the heart of freedom, hope beats: a pulse of possibility.

I am the same woman I was five minutes ago. I'm rooted to the same chair. My hands are flattened on the same scarred table. My lawyers are both still flanking me. That fluorescent light overhead is still spitting like a cockroach. Nothing has changed, and everything is different.

In a daze, I walk out of the courtroom. A bumper crop of microphones blooms in front of me. Kennedy instructs everyone that although her client is obviously delighted with the verdict, we will not be making any statements until we give an official press conference tomorrow.

That right now, her client has to get home to her son.

There are a few stragglers, hoping for a sound bite, but eventually they drift away. There is a professor being arraigned down the hall for possession of child pornography.

The world turns, and there's another victim, another bully. It's the arc of someone else's story now.

I text Edison, who calls me even though he has to leave class to do it, and I listen to the relief braided through his words. I call Adisa at work, and have to hold the phone away from my ear as she screams with joy. I'm interrupted by a text from Christina: a full row of smiling emojis, and then a hamburger and a glass of wine and a question mark.

Rain check? I type back.

"Ruth," Kennedy says, when she finds me standing with my phone in my hand, staring into space. "You all right?"

"I don't know," I reply, completely honest. "It's really over?"

Howard smiles. "It is really, truly, unequivocally over."

"Thank you," I say. I embrace him, and then I face Kennedy. "And you . . ." I shake my head. "I don't even know what to say."

"Think on it," Kennedy says, hugging me. "You can tell me next week when we have lunch."

I pull back, meeting her eyes. "I'd like that," I say, and something shifts between us. It's power, I realize, and we are dead even.

Suddenly I realize that in my astonishment at the verdict, I left my mother's lucky scarf in the courtroom. "I forgot something. I'll meet you downstairs."

When I reach the double doors, there's a bailiff stationed outside. "Ma'am?"

"I'm sorry—there was a scarf . . . ? Can I . . ."

"Sure." He waves me inside.

I'm alone in the courtroom. I walk down the aisle of the gallery, past the bar, to the spot where I was sitting. My mother's scarf is curled underneath the desk. I pick it up, feed it like a seam through my hands.

I look around the empty chamber. One day, Edison might be arguing a case here, instead of sitting next to a lawyer like I have been. One day he might even be on the judge's bench.

I close my eyes, so that I can keep this minute with me. I listen to the silence.

It feels like light-years since I was brought into another courtroom down the hall for my arraignment, wearing shackles and a nightgown and not allowed to speak for myself. It feels like forever since I was told what I could not do.

"Yes," I say softly, because it is the opposite of restraint. Because it breaks chains. Because I *can*.

I ball my hands into fists and tilt back my head and let the word rip from my throat. *Yes.*

Yes.

Yes.

stage three

Afterbirth

SIX YEARS LATER

People must learn to hate, and if they can learn to hate,
they can be taught to love.

—NELSON MANDELA, *Long Walk to Freedom*

Turk

IN THE EXAMINATION ROOM AT THE CLINIC, I TAKE A RUBBER GLOVE OUT
of the dispenser and blow it up, tying off the bottom. I take a pen and
draw eyes, a beak. "Daddy," my daughter says. "You made me a
chicken."

"Chicken?" I say. "I can't believe you think that's a chicken. That is
clearly a rooster."

She frowns. "What's the difference?"

Well, I walked right into that one, didn't I? But there's no way I'm
going to describe the birds and the bees to my three-year-old while
we're sitting waiting for her to get tested for strep. I'll let Deborah do
that when she gets home from work.

Deborah, my wife, is a stockbroker. I took her last name when we
got married, hoping to start over as someone new, someone better. She
is the one with the nine-to-five, while I stay at home with Carys, and
fit my speaking gigs around her playdates and her nursery school. I
work with the local chapter of the Anti-Defamation League. I go to
high schools and prisons and temples and churches, talking about hate.

I tell these groups about how I used to beat people up because I was hurting so bad, and either I was going to hurt them, or I was going to hurt myself. I explain that made me feel like I had a purpose. I tell them about the festivals I went to, where musicians sang about white supremacy and children played with racist games and toys. I describe my time in prison, and my work as a webmaster for a hate site. I talk about my first wife. I say that hate ate her from the inside out, but what really happened was more mundane: a bottle of pills, swallowed with a bottle of vodka. She could never handle seeing the world as it really is, and so finally, she found a way to keep her eyes closed forever.

I tell them that there is nothing more selfish than trying to change someone's mind because they don't think like you. Just because something is different does not mean it should not be respected.

I tell them this: the part of the brain, physiologically, that allows us to blame everything on people we do not really know is the same part of the brain that allows us to have compassion for strangers. Yes, the Nazis made Jews the scapegoats, to the point of near extinction. But that same bit of tissue in the mind is what led others to send money and supplies and relief, even when they were half a world away.

In my talk, I describe the long road to leaving. It started with a visit in the middle of the night—hooded, faceless individuals sent from others in power who broke down our door and beat us. Francis was thrown down a flight of stairs: me, I had three broken ribs. It was our bon voyage party, I suppose. I shut down Lonewolf.org the next day. Then there were the divorce papers I was having drawn up when Brit killed herself.

Even now, I make mistakes. I still feel the need to slam into something or someone from time to time, but now I do it on the rink in an ice hockey league. I'm probably more cautious than I should be around black dudes. But I'm even more cautious with the white ones in the pickup trucks with Confederate flags hanging in the back windows. Because I used to be who they are, and I know what they are capable of.

Many of the groups I meet with do not believe that I could possibly have changed so dramatically. That's when I tell them about my wife. Deborah knows everything about me, my past. She has managed to forgive me. And if she can forgive me, how could I not try to forgive myself?

I do penance. Three to four times a week, I relive my mistakes in front of an audience. I feel them hate me. I think I deserve it.

"Daddy," Carys says, "my throat hurts."

"I know, baby," I tell her. I pull her onto my lap just as the door opens.

The nurse comes in scanning Carys's intake form at this walk-in clinic. "Hello," she says. "My name is Ruth Walker."

She looks up, a smile on her face.

"Walker," I repeat, as she shakes my hand.

"Yes, as in the Walker Clinic. I own the place . . . but I also work here." She grins. "Don't worry. I'm a much better nurse-practitioner than I am a bookkeeper."

She doesn't recognize me. At least I don't *think* she does.

To be fair, it's Deborah's last name on the form on the clipboard. Plus, I look very different now. I've had all but one of my tattoos removed. My hair has grown out and is conservatively trimmed. I've lost about thirty pounds of muscle and brawn, ever since I've taken up running. And maybe whatever's inside me now is casting a different reflection, too, on the outside.

She turns to Carys. "So something doesn't feel good, huh? Can I take a look?"

She lets Carys sit on my lap as she runs gentle hands over my daughter's swollen glands and takes her temperature and teases her into opening her mouth by staging a singing contest that Carys, of course, wins. I let my gaze wander around the room, noticing things I hadn't seen before—the diploma on the wall with the name Ruth Jefferson written in calligraphy. The framed photo of a handsome black guy wearing a graduation cap and gown on the Yale campus.

She snaps off her gloves, drawing my attention. I notice that she is wearing a small diamond ring and wedding band on her left hand.

"I'm ninety-nine percent sure it's strep," she tells me. "Is Carys allergic to any medications?"

I shake my head. I can't find my voice.

"I can take a swab of her throat, do a rapid strep culture, and based on those results, start a course of antibiotics," she says. She tugs on Carys's braid. "You," she promises, "are going to feel *excellent* in no time at all."

Excusing herself, she walks toward the door to get whatever she needs to do the test. "Ruth," I call out, just as she puts her hand on the knob.

She turns. For a moment, her eyes narrow the tiniest bit, and I wonder. I wonder. But she doesn't ask if we have met before; she doesn't acknowledge our history. She just waits for me to say whatever it is I feel the need to say.

"Thank you," I tell her.

She nods, and slips out of the room. Carys twists on my lap. "It still hurts, Daddy."

"The nurse is going to make it better."

Satisfied with this, Carys points to the knuckles of my left hand, the only tattoo that remains on my body. "That's my name?" she asks.

"Kind of," I answer. "Your name means the same thing, in a language called Welsh."

She is just starting to learn her letters. So she points to each knuckle in turn: "L," she reads. "O. V. E."

"That's right," I say proudly. We wait for Ruth to come back to us. I hold my daughter's hand, or maybe she holds mine, like we are at an intersection, and it's my job to take her safely to the other side.

Author's Note

About four years into my writing career, I wanted to write a book about racism in the United States. I was drawn by a real-life event in New York City, when a Black undercover police officer was shot in the back, multiple times, by white colleagues—in spite of the fact that the undercover cop had been wearing what was called "the color of the day"—a wristband meant to allow officers to identify those who were in hiding. I started the novel, foundered, and quit. I couldn't do justice to the topic, somehow. I didn't know what it was like to grow up Black in this country, and I was having trouble creating a fictional character that rang true.

Flash forward twenty years. Once again, I desperately wanted to write about racism. I was uncomfortably aware that when white authors talked about racism in fiction, it was usually historical. And again, what right did I have to write about an experience I had not lived? However, if I'd written only what I knew, my career would have been short and boring. I grew up white and class-privileged. For years I had done my homework and my research, using extensive personal interviews to channel the voices of people I was not: men, teenagers, suicidal people, abused wives, rape victims. What led me to write those stories was my outrage and my desire to give those narratives airtime, so that those who hadn't experienced them became more aware. Why was writing about a person of color any different?

Because race is different. Racism is different. It's fraught, and it's hard to discuss, and so as a result we often don't.

Then I read a news story about an African American nurse in Flint, Michigan. She had worked in labor and delivery for over twenty years, and then one day a baby's dad asked to see her supervisor. He requested that this nurse, and those who looked like her, not touch his infant. He turned out to be a white supremacist. The supervisor put the patient request in the file, and a bunch of African American personnel sued for discrimination and won. But it got me thinking, and I began to weave a story.

I knew that I wanted to write from the point of view of a Black nurse, a skinhead father, and a public defender—a woman who, like me, and like many of my readers, was a well-intentioned white lady who would never consider herself to be a racist. Suddenly I knew that I could, and would, finish this novel. Unlike my first, aborted foray, I wasn't writing it to tell people of color what their own lives were like. I was writing to my own community—white people—who can very easily point to a neo-Nazi skinhead and say he's a racist . . . but who can't recognize racism in themselves.

Truth be told, I might as well have been describing myself not so long ago. I am often told by readers how much they've learned from my books—but when I write a novel, I learn a lot as well. This time, though, I was learning about myself. I was exploring my past, my upbringing, my biases, and I was discovering that I was not as blameless and progressive as I had imagined.

Most of us think the word *racism* is synonymous with the word *prejudice*. But racism is more than just discrimination based on skin color. It's also about who has institutional power. Just as racism creates disadvantages for people of color that make success harder to achieve, it also gives advantages to white people that make success easier to achieve. It's hard to see those advantages, much less own up to them.

And that, I realized, was why I *had* to write this book. When it comes to social justice, the role of the white ally is not to be a savior or a fixer. Instead, the role of the ally is to find other white people and talk to make them see that many of the benefits they've enjoyed in life are direct results of the fact that someone else did *not* have the same benefits.

I began my research by sitting down with women of color. Although I knew that peppering people of color with questions is not the best way to educate oneself, I hoped to invite these women into a process, and in return they gave me a gift: they shared their experiences of what it really feels like to be Black. I remain so grateful to these women—not just for tolerating my ignorance but for being willing to teach me. Then I had the pleasure of talking to Beverly Daniel Tatum, former president of Spelman College and a renowned racial educator. I read books by Dr. Tatum, Debby Irving, Michelle Alexander, and David Shipler. I enrolled in a social justice workshop called Undoing Racism, and left in tears every night, as I began to peel back the veneer of who I thought I was from who I truly am.

Then I met with two former skinheads, to develop a vocabulary of hate for my white supremacist character. My daughter, Sammy, was the one who found Tim Zaal—a former skinhead who had Skyped with her class in high school. Years ago, Tim beat up and left a gay man for dead. After getting out of the movement, he started to work at the Simon Wiesenthal Center talking about hate crimes and realized one day that the man he had nearly killed worked there, too. There were apologies and forgiveness, and now they are friends who talk about their unique experience to groups every week. He also is happily married now, to a Jewish woman. Frankie Meeink, another former skinhead, works with the Anti-Defamation League. Although he once recruited for hate crews in Philly, he now runs Harmony Through Hockey—a program to promote racial diversity among kids.

These men taught me that white power groups believe in the separation of the races and think they are soldiers in a racial holy war. They explained how recruiters for hate groups would target kids who were bullied, marginalized, or who came from abusive homes. They'd dis-

tribute antiwhite flyers in a white neighborhood and see who responded by saying that the whites were under attack. Then they'd
approach those folks and say, *You're not alone.* The point was to redirect
the recruit's rage into racism. Violence became a release, a mandate.
They also taught me that now, most skinhead groups are not crews
seeking out violence but rather individuals who are networking underground. Nowadays, white supremacists dress like ordinary folks. They
blend in, which is a whole different kind of terror.

When it came time to title this book, I found myself struggling
again. Many of you who are longtime fans of mine know this was not
the original name of the novel. *Small Great Things* is a reference to a
quote often attributed to Reverend Dr. Martin Luther King, Jr.: "If I
cannot do great things, I can do small things in a great way." But as a
white woman, did I have the right to paraphrase these sentiments?
Many in the African American community are sensitive to white people using Martin Luther King, Jr.'s words to reflect their own experience, and with good reason. However, I also knew that both Ruth and
Kennedy have moments in this novel where they do a small thing that
has great and lasting repercussions for others. Plus, for many whites
who are just beginning to travel the path of racial self-awareness, Dr.
King's words are often the first step of the journey. His eloquence
about a subject most of us feel inadequate putting into words is inspiring and humbling. Moreover, although individual changes cannot
completely eradicate racism—there are systems and institutions that
need to be overhauled as well—it is through small acts that racism is
both perpetuated *and* partially dismantled. For all of these reasons—
and because I hope it will encourage people to learn more about Dr.
King—I chose this title.

Of all my novels, this book will stand out for me because of the sea
change it inspired in the way I think about myself, and because it made
me aware of the distance I have yet to go when it comes to racial awareness. In America, we like to think that the reason we have had success
is that we worked hard or we were smart. Admitting that racism has
played a part in our success means admitting that the American dream
isn't quite so accessible to all. A social justice educator named Peggy

McIntosh has pointed out some of these advantages: having access to jobs and housing, for example. Walking into a random hair salon and finding someone who can cut your hair. Buying dolls, toys, and children's books that feature people of your race. Getting a promotion without someone suspecting that it was due to your skin color. Asking to speak to someone in charge, and being directed to someone of your race.

When I was researching this book, I asked white mothers how often they talked about racism with their children. Some said occasionally; some admitted they never discussed it. When I asked the same question of Black mothers, they all said, *Every day.*

I've come to see that ignorance is a privilege, too.

So what have I learned that is helpful? Well, if you are white, like I am, you can't get rid of the privilege you have, but you can use it for good. Don't say *I don't even notice race!* like it's a positive thing. Instead, recognize that differences between people make it harder for some to cross a finish line, and create fair paths to success for everyone that accommodate those differences. Educate yourself. If you think someone's voice is being ignored, tell others to listen. If your friend makes a racist joke, call him out on it, instead of just going along with it. If the two former skinheads I met can have such a complete change of heart, I feel confident that ordinary people can, too.

I expect pushback from this book. I will have people of color challenging me for choosing a topic that doesn't belong to me. I will have white people challenging me for calling them out on their racism. Believe me, I didn't write this novel because I thought it would be fun or easy. I wrote it because I believed it was the right thing to do, and because the things that make us most uncomfortable are the things that teach us what we all need to know. As Roxana Robinson said, "A writer is like a tuning fork: we respond when we're struck by something. . . . If we're lucky we'll transmit a strong pure note, one that isn't ours, but which passes through us." To the Black people reading *Small Great Things*—I hope I listened well enough to those in your community who opened their hearts to me to be able to represent your experiences with accuracy. And to the white people reading *Small Great Things*—we are all works in progress. Personally, I don't have the answers and I am still evolving daily.

There is a fire raging, and we have two choices: we can turn our backs, or we can try to fight it. Yes, talking about racism is hard to do, and yes, we stumble over the words—but we who are white need to have this discussion among ourselves. Because then, even more of us will overhear, and—I hope—the conversation will spread.

—JODI PICOULT
March 2016

Acknowledgments

If not for a host of people and resources, this book would never have been written.

Thanks to Peggy McIntosh for the concept of the invisible knapsack. Dr. Beverly Daniel Tatum literally braved the ice storm in Atlanta to meet with me, and is one of my heroes—I hope she doesn't mind that I borrowed the explanation she gave her own son about the color of his skin being something *more*, rather than something *less*. I also must thank Debby Irving for her expertise as a social justice educator, for being available all hours of the day and night to vet my words, and for so graciously letting me steal her metaphors and best lines, including the concepts of headwinds and tailwinds of privilege (as brilliantly described by Verna Myers) and *ignorance* having the word *ignore* in it. Thanks, too, to Malcolm Gladwell, who on *Q&A* on C-SPAN on December 8, 2009, used an example from his book *Outliers* examining birth-date cutoffs for young Canadian hockey players and how that translates into NHL success—the premise of which I used for Kennedy's closing argument. Thanks to the People's Institute for Survival and Beyond, which ran the Undoing Racism workshop sponsored by the Haymarket People's Fund in Boston, which encouraged me to notice my own privilege—they get full credit for Kennedy's metaphor about throwing away the babies.

I am grateful to Professor Abigail Baird, for the research on bias she provided (as well as the introduction to the remarkable Sienna Brown). To Betty Martin, the woman I'd always call first if I wanted to kill a fictional newborn. To Jennifer Twitchell of the ADL, Sindy Ravell, Hope Morris, Rebecca Thompson, Karen Bradley, and Ruth Goshen. Thanks to Bill Binnie, for his name and his donation to Families in Transition, which provides safe, affordable housing and comprehensive social services to individuals who are homeless or at risk of becoming homeless in southern New Hampshire. For McDonald's advice: Natalie Hall, Rachel Daling, Rachel Patrick, Autumn Cooper, Kayla Ayling, Billie Short, Jessica Hollis, M.M., Naomi Dawson, Joy Klink, Kimberly Wright, Emily Bradt, Sukana Al-Hassani.

Thanks to the many doctors and nurses who shared their experience, their lingo, and their best stories with me: Maureen Littlefield, Shauna Pearse, Elizabeth Joseph, Mindy Dube, Cecelia Brelsford, Meaghan Smith, Dr. Joan Barthold, Irit Librot, Dr. Dan Kelly.

To my crackerjack legal team, who swore that race is never brought into a courtroom—I hope I've changed your mind. Lise Iwon, Lise Gescheidt, Maureen McBrien-Benjamin, and Janet Gilligan—you are all way too fun to simply be considered work colleagues. Jennifer Sargent, many thanks for coming in at the eleventh hour and vetting the court scenes for accuracy's sake.

Thank you to Jane Picoult and Laura Gross, for being outraged and moved and humbled at all the right places when you read early drafts. Auriol Bishop gets credit for finding the title. And thanks to the best publishing team on the planet: Gina Centrello, Kara Welsh, Kim Hovey, Debbie Aroff, Sanyu Dillon, Rachel Kind, Denise Cronin, Scott Shannon, Matthew Schwartz, Anne Speyer, Porscha Burke, Theresa Zoro, Paolo Pepe, Catherine (I-secretly-run-Jodi's-life) Mikula, Christine Mykityshyn, Kaley Baron. Special thanks to the incomparable editor Jennifer Hershey, who challenged me so that every word on these pages is earned, and right. I'm also indebted to head cheerleader–

road warrior–de facto non-*Scandal*ous Chief of Staff Susan Corcoran, who has become so indispensable I truly don't know how I've survived this long without her.

To Frank Meeink and Tim Zaal—your courage and your compassion are all the more inspiring because of how far you've come. Thank you for walking me into the world of hate, and for showing so many others how to leave it.

To Evelyn Carrington, my Sister Friend, and Shaina—and to Sienna Brown—one of the great joys of writing this book has been getting to know you. Thank you for your honesty, your bravery, and your open hearts. To Nic Stone—who knew when I was trapped in Atlanta that I would be making a friend for life? I could not have written this book without you holding my hand and telling me not to second-guess myself. All those frantic late-night texts have led to this version. Thanks for giving me confidence, for fixing my white girl mistakes, and for believing that I could and should write this. I can't wait for *your* novel to hit the shelves.

To Kyle and Kevin Ferreira van Leer—you two are what I want to grow up and be: models for social justice. Thank you for being the ones to open my eyes to those tailwinds. To Sammy: thanks for coming home from school and saying, "You know, I think I have someone you should talk to about your book." To Jake: thank you for knowing what parking lot is behind the New Haven County Courthouse and for explaining Supreme Court decisions to me; I know you will one day be the kind of lawyer who changes the world. And to Tim, thanks for serving me my coffee in the Harvard "white privilege" mug. I love you for that, and for everything else.

Bibliography

The following books and articles were used as research and/or inspiration.

Alexander, Michelle. *The New Jim Crow: Mass Incarceration in the Age of Colorblindness*. New Press, 2010.

Coates, Ta-Nehesi. *Between the World and Me*. Spiegel & Grau, 2015.

Colby, Tanner. *Some of My Best Friends Are Black: The Strange Story of Integration in America*. Viking, 2012.

Harris-Perry, Melissa V. *Sister Citizen: Shame, Stereotypes, and Black Women in America*. Yale University Press, 2011.

Hurwin, Davida Wills. *Freaks and Revelations*. Little, Brown, 2009.

Irving, Debby. *Waking Up White: And Finding Myself in the Story of Race*. Elephant Room Press, 2014.

McIntosh, Peggy. "White Privilege: Unpacking the Invisible Knapsack," *Independent School* 49, no. 2 (winter 1990): 31. Excerpted from "White Privilege and Male Privilege: A Personal Account of Coming to See Correspondences Through Work in Women's Studies" (Working Paper 189, Wellesley Center for the Study of Women, 1988).

Meeink, Frank, and Jody M. Roy. *Autobiography of a Recovering Skinhead*. Hawthorne Books, 2009.

Phillips, Tom. "Forty-two Incredibly Weird Facts You'll Want to Tell All Your Friends," http://www.buzzfeed.com/tomphillips/42-incredibly-weird -facts-youll-want-to-tell-people-down-the#.kuYgj5yGd.

Shipler, David K. *A Country of Strangers: Blacks and Whites in America*. Vintage Books, 1998.

Tatum, Beverly Daniel. *Assimilation Blues: Black Families in White Communities: Who Succeeds and Why?* Basic Books, 2000.

———. *Can We Talk About Race? And Other Conversations in an Era of School Resegregation*. Beacon Press, 2008.

———. *"Why Are All the Black Kids Sitting Together in the Cafeteria?" And Other Conversations About Race*. Basic Books, 1997.

Tochluk, Shelly. *Witnessing Whiteness: The Need to Talk About Race and How to Do It*. Rowman & Littlefield Education, 2010.

What follows is a short story featuring characters from the novel you've just read, *Small Great Things*. Chronologically, it takes place before the action of *Small Great Things* begins.

Shine

ON THE MORNING OF RUTH BROOKS'S FIRST DAY OF CLASS AT THE PRES-
tigious Dalton School, she sat in the kitchen of another family's house,
waiting for her mama to finish packing her lunch. "You act like a guest,"
her mama instructed, spreading the same peanut butter on the same
kind of bread that would be tucked into Christina's lunch, too. "You
don't give them any reason to not invite you back."

In the past, Ruth had come only occasionally to the Hallowells'
home, but all that was going to change. Now, every morning, Sam
Hallowell's chauffeur would take her and Christina in a shiny black car
through Central Park to the Upper East Side—Ninety-first Street—
where she would be enrolled in third grade. At the end of the school
day, she would return and play with Christina in her room or do homework in the kitchen until her mama finished working. Then they'd
take the bus to Harlem, back to their own place, where Granny and
Rachel would be waiting.

Ruth knew that it was a blessing to go to this fancy school. In first grade, she and her sister, Rachel, had both gone to a school that was mostly Orthodox Jewish kids. Ruth had loved it—everything from the snap-together cubes for counting to the felt board with a floppy sun, a listless cloud, a thunderbolt, a snowflake. But it was a two-hour commute each way on the bus. In second grade, Ruth had gone to public school in Harlem. It was as different from her first school as possible. There were no books in the school library that didn't have most of their pages ripped out. The teachers spent more time yelling than teaching. Rachel had never been an engaged student, but Ruth was having the life sucked out of her. She didn't know what conversation between Ms. Mina and Mama had led to this full scholarship, but she had taken a test and done well, and that was that—she was in. And she was grateful.

At least, she was supposed to be.

She swung her feet on the kitchen stool, thinking of Rachel, who didn't have to get up at 5:30 A.M. to go to school. Rachel was in fifth grade this year, and thought she knew everything. Like last night, she told Ruth that she would probably be the only Black girl in the whole school and nobody would talk to her. Ruth had asked her mama on the bus ride in whether that was true. "Ms. Christina will talk to you," her mama had said. "You two have known each other forever."

But there was a difference between visiting the brownstone on a random Saturday and playing with Barbies, and actually attending the same school as Christina. Plus, Christina had gone to this school since kindergarten and already had friends. Just thinking about it made Ruth's throat feel too tight.

Christina bounced into the kitchen. Her hair was caught back in her favorite barrette, the one with silk roses glued to it. She carried a spotless pink backpack.

"It's time to go," she said, her voice a musical scale. "You ready, Ruth?"

Ruth hopped off the chair. Her mama straightened her cardigan and handed her one of the bag lunches. "Baby girl," Mama said to Christina, "don't you forget this."

Christina took the matching lunch. As Ruth followed her into the parlor, Ms. Mina was waiting with little Louis in her arms. He was only three, not even in preschool yet, and he was not having a lot of success at potty training. "Are you excited, Ruth?" Ms. Mina asked. "First day!"

"Yes, ma'am," Ruth said. *Excited* and *terrified* felt as if they might be one and the same.

The sedan was already in front of the brownstone. The minute they walked outside, a man burst out of the car like a kernel of popcorn exploding. He opened the back door and gave a little bow. "Ms. Christina," he said. "Ms. Ruth."

If Rachel could see this, she'd bust up. *Can't they open their own car doors?*

Ruth just said thank you and buckled herself in. She and Christina waved to their mothers on the stoop until they couldn't see them anymore. "Wait till you meet Lola," Christina said. "Lola has a pet monkey. I swear. It's part of her dad's work or something." She leaned toward Ruth. "It wears a *diaper*."

Ruth imagined going to a new friend's house and meeting this monkey in a diaper. She pictured teaching it a trick, like how to clap or something, and her new friend telling everyone else what Ruth had done.

And suddenly, they were there. The driver opened the door and Christina bolted from the car, shrieking and throwing her arms around a girl who had silvery blond hair. Lola, maybe? She didn't look back. They were talking so fast that it sounded like a different language.

The driver handed Ruth her backpack, which had been Rachel's last year. "You have a nice day, Ms. Ruth," he said gently.

It was at that moment that Ruth realized her mother had never answered her *other* question on the bus: would there be anyone else at Dalton who looked like her?

Ruth stepped onto the curb. Then she took a deep breath and dove into a wave of white.

AT DALTON YOU DIDN'T GET assigned to a teacher's classroom, you got assigned to a house—which, Ruth figured out quickly, was just a fancy word for a bunch of kids who were all the same age.

Christina was in her house, and so was the girl with the silvery hair—Lola. Ruth trailed them inside to Ms. Thomas's room, waiting for a break in the conversation so that she could introduce herself, like Mama told her to do. She waited for Christina to come to her rescue, to say, *This is Ruth*. But instead Christina ducked into the room and ran to the neat row of cubbies. "Lola," she called. "We're next to each other!"

Last year, Ruth had not had a cubby. She put her lunch neatly in the bottom and hung her jacket up on a hook. When she turned around, there was a pretty redheaded lady crouched down, holding out her hand. "I'm Ms. Thomas," she said. "I'm the house adviser." Ruth guessed that was the Dalton word for *teacher*. "What's your name?"

"Ruth," she said.

"Well, Ruth, we are so glad to have you with us this year."

Ruth nodded. But she wondered who else Ms. Thomas was speaking for; who was the *we* in that equation.

They played a game where everyone clapped a rhythm that went with their name, and everyone else in the class had to mimic it. Ruth tapped her right knee, left knee, then waved her hands like she was singing hallelujah at church. *Ruth*, everyone said, and they did the same motion she had done. It made her think of her granny's story about going to the French part of Canada once, and how she had to do charades just to ask where the toilet was.

Ms. Thomas wore a double strand of pearls that had a glittery spider clasp in the back, and Ruth counted the number of times that the spider slipped down her neck and Ms. Thomas had to tug it back into place. Ms. Thomas showed everyone a picture of herself in a white princess dress, with a handsome man beside her in a tuxedo. It looked like snow was falling on them, but it was rice. She told everyone that her husband's name was David and then she showed another picture, this one of a very small dog called Caesar. "That's my family," she said. "Now I want you to draw me a picture of yours!"

Ruth was placed at a table with a boy named Marcus (clap up high, clap down low) and a girl named Maia (tiny claps all around her face, like the petals of a sunflower). Ruth had seen Marcus pick his nose during the circle time, and between that and the fact that he was a boy, she had very little interest in him. Maia, though, was the only other student in the house who was new to Dalton. She had moved from Dallas. She had red hair like a molten river that was held back by a rhinestone headband. She had an accent, and when she spoke, her voice was full of music.

At each seat was the kind of thick vanilla drawing paper Ruth remembered from her year at the Jewish school. A confetti of crayons splashed the center of every table. "We have to share," Maia announced. She took the crayons and rolled a few toward each of them, divvying up the colors.

Christina was all the way across the room. Ruth wondered what she was drawing to illustrate her family, whether Mama would be part of it. After all, Mama spent more hours taking care of Christina than her own mother did; it was her job. And Ms. Mina was always calling Mama *family*. But could Mama be on Christina's drawing *and* Ruth's? Didn't Ruth get first dibs?

Or what if Christina left Mama out of her drawing? Did that suggest family meant different things to different people?

Honestly, Ruth couldn't figure out what would make her more upset: seeing Christina's finished drawing with Mama in it, or not.

"You get these," Maia announced, pushing a bunch of crayons toward Marcus and another group toward Ruth.

"No way," he said. "I need flesh color." He grabbed the peach crayon that was in front of Maia.

Ruth looked at the crayons in front of her. She picked up the dark blue, because Maia had saved the black for herself. She made the outline of Mama, and then drew in Rachel and herself and Granny. Then she picked up the brown crayon.

Marcus was coloring in his family with the peach crayon. Maia was making a big deal of having to wait for it.

Ruth colored her mother's face. She forgot to leave white for the eyes, and couldn't go backward, which left Mama looking angry. So she was more careful as she drew her own face. She touched the brown crayon gently to the page, shading so faintly she could barely see the pigment.

RECESS HAPPENED ON THE ROOF of the school building, an artificial garden in the middle of the city. Maia had drawn the girls in the house to her like filings to a magnet. She told them that in Texas she had lived on a ranch and ridden horses every day, something New York City girls did only during summer camp and something Ruth had never done. Horses frightened her. She didn't like the yellow of their huge teeth.

She took a deep breath and sat down just behind Christina, as if she were about to start a second concentric circle, even if she was the only member. Christina glanced over her shoulder and then scooted to the right, creating a few inches of space that couldn't fit Ruth's leg, much less her whole body. Maia was designing some sort of game: "And this is the castle, and the boys over there are the trolls that can't ever touch you, and if you cross the line by the bench you're out of the whole kingdom, and—"

Ruth wedged her feet into the spot Christina had created and scooted as far forward as she could. "Can I play too?"

Maia stared at her and scrunched her nose. "But we're playing *Princess*," she said. "You can't be a princess. You don't have the right hair."

Instinctively, Ruth touched her hair. It curved in a bob to just above her chin. Lola touched it. "I like your hair," she said. "It's pretty."

"My granny used the hot comb," Ruth said, and all six girls in the circle looked at her blankly.

Ruth puffed up a little, excited to know something they didn't. "Yeah," she continued. "You heat it up on the stove, and while it's getting ready Granny puts green Super Gro grease on my hair, and then when the comb's really hot, she runs it through to get it all straight."

Lola stared at Ruth. "And it just stays like that?"

"Yeah. Till she washes it again in a couple of weeks."

Maia's eyes widened. "You don't wash your hair every day?" she said. "Do you even *shower*?"

The others girls laughed. Ruth couldn't see Christina's face, couldn't hear whether she was laughing, too. She felt tears cutting the tunnel of her throat, and stood up fast, her fists at her sides. "I don't want to play your game," Ruth said, and she looked down at Christina. "You want to go over there and play something else?"

Christina hesitated. She looked up at Ruth, but her eyes weren't full of *I'm sorry*. They were angry, as if she blamed Ruth for making her the rope in this tug-of-war. Christina ducked her head without answering.

Ruth ran to the far corner of the rooftop garden. She lay down on the ground, staring up at the clouds so that it was easy to think that they weren't even in the city anymore, if you blocked out the sound of the car horns from below. She blinked fast, and kept her eyes extra wide, and all the other tricks she knew to keep from crying.

She could hear Maia assigning character names. Princess Marigold. Princess Daffodil. Princess Ivy.

Ms. Thomas walked toward Ruth and sat down beside her, following Ruth's gaze up to the sky. "You know," she said, as if they had been in the middle of a conversation, "there are stars there right now. You can't see them, because they're obscured by the sun. But the minute the sun goes away, wow—they're as bright as jewels."

Ruth didn't know why Ms. Thomas was telling her this. She didn't know why Ms. Thomas had come over here in the first place. She just wanted to go home. She wanted to be in Harlem in school with Rachel. Except she didn't really want to be there, either. So where did that leave her?

"Can I tell you a secret?" Ms. Thomas whispered. "We're going to study stars this year. But I'm trusting you not to tell anyone else, all right? It's going to be a surprise."

Ruth sat up, hugging her knees to her chest.

"Deal?"

"Yes, ma'am," Ruth said.

Ms. Thomas put her arm around Ruth's shoulders and squeezed. "Would you be the leader for me today, when we line up to go downstairs?"

Ruth nodded.

Ms. Thomas stood up and clapped. "Okay, boys and girls! Line up behind Ruth!"

Ruth stood at the door that led into the building and down the stairs. She thought about the secret Ms. Thomas had told her. She liked holding on to it. Sometimes at Ms. Mina's she took a hard candy from the bowl in the foyer and kept it in her pocket and didn't eat it, because she liked to stick her hand inside hours or even days later and know she had a surprise nobody else had.

"Everyone line up behind Ruth," Ms. Thomas repeated, and Ruth stood a little taller.

On the bus that night, headed back home, Mama wanted to know everything: What were the names of the friends she made? What did she learn in school? What was her teacher like?

Ruth told her about the clapping game and Marcus picking his nose and how she got to be the recess leader.

"And what about the other girls?" Mama asked.

"There's Maia," Ruth replied. "She's from Texas and she used to ride horses every day. We played Princess during recess."

Mama smiled so wide Ruth could see the pink of her gums. "Isn't that fine," she said.

It was the first time, Ruth realized, that she had ever lied to her mama.

But then, was it so bad to lie if you told someone what you knew they needed to hear?

The amount of freedom at Ruth's new school was staggering. As long as you weren't making trouble, you could just get up and go to the bathroom, without raising your hand first. There were breaks and free periods and recess and times when students were working on individual projects. Even in third grade, the Dalton administration believed, children could and should choose their own paths.

Ruth's path was unobtrusive. She stuck close to Christina, if Christina let her—which was usually when no one else was around. Maybe out of guilt and maybe out of kindness, when Maia and the others *did* show up, Christina made sure that Ruth was still included, even if it meant just tagging along with the rest of them and laughing when the others laughed, although she hadn't heard the joke. Maia was the sun and they were all in orbit; Ruth happened to be on the outskirts of the universe.

Maia's birthday was the second Friday of school, and her mother brought in cupcakes. Each one had a maple leaf poking out of the icing. The leaf was translucent, made of sugar, and was painted with some kind of edible paint so that it looked real. Ruth had never seen anything like it, and she wanted to show her mother and Rachel, so she carefully wrapped hers in a paper towel and tucked it into the pocket of her sweatshirt.

Because it was Maia's birthday, she was the leader of the recess line that day. Everyone fell into place behind her, snaking down the hallway. From her vantage point farther back in the line, Ruth could see that Maia was wearing her sparkling rhinestone headband. But now, Ruth realized, there were three other girls in the class who had matching ones. They looked like halos.

Ruth turned away and focused her attention instead on the bulletin board that was on the wall. Ms. Thomas had hung up the family portraits they'd drawn on the first day of school, which felt like a thousand years ago. It was easy for Ruth to find hers, because it was the only picture with brown faces.

Well, actually that wasn't true. Ruth let her eyes hopscotch over the other drawings until she found Christina's. There was Christina, front and center, with Ms. Mina and Mr. Sam. There was her little brother, Louis. And in the far right corner, much smaller than the other bodies, was a brown woman wearing an apron and holding a plate of cookies. Ruth knew it was supposed to be Mama. Her mama floated there like an untethered astronaut.

Ruth imagined her swimming off the edge of Christina's page, across the bulletin board, and settling into Ruth's drawing, where she belonged.

Ruth felt a shove in her back and realized that while she had been busy daydreaming the line had started moving. Ruth muttered an apology to Lola, who stood behind her, and hurried to catch up to the others.

To be honest, Ruth had never really thought about the fact that her mama had to cook dinner for Christina's family and then come to Harlem and cook all over again for her own. Maybe it was Christina's drawing that got her thinking about this, but that night at home, she found herself watching Mama cook chicken in the pan. As usual, Granny was dozing in front of the TV; she helped out where she could but that was less and less as she got older. "Mama?" she asked. "Don't you get sick of doing everything twice?"

"What do you mean, baby?"

"You have to take care of Christina's house and our house too," Ruth said.

Her mama smiled. "Well, now," she replied. "One I do for work. The other I do for love."

Just then Rachel walked into the kitchen and snorted. "It's still double the dishes," she said.

Mama gave her a sharp glance. "Then maybe you should start doing your share of chores?"

It was at that moment Ruth remembered the maple leaf candy. "I have something to show you," she announced. "They were on top of Maia's birthday cupcakes."

She dug her hand into her sweatshirt pocket and unwrapped the paper toweling. The leaf, however, had broken into pieces, some so fine they'd turned themselves back into granulated sugar.

"What's that?" Rachel asked.

"A leaf made of candy," Ruth answered.

"Okay." Rachel laughed. "If you say so."

After dinner, Mama told Rachel to take Ruth with her to play outside so she could sit down with Granny in the living room and put her feet up for a hot second. Ruth sat on the curb while Rachel and two of her friends giggled over the older boys shooting hoops in the lot across the street. "You see Joziah?" Denyce said. "He all that."

Nia popped a bubble with her gum. "I heard he's strapped."

"What?" Rachel said. "That's wack."

Sometimes it seemed to Ruth that Rachel and her friends spoke a different language.

"He ain't got no gun," Denyce said. "He just like to tell people he do."

A gun? Ruth didn't realize she'd spoken out loud until the girls all stared at her. "Oh, look," Nia said. "We shocked your baby sister."

If Mama knew Rachel was anywhere close to the boys in this neighborhood who got into trouble, she would whup her and keep her locked inside.

"Leave me alone, Nia," Ruth said. "I'm not bothering you."

Nia smirked. "So what you sayin'?"

"Hey, Ruth," Denyce asked. "How's your fancy school?" She got up from the stoop and sat down next to Ruth. Nia followed suit, sandwiching her on the other side.

"Look at that," Nia said, grabbing Ruth's wrist. "I think your skin's getting lighter."

"You practically a ghost," Denyce said, and both girls broke up laughing.

"Aight, you fools," Rachel interrupted. "Leave her be. It ain't her fault she smarter than both your brains put together."

"I'm going inside," Ruth announced, but she was pretty sure no one cared.

Her mama and Granny were on the couch, watching *Wheel of Fortune*. "What's the matter, baby?" Mama asked.

"Nothing," Ruth said. "I just wanted to take a bath."

She went into the bathroom the four of them shared. The tub had a crack in it that was the shape of a lightning bolt, and Ruth used to think that the water would run right through Mrs. Nattuck's ceiling, but since she'd never complained and they bathed every night, that probably wasn't the case. She ran the water and put on a shower cap to cover her hair and sank down to her shoulders. Then she lathered up soap on her washcloth. Her palms were pink, as pink as Christina's. She flipped her hand over, to the light brown of her wrist and forearm. Her skin had always been lighter than Rachel's; her sister had been dark as a berry her whole life. Was that why Ruth was the one who was going to Dalton?

Ruth picked up the washcloth and scrubbed at her left shoulder. She scrubbed so hard she could see the pink bloom of irritation under the brown of her skin.

It hurt.

It was beautiful.

ON MONDAY, RUTH WOKE UP before her alarm. She had brushed her teeth and dressed and packed up her schoolwork before her mama even came out of her bedroom. "Isn't someone in a hurry!" Mama said, but she smiled.

Ruth couldn't wait to get back to Dalton. Today they would be playing a math game and the winning team would get Halloween candy. She had practiced her times tables all weekend. She would win, and then she would share the candy with Maia and the other girls, and this time they would not just tolerate her, they'd welcome her.

When they reached Ms. Mina's brownstone and went in the service entrance, Ruth raced up the stairs. She sat on a kitchen stool, kicking her legs, and printed out multiplication equations on a napkin. Ms. Mina came into the kitchen for a cup of coffee. "It's just finished brewing," Mama said. "I would have brought it up to you."

"Oh, I know that, Lou," she answered. "I was up all night with the baby and my body simply couldn't wait another second." She glanced at Ruth, who was now solving her equations. "Well, look at *you*!" Ms. Mina said. "And I can barely get Christina out of bed!"

But this wasn't true because at that moment Christina came into the kitchen, wearing a rhinestone headband, to pick up her school lunch from Mama.

* * *

THERE WERE TWO TEAMS. Ms. Thomas randomly divided the students in half, and set up a buzzer on a desk in the middle of the classroom. One member of each team would face off as she recited a multiplication equation. The first person to hit the buzzer and say the correct answer would get to shoot a ball made of masking tape into one of three baskets. The farthest one was worth the most points. At the end of the game, the team with the most points would win.

Ruth faced off against Marcus first, and was given a cream puff of a question: 3 x 4. She rang the buzzer and tossed the tape ball into the trash can that was closest, because she didn't want to risk missing completely and they were better safe than sorry. They rotated through two more times, and each time, Ruth won her heat (6 x 6, and the very tricky 8 x 9). Maia was on the other team, along with Christina. Ruth knew it wasn't charitable, but when Maia screwed up and said 4 x 7 was 24, her stomach flipped with satisfaction.

Finally it was tied, and Ms. Thomas said they had to choose a designated shooter from each team to make a winning basket. It would be sudden death—the person who was picked would throw the tape ball and then the opposing team's pick would do the same, until one of them missed. Ruth leaned back against the wall, waiting for her team to rally around Edward or Lucas, who were the most athletic in the class. But instead, someone suggested her name.

At first, she flushed with pride—was she being chosen because her team recognized her as an MVP? But then she realized that wasn't what was going on here. "Yeah, Ruth," Edward said, nodding. "You know how to play basketball, don't you?"

Ruth nodded. She did know *how*—she'd watched neighborhood kids for years. But she'd never actually played the game herself.

"Of *course* she does," said Lucas. "Duh."

Reluctantly, Ruth took the tape ball and sank a basket into the farthest trash bin. Her team shouted and Lucas even gave her a high five.

The designated shooter for the other team was a tall boy named Jack who stuck out his tongue when he was concentrating, which wasn't often. He narrowed his eyes and let the tape ball roll off his fingertips. He, too, made the farthest basket.

Ruth took the ball again. She was not an athlete. She could barely walk and sing simultaneously during the Christmas pageant at church. There was absolutely no way she could be lucky enough to succeed a second time around. Then she remembered how Mama said there was no such thing as luck, just prayers being answered. So even though Ruth was certain God had more important things on His mind, she called on Jesus under her breath, and made a second basket. A third. Her teammates went wild. *Water into wine? Ha*, Ruth thought. This newfound athletic skill was a true miracle.

Jack took the ball, bounced on the tips of his toes, and stuck out his tongue. He arched one arm up, but the tape got snagged on the cuff of his sweater and fell about six feet short of the closest trash can.

"We have a winner!" Ms. Thomas sang, above a chorus of *Do over!* and *Not fair!* Ruth's team was hollering, patting her on the back and the shoulder, shouting her name. The teacher took out a bag of candy— Reese's peanut butter cups and Nestlé Crunch bars and Gobstoppers— and everyone on Ruth's team was allowed to stick their hand in and take a fistful.

Ruth made sure she got extra Reese's, then walked to Christina's desk. Maia was sitting on the top of it, whispering to Christina. "Want some?" Ruth asked, and she held out her cupped hands, letting them choose first.

"Everyone knows why you won," Maia said.

Ruth lifted her chin a notch. "Because I knew my times tables."

"More like because of how you look." Maia tossed her hair. "I don't want your dumb candy," she said, and she walked away.

Ruth stared at her. Christina fished through the candy Ruth held, choosing a Reese's. She unwrapped it and took a bite of the candy, leaving little ridges in the wake of her teeth. "I knew my times tables," Ruth murmured.

"It's not you, Ruth," Christina said. She popped the rest of the candy into her mouth. "She just doesn't like Black people."

* * *

RUTH WATCHED HER GRANNY'S HANDS twist Rachel's hair, pulling and crisscrossing to magically create the neat cornrows that weaved across her scalp in parallel zigzags. Rachel winced and whined, like always, but the end result was the same: tight, even braids that fell down to her shoulders. "Done," Granny pronounced, holding up the big hand mirror so that Rachel could see the back. "Ruth?"

Every other Sunday night, Granny washed and styled her granddaughters' hair. Granny had run her own place for years before it got to be too much for her to stand on her feet all day. Ruth climbed onto the stool, her hair still damp under the towel.

Granny's hands rooted through Ruth's hair, her fingernails scraping the scalp in a massage. She took her comb and made the first part.

"Wait—can you put the hood thing on and use the hot comb instead?" Ruth blurted out. "Please?"

Granny laughed, her hands on her wide hips. Ruth had always thought her granny looked like the sail of a ship—heavy-masted, wide, implacable. "Lou, you hear this? Queen of Sheba here wants a press."

Mama, who was sewing a button onto one of Ruth's white school shirts, looked up from where she sitting at the kitchen table. "You should be grateful your granny's doing *anything* to your hair," she said. "We're not running a salon."

Granny was pulling tighter on her hair. "Ain't never had no complaints before from my own grandbaby . . ."

"It's not you," Ruth said, hearing Christina's words beneath her own. "It's that I want to look more . . . grown up."

What she wanted was to look like Maia, with her river of shining hair. But that was about as likely as Ruth waking up in a millionaire's penthouse. Granny and Mama exchanged a look, and then Mama shrugged.

"Fine," Granny sighed. "Go get the comb."

Ruth scrambled to the cabinet where they kept the bonnet dryer and hot comb. Granny set the drying cap over her head and then placed the comb on the metal coil of the stove. After the bonnet cut off, she ran the Super Gro through a section of hair. Ruth tried not to think about how she had explained this to the other girls; how they had looked at her like she was an alien.

She held still as Granny ran the comb through her hair; she'd been burned enough to know the consequences of fidgeting. By the time she was finished, Mama had mended two more shirts, let out one of Rachel's skirts ("That girl grows like a weed," she muttered), and darned a sock. Rachel walked into the kitchen to get an apple out of the refrigerator and looked at Ruth. "You goin' somewhere special?" she asked.

"Just school."

"It looks good," Rachel said, as Ruth narrowed her eyes, suspicious. "Like that skater lady. Dorothy Hamill."

"For real?" Ruth asked.

Rachel took a bite. "Nope," she said.

"Rachel!" Mama warned, but her sister was already cruising out of the kitchen on a laugh.

"Don't you listen to her, baby," Granny said. "You beautiful, inside and out."

She held up the mirror so that Ruth could see both the front and the back. Her hair was straight and shiny, curving just slightly at the bottom. "You know what would make this even more perfect?" Ruth said. "A headband."

"So go get a headband," Granny said. "You got that nice red one you wore at Easter."

"Some of the girls in my class have the kind that sparkle," Ruth said, as casually as she could manage. "I wish I had one."

Mama didn't even look up from the sock she was mending. "We're not made of money, Ruth," she said, and she bit off the thread with her teeth.

On Columbus Day, Dalton was closed, but Mama still had to work. Rachel was invited to Nia's apartment and Ruth tagged along to the Upper West Side to play with Christina. Since Mr. Sam was out, Christina had Mama set up his movie projector, so that she and Ruth could watch the *Wonderful World of Disney* films that lined his shelves in their round metal tins. He worked in television, and their house was full of treasures Ruth could appreciate, like that, and others she couldn't—like the framed, signed photographs of movie stars she didn't know: Doris Day, Jack Lemmon, Steve McQueen.

Ruth and Christina ate grilled cheese sandwiches and tomato soup that Mama had made, and watched *Cinderella*. Christina was the only person Ruth knew who could watch a movie in her house and not have to go to a movie theater. They sat on Mr. Sam's red leather couch and shared an afghan that Ms. Mina had knitted when she was going through a crafty phase.

When the prince kissed Cinderella at the end, Christina said, "You know, it doesn't just work like that."

"Like what?"

"Like you can marry a prince if you're some nobody. You have to have a title."

Ruth thought about this. "Like a book?"

"I don't know," Christina admitted. "But not everyone has one. Maia said."

Maia said. Of course. "Does *she* have a title?" Ruth asked.

Christina considered this. "Bossypants?"

A surprised laugh bubbled out of Ruth. Then Christina was laughing, too, and it was the two of them and no one else, like it used to be.

Christina turned to her when the projector started flapping, the film having run its course. "Now what should we do?" she said. "Want to see my new Malibu Barbie?"

We. Was there a better word in the English language?

"Christina?" Ruth said hesitantly. "This is fun, right?"

Christina looked at her sidelong. "Yeah, weirdo," she said, grinning.

"So when we're at school, then . . . are you mad at me?"

There was a pause. "No," Christina said, but in that hiccup of time, Ruth heard a thousand yeses. "Why would you even think that?"

"Because you act different when it's not just us."

"No I don't!"

"You do," Ruth said, but now she was second-guessing herself. Was she imagining it? Christina had been nothing short of nice all day. Maybe the problem wasn't Christina, but Ruth herself. It wasn't like it was Christina's job to defend Ruth from Maia; Ruth had to do that on her own. So why was she blaming Christina?

Suddenly she realized Christina was crying. "Why are you being so *mean* to me?" she said, just as Mama walked in to take away their empty plates.

"Christina?" Mama said, alarmed. She crouched down and gave Christina a tissue from her own pocket to dry her face. "What happened?"

"I don't want to play anymore," Christina sobbed, red-faced, not even looking at Ruth.

"Okay, then, you go on up to your room, and I'll bring you some dessert. I baked fresh blondies. That sound good to you?"

Christina sniffled and nodded, and a minute later, she was gone. Mama folded her arms. "What did you say to upset Ms. Christina?"

The truth? Ruth thought. But instead she lowered her eyes. "Christina's only my friend when we're here," she confessed. "The minute we walk through the door of school, everything changes."

She expected Mama to get mad at her for lying. After all, it had been nearly six weeks and Ruth had gone on and on about how great school was, how many friends she had made. But instead Mama sighed and took Ruth's hand. "Baby girl," she said, "*nothing* changes."

TWO DAYS LATER, Ms. THOMAS got a student teacher. Miss Van Vleet was in college and would be coming to their classroom only on Tuesday and Thursday mornings. She would help the students who needed extra work with their writing, and she would be teaching some of the lessons. But that first day, her main job was to learn everyone's name, and she was really, really bad at it.

She called Maia *Mara*, and Lola *Lulu*. She mixed up Edward and Lucas.

Ms. Thomas tried to help her by giving her a stack of graded papers to hand out after recess. Miss Van Vleet wandered around the classroom, sometimes asking other students for help. Some of the boys tried to confuse her as a prank, and after that, when she had a question, she went straight to Ms. Thomas.

"Which one is Ruth again?" Miss Van Vleet asked.

Ms. Thomas looked up from where she was marking papers. She glanced around the room to see where Ruth was sitting, and Ruth met her gaze. Instead of pointing, she turned to Miss Van Vleet and hesitated for a moment. Then she said, "She's the girl with the red sneakers."

Ruth looked down at her red Keds. There were three other girls in her classroom who had the same shoes.

On the other hand, she was the only Black student.

That night, Rachel was being grounded without television privileges because she'd decked a girl for stealing her HoHos at lunch. That punishment wouldn't have bothered Ruth, who would have happily sat in her room reading, but Rachel had never willingly picked up a book, as far as Ruth could remember. So instead, while Ruth tried to memorize words for her spelling test, she had to block out the sound of Rachel galumphing around the room they shared, trying to find some other way to occupy her time.

"You want me to test you?" Rachel offered.

"Why?"

There was probably a catch. With Rachel, there was always a catch. It wasn't that she didn't love her sister; it was just that they saw the world through two different lenses.

"Because I'm being nice. And because I'm bored as all get out." She reached out her hand, and hesitantly Ruth gave her the list of words. Rachel climbed onto her bed and stuffed a pillow behind her head. "Baby words," she muttered, reading them over. "*Means.*"

"M-E-A-N-S."

"*Corn.*"

"C-O-R-N."

"*Argue.*"

"A-R-G-U-E."

"This is stupid," Rachel said. "You don't even have to try. Why doesn't your teacher bump you up a level?"

Ruth didn't know the answer to that; there were other students who had more challenging words, although she had never gotten less than a 95 on a spelling test.

"Well, *I* know why, even if you don't," Rachel said. "Because your teacher doesn't think a Black girl can be at the top of the class."

"That's not true," Ruth immediately said, defending Ms. Thomas. "She knows I'm smart."

"Uh-huh," Rachel answered, in a way that meant anything but that.

"She doesn't even see me as Black," Ruth countered.

Rachel laughed. "Yeah, 'cause she's too busy seeing you as a charity case."

Ruth knew that her sister meant this as a dig, but she fiercely believed that Ms. Thomas saw more than just her skin color. She saw a girl who always said please and thank you and who never interrupted someone else if they were talking. She saw a student who was one of the best readers in the class, who loved learning astronomy. She saw a good listener, a willing friend.

She saw someone who was one of them.

Smugly, Ruth told Rachel what had happened that day at school. How Ms. Thomas had identified her.

"You really think the reason she pointed you out by your sneakers was because it was the only thing she could use to describe you?" Rachel asked.

That was all it took—that chink in the foundation, that worm of a question—for Ruth to peek behind the fancy wrapping of the story she'd created in her own mind. The justification, the wishful thinking—it was swept away by the broom of doubt like so much smoke.

Ruth knew she was partly right: Ms. Thomas had been showing a kindness by not singling Ruth out for her appearance. She was trying to be inclusive by not calling Ruth "the Black girl."

But that was because to Ms. Thomas, to Maia, to Miss Van Vleet—to everyone in that school—Black wasn't just any adjective.

It was something they'd never want to be.

"I KNOW YOU DON'T WANT to be my friend," Ruth said by way of prefacing her conversation with Christina in the sedan on the way to school. "But can I ask you something?"

For almost a week now, they had moved in similar orbits, but they had not interacted unless they were forced to in a group project. Christina didn't look at Ruth, but she jerked her chin: *Okay.*

Ruth explained what had happened with Ms. Thomas and Miss Van Vleet. "If you were in a crowd with a lot of people and someone asked me who you were, I wouldn't say you're the one with the scar on your ankle from where you fell last summer. I'd use something everyone would see right away, like . . . your purple shirt or your Holly Hobbie lunch box. Doesn't it seem weird?" Ruth asked. "To not call something what it *is*?"

Christina didn't answer, and Ruth thought it was because she was still mad at her. But then she turned in her seat so that she was facing Ruth. "Maybe no one notices that you're Black," she said. "I mean, you act and sound just like *we* do."

Ruth thought about this. It couldn't really be true, could it? If she dressed in pants and played baseball and did gross things that boys did, like have burping contests, would teachers not know that she was a girl? You couldn't *unsee* what was right before your eyes, could you?

Before she could mull on this further, Christina spoke again. "I never said I didn't want to be your friend," she said, her voice small. "It's just . . . all of a sudden you're at *my* school, with *my* friends, and I thought . . . I thought . . ." She raised her hand to the window and spread her fingers like a starfish. "What if they liked you more than they like me?"

Ruth didn't know what to say. It was the first time she realized that a person might look like Christina, and live in a fancy home, and dress in designer clothing, and have everything her heart desired, and still go to sleep at night worrying.

Maybe we are *more alike than we're different*, Ruth thought.

WHEN MS. THOMAS TURNED OFF the lights in the classroom, everyone got quiet. Then she flicked them back on again. "Now," she asked, "how long did it take for the light to come back?"

It was instantaneous, immediate. There was probably a word for faster-than-a-heartbeat but Ruth didn't know it.

"Light moves fast. It can move 186,000 miles per second," Ms. Thomas said. "The reason it seems like we see light the instant I turn on the switch is because light is so quick, and because we're so close to it. But some light comes from much farther away—light from stars. They're so far away, in fact, that we don't even measure the distance in miles. We measure it in light-years—the amount of time it takes for light from that star to reach us, on earth. The reason stars look so small in the night sky is because they're so far away from us."

Ms. Thomas talked about the star that was closest to earth—the sun. She made Marcus stand at the front of the class with a flashlight and told him to turn it on. "If he was on the sun, and turned on a very bright flashlight . . . and we were all waiting in the classroom, we wouldn't see that light for eight minutes. *That's* how far away the sun is from us." The next closest star was called Proxima Centauri. It was 39.9 trillion kilometers away from us, or 4.2 light-years, which meant that it would take four years—not just eight minutes—for Marcus's flashlight to reach us on earth from there.

Ms. Thomas said that when we look at a star, we're looking backward in time. We're seeing a moment that happened millions of years ago.

Ruth thought about that. She knew Marcus's little flashlight wasn't powerful enough, but even so. What if there were kids on another planet who, years from now, saw it flash? What if, in the future, they had a piece of the moment Ruth was living right now?

It made her feel like yesterday and tomorrow weren't all that far away from each other.

Then Ms. Thomas gave everyone a toilet paper roll and a circle of black paper. Each student could choose to create either the Canis Major constellation or Orion. Ruth looked over and saw Maia pick Orion. She reached for the other one.

They had to trace the spiky limbs of the constellations, and poke tiny holes in at their joints to make the stars. Ruth carefully drew the T of Canis Major, and its split legs. It looked to her like a stick figure without a head. She used a pin carefully to mark the stars. Then with Ms. Thomas's help she affixed the black circle to one end of the roll, with electrical tape to seal the edges. When everyone in the class had finished, Ms. Thomas gave each of them a small penlight and pulled the drapes shut and turned off the classroom fluorescents. Everyone lay on the floor, shining their penlights through the toilet paper rolls, projecting their constellations onto the ceiling.

Ruth felt someone lie down beside her, and she turned to find Ms. Thomas staring up at the ceiling. "You see that star in the middle on top?" she asked, pointing, and Ruth nodded. "That's called Sirius. It takes light from that star eight and a half years to reach us here."

"That's how old I am," Ruth said.

"Well, then." Ms. Thomas laughed. "If you can see it in the night sky, you're looking at light that's the same age as you."

Ruth liked the idea of a star that she had something in common with. She wondered if she could convince her mother to let her out on the fire escape tonight to try to find it.

"It's easy to find Sirius," Ms. Thomas was saying, "because it's the brightest star we can see." She rolled to a sitting position and squeezed Ruth's shoulder. "Sometimes, it even casts a shadow."

The whole rest of the day Ruth found it hard to concentrate. She kept looking out the window at the cars below, and the people walking their dogs, and the ladies pushing strollers. She pictured a world bigger than the classroom, bigger than Manhattan, bigger than the boundaries of her imagination.

THE SCARIEST PART OF THE Presidential Physical Fitness Test was climbing the rope that hung from the ceiling of the tiny gymnasium. There were two: one with knots, and one without. Ruth was worried she couldn't even shimmy her way up the one with knots. You had to excel at all the sections: the shuttle run, the one-mile run, the curl-ups, the pull-ups, the rope climb, the V-sit reach. If you did, you got a gold certificate as an award.

Ruth, who got straight As, didn't like failing at anything, even gym class.

Because of their last names, it was Maia's turn just before Ruth's. She picked the rope with the knots (girls had a choice, boys didn't) and made it halfway up before she started to panic. Her eyes squirreled shut and her face went red and she clutched the rope like it was a lifeline. Even when Mr. Yorkey, the gym teacher, told her to come on down, she couldn't unhook herself. It took two other teachers to help pry her off the rope, and when Maia reached ground level the other girls flocked around her like worker bees to the queen. Lola was chosen to help walk Maia to the nurse's office.

When it was Ruth's turn, she wiped her hands on her shorts and pulled with all her might to anchor her feet to the bottom knot. Then she closed her eyes and inched her right hand up to the next highest knot, and then her left, and then she crunched her legs up until her feet found their next hold. She did this again, picturing herself as a caterpillar, bunching and relaxing, concentrating only on getting to a knot higher than the one Maia had reached. When her hand reached up to grab the next knot and instead she found the bell on the ceiling to ring, signaling that she'd reached the top, she was surprised. She skittered down the rope, flushed and proud, and imagined coming home with that gold certificate. Mama would put it up on the refrigerator.

About fifteen minutes later Maia walked back into the gymnasium, this time accompanied by the school nurse. Ruth heard the nurse say words like *panic attack* and *heights* and *sue*, and Mr. Yorkey agreed to let Maia sit out the rest of the test, and to be his assistant instead. He showed her how to work the stopwatch, and she sat on the start line of the mile run (eight laps around the gym track).

"Seamus, you're up," Mr. Yorkey said. "Ruth, on deck."

Ruth stood awkwardly next to Maia, not sure if she should say something like *I hope you're feeling better now*. But she didn't know how without it coming out sounding like Ruth was lording over her the fact that she had rung the bell and Maia hadn't, and pride was a sin, so instead, she just tugged at the bottom of her shorts and scuffed her sneaker on the squeaky polyurethaned floor. It sounded like a chipmunk.

Maia pushed the button on the stopwatch to get it ready. Ruth put her toe on the red starting line, as close to the inside edge as she could, without cheating.

"On your mark," Mr. Yorkey called out.

"Hey, Ruth?" Maia said quietly.

"Get set . . ."

Ruth twisted her neck.

"You're gonna ace this," Maia said, smiling. "Just run like the KKK is chasing you."

"Go!" Mr. Yorkey shouted.

LAST YEAR GRANNY'S BEST FRIEND in the world had died of cancer. She and Miz Lonnie had come up north from Mississippi when they were seventeen and had gotten jobs in a factory together and got married a year apart. Miz Lonnie was the sister she'd never had, and at her funeral, Granny wept so hard that she had to be helped out of the church.

She took to her bed, drinking the medicinal whiskey. An hour later Ruth cracked the door open to make sure she was all right, because it was scary to see someone you were used to envisioning as the very definition of solid break into pieces before your eyes. Granny was sitting on the bed, still in her black lace dress, a shoe box in her lap. Spread all around her were photographs so old that they had wavy edges, with handwritten ink on the back that had turned brown with age. "Baby girl, you come sit with me," Granny said, and Ruth crawled onto the mattress and tucked herself tight underneath the old woman's arm.

Ruth pointed to one scalloped photo. "Is that you, Granny?"

The picture was of a woman younger than Mama, even, with hair pulled back into a bun and a crisp white shirt tucked into her skirt. She was pointing at the camera and laughing.

"That's me," Granny said. "And look, in the background here, that's your great-granny." Ruth looked closer and saw a woman with a pinched mouth standing on the porch in the background, her arms crossed. "She was mad because Lonnie and me, we were always foolin' around."

"Where's Miz Lonnie?" Ruth asked.

"On the other side of the camera," Granny explained. "She had just got it that day, and she said I could be her model."

Ruth snuggled closer. Granny smelled of talcum powder and rosewater and Maker's Mark. "What about this one?" she said, holding up a picture of four austere youths—two young men stiffly holding the elbows of Granny and Miz Lonnie, who wore flower corsages that had been bleached white by the exposure process.

"Well, that was a church social. Lonnie, she was wild for that boy, but she wasn't allowed to go on her own, so he brought along a friend as my date. Go figure, I fell hard for him."

"That's Granddaddy?" Ruth asked.

"No, his name was Jerald. He was the first boy I loved. Granddaddy was the last."

They sat on the bed sifting through the entire shoe box, each photograph a memory. Granny talked about creeks she used to swim in with Miz Lonnie and the coonhound her family had that used to attack porcupines. She pointed to a gold cross Ruth's great-granny wore in one picture, which was the same gold cross Granny had around her neck at that very moment. There was a photo of her and Miz Lonnie in Times Square with old-time cars that Ruth had seen only in movies, and one of Granny pregnant with Mama, holding Miz Lonnie's toddler son, Abraham, like he was a practice run. Then Ruth found a picture that had gotten wedged in the cardboard at the side. This one, though, wasn't from Miz Lonnie's camera. It was a newspaper clipping of a hanged man. "What happened to him?" Ruth asked.

"The KKK happened to him," Granny said. She reached for her bottle of whiskey and took another shot. "White men, with their pointy hoods, burning their crosses." She breathed fire at Ruth, who closed her eyes and held her nose. "They killed him. Lonnie and me, we saw it on the way to school. And I near passed out, but Lonnie, she caught me and she told me we had to get away. We were gonna leave town and go somewhere things like this never happened—"

Just then, Mama came into the bedroom. "What on earth is going on here?" she demanded, as Ruth slipped the newspaper clipping under her leg. Mama sniffed the air and frowned, taking the whiskey bottle and the shot glass off Granny's nightstand. "What kind of example you setting?" she chided, and to Ruth she said, "That's enough. You leave Granny to get some rest." As Ruth curled the newspaper clipping into her hand, Mama pulled back the covers and took off Granny's shoes, helping her get to bed. "Why you telling Ruth about all that?" Mama said. "She's a baby!"

By now Granny was slurring her words. "Them crackas wasn't shit," she muttered. "We left town and didn't look back. We left before Jerald even got buried."

Ruth hid the newspaper clipping underneath her mattress. Sometimes she would take it out and look at it, but the image was grainy and she couldn't connect that poor man with the one in a suit and tie who had stood for a formal photo holding Granny's arm like it was made of fine china. She couldn't imagine the man twisting on that rope picking out carnations and baby's breath for a pretty corsage.

Sometimes at night, Ruth would wonder: If not for the KKK, would Granny have stayed in Mississippi and married Jerald? If not for the KKK, would Ruth even be here?

* * *

"Go!" Mr. Yorkey shouted, and Ruth did.

She pivoted on her foot, and instead of running the mile to get a gold certificate of presidential fitness, she threw herself at Maia, yanking at her glossy ponytail, rolling with her on the floor until Ruth had her pinned down, one forearm across Maia's collarbones while the other hand drew back in a fist.

"Go ahead," Maia dared. "Punch me."

Ruth was so surprised, she hesitated.

"Because then you'll just wind up cleaning toilets like your mother."

Ruth could feel her heart beating so hard, it was practically external. She was sweating, her hair coming out of its elastic to curl natural around her face. It was like Cinderella all over again, turning back into her rags with her pumpkin.

She let go of Maia abruptly and walked away from her, her back to the rest of the class, which had gone absolutely silent watching the show.

Mr. Yorkey grasped her arm firmly. "Ruth," he said, "would you like to go sit down and control your emotions?"

She faced the gym teacher. "No," Ruth said honestly, because what she really wanted to do was smack Maia. What she really wanted to do was go back in time ten minutes to the moment before Maia had said anything. Or maybe further—say, two months—before she had ever set foot in this school.

"Go to the program director's office," Mr. Yorkey said tightly. "Now."

The director of First Program at Dalton was a very thin woman named Mrs. Grau-Lerner, who smelled of mothballs and peppermint. Ruth, who had never been sent to the principal's office in her life, was shivering.

"Do you know what you did wrong, Ruth?" Mrs. Grau-Lerner asked.

Ruth shook her head. She hadn't hit Maia, although she had wanted to, so why was she being punished?

"Not only were you involved in an altercation . . . you also were rude to Mr. Yorkey."

Ruth looked up at her. She thought Mr. Yorkey had been asking her a question. She didn't realize it was actually a test.

If Mr. Yorkey had wanted her to sit down and cool off, he should have told her so. Had it been Mama, for example, she would have said, *Do your homework.* No wiggle room there, just a direct order. Instead, Mr. Yorkey had given Ruth a choice, and now she was being disciplined for taking it.

"Mrs. Grau-Lerner, Maia said—"

The woman held up her hand. "Ruth," she replied, "we don't blame others at Dalton. We take responsibility for our own actions."

Ruth looked into her lap. "Yes, ma'am," she said.

Suddenly there was a knock on the director's office door, and a secretary opened it. "Ms. Brooks is here," she said, and through the slice that was opened Ruth could see Mama still in her uniform, crackling with questions.

"Why don't you wait in Ms. Thomas's room while I speak with your mother?" Mrs. Grau-Lerner said.

Ruth slipped out of the office and past her mama with her eyes cast down. She knew there would be a reckoning in private. She walked to the classroom, which was empty because all the other students in Ms. Thomas's class were still getting tested in the gymnasium. She sat down at her desk, and then stood up and walked toward the front of the classroom.

She picked up the chalk and wrote her name on the board, underneath that night's homework assignment. Then she erased it, so that you couldn't see the letters. Just a ghost that let you know something had been there.

Mama was mad, all right, but not at Ruth. "Social difficulties, my foot," she muttered under her breath, as they boarded the bus together. "More like they're the ones who are having trouble adjusting. Can't deal with the *climate*, what does that even mean?"

Ruth was afraid to speak. If she did, then she would have to tell Mama about Maia and what she'd said, and she didn't want to do that.

But the bus stopped at the spot where they should have gotten off to go to Ms. Mina's, and they stayed on. It wasn't following the uptown route to Harlem. Ruth had no idea where they were headed.

Maybe Mama was so angry she had forgotten to get off the bus.

"Mama," Ruth asked in a small voice. "Where we going?"

In response, Mama pushed the cord for the next stop and took Ruth's hand. They got off the bus, belched into the frenetic hurry of Forty-second Street. Ruth huddled closer to Mama, avoiding tourists who were pointing at the lighted billboards and the girls in too little clothes and too much makeup who checked their reflections in the windows of fancy restaurants.

"Here we go," Mama announced, walking into a small store that sold gloves and barrettes and scarves and any other accessory you could think of. Maybe Ms. Mina had been sending Mama on an errand when she got diverted to the school. Ruth trailed her fingers along a display of hanging earrings that were made of feathers and tiny woven dream catchers.

"Ruth," Mama called, and she turned around. "Is this what you were talking about?"

She was pointing to a case of glittering rhinestone headbands, each brighter than the next. On their blue velvet field, they looked like constellations.

Sirius, Ruth thought.

"Pick one," Mama said.

Ruth blinked, shocked. Of all the outcomes she could have imagined, being rewarded for getting sent to the program director's office was not one of them. "Mama," she said, "I don't need it . . ."

"Oh yes you do," she said. She pointed to one that looked like a string of daisies, made of crystals. "That's pretty."

Ruth nodded.

"You know how I wear a uniform? It's so Ms. Mina and Mr. Sam and everyone else in that building recognizes who I am. This is *your* uniform." Her mama picked up the daisy band and settled it gently on Ruth's head, like she was being crowned. "If this is what it takes to make them see you," she said, "then so be it."

* * *

ALTHOUGH RUTH KNEW SHE WASN'T allowed out on the fire escape because Mama thought it was unsafe, she waited until everyone was asleep and then crawled outside. She lay on her back, careful not to get too close to the edge, and stared up at the stars. It was easy to find Sirius, as Ms. Thomas had said. It was by far the brightest, shining even through the smog and the clouds and the ambient light of the city.

Ruth reached up and touched her rhinestone headband. She thought about the bright beam that had left Sirius eight and a half years ago. It was reaching her fire escape and Christina's home and Dalton all at once. No matter where you stood, you'd be underneath the same light.

small

great

things

Jodi
Picoult

A Reader's Guide

A Conversation Between Jodi Picoult and Celeste Ng, Author of *Everything I Never Told You*

Celeste Ng: How has this book changed you as a writer? As a reader?

Jodi Picoult: To be honest, this book made me take a good hard look at myself and not find a very flattering portrait. I'd spent nearly fifty years of my life not talking about racism . . . because I don't *have* to. I would never have considered myself a racist. And yet, doing research for this book involved looking into my own beliefs and actions and finding myself ignorant. Okay, so maybe I wasn't a white nationalist—but I also hadn't really considered what it might mean to be a person of color; what historical and current struggles are faced; what it means to not find representation in everything from literature to television to publishing contracts to police departments. I came to see that inaction is an action, too, and not one I was particularly proud of. I had to not just learn about the privileges I have that come with white skin—I had to *own* them, and to ask myself what I could do now with this knowledge that might make the world more equitable for those who were not born white. Every day, since writing this book, dismantling racism is part of my consciousness, my dialogue with others, and my actions.

CN: You have discussed the importance of reading books by writers of color. What authors top that list for you?

JP: So many! Toni Morrison is, of course, the queen of all things literary. I heard her read from *Beloved* as a work in progress and it nearly stopped me dead. Other favorites: Colson Whitehead, Jesmyn Ward, Jacqueline Woodson, Nicola Yoon, Brit Bennett, Ta-Nehesi Coates, Jason Reynolds, Zadie Smith, Cristina Henríquez, Jhumpa Lahiri, Junot Díaz, Ellen Oh, Sabaa Tahir, Chimamanda Ngozi Adiche, Lisa See . . . and Celeste Ng. (And, no, I'm not just saying that because you asked the question. I really, really, really have been a fan for a while, and your new novel knocks it out of the park.)

CN: Has anything about readers' reactions to the book been a surprise for you?

JP: I was expecting a lot more criticism from the African American community than I received. I thought there might be a lot of side-eye for a white author writing about racism—after all, there is an argument to be made that it's not my story to tell. Believe me, I thought a lot about that before writing the book, because cultural appropriation is a real and awful thing. Ultimately I had to ask myself why I was writing the book: Was it to profit off someone else's pain? Or was it to tell a story to people who look like me, and the best way to do that was to use a voice of color? I did so much research and worked with sensitivity readers to "get it right" when I was writing Ruth's voice, and I guess it paid off, because to a fault, the African American readers who have contacted me have said that the voice of Ruth was spot on, and that they themselves had experienced acts of microaggression as had Ruth. And then they'd tell me *their* stories. One woman, I remember, had been a sign language interpreter in a white church. She had to sit across from the front row and sign, and a white elderly woman said out loud, "Can you make her stop? I can't look at her black face anymore." And this reader *had to sign those words.* Imagine the humiliation she must have felt, and then she had to get up and go to work the next day again. The stories I heard from my African American readers brought me to tears. It reminded me why I so badly wanted to write this book—so that more white people would see what they've been ignoring. Another reaction that surprised me: there was a young African American reader in LA who stood up and started to cry because she had been a fan for years, but never imagined my main character would look like her. That was pretty humbling. The reactions of white readers have also been interesting. Largely, those who read the book find it uncomfortable, but in a really important way, and realize they have some work to do. The few who have written to critique me and tell me I am wrong, and that we live in a post-racial society, have mostly been white men.

CN: What has the response been from readers in other countries?

JP: Although I think it's sometimes hard for foreign readers to understand the racial climate of America, every country I toured has had their own seedy story of racism. In Canada and Australia it is indigenous people. In the UK, it's Muslims and, interestingly, white people who were not born in the UK, thanks to the Brexit vote. So even what seems to be a very "American" story has had resonance in their own lives and their own spaces.

CN: Do you feel that where we are as a culture regarding race and racism is different now from where it was when you started writing this novel?

JP: Yes, but not in a positive way. I believe that the Trump candidacy was built on divisiveness and racial stereotyping, and the presidency seems to be continuing in that direction. I know of many friends of mine, people of color, who were the victims of active racism in the days after the election—from nooses being hung in their yards to signs left on the lawn saying "Go back where you came from." I hope that everyone who reads *Small Great Things* will make the active attempt to do at least one "small great thing" that will support a person of color in their community, whether that is making them feel wanted and welcome, or writing to a congressman to oppose legislation, or working on an upcoming political campaign, or attending a Black Lives Matter rally. The options are endless.

CN: Can you discuss the idea of parenthood as it is reflected in the experience of the three point-of-view characters in the novel?

JP: We parents want the best for our children—whatever it takes. It can be argued that Kennedy, Ruth, and Turk all abide by this standard: from Kennedy trying to sweep "embarrassing" questions about race from her child under the carpet, to Turk's active persecution of Ruth, to Ruth's decision to live in a white neighborhood and send Edison to a white school—without any say from Edison himself about what *he* might want. What I find interesting about the trope of the "good parent" is that although it can create division (as seen in the novel in all three cases), it also can provide the foundation for understanding those who are different from us. Ultimately, what all three characters have in common is that they are parents, and their love for their children causes them to act in a certain way. Parenthood is the great equalizer that cuts across differences and ideologies. Certainly Kennedy's interaction to save Edison from his actions toward the end of the novel speaks volumes to Ruth, who has already fired her. And Turk's change of heart, as well, is motivated by both the death of his child and the birth of a new one, who he doesn't want to grow up in a life of hate.

CN: You've pointed out in several interviews that racism is perpetuated—and dismantled—by individual acts. What are some acts individual readers can do to help combat racism and improve understanding between different racial groups?

JP: Find a Showing Up for Racial Justice group near you (SURJ). It is a great space for white people to talk about racism and to become allies and activists for people of color. Donate to Black Lives Matter. But on a more personal level, find a way that you can, in your own personal life, make a difference. Maybe you're a businessman or businesswoman—at your next meeting, if you notice that it's mostly white people talking, turn to someone of color and metaphorically pass the microphone ("We haven't heard from Sue yet, I'd love to hear her take on this!"). If you have a second grader, go to your child's teacher and ask if they're teaching about Heroes of Color this year—or is the entire curriculum about people of color limited to their victimization? If so, help do the research to find examples past Rosa Parks and Martin Luther King of people of color who should be celebrated for their achievements, their inventions, and their words. If you are a reader, check your bookshelf. Are you only reading white authors? Make the conscious effort to read an author of color for every white author you read. Or start a book club that reads authors of color and addresses racial issues through their writing. And if you can, reach across the racial aisle to find people of color who might join your group and offer new and interesting perspectives.

CN: What advice do you have for white readers who want to "have this discussion" about racism among themselves, as you put it in your Author's Note? How do we start those uncomfortable but important conversations?

JP: Just dive in. Talk about race when there are no people of color around—which is a space in which racism is rarely addressed. Talk about race with your kids at the dinner table. Talk to your 102-year-old grandma who uses racial slurs and explain why she shouldn't. Now, I know that when you approach someone who thinks differently from you when it comes to racism, and you announce you want to discuss it, things usually go downhill. I suggest finding a book or a movie that has some connection to understanding racism, and going to see it with that person. Then ask questions: "How did you feel when that happened to Character X?" From there, segue into a more broad discussion: "Oh, that reminds me of something that happened in the news!" That way your conversation about racism is organic and a little less confrontational. Look, there are always going to be people who are not ready to listen. But you'll never know if you don't try.

CN: Do you think writers have a responsibility to write about social issues? What do you see as the benefits of approaching social issues through fiction?

JP: I think that's the whole reason for fiction: to get readers to address a topic they might shy away from non-fictionally. You get readers invested in characters and plot, and if you do your job right, you leave them thinking about greater issues. I believe that I am lucky to have a platform—people want to read what I write, and hear what I have to say. What a gift that is! For that reason, I'm going to continue to address social issues. If you change even one mind, you've made a difference.

CN: You're active on social media (in fact, we "met" on Twitter). What do you like about using this platform to engage with readers? What challenges has it brought?

JP: I love Twitter because it allows me to be political—to be the human behind the byline, so to speak. I love that social media provides an easy way for my readers to get in touch with me, and for me to thank them for picking up my book in the first place. But of course, Twitter is also full of people whose political views are different from mine. Some write very politely to say they love my books but not my stance on politics; I thank them for reading and tell them they should probably not follow me. Others write horrible racial and homophobic slurs against me and my family—when you write about racism, you attract those who are neo-Nazis, after all. That's what the BLOCK button is for.

CN: Will you write explicitly about race in America again?

JP: I don't know if I will write explicitly about race again, but I certainly wouldn't rule it out. And more important, I think my books—regardless of subject matter—will show more of a rainbow of characters in all races. I'd like them to accurately reflect the world in which I prefer to live.

Questions and Topics for Discussion

1. Which of the three main characters (Ruth, Turk, or Kennedy) do you most relate to, and why? Think about what you have in common with the other two characters as well. How can you relate to them?

2. The title of the book comes from the Martin Luther King Jr. quote that Ruth's mother mentions on p. 173: "If I cannot do great things, I can do small things in a great way." What does this quote mean to you? What are some examples of small great things done by the characters in the novel?

3. Discuss Ruth's relationship with her sister, Adisa. How does the relationship change over the course of the novel?

4. Kennedy seeks out a neighborhood in which she is the only white person to help her gain some perspective. Can you think of an example of a time when something about your identity made you an outsider? How were you affected by that experience?

5. All of the characters change over the course of the novel, but Turk's transformation is perhaps the most extreme. What do you think contributed to that change?

6. Discuss the theme of parenthood in the novel. What does being a parent mean to Ruth, to Kennedy, and to Turk? What does it mean to you?

7. Why do you think Ruth lies to Kennedy about touching Davis when he first starts seizing? What would you have done in her position?

8. Why do you think Kennedy decides to take Ruth's case? What makes it so important to her?

9. Discuss the difference between "equity" and "equality" as Kennedy explains it on p. 427. Do you think Ruth gets equity from the trial?

10. Was your perspective on racism or privilege changed by reading this book? Is there anything you now see differently?

11. Did the ending of *Small Great Things* surprise you? If so, why? Did you envision a different ending?

12. Did the Author's Note change your reading experience at all?

13. Have you changed anything in your daily life after reading *Small Great Things*?

14. Who would you recommend *Small Great Things* to? Why?

About the Author

JODI PICOULT is the #1 *New York Times* bestselling author of twenty-four novels, including *Leaving Time, The Storyteller, Lone Wolf, Sing You Home, House Rules, Handle with Care, Change of Heart, Nineteen Minutes, My Sister's Keeper,* and, with daughter Samantha van Leer, two young adult novels, *Between the Lines* and *Off the Page*. She lives in New Hampshire with her husband and three children.

JodiPicoult.com

Facebook.com/JodiPicoult

Twitter: @jodipicoult

Instagram: @jodipicoult